The Dragon Keeper's Mark:
A Song of Fire and Stone

****

PR Garcia

Please leave an honest review on Amazon.

Contents

In the first age, when fire dimmed and stone grew restless,
the Elders cast their sight beyond the veil of time.
They beheld a world unraveling:
flame without Keeper,
stone without anchor,
dragons drifting into slumber,
humankind slipping toward ruin.

So, the Elders carved a prophecy into the bones of the world:

*"Not dragon. Not human.
One forged of both.
One who will bridge the dying flame
and the silent stone.
Only she can bear the fire that would kill a human,
and the mortal weight that would collapse a dragon."*

And they whispered further:
that the Twin Flames would not rise as one,
but as halves of a sundered fire,
each holding what the other could not survive alone.

For when the last red moon stains the heavens,
and the shadowed brother lifts his blade,
the world will call for the child of flame and stone,
the only one who can wake the Elders
and bind the fire that once devoured kings.

From *The Book of Elder Wyrms*, Obsidian Leaf I
As inscribed before the War of Ash and Ember

Chapter 1

A sound began. A low, building whisper, like wind through a graveyard. It grew louder, higher; the pitch climbing until it became a shriek that made teeth ache and eyes water. The lance vibrated as it flew forward, trembling with eagerness.

A thunderclap shattered across the sky. A keening wail came from the weapon as it tore through the air, a shriek of something joyful. Something free…and hungry. The emerald veins along its length blazed brighter, trailing light like a curse made visible.

The air parted as it advanced. The sound was no longer wind, but the world protesting from the wrongness of the weapon's existence.

Elara caught the sound before she understood it. Her eyes snapped upward, cutting across the darkness, searching until they found it. A blur tore through the night like something alive, far too large, far too fast, its shape wrong, monstrous, as if it had been forged for ruin alone. For a heartbeat, she could not move, could not breathe, could only stare as the lance carved its path through the dark.

Then instinct took over. Her gaze snapped upward, chasing its origin across the sky.

When she found it, her blood turned to ice. There, half-swallowed by darkness high above her, sat a rider astride a massive black dragon. He wore obsidian armor scored with runes that did not reflect light but consumed it, drinking in the faint glow around him until the air itself seemed to bend. His helm, shaped like a coiled serpent, revealed no face, only a narrow vertical slit where eyes should have been.

A tremor passed through her, not cold, not fear, but something hollower. Absence. The kind that stripped warmth from bone and breath alike. Whatever he had once been was gone. He had not lost his humanity; he had cut it out, piece by deliberate piece, until nothing remained but the void he had chosen to become.

The Commander.

Three days prior, he had arrived at their kingdom with false civility, offering jewels that gleamed like stolen starlight, gold enough to drown a kingdom. He would trade everything he possessed for their twin dragon eggs. But no wealth forged by mortal hands could buy a dragon's unborn fire.

The two eggs he sought were the last in existence, relics of an age all but erased. They were the first eggs known to have been laid in three hundred years. But more importantly, they were already claimed. The ancient covenant, older than kings and older than written language, awakened the moment the twins touched the shells. Their souls were woven together with the Drakes inside: one heartbeat, one purpose, one destiny.

No bargain could undo that binding. No coin could fracture it.

But the Commander had no intention of honoring covenants. He needed the unhatched wyrmlings. And he would do whatever was required to acquire them.

So, he turned to the only path left to him.

Violence.

And because victory was the only emotion he still recognized.

He launched his dark army and crossed the land to take the eggs and to kill the twins who protected them. Once they were dead, the unborn wyrmlings would be free to bond with another.

But Vaelor, the male human twin, had sworn that no blade would ever reach his sister Elara while he still drew breath.

The sound of Elara's dragon screaming in defiance reverted her attention to the Commander. She stared at a second lance the Commander held in his gauntleted hand.

Elara's lungs refused to breathe. Beneath the dark dragon's wings she witnessed a quiver of lances, twelve at least, each crafted to tear through air and flesh alike. Her mind reeled. No defense existed against such weapons.

They were obscene.

Each was handcrafted, forged from obsidian torn from the Sundered Deep during the First Dragon War. Veins of venom threaded through the spearhead. Not only poison, but distilled malice that pulsed with sickly emerald light, each throb synchronized with a heartbeat. The liquid light moved through the lance like blood through veins.

Barbs spiraled down the shaft, each one curved backward like a predator's tooth, designed not only to pierce but to anchor. To tear on exit. The tip whispered for blood, honed to a molecular edge that made the air around it shimmer and split, reality trying to pull away from something so fundamentally wrong.

Elara's eyes followed the arc of the first harpoon as it sailed across the storm-dark sky, and for one frozen heartbeat, she thought ... No; she **prayed** it would miss. That somehow, the dragons would see it, would move, would…

For one impossible heartbeat, everything held.

The impact hit the lead dragon square in the chest, the sound undeniable.

It wasn't the thud of metal striking flesh. Or the crack of breaking bone. It was the sound of something sacred being broken. A deep, resonant CRACK that split the air. The barbs bit deep, and the venom surged inward.

The dragon's roar exploded across the sky. It was not simply a cry or howl born of fury. It was agony. Pure, primal anguish that transcended sound. It became pressure. Force. It crushed the air from the lungs and made the ground shudder.

Elara's hands flew to her ears, slamming against her skull, fingers digging into her hair, pressing so hard it hurt. But it didn't help. Nothing helped. The sound wasn't only in the air; it was inside her, vibrating through her bones, her teeth, her heart.

"No, no, no…" The words ripped from her throat, broken, desperate.

Through the gaps between her fingers, she watched, unable to look away as the dragon thrashed. Its wings, vast as cathedral vaults, beat against the sky in desperation, each stroke summoning cyclones that tore clouds apart. But it was weakening. The emerald light from the lance was spreading, crawling through its chest like roots, an infection of corruption made visible.

The dragon's scales, ancient and impervious to mortal weapons, cracked like ice shattering. Spiderwebs of black spread from the wound outward. Where the venom touched, gold turned to ash-gray. With one last sigh, the magnificent wyrm surrendered and fell flightless to the earth below.

The rider clung for only a heartbeat longer before gravity tore him free. He fell alone, tumbling end over end through empty air. He struck first. The wyrm followed, and the ground answered with annihilation.

Through the haze of thick smoke, Elara scanned for Vaelor's wing mates still alive, still fighting. The majority, youths trained by her brother, seemed too young for this fight.

The Commander readied the second lance, slipping it into the launcher.

The weapon pulsed.

It wanted out.

He pushed the lever.

CRACK.

The second lance launched.

"STOP!" Elara screamed, but her voice was nothing, a whisper lost in the apocalypse.

The lance sheared too far left, slicing across a dragon's wing instead of its chest. The obsidian tip tore through membrane and muscle in a single brutal stroke, shredding the wing from shoulder to mid-span. Silver blood sprayed in a wide arc. The dragon's roar ripped through the heavens, raw and dying. Its wings convulsed, the ruined one flailing as the other fought to hold its height.

The rider clung to the saddle as the beast lurched sideways, losing altitude in a spiraling descent. They dropped fast. Two hundred feet, then three. The wind shrieked around them. The creature struggled to right itself, but pain overwhelmed it, causing its spine to buckle and release silver mist into the air. The rider's fingers slipped along the saddle grips, armor clattering as gravity dragged them downward.

Another hundred feet vanished beneath them.

The ground rushed up in a blur: trees, stone, and fire weaving together in a violent tapestry. In its final desperate act, the noble beast tucked its rider beneath its remaining wing, shielding him from the worst of the fall.

They struck the earth with a thunderous crash, flattening the surrounding brush. Dust and blood exploded upward in a violent plume. The dragon's body shuddered once, twice, then stilled. Its mangled wings splayed at an unnatural angle, its labored breaths rattling.

Its last roar faded into the storm.

The rider slipped across the bloodied dragon's wing and dropped onto the ground. He did not move.

Three dragons circled and emerged from above. They streaked toward the Commander like living comets. Each rider leaned low over their saddle, weapons drawn, faces set. The sky vibrated beneath their combined roar.

The Commander did not flinch.

Feeling a twitch of the Commander's gauntleted fingers, his Drake snapped to the side, folding one wing and dropping ten yards in an instant. The dragon's claws slashed at empty sky as the Commander slipped beneath the assailants; the maneuver sharp and well practiced. Riders shouted warnings to one another, recalibrating, diving again.

The Commander was already moving.

He reached for the mechanism at his side. The void-scarred metal split open like the jaws of a serpent, and another lance locked into place.

"Now," he breathed.

Vorthryn spun upward, a spiraling twist of corrupted muscle and shadow as the Commander fired.

The dragon on the right tried to evade the lance.

It wasn't fast enough.

The weapon struck behind the rider's saddle, punching through scale and sinking into meat. Once more, the cry of death filled the sky, raw and wet. The great dragon's body seized, and the wings collapsed mid-beat, muscle tearing from bone. Too young for the weight of his armor, the rider clamped onto the reins while the dragon's mass rolled and dragged him hard to the right.

The bond uniting the Drake and rider shattered.

As the two dropped to their deaths, the Commander turned his serpent-helm toward the two remaining riders. "Come," he whispered. "Come meet your death."

They didn't retreat. If anything, the fall of their comrade ignited something fiercer in the two remaining Keepers. Coordinating their attack, they split into a pincer formation.

The Commander's head tilted, assessing. A chuckle escaped his throat. "Futile."

From below, three more dragons burst from the churning haze. Their wings beat in synchronized rhythm, creating a vortex that rattled Vorthryn's corrupted membranes. Lightning flashed off their scale-armor, turning them into streaks of living flame as they ascended.

Five dragons now. Five riders. A formation honed over a lifetime of flying together.

They closed in, collapsing the airspace around the Commander.

Vorthryn hesitated for only a second. He twisted left to shield the Commander from the approaching riders while another vaulted upward, unseen, her bow drawn and prepared. She fired, plunging her arrow into the seam of the Commander's armor. The female Keeper screamed her battle cry and fired again.

Vorthryn jerked his head to the side, catching her off-guard with a blast of corrupt fire. A plume of blackened flame laced with emerald venom seared the air. To shield her, the rider's dragon jerked upward, absorbing the impact on its chest.

The corruption devoured both scale and flesh. The dragon's wings folded inward, membranes dissolving in midair, bone turning black and flaking away. The creature convulsed as its rider clung to the saddle straps.

"Don't falter, Haggard. We've almost got him. Please, HOLD!" she screamed.

But the dragon was already gone.

The rider tried to leap free, drawing a dagger to cut her tether, but corruption surged up the reins and into her gauntlets. She shrieked, fingers fusing to the warm leather as both she and her dragon vanished into the flames below.

As the dragon and rider dropped past the Commander, he fired another two lances, eliminating two more.

Vorthryn rolled, a sudden corkscrew dive. The corrupted wyrm wrenched sideways through the formation of the last two dragons, forcing them to scatter or collide midair. Riders shouted warnings, narrowly avoiding each other as the Commander and Drake threaded through their chaos.

The trap snapped shut.

The larger of the two remaining dragons struck like a killing beast, its jaws slamming shut around Vorthryn's throat with bone-crushing force. Corrupted blood erupted in a steaming torrent, foul, and caustic, flooding his mouth and burning down his gullet as if he had swallowed fire and rot together. The pain was blinding, but he clamped harder, teeth grinding, refusing to let go even as the poison ate at him from the inside. The second dragon attacked Vorthryn, tearing through his gear and flesh, trying to roll rider and wyrm into open sky and let gravity finish what teeth had begun.

The Commander's hand snapped to the loading mechanism. With a metallic snarl, the next lance slammed into place. He raised the weapon and cursed.

Vorthryn's head filled the sightline, held in the attacking dragon's jaws. One misfire and the lance would punch through his own mount's skull. There would be no second chance.

The Commander hooked his leg hard around the saddle horn and leaned far to the right, straining against the harness. The straps groaned. He felt the saddle slip two inches, the result of the second dragon clawing through the leather.

Fearing the loosened strap would allow the saddle to slip to the side, the Commander righted himself. He still had no angle. No opening. Only scale and bone filled the line of fire.

For a moment, nothing moved.

"Move," the Commander hissed through clenched teeth, yanking the reins with brutal force.

Vorthryn thrashed, muscles bunching, wings beating ragged and uneven. The enemy's grip faltered for a heartbeat. But it sufficed. Vorthryn yanked his neck free, chunks of flesh torn from his neck. His wing smashed into the dragon below with crushing force. The impact sent it spinning away, scales shearing, breath torn from his lungs as he was flung hard into open air. He tumbled end over end, powerless to stop his fall until he could right himself.

An opening flashed into existence.

The Commander fired.

The lance screamed past Vorthryn's exposed neck by inches and slammed into the enemy dragon's chest with a brutal, concussive impact, punching clean through its gullet.

For a heartbeat, there was no sound. Then the dragon's throat collapsed. The rider vanished into the chaos below.

Before the last dragon could gain control, the Commander reloaded and fired, eliminating both dragon and rider.

The Commander sat tall in the saddle, obsidian armor gleaming with reflected lightning. "I will have my prize."

Blood pooled on Elara's lip where she'd bitten clean through.

She tasted copper.

Then grief.

Then nothing at all.

Few Wyrms still drew breath. The War of Ash and Ember had reduced them to carrion and ash. Solarus, the First Elder Wyrm, erased what the war had spared, purging the mixed-bloods without pause or regret. Now, before her eyes, the last remnants were unmade; not slain, but removed from the world itself.

Elara searched the dense haze, trying hard to see. Below, her village was no longer a place, but an inferno painted in shades of grief.

"Has he no opponent left?" she screamed into the air.

Her fingers found the egg in her satchel and clutched it tightly.

It was warm.

Steady.

Alive.

For a moment, that was all she could feel. Then the world rushed back in. A chill crept over her skin. The tiny hairs at her nape lifted. Her breath froze.

High above her, half-veiled by smoke and drifting ash, the Commander waited. His Drake hovered on trembling, bloodied wings, blood still dripping from its neck wounds. But the Commander did not sway. He watched her with the patience of a creature that had already decided how she would die.

Only she and the Commander remained. No other dragons rose to defend her precious egg. Where was her brother? Was he dead, too? She had not witnessed Vaelor's fall, but something was different. Where his presence had always lived, only a cold, echoing void remained.

Smoke curled around the Commander's silhouette as the Drake drifted lower, its massive body angled so his line of sight never left her. He leaned forward slightly, gloved hands resting on the saddle-spine. Predators did not rush. They observed. They savored.

And he was savoring her terror now.

The Drake drifted closer. The Commander did not speak. He didn't need to.

The silence stretched.

His silence was the promise. His presence, the threat. His stillness, the sentence.

And as he watched her with that cold, consuming hunger, she knew…He had already decided who would be master over the twin eggs.

From out of nowhere, a roar split the sky behind Elara. She spun as a dragon streaked past her, its bronze wings cutting through the smoke like burnished blades. Its rider leaned low over its neck, armor scorched, helm dented, one arm hanging at his side. Blood trailed behind him in a thin, fluttering ribbon. Yet his eyes burned with a fury that refused to surrender.

"Kaios," Elara whispered.

He didn't look at her.

Kaios urged his wounded dragon higher, the beast answering with a ragged cry. Its flight was uneven. One wing trembled. But it climbed.

Smoke parted around them in a rushing spiral. And there he was.

The Commander.

Waiting.

For a breath, both remained still.

The Commander didn't load another weapon. Didn't move. His eyes remained locked on the oncoming rider with a terrible stillness. Vorthryn hovered like a shadow of death given flesh.

Kaios rose until he was level with the Commander.

"YOU TOOK THEM!" he screamed. "You took them all!"

The Commander smiled.

Kaios drew his spear. It shook in his grasp.

His dragon beat one last time upward, wings shuddering, muscles failing. The beast shrieked but did not break. Together, they surged the final few yards toward the demon before them.

The Commander watched. He did not block. He simply lifted one hand. A ripple of corrupted energy flared outward, invisible but lethal. The spear Kaios held disintegrated mid-air, dissolving into ash that blew back into his face. Kaios reached for another weapon; anything, his hands frantic, desperate. His fingers locked on the hilt of a dagger.

"Kaios!" Elara cried, her voice swallowed by the storm.

He turned and met her gaze for one impossible heartbeat.

Then the Commander moved.

With the smallest motion, no more than a flick of his finger, the Commander loosed a pulse of emerald flame into the dragon's chest. The beast convulsed. Its eyes rolled white. Its heart stopped. It fell lifeless, wings collapsing inward like broken banners. Kaios flew from the saddle. He tumbled through the air, spinning, blood trailing behind him in a crimson arc.

"Vaelor, forever yours,' he screamed.

Then he was gone.

The Commander looked to Elara.

His lips curved.

Slow.

Deliberate.

He was enjoying this.

"Kaios…" Elara's fingers dug into her armor. A tremor rippled through her. Not fear. Something deeper. Hotter.

The egg beneath her arm throbbed with a sudden pulse of heat. It answered her rage, warned her, and urged her on. She clutched it tighter, pressing it against her chest as if it were the only piece of sanity she had left.

Above her, the Commander watched.

Curious.

Confused.

What he saw made no sense.

A faint glow coiled around the girl's frame. At first, it was no more than a shimmer, a trick of the storm-light. But then it thickened. Brightened. Flickered. Not merely light, but heat. A halo of something alive.

Impossible.

Human flesh did not ignite without screaming. Human blood did not shimmer like molten ember. And yet the surrounding air warped, bent.

The Commander leaned forward, eyes narrowing to slits.

"No mortal can hold dragonfire."

The glow grew.

He could not name what he was seeing. He had no explanation for it; no prophecy for a girl haloed in fire that did not burn her. He'd seen magic that corrupted flesh, that consumed souls, that even crawled like rot through living bone. But this … this didn't match any curse or power he knew.

It was wrong. It was impossible. And yet it occurred beneath him. Surely it was an illusion, a result of the battle, energy spent, the flames altering his perspective.

The hollow in Elara's chest ignited. She raised her head, her eyes meeting the Commander's with newfound courage.

"You will answer for him," she shouted, voice shaking but deadly, "and for every life you've stolen today."

In the glow of fire, the Commander paused. A new game piece had moved onto the board.

He drove another harpoon into the cradle. The hollow, exhausted click that followed told him it was his last one. He had one last chance to grab his prize

His finger slid toward the trigger with deliberate slowness, controlled and exacting. The weapon locked onto her with a click, its silence a jarring detail amid the carnage. That single sound carried finality.

He held her gaze.

And fired.

A massive shadow devoured the sky around her.

The world went dark. Not gradually, but all at once. Night had collapsed upon her. Swallowed by the sudden eclipse, the Commander's silhouette vanished. The air changed, grew heavy, charged with the presence of something immense.

The shadow did more than pass; it swept over her and her dragon like the hand of a god. Vast wings blotted out the storm and the horror beyond. As it wheeled back, it cut through the air with a sound like thunder rolling across mountains.

Vaelor.

"Stop, Sister. Stand down. Don't let what he's done trick you into igniting your dragonfire. Keep your flame hidden. No one can know what's inside you."

Vaelor's dragon roared in defiance as he positioned himself between Elara and the Commander, wings spread wide, a living barrier of muscle and rage and desperate protection.

He had trained his whole life for this, for the moment he would prove he deserved to be called her twin. He banked his dragon hard left. His heels kicked into his dragon's flanks with the urgency of someone with seconds to live. The dragon responded, wings folding tight against its body, transforming into a living missile to intercept the approaching harpoon.

Vaelor's body pitched forward, arms spread wide. He made himself bigger, broader, became a wall of flesh and bone substantial enough to stop what was coming. His cloak whipped behind him like broken wings. The rays of fire caught his face, a face still too young for the scraggly beard he'd been trying to grow. A terrible peace flashed across his eyes.

He had already accepted the inevitable. He had already surrendered, even as his heart still thumped.

His lips moved. Through the roar of wind and dragon wings, she couldn't hear the words, but she heard them in her mind: *"Protect the flame!"*

For an instant so brief it seemed nonexistent, Vaelor felt the instinct to live.

To pull away.

To save himself.

He crushed the thought.

Vaelor closed his eyes and relaxed his body. He positioned himself with the precision of someone who had rehearsed this moment in his mind, calculating angles, ensuring the harpoon would find him instead of her.

His dragon spread its wings at the last second, an ultimate act of defiance, making them the largest possible target. Beast and rider moved as one, synchronized in their sacrifice, both choosing her and her egg's life over their own without hesitation.

Vaelor remembered her as a child, chasing fireflies she could never catch. He raised his chin, stretching his arms wider still, and met death head-on with his eyes wide open. He would buy her one more second.

The world narrowed.

One moment.

One choice.

Then…

The dragon-bone harpoon struck Vaelor square in the chest.

The disruption was immediate.

Waves exploded through Vaelor, the corruption spreading through his veins. And because he was bonded with his dragon Thymorion, the disruption flowed like poison through that sacred tether into the dragon as well.

The scream that tore from their throats wasn't human, wasn't dragon. It was the sound of a soul being ripped in half while still alive.

Vaelor's back arched, his mouth stretched wide. Blood vessels burst in his eyes, turning white to crimson. His hands clawed at his chest, at the space where his Keeper's bond lived, where it had always lived since the day Thymorion bonded with him.

But now only emptiness remained. A *violation*, as if someone had reached into his ribcage and torn out something more vital than his heart.

They fell.

Apart.

Alone.

The space between them might have been inches or miles. It was infinite. Vaelor's body tumbled, the harpoon jutting from his chest like a flagpole of defeat. With each rotation, the dark metal drank more light from his eyes, frost spreading across his skin in fractal patterns. His lips, still forming his sister's name, turned blue, then gray, then white.

"Elara, protect the flame."

Thymorion plummeted beside him. The dragon's massive form, which should have fallen faster, seemed suspended in a cruel parallel descent. They spiraled around each other in a grotesque dance, pulled by gravity and pushed by wind. Each reached out with numb limbs, knowing touch would not occur again.

Chapter 2

Inside the satchel tucked inside Vaelor's cloak, Elara's egg's twin trembled. A cry emerged from within, a noise that should not exist in the world of flesh and bone. This sound, ancient yet fresh, vibrated through magic itself, bypassing the air.

The cry pierced through the chaos of battle, through the roar of flames and the screams of the dying. Everyone, dragon and human alike, felt it in their bones, in their blood, in the deepest chambers of their hearts.

The Commander heard it. And froze. His breath stalled. His eyes widened, stripped of malice, reshaped by an emotion he had not felt in years:

Exultation.

A wyrmling's cry. Alive. Untouched. Within his reach.

He tilted his head, listening. Shock flickered across his features, then calculation, then hunger, possibility sparking like flint behind his eyes. The sound hollowed him out, then filled him with a feverish, terrible purpose.

Slowly, his expression twisted. Softness curdled into desire. Wonder blackened with intent.

A smile, devious and evil, unfurled across his lips.

He heard the future … and he wanted it.

Abandoning Elara, the Commander wrenched the reins hard, turning his Drake away from its intended kill and driving it toward the ground. "Down, Vorthryn. I want that egg."

The obsidian wyrm complied, dropping into a lethal nosedive. The world blurred into streaks of fire and shadow as he plunged through the burning ruin, a black spear cutting into the heart of destruction. The rush of displaced air tore upward in his wake.

At first, Elara couldn't understand why the Commander veered away from her, why his attack broke at the last instant. Then her gaze followed his descent, and the truth struck with sudden, breathless clarity. He wasn't coming for her.

He was diving for the egg, cradled against Vaelor's heart.

Elara screamed, her sound primal, infinite. Her voice carried such concentrated fire, such raw fury and grief, that the very air around her *combusted*. Flames erupted from nothing, reality igniting in response to her anguish.

She urged Solyndra lower. Her gaze swept the chaos, frantic. She searched for the Commander, for the gleam of Thymorion's bronze scales, for the glint of Vaelor's armor, for the unborn wyrmling, *any* sign that they had survived the fall. Somewhere in that maze of flame and shadow was her twin brother and his egg. But all her eyes glimpsed were burning timbers, collapsed walls, and bodies she couldn't identify.

The smoke shifted again, and time stopped breathing.

There, in a circle of devastation where dragonfire transformed the ground into glass, the Commander and his dragon rested.

Elara's eyes traveled downward from the destroyer's obsidian form to what lay at his feet. That familiar mop of dark hair. Those arms that had hugged her only that morning. The chest that should have been rising and falling, motionless as stone.

Her brother. He had promised her he wouldn't fall.

From this height, he looked so small. Like a discarded doll rather than the warrior who'd sworn to protect their village. The ground around him was painted dark, a spreading pool that reflected the firelight like a mirror of blood.

But even that soul-shattering sight paled against what the bringer of death held aloft above his head.

Her brother's precious egg.

It rested, cradled in the destroyer's gauntleted hand like a trophy ripped from the chest of hope. Even from the sky, Elara could see the shell's iridescent surface flickering with sickly veins of corruption spreading from the Commander's touch.

"NO!" she shrieked.

The Commander's helmeted head tilted upward, fixing her with his gaze across the distance.

"So, it seems you brought me yours as well," he whispered to himself.

Elara could feel his smile, feel his satisfaction radiating upward like heat from a forge. He stepped over her brother's body, his armored boot coming down inches from that still, beloved face, a last insult. He reached down and closed his free hand around the harpoon buried in Vaelor's chest. With a slow, grinding twist, he worked the shaft loose and tore it free. Blood streamed down the blade and ran along the length of the weapon, dark and slick as it fell.

"Shall we try this again?" he asked.

His dragon sank lower, folding its wings with predatory elegance. The Commander set the egg upon the ground, then drove the lance into the cradle, smiling as he heard the familiar click. Retrieving the egg, he vaulted back into the saddle, already turning away. Part of his work finished.

The beast's wings unfurled, massive, tattered membranes like the sails of a ship from hell. With a single beat that sent debris spiraling, they launched upward.

Straight toward Elara.

Master and serpent rose to her eye level, close enough that she could see her own reflection in his black obsidian armor. The Commander lifted the confiscated egg. The surrounding air tightened, humming with a predatory pull. The shell's veins, now black threaded with dying gold, shifted and twisted. It rotated in his palm, dragging itself toward the direction of Elara's egg with the inevitability of a compass finding north. No spell guided it, only the ancient bond of Twin Flames, a resonance older than wyrms or men.

As the stolen egg strained toward its twin, the ground answered. A deep, ancient vibration rolled up from the mountain's roots and into the air, resonating through cloud and wing. It was not a quake, but a summoned breath, a pulse of ancient awareness pushing upward from beneath the stone.

The tremor struck Vorthryn mid-flight.

His wings snapped.

The Drake shrieked in fear and lurched backward. His corrupted scales blistered where the tremor touched them; the dark veins beneath his hide recoiled from a force they could not withstand. The flame within him wavered, smothered under the weight of that ancient awareness rising from the deep.

The Commander froze, clamping one hand around the saddle-spine as the Drake thrashed. He knew this feeling.

It was a dragon's mind turning in its sleep.

Terrus.

The Stone Elder Wyrm. The Sleeper of the Mountain.

For centuries, the Commander had trusted the Elder Wyrms' silence. Their sleep was his shield; their absence his empire of ruin. But now, one stirred beneath the mountain, one who recognized the twin resonance, one that recognized *him*.

Another faint tremor rose from the mountain. Barely more than a breath. But Vorthryn perceived it as death incarnate.

Vorthryn screamed again, a ragged, terrified sound, wings convulsing. He veered, climbing in a panicked spiral, fighting to escape an enemy he could neither see nor face.

The Commander hauled on the reins. "Hold, damn you. HOLD!"

But the corrupted wyrm would not obey.

He, a being who had murdered dragons, crushed cities, and razed empires, felt the first flicker of uncertainty in centuries as his Drake fled the valley, retreating into the storm-filled sky.

Behind him, the heartbeat faded. Dragon Mountain stilled. The Sleeper sank again into the deep.

But not fully. Not this time.

A single line of prophecy whispered through the Commander's mind, unbidden and unwelcome:

"When the Twin Flames rise, even the mountains will wake."

The Commander cast one last glance back toward Elara, toward the last egg. For years, he had dismissed the prophecy as superstition. But now the words struck the one place he still bled. Not fear of destiny, but concern that destiny might still remember him. That the world he'd clawed control over could name his failures aloud.

The prophecy didn't drive him. His fear of failure did.

Elara watched the black dragon grow smaller and disappear into the sanctuary of blackness.

Tears filled her eyes. "I'm sorry, Vaelor. I failed you. But I promise I will get it back. That monster will NOT have your wyrmling."

As Elara directed her dragon downwards toward her brother, a faint disturbance stirred the air. A low thrumming vibration rippled across Elara's teeth. The sound built, rose, transformed into something alive and hungry, a keening wail, part shriek of metal, part organic scream.

"Solyndra, MOVE! Another harpoon."

Solyndra's muscles bunched beneath her, the dragon's massive body beginning a desperate roll. But she was too late. The harpoon punched through her chest with the wet crunch of splintering bone. Her scales parted. The tip erupted through her back in a spray of silver blood, corrupted by the weapon's poison.

The wyrm's wings locked mid-beat. Her head whipped back, neck forming an impossible arch, golden eyes wide with shock. No roar came. A soft exhale escaped her throat, as if surprised. Her heartbeat stuttered..

Then stopped.

Her wings fell against her body. Dragon and rider plummeted, Solyndra's dead weight pulling them into a spiraling nosedive. The wind screamed past Elara's ears and tore at her clothes. She felt the saddle lurch beneath her. Her legs lost hold. The wind pulled her free. She was falling, no longer a rider but prey to gravity's indifferent pull.

Her hand shot out with pure instinct, clutching at her satchel. Her fingers wrapped around the leather strap as the world wheeled around her.

Solyndra slammed into the earth beside Vaelor's fallen beast, the impact so violent it created a crater. Wind and dust hammered Elara, lifting and sweeping her up and out over the violent river. Her body burst into a rage of fire as gravity seized her again, pulling her down.

Her body plunged into the river, the icy current closing over her in an instant. The water surface bubbled as it drowned the fire consuming her body. A fine layer of vapor rose toward the sky.

Water rushed into her mouth and nose. The frigid waters thrust a thousand needle-pricks into her skin all at once, stinging, painful, stealing the breath from her lungs. The swift current wrapped around her, dragging her down into blackish water. She hit rock, spun, and lost all sense of up or air.

The river's icy fingers clawed at her clothes, her hair, her limbs, pulling her deeper into its lightless belly. The satchel at her chest, heavy with the dragon's egg, became an anchor, dragging her through the crushing dark.

She fought upward, kicking, clawing through the freezing black, her lungs screaming. She broke the surface, gasping for breath as soldiers' voices filled the night. But the river was stronger. It yanked her beneath the surface again.

Through the water's roar and her own thundering pulse, a voice reached her. She couldn't tell if it was real or imagined.

Protect the flame.

As if answering that whispered command, the river surged faster, its current doubling in strength. The soldiers' shouts grew distant, then vanished as the water carried her beyond their reach, beyond their torches, into the wild dark where only the river knew the way.

A wave crashed over her head. Her body tumbled beneath the surface, robbing her of more air. The world became a chaos of bubbles and blackness. Her body had gone beyond cold now, beyond pain, settling into a strange numbness that felt like warmth. Dangerous warmth. The kind that came before the end.

The egg remained warm, pressed against ribs that scarcely rose and fell. Its heat pulsed against her chest, the last living thing about her. Her locked fingers held the satchel's strap, a grip she could no longer feel or release.

A bend in the river snagged her in its grip. It swept her through a narrow channel where reeds rose thick as spears. A snarl of roots jutting from the bank smashed into her body, and bark scraped what was left of her skin. The water slowed. She drifted into the shallows, rolling until the reeds caught her in their rustling embrace.

The muddy shore cradled half of her body. The other half remained submerged, the current lapping at her ribs like a tongue, still hungry, reluctant to let go. Her body rolled back and forth, a prisoner of the river's pulse.

She tried to crawl higher. Her arms refused. Breath came in shallow sips that misted the air. The world collapsed into simple rhythms: water against stone, heart against cold.

Then something moved below.

A tug above her boot. Sharp. Deliberate.

Another, harder, biting deeper.

She looked down through the murk. Two shapes coiled against her leg above her knee. Sleek, serpentine bodies catching fragments of moonlight. Lungfish. Their jaws locked tight, teeth working deeper with each twist of their heads.

A small cry somehow emerged from her throat, a cry lost to the whisper of reeds. She kicked, but her leg moved as if through honey. Dark threads of blood bloomed in the water around her boot.

Then the venom hit.

It started as heat. Wrong and burning heat. It raced up her leg in jagged lines. Her muscles seized, then went slack. The numbness that had been creeping through her from the cold accelerated, rushing up her thigh, her hip, spreading like spilled ink through her blood. The lungfish continued their patient work, jaws grinding.

The reeds rustled above her, and for a moment she thought she heard that voice again, urgent now: *Protect the flame.*

But her eyes were already closing, the moon fracturing into a thousand pieces above the water's surface.

Chapter 3

The battle was already lost by the time Osric arrived. He crested the ridge at a dead gallop. The world below him was nothing but fire, screams, and falling shadows. He pulled his horse to a brutal stop as a shape streaked across the sky: a cursed obsidian lance.

Osric watched, helpless, as the weapon found its target.

Vaelor.

The lance punched through the young Keeper's chest, and for a heartbeat, the night went silent. Then came the Vaelor's and the dragon's screams and tore the heavens apart.

Osric froze. He knew that scream; it had once belonged to him and his Drake. It was the cry of a bond unmade, the moment the ancient thread between Keeper and Drake is severed forever. He had survived it once, and only because he had been condemned by the Great Elder Drake. He doubted Vaelor would survive.

Both Keeper and dragon fell. They struck the earth with a force that shook the trees around Osric. The ground trembled. The old Keeper waited, hoped, but Vaelor did not rise.

"Go unburdened, Keeper. Your watch is ended," Osric whispered.

Another shadow fell across him.

Osric stilled, his breath catching as the light dimmed too quickly, too completely to be cloud or smoke. He turned, instinct screaming a warning. The darkness stretched, widened, alive.

The Commander's dragon dropped from the sky in a crushing descent, landing beside Vaelor's crumpled form in a spray of embers and wind. An armored figure dismounted with slow, deliberate precision, as though savoring the devastation he'd wrought. He knelt, fingers closing around the shattered remnants of Vaelor's satchel.

The egg, Vaelor's egg, the one Osric had come to protect and train, glimmered faintly within.

Osric's stomach lurched. His throat burned with a curse he could not release.

The Commander stood with the egg cradled in one arm. Osric watched as he seized the spent lance, forcibly pulled it from Vaelor's mutilated body, and rammed it into the launcher. The hunt was not over. In one fluid motion, the Commander vaulted into the saddle. His Drake's wings spread wide, and together they surged upward, turning toward the lone figure watching in the sky above.

Elara.

Osric kicked his horse forward instinctively. He was a world away from her, and the river cut that world in two. Plus, he had no weapon to stop the Commander.

His eyes on Elara, Osric saw the lance streak through the air and strike Elara's dragon. As with each harpoon, the Keeper-dragon bond shattered. Elara was thrown from her saddle. She fell, vanishing beneath the torrent of the river.

Osric drove his horse down the ridge, weaving between broken trees and scorched earth. He reached the river only to find soldiers already swarming the shoreline, searching, shouting, spearing the water with torches and blades.

He could never reach her now. Not yet. Not without being seen.

Osric stiffened beneath the charred pines as a faint metallic whisper slid through the night. The unmistakable rasp of steel leaving a sheath.

Enemy soldiers.

He didn't turn. Didn't breathe. He let them think he hadn't noticed.

Boot steps approached through the needles, soft but hurried. Two sets. One circling left, the other coming straight behind him.

Amateurs.

The first soldier lunged from behind, sword raised high to plunge into Osric's back.

Osric snapped his reins and jerked his horse to one side. The stallion surged forward with terrifying speed, pivoting on powerful hind legs. Osric's blade was already out, a streak of silver in the firelit dark.

He slashed downward across the man's torso, steel carving through mail, rib, and lung with a wet, sickening *crunch*. The force of the strike spun the soldier to the side. He staggered. His hands pressed to the ruin of his chest as hot entrails spilled through his fingers. He collapsed to his knees, choking on his own blood before pitching face-first into the dirt.

The second soldier shouted and charged from the left, braver and faster.

Osric met him head-on.

He drove his horse forward at full impact. The stallion struck the man's chest like a hammer, the collision snapping ribs with a crack that shuddered through the night. The soldier was thrown backward, hit the ground hard, and rolled.

Osric didn't slow.

He guided the horse over the man. Hooves crashed down, crushing the soldier's forearm, then his thigh. The scream that followed was ragged, high, desperate. Osric rose in the saddle and brought his blade down in a merciless vertical stroke. Steel split helmet, skull, and spine, driving into the earth beneath. The soldier spasmed once, then went still as blood pooled beneath the crushed leaves.

Steam rose from the corpses in the chilly air.

Osric reined his horse back to the edge of the ridge, the animal snorting, flecks of gore on its legs. He scanned the darkness. No more movement, no more threats. Only silence, broken by the river below.

He wiped his blade clean on the nearest corpse's cloak and sheathed it with a sharp click.

Traveling up the mountainside, Osric searched for any vantage point, any blind spot to watch the chaos below. At last, he found it: a narrow shelf of stone beneath a canopy of charred pines overlooking the river's black ribbon.

He dismounted, muscles trembling, heart cracking open with every heartbeat he couldn't see her.

And he did the only thing he could. He waited.

The glow of torches painted shifting gold across the riverbank below, where soldiers spread out in a broken line. Their shouts carried faintly through the wind, muffled by the roar of the current. He could hear the clatter of armor, the splashing of boots in the shallows, the rasp of steel drawn and sheathed again in frustration.

He counted at least thirty men armed with crossbows and spears, moving methodically along the water's edge. And above them, circling low and slow through the smoke, came the shape of the ancient Blightfire Drake and its rider.

Whispers filled the air: thin, brittle, and mournful. At first, Osric mistook them for the wind, but his damnation had stripped him of such mercies. Cursed to walk between fire and death, he alone could hear what others could not. He heard their wailing, voices crying out in languages older than stone, pleading for release. The sound came from the Drake. The creature's scales housed the imprisoned souls of those it had slain, forced to sing their own requiem for eternity.

Osric's pulse faltered. The sound *entered* him, threading through his thoughts, clawing at his heart with icy fingers. He could feel their sorrow, their terror, their desperate need to be freed. But over it all, he felt something darker still: Vorthryn's pleasure in their torment. One day, he would free them, but today Elara was his priority.

Snowflakes drifted down from the night sky. Osric pulled his cloak tighter around his shoulders as he pressed himself flatter against the earth as the Drake's shadow glided over him.

Below, the soldiers shouted over the roar of the current, their torches sweeping frantic arcs across the riverbank.

"Spread out! She's out here somewhere!"

"The river's ripping through here. She's washed past us."

"We finish searching here before moving on. This is where she fell. Check every group of reeds. Use your swords to search the bottom. The Commander wants that egg found before dawn!"

Voices were strained, breathless, tinged with fear. Not of failure, but of the man they served.

A new voice cut through the chaos. Authoritative. Demanding.

"Have you found her?"

Every soldier froze. From nowhere, a dragon appeared on the far bank, its wings folding tight against its flanks as it settled into the mud.

"No, Commander," said a soldier running to the river's edge. "The smoke and darkness make it hard to locate her. Plus, the current is extremely strong. She's more than likely been washed further upstream.

The Commander descended from the saddle with predatory grace. His helmet turned toward the river, slowly, as though tracking sounds no mortal ear could detect.

"Call off the search," he thundered. "With the limited visibility, one of your men is likely to injure the egg."

"And what of the girl?"

"The river has already claimed her. She was no use to me. It is the egg that I want."

A soldier gathered the courage, or the stupidity, to object. "But, Commander…"

The Commander turned a fraction of an inch in his direction.

Only a fraction. No more.

The soldier's words strangled in his throat as a faint red glow throbbed beneath the Commander's armor, slow and deliberate, like the heartbeat of something monstrous chained inside his chest. The glow faded… but the warning remained.

When the Commander spoke again, his voice was quieter, and far more dangerous.

"It's too dark to find a corpse."

The Commander paused. He let the words hang like a noose.

"We resume the search at first light."

The soldiers lowered their torches and slowly withdrew, leaving the darkness behind them.

When the Commander turned and remounted, Osric witnessed the egg cradled in his hands. A dragon egg. That meant only one thing. Vaelor was dead.

The egg glimmered for the briefest instant. A flicker beneath its dulled shell, faint as a dying ember, but Osric felt it.

A pulse.

A recognition.

It was alive. And it *knew* him.

The Commander paused. He surveyed the area, searching for something hidden, something foreboding.

Did the Commander feel the egg's pulse too? Does he know I'm near?

Holding tightly onto the egg, the Commander mounted his Drake.

"The egg is connected to its twin," he shouted. "Neither can hide from the other. My egg will lead us to the other's location and the girl's body. We resume the search a mile downriver the moment the sky lightens."

Twin. The word hit Osric like a physical blow. He remembered what the Great Elder Wyrm had told him long ago:

"Keep them safe. Never allow evil to find them both. Together, their power is unstoppable, able to destroy anything and everything. Under the guidance of the Twin Flames, they will unite this world, bring back the days of harmony between wyrms and humans, re-establish the brotherhood of Keepers."

Now he understood. The eggs were two halves of the same whole, drawn to each other like lodestones. And this dark Commander who'd hunted Elara knew it. He'd use the one to find the other.

Osric's jaw clenched so hard his teeth ached. He watched as the Commander turned the captured egg in his hands, studying its surface in the limited moonlight. Each movement felt like desecration. That egg was the last hope of the Great Wyrm Solarus's bloodline, and Vaelor had given everything to protect it.

For nothing.

Osric's fingers wrapped around the knife tucked in his belt, its grip worn smooth from centuries of use. Five soldiers blocked his path to reach the Commander. He could take two, even three of them. But the others would cut him down before he reached the Commander. *Best stay hidden.*

Besides, I must find Elara and rescue her and her egg. Hold on, Little Wyrmling. I will come for you after I rescue your twin.

The Commander took one last look. The dragon roared. With a whirlwind of air, it rose into the night, trailing streams of frost in its wake. The soldiers, hesitant and weary, faded away, their torches retreating one by one into the darkness.

Osric remained hidden until the last light disappeared beyond the bend in the river. Only then did he exhale. His heart had been pounding so hard he hadn't noticed the ache in his ribs until the silence fell.

The Commander was right about one thing: the current was merciless. The girl would have been carried far downstream. Maybe too far. Maybe not far enough.

He brushed frost from his cloak and slipped the reins into his hand. "Easy, Regal," he murmured, patting the beast's neck. "They're gone now." The horse flicked its ears, nostrils flaring at the lingering scent of smoke and dragonfire.

Osric scanned the river, its dark ribbon twisting beneath the moonlight, cold and endless. Somewhere downstream, beneath its surface or along its banks, the girl or her body waited.

"Let's find her before Fate makes up its mind."

He guided Regal down the slope, keeping to the trees, letting the river's sound mask their travel. The night closed in around them, thick with mist. In the distance, thunder rumbled. Or perhaps it was the lingering echo of dragon wings. Osric didn't care to learn which was correct.

He spurred the horse onward. The hunt had ended for the soldiers, but for him, it had only begun. With the soldiers' torches gone, the valley became swallowed in shadow. Only the moon remained, pale and watchful. Its reflection trembled across the black surface of the river.

Osric followed the sound of the water downstream, the hooves of his horse muffled in the damp earth. He kept his eyes sharp, his senses stretched thin. He was determined to find her and the egg.

An owl passed overhead, its wings cutting through the air without sound, a ghost against the stars. The screech that followed barely disturbed the night, soft as a mother's warning to her young, but Osric's trained ear caught it.

"I hear you, Brother Owl." The words left his lips in a whisper. "Take me to her."

The owl banked sharply, moonlight sliding across its barred feathers as it circled once, then twice. Then it dropped low and glided south, following the river's dark ribbon back the way it had come.

Osric pressed his heels into his horse's flanks. The stallion responded instantly, picking his way through the tangled brush. The owl occasionally called back with that same low, throaty sound that pulled Osric forward. They rode hard along the riverbank. The owl disappeared into the shadow, then emerged further ahead, always leading.

Time blurred.

Minutes, maybe hours, passed.

Time was measured only in his horse's laboring breath and the burn in Osric's thighs from gripping his steed's sides.

The river changed. The violent white rush gentled to black glass, and the banks widened. Here, the current had carved a lazy bend, depositing silt and debris in a natural eddy.

The owl settled on a branch of a half-dead willow that leaned out over the water. Its talons gripped the wood with finality. "*Here,*" the gesture said. "*No further.*"

Along this part of the river the reeds grew extra thick, their stalks swayed in the current's pull, their dry stalks rubbing together in whispers that sounded like voices. Like breathing.

Osric reined the horse to a stop. Something tugged at his gaze, a brown shape where the current eddied into shadow. Something was caught against the reeds, half-hidden beneath the black water. For an instant, he thought it was driftwood. Then he saw the hand.

"Please be alive," he breathed as he jumped from his saddle.

He splashed forward, the river rising past his knees, cold enough to burn. The current tugged at him, greedy even now, as though it wanted to keep anything entering its waters. Pushing through the reeds, he reached the still form tangled among them.

It was her.

Elara lay sprawled on her side; her hair fanned across the shore like threads of silver and ash. One arm was submerged, the other entwined around a satchel strap. Her cloak billowed with the current, torn and heavy. The moonlight washed the color from her skin until she looked carved from ice.

Osric knelt beside her, turning her carefully. Her lips were blue, her eyes half-open but unfocused. He pressed two fingers to her neck. A pulse faint, but there.

"She lives," he muttered, relief rough in his voice. "Barely."

Then he saw her leg.

The water around it was dark and cloudy, and beneath the surface, the flesh looked shredded. Two long, torn channels ran side by side, the skin around them chewed into ragged flaps. Strings of tissue clung to the edges, and dark blood seeped steadily from the exposed red meat beneath. The skin was already discolored. The veins above it glowed faintly, an unnatural blue. He knew the signs. Lung fish venom. The poison would already be climbing toward her heart.

He stripped off his gloves and plunged his hands into the icy water. "Not tonight," he said under his breath. "Not to the likes of you."

He pulled her free from the reeds, lifting her into his arms. Her body was limp as he held it against his chest. He splashed through the water, and up the bank to a grassy knoll.

The satchel shifted, and the flap fell open. Inside, the dragon's egg glowed from within, casting soft light across his face. The glow illuminated her pale features, the blood on her leg, the mud and ash that streaked his own hands.

For a moment, the world held still. The fire in the egg seemed to breathe.

Osric's throat tightened. "By the wyrms," he whispered, awe and dread threading his voice. "You survived as well."

He laid the dying girl and the satchel gently on the grass. Kneeling beside her, he peeled the soaked cloak from her shoulders. Next, he withdrew the egg from the satchel and set it beside her. Its warmth spilled into the air, faint but steady, pushing back the river's bitter chill. Steam curled where warmth met cold.

Osric ran to his steed and his saddlebag. His hands shook as he retrieved a small glass bottle filled with shimmering blue powder. He hurried back and tore open the fabric of her pant leg. The wound was deep. He uncorked the bottle and poured the powder into the gash. It hissed as it met her blood, releasing a faint blue light that flickered, then dulled.

Tearing a strip from his own cloak, he bound her leg tightly above the wound to slow the toxin's advance. Her body jerked once, then stilled. Her breath came in shallow, stuttering waves, each one a fragile promise that she still lived.

He glanced briefly toward the south. The smoke of Emberhold still glowed faintly on the horizon, a dying ember against the stars. "You've survived their fire," he said to her quietly. "Don't let the river finish their job."

Osric spread a blanket across the ground. He placed Elara and the egg inside, then proceeded to pull the ends tightly around both, creating a cocoon of warmth. He lifted the bundle, cradling the wrap against his chest, and mounted his horse. He slipped his finger inside and checked her neck pulse again. Although still weak, it was stronger than the first time. He watched in awe as the egg vibrated, its beat keeping rhythm with her heartbeat, pulsing life into her frozen body.

"Brother Owl, bird of the night, lend me your eyes. Somewhere in this forsaken land is rumored to be a sorcerer, a healer educated in medicinal herbs. Take me to her so she can save this child. Time is of the essence."

The owl sprang from the willow branch, wings spreading wide as it caught an updraft from the river. It carved two perfect circles above the reeds, each pass lower than the last. It banked hard west, away from the water. Its body stretched long in flight, feathers catching the moonlight. A single hoot rolled across the night, not the soft warning call from before, but something fuller, almost mournful.

Osric wasted no time. He reined his horse toward the west, riding into the darkness, following his winged guide.

The bird dissolved into the night. But it hadn't abandoned him. Every few heartbeats, another hoot drifted back through the night, a beacon of sound in the blackness, marking its path through trees he couldn't see. Each call pulled at him, insistent, growing fainter with distance.

"Follow," the fading hoots seemed to say.

They rode through the night like creatures possessed, Regal's hooves thundering against earth, then stone, then earth again. Six hours without rest, without water, without mercy. The stallion's breath had gone from steady rhythm to ragged gasps somewhere in the third hour, but he kept running, foaming at his mouth, flecking his chest white in the darkness.

As dawn bled pale gold across the horizon, Regal's stride broke.

First came the stumble; his front leg buckled for a heartbeat. Thirty minutes later came the cough, wet and terrible, spraying blood across his lips. His great chest heaved twice more, ribs standing out like ship timbers beneath his sweat-darkened coat, and then his legs simply... stopped. He went down hard, front knees hitting first, then rolling sideways with a sound like thunder.

Osric barely managed to leap clear, landing hard in the grass as the eight hundred pounds of horse crashed into the earth beneath him. Regal's eyes rolled white, showing their rims. His sides thundered like forge bellows, each breath shallower than the last. Blood ran from his nostrils in twin streams.

"I'm sorry," Osric whispered, his hand finding his steed's neck, feeling the pulse flutter and fade beneath his palm. "You ran true. You ran brave."

One last shudder passed through Regal's magnificent body. Then stillness.

No time for grief. No time for the proper words Regal deserved. Osric wrenched his saddlebag free from beneath the horse's weight, leather straps cutting into his palms. Elara's satchel came next. Last, he gathered the unconscious woman into his arms. She weighed nothing, bird-bones and fever, her skin burning through the blanket he'd wrapped her in.

He ran.

His boots found their rhythm on the forest floor, following the path where the owl's last calls had led him westward. Behind him, Regal's body was already drawing the first flies of morning.

Within twenty minutes, his breath was ragged, his chest burning like a forge. By thirty minutes, his arms trembled from the weight of her. He hoisted her higher and forced his legs to keep moving.

He staggered down a ravine, half sliding with her tight against him. His boot struck a stone; he nearly fell. On instinct alone, he twisted his body to take the impact, shielding her, then lurched back to his feet.

He pushed on.

The forest blurred: shadows, branches, the sting of frigid air carving into his lungs. Sweat mixed with river water. Blood, hers and his, slicked his grip.

Minutes passed. Forty. Fifty. More. Time dissolved into nothing but the next step, and the next, and the next. His vision tunneled. His legs shook violently. His breath came in broken gasps. But he refused to stop.

His body screamed.

He tightened his hold on her, jaw set, a snarl breaking free as he forced himself forward through pure will.

Pain meant nothing. Exhaustion meant nothing.

Then, his knees buckled mid-stride.

He went down hard, shins cracking against exposed roots. Air tore from his lungs in desperate, whooping gasps that sounded more animal than man. The taste of copper filled his mouth. Through the blur of exhaustion, something caught his eye. A glimmer of light ahead. Could it be a campfire or a cottage? As he strained his eyes, the light disappeared, vanishing as quickly as it had appeared.

He struggled to get one foot under him. Osric pushed up and immediately crashed back down. This time, the woman rolled from his arms, the blanket unwrapping as she tumbled into the leaves. The egg spilled free, glowing faintly in the morning shadows.

His strength was gone, stripped from him so completely he could barely remain kneeling. Tears welled, hot and humiliating, carving clean lines through the grime on his face. He turned in a slow circle, breaths shallow, searching for anything familiar. Nothing. The trees were strangers, the shadows thick, the silence heavy. The owl that had guided him was gone. He saw no one who could help, no lantern light coming his way. He was alone.

A twig snapped behind him.

Close.

Through the blur of exhaustion and tears, a shadow separated from the trees, moving toward him with deliberate steps. Osric's hand fumbled for his holster, fingers thick and clumsy as sausages. The gun's grip felt cumbersome, heavy. His hand shook so violently that he couldn't even clear leather.

"Stop right there or I'll shoot you." The threat wheezed out, pathetic, barely louder than the wind through leaves.

"Don't shoot." A woman's voice broke through the darkness, steady and unhurried. "I've come to help."

The shadow moved closer. An ancient face appeared, its skin mapped with a lifetime of wrinkles, hair white as fresh snow. Her eyes were the blue of deep winter ice, but warm somehow, crinkled at the corners with what might have been amusement. On her shoulder, talons gripping the rough weave of her cloak, perched the owl. His owl.

Behind her, a mule stood patient in the traces of a makeshift stretcher composed of two poles and a stretched hide. A young stallion waited beside it, wide-eyed and steady on his feet, watching Osric with intelligent eyes.

The woman knelt beside him, joints popping like kindling, and her weathered hand found his shoulder.

"You've made it, Keeper of Old," she said. "The hard part's over. You've brought her to help." She led the stallion beside Osric's spent body. "Kashmere, kneel down so he can lie over you. Then take him home."

The horse's great head dipped as his front legs folded. His knees touched earth, his haunches following, until his belly brushed the ground.

"You are too heavy for me to lift. I need you to crawl onto the horse's back. He will take you to safety."

Osric glanced toward Elara lying on the ground.

"Do not worry. I will take her on the donkey's stretcher. Soon, both of you will be safe."

The Keeper wanted to protest, but his mouth wouldn't form the words.

He turned his eyes toward the expanse of horsehide before him, knowing what he had to do, knowing his body had nothing left to give. His first attempt failed completely. His arms folded, dropping him back into the dirt.

The elderly woman stepped forward. Her gnarled hands slipped around Osric's right hand, guiding his fingers upward. She curled his fingers through the horse's mane, then repeated the process with his left hand. She clenched her hands, adding strength to his.

"You must find the strength to pull yourself up. Otherwise, the rider and his Drake will find you come morning. Now PULL."

Osric pulled with what little strength remained in his arms. The coarse hair cut into his hands as he gripped and tugged. His body dragged forward an inch. Osric pulled again. He grabbed another handful, higher up. His legs were useless weights, dragging behind him.

Handful by handful, he climbed the living wall. When he could go no further, the woman grabbed his right leg and threw it over the horse's back. It was less of a throw and more of a graceless flop. He ended up sprawled across Kashmere's back like a sack of grain, face buried in the horse's neck, arms dangling uselessly down the far side. He couldn't even adjust his position, only lay there breathing in the smell of horse sweat and old leather.

"Stand, Kashmere." As the horse stood, Osric's body tilted but remained prone on the horse's back. The old woman removed a rope from the stretcher and threw it over Osric. She ran around to the other side and tied it tight, binding the fallen Keeper to the horse. "I think you need this more than she does. Hopefully, this will keep you from falling off until I get you home."

She scurried to where Elara lay in the leaves. Her hands worked quickly, tucking the blanket back around the young woman's still form, ensuring the egg remained pressed against her chest. With her rope now keeping Osric in place, she had no option other than to pull Elara onto the stretcher. Moaning against the strain, she tugged the bundle toward the stretcher. After a minute, she had to stop, gasping for breath.

"I am too old for this," she murmured. Kashmere gave a low whinny. "I know, I know. The sun is rising. I'm going as fast as I can."

She tugged again, then rested. On the third attempt, she pulled Elara onto the stretcher.

With the lead rope in hand, she led the mule forward. Kashmere followed, matching the woman's unhurried pace.

A cottage materialized from the shadows, its stone walls grown over with ivy, windows glowing with light, smoke rising from a chimney hidden beneath moss and climbing roses. Through the open door, herbs could be seen hanging from rafters. A warm fire crackled. Ancient bones and various colored bottles lay scattered across the counter and table.

She hurried inside, leaving both animals at the door. From a wooden chest in the bedroom, she pulled out woolen blankets, armful after armful, building a nest on the woven rug before the hearth. When the pile stood knee-high, soft and inviting as a cloud, she returned to where Kashmere waited.

"Okay, Kashmere, slow and easy," she murmured. She guided the horse into the house, around her favorite chair, and in front of the piled blankets. The moment she untied the rope, Osric's legs slid from the horse. He hung suspended against the horse's side; his fingers still tangled in Kashmere's mane. Then his fingers relaxed, and gravity claimed him entirely. He plummeted straight down, his body meeting the blankets with a soft *puff*. Air rippled outward through the layers of wool and cotton, sending a cloud of dust up into the firelight.

Osric lay exactly as he'd landed, face down, one arm twisted beneath him, legs splayed at graceless angles. Even the simple act of turning his head to breathe took great effort. The blankets had saved him from bruising, but dignity was another casualty entirely.

He sank into the softness, the warmth rising around him like water, cushioning limbs that felt like they'd been beaten with hammers.

The elder woman pulled his legs out into a straight line. She rolled him onto his back, bringing his tucked arm out from his body. Carefully, she turned his head to the right, then rolled him onto his side so he could breathe better. She untied and removed his boots, setting them before the fireplace to dry out. Lastly, she removed his weapon from his belt and laid it on the floor in front of the blankets.

The woman stepped to the stretcher next, murmuring to her donkey as she guided the creature forward. She backed the animal in carefully until the stretcher's frame pressed against the bedding on the floor. Then, she seized the corners of the blanket cocooning Elara and gave a single, steady pull.

The bundle slid smoothly off the stretcher and settled into the prepared nest beside Osric.

Elara's head rolled limply to one side, revealing the ghostly pallor of her throat. She was too pale, too still. The woman scurried into the bedroom, then returned with two afghans made of thick wool, worn soft with age, smelling of lavender and woodsmoke. She shook them out with a snap, laying one afghan over each guest. The afghans warmth settled over them like a blessing, trapping heat against bodies that had forgotten what warmth felt like.

"Kashmere, take your fellow trotters down the lane and stomp out all indication of the stretcher. Every track, every drag mark. Make it as if we never passed."

The horse snorted once and moved off. He neighed, and three mares emerged from the tree line to join him.

Ophira led the mule outside, disconnecting its lead rope and stretcher. With a soft pat on the rump, she sent him to join the horses.

The owl ruffled its feathers as the woman turned her attention to him. "Hayden, have your feathered friends lead wolves and bears to the dead horse. Instruct them to eat the carcass so no evidence remains. Have the wolves drag the saddle and any other of Osric's belongings to the back shed."

The owl blinked once. He launched himself into the morning air, wings cutting through the light with a deep, whispering sweep. His call rolled through the forest, echoing against bark and stone.

A heartbeat later, the woods answered.

Ravens lifted first, black blades slicing the sky. It was followed by the harsher cries of crows and the shrill, warning chatter of jays. They poured upward in a swirling column, their bodies blotting out the sun until the forest fell under a shifting, feathered shadow.

High above, the owl banked toward the eastern ridge, gliding like a silent herald. His call rang out again, this time deeper, more commanding.

In the thickets below, bears lifted their heads. Wolves paused. Every predator within earshot stirred. They eagerly headed toward the feast that awaited them.

The elder woman stepped back inside. Before she closed the heavy door, she peeked at the sun, it's tip now visible over the horizon.

"That was cutting it too close," she said. She closed and bolted the door, then turned to the two visitors lying on her floor. "Now then, let's see what Hayden has delivered to my door."

Chapter 4

Osric bolted into a sitting position, his vision blurred, his mind still spinning. He tried to push himself into a stand, but his muscles would not obey. He heard someone move. He moved his fingers over the place where his weapon should have been. It was gone.

"Who's there? Where is the girl?"

"You are safe, Osric of Old," came a soft, gentle voice. "The girl is safe. She is resting beside you." The elder woman walked over and took his hand, placing it over Elara. "See, she sleeps."

"Where is the egg?"

"Where you placed it. Feel for yourself." The elder guided his hand across the impression of the egg beneath the blanket. Upon reassured both the girl and the egg were safe, Osric's tense body relaxed. The old woman gently pushed his shoulders back onto the blankets. "Now rest. You spent much of your strength getting Elara and the unborn wyrmling here."

"My weapon?"

"On the floor beside you. But you are safe here, hidden within these walls."

The woman did not know whether Osric heard her answer or not. Within seconds of his head resting again on the pillows, he fell into an exhausted sleep.

*****

Osric's brain registered a sound that did not belong. It was the sound of something being chopped and cut, mingled with a voice humming softly. Motionless, he listened, pinpointing where the sound originated from.

Continuing to remain perfectly still, he breathed deeply. The smell of wood burning, fresh herbs and oils, cooking food, and the odor of his own body drifted into his nostrils. Also, the smell of lavender.

He eased his eyes open, keeping them to thin slits. The world wavered at first, shapes smeared and uncertain. He blinked once, then again. On the third, the blur sharpened into focus.

Before him stretched a large room filled with herbs and apothecary jars. An old lady with gray hair stood across the room, chopping vegetables. He watched as she scooped them up and dumped them into a boiling kettle on a stove.

"Welcome, Osric Skaldvar of Glendenhaussen," came the woman's voice. She laid her knife on the cutting board.

"How do you know my name? I do not know you."

"Your name is known far and wide; the Keeper who cannot die. And had I not known of your legend since I was a child, I would have recognized you by the sigil on your shirt and the mark on your hand. Both belong to a time centuries ago, when the Elder Wyrms lived on this earth, and Keepers reared dragons. Do you deny your name?"

"You seem to know my name, but again, I do not know yours."

A soft chuckle escaped the woman's throat. "Have I changed that much since the last time we met? I am Ophira."

"Ophira, the great alchemist?"

Again, Ophira laughed. "The same, but I haven't been an alchemist for many years. Nowadays, I putter around my house and garden and take care of a few chickens, horses, and cows. How do you not know me? You told the owl to bring you here."

"I asked him to take me to the sorceress who was rumored to live around here. I did not know that someone would be you. Besides, I'm having trouble focusing. You are only a blur to me."

"Be patient. Your vision will clear soon. I will help you stand and sit on a chair, then I will bring you something to eat. You need to replenish your strength. You are still being hunted. She and the unborn wyrm still need your protection."

Ophira pulled a wooden, slotted-back chair in front of the guardian. "Use this for support. Try to stand."

Osric gripped the back of the chair and pushed himself upright. His arms trembled, muscles knotting beneath the strain. He rose halfway before his strength gave out, dropping him back onto the bedding with a harsh exhale.

Firelight wavered at the edge of his vision. His limbs burned from the miles he'd carried her, his hands shaking with exhaustion he couldn't disguise.

He drew a steadying breath, but the tremor in his limbs betrayed him, a stark reminder of how much strength he had already spent. "Damn," he muttered. "I'm as weak as a newborn wyrm…."

He hurled his arm forward, striking the chair and sending it across the room, where it shattered against the far wall.

"What did you expect? You may not be able to die, but your body still has limits. You may be immortal in the sense that your body can rapidly repair any damage inflicted upon it. That means your muscles can still only carry so much weight, and your legs can only run for a specified amount of time. Be patient, Osric of Old. Rest. You will recover."

"I've rested long enough."

"Not long enough to undo what you've done to yourself."

Osric's gaze drifted to the small wooden table. A bowl of steaming stew, fresh bread beside it. Close enough to see, yet too far to reach. He tried again, but his legs refused to obey.

Sweat beaded along his brow. The world tilted. His vision dimmed at the edges, but he clenched his jaw and pushed.

Ophira's voice cut through the silence. "Stubbornness does not equal strength."

He ignored her. Inch by inch, he forced himself upright until he was able to sit on the chair's seat. He looked at the sorceress. "I carried her when my steed fell," he said quietly. "I won't lie here while she fights to breathe."

Something in Ophira's eyes softened. She stepped closer, took the bowl from the table, and placed it in his trembling hands. "Then eat," she said. "Did you believe you could run forever without your body collapsing?"

"One never knows what is possible until one tries."

"True." Ophira studied him for a long time. Most men would have collapsed miles back, but he had driven himself past every sane limit, carrying the girl as though he could outrun death. He would burn himself to ash before letting her go, she realized. "I added some herbs to the stew to help your muscles regain their strength faster."

Osric stared into the bowl, exhaustion pressing behind his eyes. Silently, he cursed himself. In his determination to save the girl, he had stripped them both of any real defense. If attackers came now, he would not even have the strength to push them away.

The spoon trembled in his grip.

"I assure you, you both are safe inside my cabin," Ophira said. "Heavy enchantments hide us from the eyes of the world. One day, he will discover how to break my spells and find what I have hidden from him. But that day is not today." She reached down and picked up his weapon from where it lay on the floor. "Here, perhaps this will help with your confidence."

Osric took the weapon without a word, his fingers encircling the grip. His hand fell with a *thud* to his side. *Damn, I can't even lift it. It feels like it somehow tripled in weight.* Seeing the Keeper did not yet possess the strength to lift it, Ophira took it from his hand and slid it into his belt.

His fingers were losing their hold on the spoon. He laid the utensil in the bowl and set the bowl on his lap. His stomach growled for want of more food, but he was not willing to show the old woman his weakness again.

"If you'd like, I can feed you until your hand's strength returns."

"I just need a few more minutes for my fingers to work." Osric flexed his hands, feeling life returning to his muscles.

"The moment I can stand and walk, I need to borrow your horse and donkey. My stallion's body is not far from here. It will be a beacon announcing to the world the whereabouts of your home and our hiding place."

"Do not worry, Osric of Old. Your horse has been disposed of by the animals of the forest. No skin, no bones remain to speak of you passing this way. Your saddle and belongings are hidden well in the secret room behind the root cellar."

Osric stared into the bowl and reached for the spoon again. His hand trembled, but this time he mastered it. He gathered a heavy spoonful and forced it to his lips before his strength faltered. His eyes closed as the warmth of the stew spread through him.

"Why do you call me Osric of Old?"

"Because long ago, when I was young, that is how you introduced yourself to me. Besides, you are very old. None alive has attained even a fraction of your age. Only the wyrms are older."

A smile appeared on his lips. "I am old. But I haven't gone by Osric the Old for some time. How old are you, Ophira?"

"Older than I should be." Noticing that the protector had managed to finish his stew, she took his bowl. "Would you like more?"

"About half of what you gave me before. I didn't realize how hungry I was. I already feel better and stronger."

"How long since you last ate?"

"I don't remember; two or three days." He turned to the sleeping body on the bed. "How is she doing?"

"She's very ill," Ophira said. "The venom and the river took far more than you saw. Her body needs time, and fire, to mend."

"Did the egg suffer any damage?"

"Not that I can tell."

Ophira handed Osric another bowl. This time, his hand did not shake, but he could still feel the heaviness of the bowl. He kept it on his lap.

"What do you know about this Dark Commander? I've heard whispers about him, but I thought he was a myth."

"He isn't a myth," Ophira whispered. "The Dark Commander was once a man, before the Void hollowed him. What he is now... no living thing should be."

Osric's throat tightened. "There were soldiers searching for her. Does he command an army?"

"Not men," Ophira said, her eyes seeing beyond the room. "Not anymore. They are the fallen soldiers of wars, men whose souls were scorched black by the fires they lit. Their armor carries the smell of burnt flesh, their eyes no longer reflect light. They march without rest, without mercy, without life. And they follow only him."

Ophira went still. The color drained from her face, as if drawn out by an unseen hand, feeling something deeper than fear. "He has returned to finish what the war began; to end the bloodline of the Great Elders, especially Solarus'. For those that will survive, he wants to twist them into something that was never meant to exist." Her gaze drifted to Elara and the egg. "The twin dragons will give him the power he craves. He wants to mold them into something evil, something dark like the Drake he rides. They will be his weapon to destroy this world. That's why he hunts them. That's why he won't stop until he has the second egg."

"I won't let him have her egg or keep the one he stole."

"So, my dreams are true. The Commander has Elara's brother's wyrm."

"Yes."

Osric's jaw worked once, a tiny muscle ticking. He chewed down a truth he didn't want to speak aloud. His gaze dropped; not to the floor, but to the empty space near the hearth where Vaelor's egg *should* have been. For the briefest heartbeat, the stoic Keeper looked older, shoulders drawn inward under the weight of a failure he hadn't yet forgiven himself for.

"But the Elder Wyrms will stop him," Osric said.

The words carried conviction, but his eyes didn't. A shadow flickered there, regret sharp and raw. He should have been faster. He should have been there before the thief ever reached their doorstep. He should have…

His breath left him in a slow, controlled exhale, the kind used by men who fear what will happen if they let themselves feel too much. He forced his chin up, meeting her gaze again.

"They won't allow him to use the wyrmlings for destruction and chaos. They WILL stop him."

"The Elders folded their wings long ago and sleep," Ophira said, a great sadness audible in her voice. 'They will not interfere."

"They will. I know it."

"I wish I had your faith in the Elders." The woman took Osric's bowl and walked towards the sink. She stopped partway across the room. "When Solarus cursed you, did he leave no room for redemption?"

"Not that I've discovered. For five hundred years, I've walked the earth and witnessed the crimes of men. In that time, the wyrms have grown fewer. The twin eggs are the only ones laid in hundreds of years. If they are destroyed or corrupted, I have no hope of redemption."

"Did you ever think that Solarus bestowed immortality upon you because he knew that your heart, dedication, and strength would be needed again? Perhaps there is a reason the fates have brought Elara and you together."

"Solarus cursed me because I disobeyed his orders and protected the mixed-bloods. Nothing more, nothing less."

Osric managed to slide off the chair and back onto the blankets. He laid back down, turning his back to the old woman. She spoke nonsense. There was no redemption. But as his eyes closed, her words echoed in his mind.

*****

Ophira's words flooded his dreams. The memories of his cursing, buried deep inside his subconscious long ago, surfaced.

A cry rose from his throat as he watched the Great Elder Wyrm Solarus lift his foot and crush the last two mixed-blood wyrm eggs beneath his weight. The piercing cries of the unborn dragons rang through the air as their shells burst open. Osric stood and watched, his arms restrained between two massive Drakes, unable to stop the killings, unable to stop the sound.

Solarus' voice rolled like thunder across the chamber, ancient and merciless.

"For your defiance, I strip you of your Keepership. No longer shall dragon or flame heed your call. You will walk the mortal world until you redeem the treachery that stains your soul. You shall witness the twilight of the wyrms. And be powerless to stay their end."

The air convulsed. Light flared around Osric, searing through skin and bone. A cry tore from his throat as his bond with his Drake, Kaerath, unraveled thread by agonizing thread. Power fled his veins like water from a broken water jug, leaving him hollow, trembling, less than whole. He dropped to his knees, the sound of Kaerath's screams ripping his very soul apart.

The world dimmed around him, and in that darkness, he understood his curse once more. Not death, but life without flame.

Osric snapped upright, torn from his nightmare. Sweat soaked his body. His breath came in ragged gulps, his lungs refusing to take in the needed oxygen. He turned his head towards the sleeping Elara and her egg, both an obscured blur. He raised his hand and rubbed his index fingers under his eyes, removing his fallen tears. *Could Ophira be correct? Could Elara be the redemption Solarus spoke of? Could my damnation be ending after so many years?*

Osric closed his eyes. He pushed the resurfaced memories once more into the back of his mind. As for Ophira's words? What hope they offered, he pushed aside also. He had no use for such false promises. He had been given a chance to save one, possibly two, precious dragon eggs and ensure their continuation. He would not fail again.

Chapter 5

The scent of smoke and wild sage clung to the air. Elara stirred beneath heavy blankets, her breath catching as fire crawled up her frozen leg. Her thoughts slid apart, fractured by fever, shapes flickering at the edges of her vision that were not there. Instinct rose sharp and immediate: danger. Protect yourself. Protect the egg. She didn't understand. Her mind was lost to heat and shadow, knowing only that something precious must not be taken.

A sound came next, sharp enough to cut through the fever: steel on stone, slow and deliberate. It did not belong in a world of safety.

She turned her head. A man sat by the hearth, drawing a curved blade along a whetstone with measured patience. Firelight dragged his shadow up the wall, lengthening it, distorting it, until it no longer matched the shape of a man, but something older, something that had been waiting.

The man did not look at her. If he sensed she was awake, he gave no sign. He continued to draw the blade along the stone.

Elara watched through a haze, the sound stretching and folding in her mind, as if it came from somewhere far away. Nothing felt anchored: not the man, not the blade, not even herself. Yet his presence held, heavy and certain, pressing through the fog as the only thing that might be real.

The shape of him shifted. No longer a man, but something sharper, colder. A master willing to take what was hers.

Elara's hand slipped beneath the blanket, searching for the dagger hidden inside her shirt. Her chest tightened as her hand frantically searched for the hilt. She could not find the coldness of its steel. Someone had taken it, stripped her of her protection. Her eyes swept across the bed, frantic, pleading. Her eyes caught another knife's hilt protruding from beneath the pillow beside her. The familiar sight steadied her. Her pulse hammered high in her throat as she reached across the bedding with slow, deliberate care. Her fingers closed around the hilt, gripping it hard, reclaiming the one sliver of control she had.

She closed her eyes, doing her best to remember the past events. But her mind was foggy, unsure what was real and what wasn't. She remembered Vaelor's death, her dragon being harpooned. Then she fell, the egg's glow beneath her arm. There was coldness and not being able to breathe. But nowhere in her muffled memories was there a stranger. Was he the one who stripped her boots, tended her wounds, and removed her weapon?

Her fingers closed around the dagger's hilt.

"Your breathing changed," the man said without turning. His voice was low, edged like tempered steel. "You're awake."

Elara froze, heart thudding.

Osric set the blade aside, wiped the sharpening stone clean with a piece of cloth, and then looked at her. His eyes were gray, the kind of gray that comes before storms.

"Where's my egg?" she rasped.

"Alive, beside you," he said simply. "You were half frozen when I found you. The heat from that egg kept your heart from stopping."

She tried to rise, but her leg betrayed her. Pain shot up her side, sharp and searing, like fire consuming muscle and bone. The world tilted. A cry escaped her throat.

The man crossed the room in three strides, his shadow spilling across her like a storm. "Stay still," he said, dropping to his knees beside her. "Lung fish attacked you while in the river. They did some intense damage to your leg."

"Don't touch me!"

She scrambled backward, blankets tangling around her legs, vision tunneling, breath coming in rapid, shallow gasps. Pain roared through her head, but it couldn't drown out the terror, the absolute conviction that this stranger was here to finish what the river, the fire, the darkness had started.

Her eyes, wide and wild, locked on him with the desperate vigilance of a trapped animal expecting the next strike.

Her hand erupted from beneath the blanket before either of them understood what she was doing.

The dagger punched into him with a sick, wet thud. Osric's entire body jerked, breath ripped from his lungs in a harsh, ragged exhale. He stared down in disbelief as the hilt jutted from his chest. His dagger, the one he'd hidden beneath his pillow, was now buried beneath his ribs.

Elara froze; fingers still wrapped around the handle. Warm blood surged over her hand, pulsing in time with his slowing heartbeat. She didn't breathe. Didn't blink. Didn't even *realize* she'd moved. Terror and instinct had fused, hijacking her body, driving the blow home before thought could intervene.

Osric staggered back two steps, eyes wide. A fury born of betrayal tightened his features until every line on his face trembled with restrained violence. He took another unstable step, his body swaying. Blood ran down his torso in dark rivulets.

Elara watched as if inside a dream. The being stood there, the knife's hilt keeping rhythm with the stranger's heartbeat. Blood flowed down his chest. Her hands trembled violently, slick with his blood.

Confused, she reached to pull the dagger free. Osric seized her wrist with surprising strength. "Don't," he rasped. "You'll make it worse."

His grip tightened, forcing her fingers to stay locked around the knife's hilt. "Look past what your fever is telling you. Look with your eyes."

Elara stared, trying to focus.

"Look at ME." Osric's voice cut through the room, hard and commanding, echoing off the walls with a force that demanded obedience.

Her gaze snapped to him. The distortion shattered, the fever loosening its hold just enough to let him in.

Osric swayed, his hand catching the chair before he could fall. "If I meant you harm," he forced out, each word dragged through failing breath, "you wouldn't still be breathing."

He let the silence carry the truth of it.

His grip on her wrist eased, not weak, but measured. Intentional. He released her as though any sudden move would make matters worse.

He wrapped his fingers around the dagger. His arm tightened. Not with strength, but with effort. With deliberate calm, he drew the blade free.

Inch by inch.

The blade broke free with a slick, wet sound. Blood flowed freely from the wound, staining his shirt as it slid downward and dripped onto the floor.

He winced, his breath sharp through his teeth, but he didn't cry out. Instead, he pressed his palm over the wound, blood seeping through his fingers, and met her gaze again. The dagger slipped from his grasp and hit the floor with a dull clang.

Osric watched the blood spill through his fingers. He raised his eyes to meet hers. "I can't believe you stabbed me, you impotent, spoiled brat."

Ophira came in from the outside, her apron filled with all types of medical herbs. Upon seeing the scene in the room, she dropped the plants and rushed to Osric.

"Sit, sit," she said, helping him into the chair. "By all the Elders, what happened? I've been gone only ten minutes."

"She stabbed me," Osric muttered, sagging as his strength failed.

Ophira tore open his shirt, her fingers already pressing a thick pile of cloth to the wound. "You're lucky, Keeper. Another inch and you'd be bleeding out on my floor." She shot Elara a look of fear, judgment, and a warning all at once. But the young woman had already returned to the world between life and death, unaware of what had transpired.

"Keep pressure on that wound, Osric. I need to check Elara." The woman scurried over and lowered her body to her knees. She checked Elara's eyes and felt her forehead. "She's burning up. I need to bring her fever down. Can you wait a few minutes for me to treat you?"

"It's not the first time I've been stabbed, I assure you."

Ophira grabbed the spilt herbs and scurried over to the kitchen counter. She broke off leaves and flowers, placing them inside a pot of water she turned on to boil. From her cupboard, she brought three bottles of powder and elixirs and added them to the brew. When the mixture was ready, she poured it into a glass along with icy water from her well. Rushing to the girl's side, she lifted Elara's head into her lap.

"Here, drink this. It will bring down your fever and take away your nightmares."

The sorceress managed to get the entire glass down Elara's throat. As she lay her back down and covered her with the blanket, she could already feel the girl's body cooling.

"Now for you." She glanced at Osric. His skin was pale, his breathing shallow. His body leaned toward the floor, unable to maintain the strength to remain seated.

Ophira scurried to the kitchen and poured another glass of the mixture for Osric. "Drink this." She lifted the glass to his mouth, assured that his bloody fingers were incapable of holding on to the slippery surface.

Osric took a gulp. He swallowed it, making a gruesome face. "Taste like worm guts."

"Drink it! It will slow your bleeding and keep the wound from getting infected."

"You gave us both the same drink. How can it bring down her fever and slow my bleeding?"

Ophira gave him a stern look. "Who's the alchemist here? You or me? Now I'm not going to tell you again to drink it unless you want me to pour it down your gullet."

"You think you're strong enough to do that?"

"In your present weakened condition, yes!"

Osric chuckled, a rare thing for him. "You're probably right."

Ophira wetted a cloth in the sink and brought it to the Keeper. "Wipe one of your hands so you can hold the glass. While you finish drinking the mixture, I'll tend to your wound."

She removed the cloth to examine the wound. Blood spilled out immediately, making it impossible to ascertain what damage was done. She pressed the blood-soaked cloth back on the wound. "Continue with the pressure. It's bleeding too much to determine the extent of the damage. But it's deep. I'm afraid the only way to stop your bleeding is to cauterize it."

"I already figured that."

Ophira gathered up her cauterization powder and a fire stick. She patted away as much blood as she could and filled the wound with the powder. "What happened? Why did she stab you?"

"I don't know. She woke and tried to sit up. When she screamed out in pain, I went to assist. Next thing I knew she had plunged my knife into my chest."

"She must have been delirious from the high fever. I don't think she had any idea of what she was doing or why. She acted on pure fear and adrenaline."

The alchemist struck the firestick and held it to the powder. A blue flame erupted, sealing the wound from the inside out.

Osric grabbed both sides of the chair seat. He lifted his buttocks up an inch, his face grimacing in pain. Beads of perspiration flowed down Osric's face. Ophira leaned down and blew out the flame.

"You still with me?" Ophira asked.

He nodded. After two minutes, he softly said, "Even if the knife can't kill me, it still hurts like hell."

"Thus is the price for immortality."

"Next time I'm cursed, I'll make sure to ask for no pain." Ophira looked at him, seeing the twinkle in his eyes.

After smearing a glob of salve over the burn, Ophira covered it with a cloth, then wrapped a bandage around his chest.

"Now to bed with you, too. Your body must rest to heal."

As with Elara, the mixture put Osric into a deep sleep. Ophira watched the two slumber. "This stabbing is most unfortunate. Your body is now weaker than it was before. And time grows short. I can't elude him much longer."

*****

Osric stood inside the outer door frame; his fingers wrapped tightly around the wood. The cool, moist air whispered across his bare chest, causing little goosebumps to form across his upper body. Rain cascaded in silver sheets beyond the sagging eaves. The storm rolled across the valley like a living thing, dark and hungry. Lightning split the sky, a jagged wound of white fire. His eyes caught it, held it. When thunder broke overhead, rattling the ancient timbers, he remained motionless as carved stone.

"Still the same fire; too bright to cage, too wild to tame." he murmured, as Ophira stepped outside. "How's she doing?"

"She sleeps. The medicine is warring inside her against the poison and torn tissues. But she is alive." Ophira looked down at Osric's blood-soaked shirt in her hands, turning it over thrice, evaluating the blood stain. "It's going to take a barrel of kickleberry seeds to get this blood out."

"Do the best you can. I'm used to bloodied clothing. If nothing else, stitch up the tear. It will be sufficient."

"You know, she didn't mean to hurt you. She honestly believed you were her enemy."

"Acting without thinking sets a dangerous precedent. She's impulsive, stubborn, and reckless. And that combination will make our training hell."

"Weren't we all at her age?"

"No, I never was."

"I doubt that." Ophira paused, looking out at the rain. "You asked me what I knew about the Commander. I did not tell you everything I know."

Osric turned and gave her a disapproving look. "What haven't you told me?"

"Ever since the Dark Commander appeared, I've been trying to trace his heritage, figure out where he came from. He has hidden his past well. But the other night, the night he attacked Vaelor and Elara, something happened. The Great Elder Terrus stirred, his conscience awake by the Commander's taking of the other egg. He was awake for only a second. But in that second, he revealed the truth to me. The Commander is Malachar."

Osric's eyes grew wide. Surely, the woman was joking. "That's not possible, Ophira. The Commander is too young to be Malachar."

"Says the man who has lived for five centuries and never ages. I tell you, he's the same being. Malachar is the Commander. The Commander is Malachar. He follows the signs, hunts the Twin Flames."

"If what you say is true, Elara and her wyrmling are in greater danger than I imagined."

"As are you." Ophira turned, heading back inside to start dinner. She didn't mean to look toward the root cellar, but her eyes betrayed her, sliding toward the back of the cottage as though tugged by an unseen thread. The heavy wooden door sat in silence, yet the air around it felt… watchful. Beneath the floorboards, in the cold hush of the earth, lay a secret she had hidden for years. It seemed to stir, sensing its moment drawing near. She wondered what Osric would say.

Chapter 6

Elara's fever surged again that evening, heat rolling through her until the blankets clung to her damp skin. Her dreams wavered between fire and frost: hands lifting her from mud, salve pressed into her wounds, a woman's voice murmuring words she couldn't hold onto.

Protect the flame.

Through the haze, one face kept returning: gray eyes, streaks of ash in his hair, the Keeper's mark glowing faintly on his hand.

"You're safe," his voice whispered, finding her even here. *"I will protect you."*

The words settled inside her like a spark waiting for breath.

*****

A crow slammed onto the windowsill, its talons screeching across the stone. It leaned forward and pecked hard against the glass, a sharp, hollow strike. It cawed only once.

Ophira walked toward the window without a word. The moment she pulled it open, the crow hopped inside. Its feathers shuddered in sharp, nervous ripples. It chattered in a harsh, broken burst of sound that was nothing like the sound of a normal bird. This was clipped. Urgent. A message formed of dread.

The crow lurched into the air and vanished back through the window, leaving the room trembling with the echo of danger.

"Is everything okay?" Osric asked.

"My scouts say the Commander's forces are thirty miles out," Ophira said. She didn't stop moving. Her hands worked quickly, gathering vegetables and chopping without looking. "They will reach the valley soon."

Osric's shoulders stiffened. "Will your enchantments hold?"

"No," she said. "He is too strong for me. He will soon break my defenses."

"Any idea when she might be strong enough to be moved?"

"The lung fish poison has taken a heavy toll upon her body," Ophira said. "If it were not for the unborn dragon's healing power, she would already be dead. It will be months before she is fully recovered."

"We can't wait that long. I need to get her somewhere safe now, then hunt for the egg the Commander stole."

"You are correct; you cannot wait." Ophira dropped the potatoes into the boiling chicken broth. "You must leave two days hence."

"She's too weak. She'll never survive the journey."

"With the egg's power of healing, I believe she can."

"And where do we go? If he can find us hidden here, he can find us anywhere. The egg he stole will lead him straight to Elara."

Ophira reached over and withdrew five carrots from her basket. She sliced off the tops and bottoms, then sliced them into small discs. "There is only one place you can go where he cannot follow, where she will be safe until she recovers. You must take her into the Dragon Mountains, to the hidden cave in the highest mound. The cave of the Elder Wyrm, Terrus."

"Terrus' cave?" Osric shouted, jumping to his feet. "Are you crazy, Old Woman? Terrus is one of the wyrms who agreed with Solarus to condemn me to this cursed life."

"It is the only safe place, and you know it. When Terrus folded his wings and became Dragon Mountain, he sealed all his powers inside until he and the other wyrms are once more needed by man. His fire keeps the cave warm in a frozen world. Edible plants and roots grow in the fertile ground. A pool of water offers a warm healing environment to heal and cook. Plus, his scales will prevent Vaelor's stolen egg from locating Elara's unborn wyrmling."

Osric flung the rag he was using to clean his sword on the floor. "No, I won't go."

"Then Elara will die, and the unborn wyrmling will be Malachar's to corrupt. It is your only choice, Osric."

His boots hammered against the floorboards as he walked to the window. He stared in the direction of the mountains. The trees beside the cottage hid Terrus' home from view, but the Keeper did not need to see the mighty mountain to know the fortress was there.

The world beyond the glass seemed to pulse. He felt it in his bones, in the old mark burned into his hand, in the breath that caught in his chest. A pull, subtle yet vast, reached out to him.

He knew.

He *always knew* where they slept: Terrus, Solarus, Noctis, and the remaining four Elder Wyrms.

Osric sensed each dragon's minuscule heartbeat as they slumbered. Their dreams pressed against his awareness like heat against skin: slow, mighty, rumbling with the weight of creatures older than history.

He drew in a sharp breath, tilting his head, listening. *Something is different this time. Something has changed. The dragons are not as deeply asleep as they should be.*

He kept his focus on the outside world, his back to Ophira. "It doesn't matter, anyway. The cave doesn't exist. It's a myth, Ophira. A story old men tell around campfires to children."

"You're wrong, Osric Skaldvar of Glendenhaussen. It exists. I have been there."

Osric pivoted sharply; the room seemed to tighten around him. His eyes widened, bright and cold. "You've been to Terrus' sanctum?"

"Yes, when I was a young Greenwitch. It was late fall, and I became lost in the mountains. An early snowstorm swept in, and I would have died except for the fact that a flock of crows led me to the cave. There, I met the sleeping Elder Wyrm and had many conversations with him while the snow piled up outside. I wasn't able to leave for five months."

Osric's eyes narrowed; one brow arched slightly higher than the other.

"You doubt me. Ask me something only Terrus and you would know."

The protector thought hard. *What would only the wyrm and I know?* Osric took a step forward, placing his hands on his hips. A smirk crossed his face. "What was the last thing Terrus said to me when Solarus cursed me?"

"You will bear witness to the end of the wyrms and be helpless to stop it. You will know their silence in your soul until the hour you redeem the balance you have broken. You will remember this, Osric Skaldvar, until the stars forget their names."

Osric froze, the words hitting him like a physical blow. His eyes widened, pupils shrinking to pinpricks as the color drained from his face. For a heartbeat, he didn't breathe. His mouth parted slightly, trying to form words that refused to come.

Then he stumbled back, one hand groping blindly for balance. The chair caught the back of his knees, and he collapsed into it with a dull thud.

His jaw worked soundlessly. A muscle twitched along his cheek. Disbelief warred with dawning horror in his eyes; the look of a man whose foundation had shifted beneath him.

"How…how could you possibly know that?" he whispered, voice raw, the question more a plea than an accusation.

"As I said, we had many conversations over those five months. Many, unbelievably, about you. Was I correct?"

"Yes," came a haunting sound.

"Then you believe I speak the truth?"

Tears slid down the former keeper's cheeks. "I can still hear his words like it was yesterday. They are carved into my heart, my soul. They are with me the moment I wake and haunt my dreams at night. Yes, you are correct. I believe you have entered Terrus' sanctum."

Ophira walked over to the window and looked outside. "Clouds are building in the east. Winter comes early in the mountains. The cave will sustain you. Food. Warmth. Protection."

"And how do you propose we make the journey?" Osric asked. "I can't carry her all the way. We've already seen what happens when I try that."

"The mare will carry you there," Ophira said, tone hardening, "She is young and strong. She'll make the journey within a week. Plus, you'll need her for meat once winter traps you in."

Osric grimaced but said nothing. He knew the mare must be sacrificed if they were to live.

*****

They ate quickly. Ophira cleaned the bowls and set them on a towel to dry.

"Your strength is returning," she said. "But time is against us. He draws ever closer." Ophira motioned her hand. "Come to Elara's bed. I will teach you how to tend to her wounds."

"I can assure you, I've attended many wounded Keepers and soldiers during my five hundred years of exile."

"Have you ever treated lung fish venom?"

"No. But it can't be much different than other poisonous animal bites."

"It is thinking like that that has put many men, women, and children in their early graves." Ophira walked over to Elara and rolled the cover away from her leg. She cut away the bandages, revealing an ugly wound.

"You can see where I sliced open her leg to drain the poison. Thankfully, the oozing has lessened, but the flesh is still angry."

The wound was an ugly swelling of tissue, flushed deep red and rimmed with sickly yellow. Heat rolled off it, the skin stretched tight and glistening, pulsing faintly with each sluggish beat of her heart. A thin thread of pus traced a line through the blood.

Ophira handed him a cloth. "Put pressure here," Ophira murmured, pointing to a discolored area. "Push hard. You must press until it runs clean. You need to draw out what's left of the infection."

Osric braced himself and pressed down, feeling the resistance give way beneath the soaked linen. A sickly warmth spread under his palm as thick pus oozed from the edges of the wound, yellowish green, the stench of decay rising from it like a living thing. It reminded him of the swamps of Vanguard after a storm when the stagnant waters turned black and the air reeked of rot and death. He swallowed hard against the bile creeping up his throat. *How is she still alive?*

He glanced up, meaning to ask Ophira how long the venom would linger. But then he saw Ophira's eyes staring in disbelief. He followed her line of sight. Above the wound, her skin was darkening; first to a warm tan, then to a soft bronze sheen that caught the lamplight. Tiny scales shimmered beneath the skin.

Ophira looked up sharply. "What is that?"

By the wyrms. I don't believe it. Osric reached out, his fingertips brushing the scaled pattern spiraling down her thigh. *It's smooth and warm. I can feel it pulsing faintly beneath my touch.* "I've seen this before," he murmured.

"In a wound?"

He shook his head. "No. In the Riders. Those whose bond with their wyrm was too strong." He swallowed. *How could I ever forget? Those keepers shared too much of themselves with the creatures they rode.* "The dragon's essence seeps into the flesh. Their bond becomes more than spiritual."

Ophira's brow furrowed. "But her dragon is not yet born."

Osric looked at the egg resting beside her, its surface veined with faint light, pale gold moving like breath beneath a shell of stone. "That doesn't matter," he said softly. "The bond's begun. The unborn is drawing strength from her now that its twin is gone."

Ophira's eyes flicked from Elara's leg to the egg. "Then she's feeding it?"

He nodded. "In part. It's how an unborn dragon survives when its other half is gone. That's why twin dragons are seldom born. It's too dangerous. The unborn dragon will keep taking what it needs until the balance shifts. Or until Elara has nothing left to give."

He looked at Elara's face. Her lips were pale, her lashes trembled against her skin. *You do it without hesitation, don't you? You'll give your last breath if it means your wyrmling lives?*

A warmth pulsed beneath his hand, spreading from her leg into his own fingers. It wasn't heat, not exactly, but something deeper. A hum of life that made his heart stutter. *It's reaching through her. It's trying to communicate.*

Ophira moved closer, her voice hushed. "I thought the egg was healing her, not draining her. We need to separate them."

Ophira reached out to remove the egg. Osric hand stopped her. "No, she still needs the wyrmling's healing power. And it needs her. If we break the connection, chances are both will die."

"Then what do we do? Allow the egg to weaken her to the point of no return? I will not agree to that."

Osric hesitated, thinking. "I suggest we separate them for a few hours each day. We can set the egg by the fireplace to keep it warm. The bond won't be broken, but it will be lessened. And that might be enough to help her live. Plus, there's the possibility the unborn will hatch before it kills her."

"You said the unborn dragon is drawing strength because the bond with its twin has been severed?"

"Yes. Like Elara and her brother, the two eggs depended on each other to exist. One cannot develop without the other. If the bond is broken, and it is strong enough, the surviving wyrmling will seek another to bond with. The embryo is trying to survive."

"Is Elara drawing strength from the wyrmling?"

"I believe so. All Keepers and their bonded dragons share a beneficial strength. But I've never seen it before between a Keeper and an unborn dragonet. I've never encountered anything like this before." He lifted the cloth. "The pus has stopped draining. What do I do now?"

For the next forty minutes, Ophira taught the Keeper how to dress and tend to Elara's wound. When he was finished, and her leg was rewrapped, he removed the egg and placed it in its satchel before the fireplace. Within minutes, Elara's body was cooler to the touch.

"Let's get more supplies packed," Osric said. "We need staples such as flour, salt, and blankets."

"In a moment. I have something I must show you first."

Ophira walked across the kitchen and slipped through the root cellar entrance. Within seconds, the sounds of stored supplies being dragged across the floor reached Osric's ears.

"What are you doing in there?" Osric shouted.

No answer came back; only the steady disturbance below. Items being moved, not in haste, but with intent. The muted knock of jars, the low grind of weight shifting across the cellar floor.

Osric listened, every sound sharpening, separating.

The noise dropped lower, deeper, as if it had slipped beneath the room itself. A strained creak followed, wood resisting, then yielding, a sound that did not belong to anything meant to be opened.

A trap door.

A faint wind rose through the floorboards, cold and old, blowing across his feet.

Then came a new sound of iron. A slow, deliberate scrape. Metal against stone, heavy but controlled. A soft clink followed, then the careful lift of something that carried weight beyond its size.

Osric's breath stilled.

Whatever she was getting down there… it had been hidden for a reason.

"Do you need help?"

"Nope." Ophira shouted. She stepped out, dragging a large, iron cradle from the room.

Now what is that old lady up to?

"You said Elara's egg needs another egg to bond with?"

"Yes, but there are no others."

"That might not be true." Ophira yanked the cradle across the room, her robes trailing ash as she knelt beside the hearth. From within a blackened iron cradle, she drew back a layer of charred cloth. A gray, stone-like oval rested within. As large as a man's skull, dull as weathered bone. It bore no glow, no warmth, only the stillness of centuries.

Osric stared, his throat tightening. At first glance, he didn't recognize it. But as the firelight shifted, faint veins glimmered beneath its surface. Thin, branching filaments of gold fossilized into the shell-like veins of buried light. The pattern was unmistakable.

He stepped closer, disbelief hardening into awe. "Where in the hell did you get a dragon's egg?"

Chapter 7

"Do you not recognize the reason for your damnation?" Ophira asked softly. "Legend says a Greenwitch found it beneath the Dragon Vaults almost five hundred years ago. The egg called out to her, telling her it was meant for a Keeper in the future."

Osric reached toward the egg but stopped short. The air around the second egg shimmered faintly, holding its own breath. "It shouldn't exist," he said, voice trembling. "It CAN'T exist! They were all destroyed. I saw Solarus crush every egg."

Ophira looked into his eyes. She could see them filling with tears. "Some fires refuse to die, Osric. I thought it could bind with Elara's egg, to help it grow. Perhaps even help you."

Osric's hand trembled as he placed it in the air beside the gray egg, cold with memory. *Could you be the egg I saved and was cursed for?*

"Do you not see the truth? Your flame was not extinguished as you thought. It's been waiting, trapped, and forgotten. And now it calls again to be released."

"Who was the Keeper it was waiting for?"

"If the egg told her, the Greenwitch never revealed the name. All I remember is that the one it sought would bear the echo of flame and mercy both, the touch of destruction and deliverance intertwined. She wrote that when that soul drew near, the stone would remember its purpose." Ophira's eyes lifted to Osric then, the firelight catching in their depths. "It has waited for you for a long time."

Osric crouched beside the cradle, his breath shallow. The air surrounding the egg was cold and heavy, the kind of cold that came from places the sun forgot. *It can't be alive. Not after all this time.*

He reached out his fingers. The egg was rough. Stone, not shell.

No pulse. No heat. Only silence.

Osric rose, his boots stomping across the stone floor as he headed toward the front door. "You're crazy, Old Woman. The wyrmling inside this egg died centuries ago. It was not meant for me. It's useless."

"So, I thought too," Ophira murmured behind him, "It has never stirred since I've had it. Not for my mom, grandmother, or great-grandmother either. I thought it was dust until this mark appeared."

Osric froze mid-step. Air refused to enter his lungs.

A mark? Is it possible?

He turned, every movement taut with disbelief. Ophira gently rotated the egg, revealing the truth he had never expected to face again. Across the surface, a faint shimmer traced the outline of something once hidden; a symbol etched not by hand but by memory. It curled like smoke, forming the silhouette of a dragon in flight, wings unfurled in an endless arc that circled back upon itself. The mark seemed to breathe, half illusion, half miracle, as though the shell remembered the creature it once promised to bear.

Slowly, Osric lifted his right hand into the light.

There, inside his palm above his wrist, a faint mark gleamed through the grime, so faint he might have thought it a scar, half-healed and almost gone. But a faint glow stopped his breath. A branching line of gold faintly glowed, curling like the veins on the fossilized shell. It pulsed across his palm.

It cannot be. Solarus erased my binding mark.

When Osric was cursed, his fire bond faded with his dragon's hibernation; the last of the bond-blood burned away and took every trace of the bond with it. For 500 years his palm remained dark. Yet here it was again, faint, ghostlike.

Awake.

He glanced back at the egg. The veins caught the firelight, matching his mark exactly, curve for curve.

A cold sweat broke across his brow. *It knows me.*

Ophira noticed the shift in his expression. "What is it?"

He dropped his hand quickly, curling his fingers into a fist. "Nothing." His voice came out too fast. Too defensive.

Ophira saw what he tried to hide: a faint tremor in his hand, a quickness of his breath. Her gaze drifted to the light glimmering through his fingers, faint but unmistakable.

Her eyes narrowed. "You may be able to hide your mark, but not its glow. You've carried it before."

Osric didn't answer. He kept his hand clenched, the scar hidden in his palm. A moment of hope burned through him all the same.

Ophira rose slowly, her expression unreadable. "You're connected to it."

"No," he said. "I can't be. All bonds were severed long ago."

But even as he spoke, the lie soured in his mouth. The air near the egg seemed to grow heavier, the shadows thicker, as though listening. *How did you live when the others didn't?* The thought rose uninvited, sharp, and merciless.

Ophira stepped closer, voice softer now, but edged with awe. "You are one of the original Keepers."

His jaw tightened. "Once, but no more."

"You were there," she said. "You witnessed Solarus give the order to crush the mixed-blood eggs and destroy any born hatchlings."

Osric looked away, the fire casting molten light across his face. "I followed my orders," he said hoarsely. "Until I didn't."

Silence stretched.

Ophira's eyes darted to the egg, then back to him. "You defied Solarus."

He exhaled through his nose, the memory clawing its way up from the darkest corners of his mind.

The screams of the young dragons filled his ears. He felt them, vibrating through his ribs and burrowing into his bones. The air burned sharp and dry. Heat clawed at the corners of his eyes. Tears welled unbidden, obscuring the world in a blurry smear. He tried to blink them away, but each blink only dragged the sting deeper.

The air grew dense and oily, coating his tongue until he could almost taste the young wyrms' death.

I couldn't watch them die. Not the children. Not when they bore no fault but their blood.

"I tried to save them." His throat tightened before his words found air. When they came, they barely stirred the space between them. More breath than sound. His vocal cords loosened, the muscles in his neck slackened, and the words slipped out on a thin exhale. "The flames took the nursery, and the vault collapsed. I believed all had died."

Ophira's gaze slid toward the dull, veined shell in the cradle. "It appears one survived."

He looked back at the egg. *No… you can't be the one I saved. No dragonet survives dormant for five hundred years.*

The mark on his wrist burned brighter. *Yet there you are. How can I not believe my eyes? How can I ignore the truth inside that cradle?*

"The shell was never shattered," Ophira went on, almost to herself. "The fire petrified it instead. Trapped it between life and death. You were cursed by Solarus that day. Perhaps it was not condemnation, but design."

He sank to one knee before the cradle, the truth settling in like ash. *All this time, I thought my curse was survival. But it was remembrance.*

The silence pressed down between them, thick with old sins.

Ophira's voice dropped to a whisper. "You carry the blood mark of its Keeper. If it lives, it will know you."

"If it does live, then I owe it the truth. And the dead their answer."

"You will have both soon enough. The past is stirring, Osric. You can feel it, can't you? The day of your redemption is at hand. "

He didn't deny the possibility.

"I never…"

The high screeches of crows cawing sounded.

"Something's wrong," Osric said, running his hand across his eyes to dry his tears.

"Soldiers," Ophira said, rushing to the window as the flock circled her cottage. "At least twenty. And …" Her face blanched, lips paling, the warmth vanishing from her cheeks. The skin stretched taut over the bone. She turned her gaze to Osric. "Hurry, take Elara and the eggs to the hidden room behind the back storage area. He's coming."

Osric slipped Elara's egg into its satchel. He shoved his weapons into his waistband. "You think they'll find your cottage?" He slipped the egg carrier over his shoulder, then lifted Elara into his arms along with her blankets.

"They won't, but HE will. The Commander has found me. Somehow, he's finally penetrated my defenses as I feared. He rides upon his black wyrm, drawing closer."

Ophira tossed the medical supplies into a basket and pushed them beneath Osric's arm. She grabbed the soiled bandages and tossed them into the fire, stoking the charcoals to make sure they burned.

"Quick, into the secret room behind the cellar. If things go wrong, follow the tunnel in the back room to the outside. It opens far enough out that you should be able to get away."

"But we won't have any food or supplies."

"No, but you'll have your lives and both eggs. Head toward the Dragon Mountains. Halfway there, you will discover a hidden cellar buried beneath a dragon-shaped rock. There are limited supplies there that will last you a few days, and some medical supplies. With luck, they'll see you or Elara aren't here and will leave without an incident."

Osric reached into his side pocket and withdrew a small weapon. "Take this in case things do go wrong."

"No. If they see me with a weapon, things WILL go wrong." The crows cawed again, this time even louder.

Cradling the orphaned egg, Ophira followed Osric into the root cellar. She reached for a concealed panel and tore it open, revealing a second room that stretched back into darkness. Small illuminating bulbs lined the ceiling, casting an eerie glow down the tunnel.

"Remember, you must make it to Dragon Mountains and seek Terrus. He will protect you from the Commander. He is obligated to protect Solarus' lineage." The sorceress set the second egg on the floor beside a pile of grain sacks.

"Good luck," Osric said. He placed Elara's egg beside the other on the floor, then sat down on the sacks, holding Elara tightly.

"No matter what you hear, do not emerge. My life is nothing compared to theirs." The sorceress looked at the woman and the two eggs. "Together, they are capable of defeating him."

Without another word, Ophira darted into the root cellar and hauled the inner door shut behind her. The metal groaned as it sealed, a heavy, protesting sound. Dust broke loose from the ceiling, drifting down in a fine veil that settled over the fugitives.

The air turned musty and stale, thick with earth and long neglect. Elara's egg burned brightly at Osric's feet, its glow steady, alive. Beside it, another light answered, its glow barely visible and struggling. The light from the hairline cracks of the second egg were too weak to claim the space, yet it refused to fade.

Ophira ran her fingers along the frame, whispering the words that blurred the seams until the door vanished into the wall. She sealed it with an invisibility lock, then dropped two tarps from the hooks above, letting them fall in careless folds.

She dragged crates into place, six in all, stacking them with just enough disorder to look unplanned. Two sacks of grain followed, slumped against the pile as if they had always been there.

Taking up the broom, she swept away the loose dirt and the deeper marks of Osric's boots. When the floor was clean, she stepped through it herself, again and again, crossing her own path until no single trail could be followed.

At the threshold, she paused and looked back.

Nothing drew the eye. Nothing asked a question.

She ran to the kitchen sink and quickly washed, dried, and put away Osric's bowl and utensils. Hers, she left as an indication she ate alone. Taking the remaining bedding, she rushed into her bedroom and threw it over her bed, then hurried back, folding up the cot and shoving it into a corner.

The crows sounded their warnings again, accompanied by the sound of large wings moving through the air. The Commander, on top of his dragon, was close.

Ophira hurried into the kitchen, forcing her hands to stay busy. The stew went on to simmer, its soft bubbling the only sound in the cottage. A cutting board and three potatoes landed on the table.

She steadied the first potato beneath her fingers and dragged the flat of her knife across the skin. A single curl lifted, slow and perfect. The second peel fell. Then the third. Each motion sharper, quicker, hoping speed alone could drown out the uneasy quiet gathering in the room.

A violent knock crashed against the door, rattling the hinges and freezing her breath in her lungs.

"Who is it?" she shouted.

Another knock, harder and louder.

She wiped her hands on the kitchen towel hanging from her waistband, although they were already dry. The silence in the cottage pressed close. Even the fire had dimmed to a faint orange pulse.

She forced her feet to move toward the door. Each step felt heavier than the last. Her fingers brushed the cold iron latch, and the chill bit into her skin.

Click.

The sound of the lock releasing cracked through the quiet like the snap of a breaking branch. For a breath, she hesitated, her palm resting against the door, then she drew it open.

The hinges gave a long, low groan, the kind that sounded too human to be metal. The door swung wide, letting in a rush of frigid air and the smell of damp earth.

Three soldiers stood on her doorstep, armor dull beneath the morning light, their faces half-shadowed beneath their helmets. Behind them, the field was alive with movement. Two dozen more soldiers arrayed in a loose semicircle, their spears catching the faint gleam of the rising sun. Beyond them, barely visible through the thin haze, loomed Malachar's Drake, its wings folded, its eyes burning faintly red as it watched.

And beside the beast, still as a statue, stood the Commander himself, his gaze fixed on her cottage.

Ophira steadied her breath, her fingers tightening around the towel. "How may I help you, gentlemen?" she asked, her voice calm even though every instinct screamed to bolt the door and bar it again.

"Stand aside for Commander Malachar, the Keeper of Dragons," stated the soldier on the right, his voice steady and firm.

The Commander's shadow stretched long before him, his boots striking a rhythm that echoed through her chest. Her pulse hammered, but her breath came slow, controlled. She could not let him see the tremor beneath her calm. Curiosity was his weapon; silence, hers. She steadied her gaze on him, eyes cool as tempered glass, her expression composed into something unreadable. Whatever storm roiled inside her, she buried it deep, giving him nothing.

"I did not know there were any dragons still alive one could be the keeper of."

No fear.

No flicker.

She watched him come closer, his strides long and unrelenting, each one eating away the space between them. Dust rose behind him, curling through the air like smoke from an approaching storm. Four minutes, no more, and he would be at her door. The ground seemed to shrink beneath his boots, the air heavier with every step. By the time he reached the front step, the silence felt brittle. Even the wind dared not move.

"Who's to say what exists and what does not," came the Commander's voice.

"Good day, Commander," Ophira greeted. "How can I be of service?"

The Commander's gaze swept over the cottage with thinly veiled disdain. "So, this is why your little dwelling hides behind an invisibility spell?" he said, his tone sharp with accusation. "I've flown patrols over this sector for years and never once saw so much as a roofline…until yesterday."

His eyes narrowed, lips curling in faint contempt as though her mere existence offended him.

Ophira met his gaze; her hands folded neatly before her. "That's strange? I know of no spell hiding my home. It is set back a way, hidden by trees and bushes. Often the mountain's shadow bathes it in darkness. Perhaps that is why you did not see it before."

He studied her for a moment, eyes cold, unblinking. A faint sneer tugged at the corner of his mouth. "Darkness," he said, tasting the word and finding it beneath him. "Perhaps."

He stepped closer, the earth crunching beneath his boots, his shadow sliding across the threshold to meet her feet.

She did not step aside.

The Commander's gaze drifted past her shoulder, past the closed doors, suspicion sharpening his features. "You live alone?" he asked, though it wasn't a question. It was a challenge; an accusation wrapped in civility.

"I do," Ophira replied evenly. "The solitude suits me. I did have a cat, but he disappeared a few weeks back. You didn't happen to see a white cat on your way here, did you?"

He took a step forward, ignoring her question. Again, she blocked his entrance. "That strains belief," he said. "A woman alone, in a wilderness such as this?" His tone carried the same derision he might use on a lying child.

She allowed herself the smallest smile, faint, and patient. "I expect you to think whatever you wish, Commander. My life requires no defense."

His eyes narrowed. "But it does require explanation." He pushed past her without permission. The scent of leather and metal filled the air as his shoulder grazed the doorway. "A woman such as yourself is not safe."

Ophira followed behind him, her steps soundless. Every instinct screamed for her to act, to protect what lay hidden beyond the inner door. But she did not falter.

Chapter 8

The Commander prowled through the cottage like a man inspecting a conquered land, each step deliberate, each glance heavy with judgment. His armor scraped against the walls as he moved, the scent of metal and dust trailing behind him.

He ran a gloved hand over the mantle, smearing the thin film of ash that coated the stone. "A lonely life, I see," he said. "Unless, of course, you keep company with shadows."

"The mountain provides all the company I need," Ophira replied evenly.

He grunted, unconvinced, his eyes darting to a door on the left. Her bedroom? Without asking, he marched over and pushed it open. The hinges gave a long, weary creak.

The small room was tidy but lived-in: a single unmade bed, several wool blankets lying across it, a candle half-burned on the bedside table. The faint scent of lavender lingered in the air.

He stepped inside, his boots leaving dark marks on the woven rug. His gaze swept across the walls, the trunk at the foot of the bed, the pitcher of water on the washstand. He flipped open the trunk with a rough hand.

Folded linens. A shawl. A pouch of dried herbs.

He closed it again with an unimpressed snort. "For a woman of magic, you live simply."

"I find simplicity keeps the mind clear," she said.

"So, you do perform magic?"

"Your words, not mine."

The Commander's inspection grew bolder. Finding nothing but linens and herbs in the bedroom, he returned to the living area. He fixed his gaze on the last unopened door near the rear of the cottage.

"And this one?"

Ophira's throat tightened. "Storage. Roots and vegetables. Nothing of interest."

He took a slow step toward it, gloved hand brushing the latch. "We'll see." He turned to his men. "Check it."

The three guards moved past her, their boots thudding against the floor. One of them unlatched the door and pulled it open. A breath of cold, earthy air spilled into the room. The guards slipped down the narrow steps.

Ophira remained motionless, her palms damp against her apron. Would they find the hidden door concealed behind the far wall?

She locked her eyes on the Commander, not daring to glance toward the open doorway. He held her in his gaze, measuring the space between her words, the moments when her breath came too late, marking each one, waiting for the smallest flicker of fear to betray her.

The scrape of boots against dirt and stone drifted up the stairs from below. The sound of crates shifting filled Ophira's ears. Wood complained softly before falling still again. Burlap rasped as it was lifted, its coarse fibers dragging against wood with a dry, gritty whisper. Grain settling inside with a soft, muffled slide.

Then a heavy, blunt thump sounded as the sack was dropped. It was followed by a loose, collapsing hush as the sack slumped and spread, the fabric sighing as it settled into place.

Ophira listened intently, holding herself motionless as the sounds rose and faded, each one lingering a moment too long. She forced her lungs to breathe normally, afraid to show any signs that the Commander would interpret as lies.

"Well?" the Commander called down. "What did you find?"

A moment of silence. Then one of the guards poked his head out. "Nothing of importance, sir. A few roots, grain, and a few tools."

"Check again," the Commander barked. "I sense something, like a presence hidden behind fog."

The minutes ticked by. They were taking too long, searching too hard. Ophira's resolve began to falter. She fixed her gaze on the far wall, counting the shallow lines in the stone, willing herself not to turn. The sounds from below tugged at her attention, each scrape and thud tightening the muscles in her neck. Her eyes flickered despite her effort, beginning to betray her.

"We don't find anything, Commander."

The words cut through the moment, stopping her before she turned.

The men reappeared one by one, brushing dirt from their armor. The Commander's scowl deepened. He hated being wrong.

"I must have imagined a presence." He cast Ophira a long, cold look. "Seems your shadows are harmless after all."

She met his gaze steadily. "I told you. Only roots."

He lingered a heartbeat longer before brushing past her toward the exit. At the door, he looked back once. "It is not safe for you out here. We came across a band of thieves two days prior. I am leaving these three soldiers to ensure your safety."

"That is not necessary, Commander. I assure you that I am safe inside my cottage."

"I have decided. You WILL have protection."

The Commander stepped one foot across the threshold. Then stopped.

He turned his head slowly, nostrils flaring, then pressed his face to the doorframe. The sound that followed, a deep, deliberate inhale, turned Ophira's blood to ice.

The Commander drew another breath, longer this time. Then something *shifted*. His lips parted, and from within his mouth slipped a forked tongue.

Long.

Glistening.

Serpentine.

It slithered over the grain of the doorway in a slow, deliberate stroke, leaving behind a glistening trail that caught the light like oil on water. The sound was wrong, wet, and intimate. It was half hiss, half sigh, as though the wood recoiled beneath his touch.

Ophira watched, refusing to react.

A smell reached her next; the bitter scent of old magic stirring where none should exist. It crawled into her lungs, sharp and metallic, coating her throat. Her stomach turned. Every instinct screamed to step back, to run, but she dared not move.

It was more than a tongue tasting timber. It was something darker, something that *fed*. An ancient hunger tasting not the wood, but its memories. The laughter, the tears, the lives that had passed through the threshold.

The Commander's eyelids fluttered shut, his pupils thinning to slits when they opened again. A faint smile curved his lips, cold and knowing.

A slow, serpentine hiss sounded as his forked tongue slipped back inside his mouth. He straightened, the faint creak of his armor the only sound in the room. He looked at her, those slit-pupiled eyes narrowing, a faint gleam of knowing cutting through the gloom.

From deep within his throat, low and deliberate, three words slid free.

"A Dragon Keeper."

Ophira almost collapsed but somehow remained on her feet. When Osric went out onto the porch earlier that day, he wrapped his fingers around the doorframe to steady himself. Unknowingly, he left a memory. Somehow, as impossible as it sounded, the Commander's tongue possessed the ability to taste memories. Which meant that somewhere in Osric's past, he and Malachar had crossed paths. And he remembered the Keeper's taste.

Without another word, he abruptly turned and walked through the door.

The soldiers shifted, straightening as he passed. In the distance, the Drake cried and unfurled its wings. The Commander walked toward the Drake, then mounted. With one beat of the beast's monstrous wings, they rose into the sky, sending a gale through the yard, scattering dust, rattling the shutters.

And then he was gone, ascending into the clouds. The sound of those three words lingered in Ophira's mind.

A Dragon Keeper.

All their efforts to hide him and Elara were shattered with his tongue's one taste.

She chanted a spell under her breath, the old words trembling against her lips. She doubted it would be of any use, but she had to do something to keep her guests hidden. Faint sparks shimmered around her fingers.

Too weak.

Too late.

*****

Osric pressed his ear to the worn plank, feeling the grain against the shell of his skull. The wood throbbed faintly under his jaw; tiny, maddening vibrations that might be nothing or everything. He wanted sound to come: a boot, a cough, Ophira's voice. Anything to split the dark with truth.

He laid his fingers aside the hilt of his weapon. Its weight was a cold, steady promise against his palm. Heat prickled along his neck and behind his eyes, a tide of adrenaline that sharpened his vision and left a tang on his tongue.

Smells told him more than sounds: the odor of men's sweat, the smell of worn leather, the faint copper of recent wounds. He flattened his ear harder, hoping to coax sound from the wood. Nothing answered.

He imagined the door splintering, his body a thin line between Elara and the world. *I should break it down. Save Ophira. Save Elara.* But beneath that surge, something cold wound around his spine: the not-knowing. What if the Commander waited beyond the frame, patient as poison? The image of a blade catching light in that man's hand made his stomach drop.

How long should I wait? Twenty more minutes? An hour? Should I take Elara and escape through the back passage? A horse waits for us, hidden amongst the trees behind the cottage, along with a few supplies. There might be enough for several days, but not enough to ensure our survival for long. We need more. But if I leave now, I must go with what's already in the saddlebags.

Osric sank back onto the grain sacks; the burlap rasped through his trousers and anchored him with its ordinary smell of yeast and straw. Time passed. How long, he could not estimate. A small voice insisted that he trust in Ophira.

Two sharp raps against the door broke the silence. Osric violently jerked into a standing position, Elara heavy in his arms. His sword thudded against his leg.

Relief, immediate and aching, flooded him. Another two knocks. Ophira's signal. She was alive, but it was not safe for him to emerge yet.

He pressed his palm flat to the wood, feeling the echo of those raps vibrate through his bones. He swallowed, unclenched his fists, and settled his breathing. He eased his body back onto the grain sack, his weight settling into the worn hollow. Once more, he waited.

*****

As Ophira scurried to the root cellar, she turned the stove knob on, reheating the kettle of stew. From the cellar, she grabbed a handful of potatoes, carrots, and an onion. She pounded the onion twice on the wall to knock off a chunk

83

of old, dried dirt. She did the same with a turmeric root, signaling to Osric that it was not yet safe to exit.

She moved like a woman possessed. Osric and Elara could not leave until she disposed of the three guards outside. But how? She scurried to her herb cupboard and rifled through the various bottles. Her eyes locked on a tiny bottle of ground powder.

"Dreamthorn seeds. A single pinch in each bowl will put them into a deep, deep sleep. Then Osric and Elara can escape out the back with no chance of being caught."

Grabbing the ground seeds, she returned to the stove and set the vial on the counter. Her knife flashed as she sliced vegetables and tossed them into the pot. The kitchen filled with the sweet, sharp chorus of onions, carrots, and celery meeting heat in a hiss and bloom of steam.

Once it was ready, she ladled the stew into four bowls. In three of them, she dropped a pinch of the ground dreamthorn. Cramming three spoons inside her skirt pocket, she balanced the three tainted bowls on her arm. Using her foot to open the door, she carefully meandered to where the three soldiers were setting up camp. She smiled as she saw their meager excuse for dinner: three field rats cooking on a metal spit over a small fire.

"I thought you three might be hungry," Ophira said, handing each soldier a bowl and spoon. "I have plenty. I often cook more than I need. I used to throw the leftovers to the pigs, but I ate them last winter." She saw their hesitation. "Unless you'd rather eat your roasted rats."

"No, ma'am. We welcome your stew," said one guard who Ophira thought had a kind face.

Another guard investigated his bowl, then looked up at Ophira. "Why aren't you eating any?"

"Mine's waiting for me inside."

He sat his bowl on the ground and tried to grab the other two guards' stew. "Don't eat that. She could have poisoned it."

The kind guard grabbed his back. "I don't care if it's poisoned or not. It's the best meal we've had in months. I'm eating it!"

"So am I," said the third guard.

The callous guard watched. When neither of the other two guards tumbled over, he picked up his bowl and devoured its contents. The three shoveled the stew spoonful after spoonful into their mouths.

"This is delicious, ma'am. Thank you."

"If you'd like more, there's plenty on the stove. You're welcome to it." She pulled her wrap tighter around her shoulders. "It's getting cold out here. I'm going to go back inside and eat my dinner. Please come inside if you want more. No need to knock. I'll leave the door unlocked."

Ophira turned and headed back to the cottage. When she reached the threshold, she turned. The three soldiers lay on the ground sound asleep; their empty bowls scattered across the grass beside them.

She waited five minutes, eyes fixed on the slow rise and fall of their chests, counting each breath until it settled into the deep rhythm of sleep. When she was certain, she lifted her gaze and scanned the surroundings. No movement. No voices. Far off, the smoke of bonfires rose into the damp air, their glow pulsing against the dark. She detected no soldiers, nor any trace of the Commander or his Drake. It was now or never.

Praying she was right, Ophira closed and locked the door. She hurried down into the root cellar, breath tight, hands already moving. Crates scraped as she shoved them aside. She struck the hidden door twice with her fists, then dragged the grain sacks left and tore the blankets free. She unlocked the door and pulled it open.

Osric greeted her on the other side, weapon in hand. He lowered his gun when he saw Ophira standing there, her breath coming in gasps.

"You …have to…leave now." Ophira collapsed on two of the grain sacks.'

"You need to catch your breath," Osric said.

Ophira looked up into his eyes. He saw their change. Her eyes no longer displayed her warmth and calmness. It had been replaced with something cold, evil, terrorizing.

She closed her eyes and slowed her heart and breathing. After a minute, she murmured. "He knows you're here. It's not safe. You must go immediately."

"Ophira, Elara's not strong enough to make the journey today. She needs at least one or two more days before I try to take her to the mountain. A trip now will kill her."

"She's dead if she remains here, as you will be. The Commander will get the egg. To save all, you must leave. Lay Elara on the grain sacks and take these." Ophira shoved two filled saddlebags into his hands. In the crook of his arm, she piled bunches of carrots and a small sack of potatoes. With a shove, she attempted to push him towards the tunnel.

"You're scared," Osric said, refusing to move. "We've got time. He can't possibly know that we're here."

"I don't have time to argue. He possesses dark magic. I saw him taste your presence on the front door frame."

Osric's forehead wrinkled. "How could he taste me?"

"Why do you question my words?" Ophira asked, doing her best not to scream at the Keeper. "Just trust me when I said he did."

A floorboard complained above her, long and low. Ophira took the steps two at a time, heart loud in her ears. She burst into the living area, already bracing for a voice, a shadow…

Nothing.

The room lay empty. The breath she had been holding slipped free, only to catch again as Osric came up behind her, close enough that she felt him before she saw him, his weapon already in hand, angled toward the open space as if he trusted silence no more than she did.

"I can feel him. He's watching this cottage. You must exit through the tunnel where the young mare waits. Leave Elara in the root cellar while you finish loading your mount with the needed supplies. Take the saddlebags I just gave you, the food, and those blankets. I'll pack you some food from the kitchen for your journey, along with the medical supplies. Now, hurry."

"What about the donkey and the supplies we were going to load her with? I can't take enough supplies in the saddlebags to get us through the winter."

"We no longer have the luxury of time to load Mistie with the supplies. Plus, she'll slow you down too much. You've got to reach the mountain before he finds you two. The mountain will provide you with food."

How is the mountain supposed to feed us? Winter will soon be here.

Osric didn't question Ophira. He picked up the dropped saddlebags and slipped them over his shoulders, along with the food and the blankets. He ran down the long tunnel, the small luminous bulbs lighting his way.

Osric eased out from beneath the bramble and stopped. Voices? Or sounds echoing in his mind? He knew better than to trust the quiet now settling around him. He waited, listening, not for sound, but for the moment silence broke.

Nothing moved. Nothing spoke.

He advanced, step by measured step, weapon lifted, every instinct warning him this stillness had been arranged. The mare stood ahead, rope cinched tight to a low tree limb. Too neat. Too exposed. Osric slowed, circling her without closing the distance. Bait, his thoughts shouted.

But no attack came, no approaching bootsteps broke the stillness, no sound of dragon wings scouring the sky.

Still mistrusting the night, Osric approached the mare slowly. "Hello, girl. Ready for a long ride?"

He lifted the leather saddlebags and settled the center strap over the mare's cantle, redistributing the weight until it fell evenly across her back. Behind the saddle, he rolled the blankets into a tight bundle, tying it with a strip of braided leather and looping it through the rear saddle rings so it rested snugly across the mare's haunches.

When everything was secure, he hurried back inside for the items Ophira had packed for them, plus two smaller bags of food and a full skin of water. The water he fastened to the offside D-ring, along with the bag of medicine and the food Ophira packed. His fingers brushed the flint kit Ophira had stuffed into his pocket. He slipped it into a side pouch, then added a twist of oiled tinder. In an already crammed larger pocket, he pushed in two pans and a small bag of salt. Lastly, he added a narrow tin cup and a length of cloth that could serve as a bandage, a mask, or a signal.

He looked at a third blanket lying on the ground. Two were already packed. His hand settled on it, feeling the weight, the warmth it promised. Then he let it go. Instead, he took his dark cloak, rough and scentless, and rolled it tight.

With the mare packed with the bare necessities, Osric returned at last for Elara and the eggs. Although her fever had broken, she was still extremely weak, more asleep than awake. He slid his arms beneath her and lifted her against his chest. Her head fell softly against him, a faint sigh escaping her lips as he adjusted his hold.

He bolted down the tunnel, Elara snug in his arms, Ophira following with the two dragon eggs inside their satchels and the bear skin.

Osric lifted Elara onto the mare's back. Her head lolled forward, resting across the animal's flowing mane.

"Hand me the eggs," Osric whispered.

"In a moment. I have something for you." She sat the satchels on the ground and reached into her pocket, withdrawing a silver amulet.

"Is that what I think that is?" Osric whispered.

"The Veil of Noctis, forged by the great Elder Wyrm herself. When bound with silver and worn near the heart, it renders the wearer invisible. It is designed to wrap you in Noctis' shadow of darkness. Even dragons will not sense you, see, or hear you."

"What about the Commander?"

"Not even he can penetrate the veil's ability to hide one in shadow. But to be sure you are hidden, I will also cast a spell around your horse to render her invisible. If you bend down, I will place it around your neck."

Osric bent low.

"I protect you with the Veil of Noctis. May it hide you from those who mean you harm." Ophira slipped the amulet around the Keeper's neck.

He straightened. A faint hum radiated through his chest, and a warm glow drifted across his body.

"Thank you, Ophira."

"Remember, when you reach the safety of the Dragon Mountain, you must slaughter the mare."

"I will do as you ask."

Osric steadied Elara with one arm as he grabbed the saddle horn, slipped his foot into the stirrup, and swung up into the saddle behind her. He felt the young mare's muscles tense under the sudden double weight.

"Easy now," he murmured, his voice low.

He wrapped a wrap around Elara, tying it behind his back. Ophira handed him the two eggs. He slipped each one inside the cloth, nestled against Elara. The heat both radiated would help keep her warm across the tundra.

"Osric, one more thing," Ophira said as she wrapped the bear skin around Elara's shoulders. "No matter what, do not look back. No matter what you believe has happened, you cannot return. Promise me."

"Why? What is going to happen?"

"PROMISE ME!"

"I promise."

The night wind brought with it the sound of voices.

"Hurry. They are coming." Ophira pivoted, then vanished within the tunnel's darkness without another word. As she ran down the narrow tunnel, she smashed the bulbs, plunging the escape into total darkness. Upon entering the root cellar, she didn't bother to close or lock the secret door.

Osric nudged the mare forward. Her hooves broke through the late afternoon hush, sinking into dew-soaked earth. Behind them, the fog swallowed the cottage and the last light from Ophira's window.

The forest closed around them. Branches knitted overhead, their leaves slick and whispering as the wind shifted, bringing with it the cold scent of rain. Osric guided the mare onto a narrow, well-worn animal trail, barely wide enough for hoof and boot. The trees grew denser here, ancient trunks leaning close.

Above, a faint rustle of wings stirred the air. The owl, his former shadow, once again glided ahead, silent as thought, its pale form flickering between branches. Every so often, it would circle back, hovering long enough for Osric to glimpse the glow of its eyes before vanishing again into the darkness of night.

"Lead true, old friend," he whispered.

Elara sagged against him; her small hands slack over the saddle's horn. Each time her body tilted, he tightened his arm around her waist, feeling the fragile rise and fall of her breathing.

A low rumble shivered through the clouds above. He looked up, though the canopy gave no view of the sky, only shifting darkness and the occasional drip of water through leaves. Somewhere far off, thunder answered.

Osric's thoughts turned upward, to what might be flying there. The Commander's dragon, black against the storm, could be circling even now, its eyes cutting through shadows. The thought chilled him more than the wind. He wrapped his hand around the Veil of Noctis. *I hope the Great Elder*

Wyrm Noctis' power to conceal still lives in this crystal. If so, hide us well, Noctis. If not, pray we have a swift death.

*****

Ophira emerged from the root cellar. Her heart pounding, she rested her hand on the kitchen wall for a moment, trying to calm her nerves and steady her breath. A tremor traveled through the wood into her palm, a low, living vibration she knew too well. Dragon wings.

"I knew you were close by," she whispered, her gaze lifting toward the trembling rafters. "Your power is too strong for me to continue to hide Osric and Elara's shadows. No spell will hold you at bay. There is only one choice left to me. I must make sure that no part of my memory or the cottage's shadows will give you the answers you seek."

She turned slowly, eyes sweeping the rooms that had been her home for so many years. Every shelf, every crack in the stone walls carried a memory. "You've been a good companion," she murmured to the empty room. "Forgive me for being the bearer of your end."

She crossed swiftly to her apothecary cupboard. She reached inside. For a moment, she rested her hand on the small emerald vial tucked away on the second shelf. Its emerald vapor swirled like trapped mist. She always prayed she would never have to use it. There were dissolving spells, and there were endings.

Grabbing the bottle, she slipped it into her pocket and set to work. She stacked aspen logs before the hearth, scattering kindling with quick, sure hands. The air filled with the scent of resin and ash as she seized the fireplace shovel, scooping glowing embers into its pan and spreading them across the wood.

The moment the embers touched the kindling, thin ribbons of smoke curled upward. Flames bloomed hungrily, crawling across the wood and reaching for the ceiling. Ophira seized a burning log and tossed it aside. It rolled across the floor, setting the rug ablaze. Within moments, fire swept through the room, devouring years of her life in a roar of orange light.

She ran to the door, cloak whipping around her, and grabbed Mistie's bridle from its hook. Outside, she whistled sharply into the dusk. The donkey's bray answered, distant, fearful. Ophira called again. Silence.

Her heart clenched. Had the soldiers already taken her?

She pulled her cloak tighter and turned from the burning cottage, the inferno's glow licking across her face as she started down the narrow path. Behind her, the flames consumed all traces of her guests' presence.

The flames surged higher than she'd intended, roaring to life and devouring the darkness. Firelight spilled across the clearing, searing away every shadow until none remained. The night no longer offered her refuge. She stood exposed, bathed in gold and flame, with nowhere left to hide.

A faint whistle cut through the air. Then, pain. A searing line tore through her leg. Ophira gasped and fell to her knees. She looked down to see an arrow buried deep in her thigh, the fletching still quivering. She scanned the area. From the forest's shadows emerged Malachar's army, weapons drawn. Several soldiers were examining the three soldiers asleep on the ground.

The ground convulsed. Soil split and stones leapt as the black wyrm landed in front of her like a falling mountain. Its talons gouged deep furrows into the earth. Its wings blotting out the last light of dusk. Wind whipped around Ophira, tearing her hood back as the wyrm screamed, a sound that made the world flinch.

But Ophira did not. She lifted her face to the beast, calm in her final defiance.

As the Commander slid from the wyrm's back, she reached into her pocket, drew out the emerald vial, and pulled the cork with steady fingers.

"Neither I nor my home," she shouted, "will ever reveal the secrets you hunt."

She lifted the vial, pouring the emerald vapor down her throat.

The liquid hit her tongue like liquid winter. Ophira gasped violently as the magic seized her throat. She clenched her abdomen. The vial slipped from her fingers and fell to the ground.

Light did not take her cleanly. It tore her apart.

Her outline cracked like glass under pressure, fissures spidering through her flesh as threads of her breath, thought, and memory peeled away in drifting, painful strands. She cried out in agony, as if each thread ripped a seam from her soul.

Malachar lunged forward, screaming incantations, fingers carving desperate sigils into the air.

But he was too late.

The enchantment clawed through Ophira's body, unraveling her faster than he could bind her. Her clothes, her hair, even her shadow frayed into smoke. Her form collapsed inward, the last pieces tearing apart like burning paper.

Malachar roared, struck by the backlash of her spell's final surge. Sparks burst across the clearing as the cottage roof caved in before him. He staggered back, gasping. The trail was gone. Her memories, every secret he hungered for, were ash in the wind.

He screamed again, the sound cracking the air like a wound.

Chapter 9

The night shattered under a cry so inhuman, so piercing, it felt as though the world was being torn in two. From somewhere beyond the trees came a shriek of anguish, wild and consuming.

The mare sidestepped, her ears lying flat against her head. Osric yanked her reins, forcing her to halt, his eyes snapping toward the east. Through the dark tangle of forest, a faint glow bled upward. Fire.

But the cry. That wasn't fire. Fire roared; this sound *screamed*... in frustration, in anger.

A chill worked its way beneath his skin. He couldn't say how he knew, only that the truth settled over him like a weight. Something had happened to Ophira. *The Commander returned as she had said he would.*

He stared toward the distant light, his chest tightening. *She's gone. She gave herself for Elara, for the unborn wyrms... for me.*

The mare shifted restlessly beneath him, ears flicking toward the sound that still echoed faintly through the trees. Osric swallowed, his throat dry. He whispered into the wind, "Good journey, my friend. May the fire hide your secrets well."

Osric urged the mare deeper into the trees. The forest swallowed them whole.

When the horse tired, Osric stopped, allowing the horse to drink from a small stream and chomp on some new grass. He softly pressed his fingers to Elara's neck. Her skin was warm, but not from fever. Her heartbeat was strong and regular. He noted a small crack in the new egg. *Looks like it won't be long before you hatch, Little One.*

He wrapped his feet around the stirrups, locking his feet to ensure he remained in the saddle. He encircled Elara with his arms, locking his fingers together. They he closed his eyes, allowing sleep to take over his body. Osric slept for two hours, until the owl's hoot broke his rest. He listened to the sounds of the night. Except for a few small critters scattering through the underbrush, the air was silent.

He pulled on the mare's reins and softly pressed his heels into her side. Without hesitation, she continued their journey to Dragon Mountain. As the mist dispersed, so did the forest. They survived the night.

The air thinned and grew colder as the trees fell away. Before them stretched a vast meadow, white and silent beneath a fresh sweep of snow. At its center stood a lone oak, its red-gold leaves trembling against the wind like a beacon in the emptiness.

Beyond it, Dragon Mountain rose faintly through the clouds; too distant to offer protection, close enough to feel like salvation.

"If we cross this field," Osric murmured, "we expose ourselves. No trees. No stone. Nothing to break a Drake's sight."

Osric's eyes scanned the horizon: the open sweep of grass, the low folds of land that could hide anything, and above it all, the heavy, rolling clouds that mirrored the churn in his gut. He could feel the weight of the sky pressing down, as if the storm had only been a warning, not an end.

"But we're still too far from the mountain," he said. "Its protection won't reach us here."

Elara shifted. Osric caught her gently, keeping her close. "If we cross this meadow," he went on, "we might be seen. If Ophira's spells and amulet do not hide us, the Commander's wyrm will spot us from leagues away."

A gust swept through the grass, rippling it like water. He imagined the beast's shadow sliding across the open plain, vast wings blotting out the light, its scream tearing the clouds apart, its talons outstretched ready to tear them to pieces.

Duty told him to wait, to circle wide and lose time for the sake of stealth. But instinct whispered something else: *Delaying will surely kill us as surely as exposure will. The Commander won't rest. He will sweep the forest, even scorch the edges until nothing remains. He knows we're out here.*

Osric closed his eyes briefly, weighing the silence. *If I fail her, she dies. If I act, we both might.*

The owl settled on the branch of a sapling beside them; feathers damp and gleaming. It looked toward the meadow, then back at him, head cocked, asking what courage he had left.

He exhaled slowly. "We ride fast and low," he said at last. "If the skies stay heavy, the clouds may cover us. That, along with Ophira's magic and the Veil of Noctis, might save us."

He tightened his grip on the reins, tapping his heels into the mare's flanks. The young horse snorted, gathering herself, her muscles coiling under damp leather. The owl took flight, cutting a pale arc into the gray morning.

The mare broke into a gallop the instant Osric gave her the reins. The meadow unrolled endlessly ahead. Large, fluffy snowflakes drifted down. The lone oak tree stood at the center, massive and ancient, a beacon of safety calling to him. That was his goal, the only cover between the forest and the distant shadow of Dragon Mountain.

Then the sky shifted.

The mare's ears flicked, catching a tone too low for human hearing. Osric felt it next: a vibration, deep and resonant, rippling through the ground. He looked up.

The clouds moved. Not with the wind, but against it.

From the folds of the storm came a vast and terrible shape, a wyrm's silhouette, black wings unfurling across the sky. It rode the air with predatory grace, its movements slow, deliberate, knowing. Osric's breath snagged in his throat as the beast's cry split the heavens.

"Faster!" He drove his heels into the mare's sides. She lunged forward, mud flying from her hooves. The field blurred, the oak surged closer, its massive branches beckoning like sheltering arms.

The wyrm's shadow swept across the grass. It passed over them like a curse. The mare screamed, her stride faltering for half a heartbeat before Osric steadied her. "Don't break, girl. Not now. Not now!"

Wind clawed at Osric's face, tearing through his hair. The oak loomed near enough now that he could see the snow collecting on its branches.

The wyrm screamed again, closer this time, the sound rolling over the meadow. He didn't look up; he couldn't. To see it was to freeze and freezing meant death. Instead, he focused on the oak, on the dark sanctuary beneath its roots, on the faint shape of the owl circling wildly above it.

The mare gave one last surge, muscles burning under her slick hide. They reached the tree as the air behind them split with heat and sound. A blast of fire erupted across the meadow, charring the wet grass to steam. The shockwave hit like a hammer. Osric shielded Elara with his body as the mare stumbled, half-falling into the shelter of the oak's enormous roots.

Smoke and water drops from melted snow tangled in the air. The world smelled of sulfur and fear.

Osric dismounted in one motion, dragging Elara with him beneath the gnarled trunk. The mare trembled but stayed, chest heaving. Overhead, the wyrm circled once, its massive wings beating the mist apart, the thick smoke and spreading fire blurring Osric's sight.

Osric held his breath, his hand over Elara's heart. The owl perched above them in silence.

Then, slowly, the wyrm's shadow shifted east, fading into the cloudbank.

The Veil of Noctis held. Thank you, Elder Noctis. You kept us wrapped inside your perpetual darkness.

Osric's shoulders sagged. He hadn't realized until then how hard his heart had been hammering, how tightly his jaw was clenched. But for the first time since leaving the cottage, he allowed himself to hope.

From above, the tree appeared as a withered ash; half-rotted, hollowed by centuries, a dying relic clinging to the last embers of life. Yet those who stood upon the earth before it, hearts pure and spirits unbroken, beheld something far older. The bark glimmered with the faintest trace of starlight; its roots hummed with the deep, slow pulse of ages long forgotten.

It was no mere tree, but one of the Elder Wyrm Noctis's first gifts to the mortal realm. Clouded to the fallen but revealed in truth to the chosen hearts.

The roots of the oak formed a shelter. They twisted and arched into a hollow, large enough for the mare to stand partly beneath and for Osric to kneel beside Elara. He sank to one knee. Elara's skin was pale, her lips faintly blue. He brushed her cheek with the back of his knuckles, trying to coax some color into her face.

"You're safe now," he murmured, though the words tasted hollow. Safety was an illusion. The wyrm would circle back; the Commander would never abandon his prey.

We must reach the mountain!

Osric dug into his saddlebag, pulling free a flask, a strip of dried cloth, and a pouch of herbs Ophira had given him. He crushed the leaves between his fingers, releasing their sharp scent into the damp air: lavender and something bitter, like pine resin. He wet the cloth, wrung it out, and laid the crushed leaves inside. He pressed it gently to Elara's lips. Holding her head up, he poured a tiny amount of water over the cloth. It flowed through the herbs and dripped into Elara's mouth.

Her eyes fluttered. "Vaelor?"

"No, My Lady," he said. His voice was softer now, stripped of command.

Her hand found his wrist, weak but warm. "My brother? My egg?"

He looked away, jaw tightening. "Your egg is beside you," he said, lifting her hand and placing it on her egg. "I don't know about your brother."

The silence stretched between them, filled only by the faint rustle of the mare shifting her weight and the low, rhythmic *whoo* of the owl perched high in the oak's branches. The bird's eyes gleamed pale gold in the half-light, ever watchful, turning toward every whisper of wind.

Osric followed its gaze. Through a gap in the branches, he saw that the clouds had begun to thin. Far beyond the meadow's edge, Dragon Mountain rose, its black slopes rimmed in faint crimson light.

He stared at it for a long time, feeling the old pull, the promise of protection, the weight of oaths he had long since broken.

Elara stirred again, drawing him back. Her breathing had steadied, her fever still gone. He rested his hand lightly over hers. He could feel the beating of the unborn dragon's heart.

"Rest, Elara," he said quietly. "For now, you are safe." He pulled the bear skin from the mare's neck and placed it over Elara. Then, he lay beside her, crawling beneath the skin's warmth.

He loosened the satchel flap and peered inside at the orphaned egg. The crack he'd noticed earlier had widened a hair's width, a jagged vein running across its shell. Whether it was from the relentless pounding of the horse's gallop, or the stirrings of life within, he couldn't tell.

Does your heart still beat inside your tiny body? Then he remembered Ophira's words. *Have you been waiting for me?*

Outside, the snow deepened, drumming against the meadow like distant footsteps. Osric's eyes shifted once more toward the mountain. For the first time, he wondered if Dragon Mountain would offer him sanctuary or judgment. It had been over five hundred years since he stood in the presence of one of the ancient wyrms. Ophira said the mountain was the resting place of Terrus. Although Terrus had sided with Solarus regarding the half-bloods, he defended Osric when Solarus cursed him. Somewhere inside the sleeping wyrm that kindness remained. *But I have no time to worry about that. It's Dragon Mountain or certain death.*

Night descended softly, though Osric barely noticed as he slept. Storm clouds thickened the sky again, pressing low, turning the air heavy with snow. Beyond the oak's shelter, the meadow had gone eerily still, buried in several inches of snow.

A tremor shook the tear roots.

Osric's mind snapped alert. Slowly, he opened his eyes, alert, not moving. Something besides nightmares disturbed his rest. He shifted his gaze, glancing toward the meadow. The grass moved, though no wind touched it. A ripple, subtle but wrong, ran across the field, signaling something vast and unseen brushed beneath the surface of the world.

Osric stilled, every sense sharpening. The mare raised her head, nostrils flaring. The owl gave a low, throaty hiss. *One of the Commander's tricks?*

The sound came again.

Faint.

Rhythmic.

Like distant breathing.

It rolled across the meadow in long, measured waves. Osric rose slowly, hand on his sword hilt. His gaze followed the direction of the sound, to where Dragon Mountain loomed against the sky. There, through the haze, a faint pulse of red deepened, steady, and deliberate, echoing that strange rhythm in the ground.

This is not the Commander's doing. The mountain calls and something beneath it is answering.

Behind him, Elara stirred, murmuring in her sleep words that made no sense, old syllables that didn't belong to any human tongue. He knelt quickly, pressing a hand to her shoulder.

Your heat is not from a fever. A faint orange glow of fire lies beneath your skin. I don't understand what is happening to you or what to do to stop it.

Elara's eyes snapped open. They were unfocused, glassy, reflecting the same faint red glow that shimmered on the horizon. She stared past him, toward the mountain, her expression of one bordering on the next plain of existence.

"He's awakening," she whispered. "The old one. He stirs because I allowed the fire to answer my fear."

The words chilled Osric. Before he could ask what she meant, the ground beneath them gave a faint tremor, soft but certain, like a warning. A coldness threaded through him. This presence wasn't hunting; they would have felt teeth by now. It was studying them.

Ophira's warning surfaced in his mind. She had spoken of an ancient presence, guardians that lived beneath the mountain and safeguarded Terrus.

Have we awakened a guardian?

He exhaled slowly, the taste of uncertainty lingering. "We move now," he murmured, eyes fixed on the ground. "Whatever's calling… it's reaching. Searching." His jaw tightened. "But when it stops, it won't be because it's gone. It'll be because it no longer needs to reach. And when that happens, we won't see it coming."

He lifted Elara into the saddle, once more tying the blanket around her with the two eggs tucked inside. Then he mounted behind her. Wrapping one arm firmly across her abdomen, Osric guided the mare from the oak's shadow.

Once clear of the roots, he spurred the steed into a swift canter. The meadow was a wasteland of ashed snow and smoke now, the scorched patch still steaming faintly. The mare's hooves struck the crusted ground with a hollow, cracking rhythm, each step breaking through the brittle surface with a sharp *crunch* and a dull, echoing thud beneath. The sound carried too far in the open silence.

The mare's ears twitched constantly, nostrils flaring, and more than once she stumbled for no reason Osric could see.

Behind him, the earth tore with a low, splitting groan. Osric turned. He watched as the ground heaved in a slow, deliberate roll.

Something vast has shifted beneath the skin of the world.

Fine cracks raced across the frozen grass in jagged lines, chasing one another outward, then sealing just as quickly.

It was no longer observing. It was advancing.

Chapter 10

Morning broke over the horizon in a feeble flicker, its weak light doing little to warm the trembling plain. The sky was dark and angry, promising to deliver more snow before the day was done.

As far as his eyes could reach, the plains lay bare, stripped of shelter, stripped of mercy. There was nowhere to hide, nowhere to turn, only an endless stretch of open ground that must be crossed before the Drake wheeled back for another pass.

Osric pulled the bearskin tighter around Elara and himself. The wind cut hard and mercilessly, scouring the snow-covered plain. It was a cruel ally; one he both welcomed and feared. Each bitter gust erased the horse's tracks, smothering their passage beneath drifting white, but it also gnawed at Elara's failing strength. Her weak body still fought the lung-fish poison. Her breath was shallow, her body barely holding its claim on warmth even with both eggs tucked beside her. He knew that the cold could take her as surely as the toxin had tried.

Unlike Elara, the Keeper was forged in hardship. He had been cursed to endure, not to be spared. Pain, cold, consequences; these were debts the world collected from him repeatedly. If suffering was the price of hiding her from the Commander, he would pay it without question. Let the wind strip the heat from his bones if it must. He would bear it. Elara could not.

He nudged the horse forward.

The owl pressed on toward the mountains, circling high above them. When they lagged, it dipped low, close enough for the beat of its wings to stir the air around them, then climbed again, urging them onward.

Hours passed.

The sun climbed and began its slow descent. The mare's hoofs crunched the hardened snow. Faint tremors beneath the soil continued. Whatever crept beneath the soil continued its pursuit of them.

Osric scanned the empty reach ahead, measuring distance the way a condemned man measures time. He saw nowhere to bed down: no trees, no rock outcropping, no hollow to break the wind. Only frozen ground and drifting snow. He could dig a shallow den if he had to, carve a pit with his hands, but it would become a tomb for Elara before morning. Driving the horse through the night was not an option, and sleeping upright offered no better relief.

By late afternoon, dread settled deeper into Osric's bones. He watched as the sun sank toward the horizon and the cold rose to meet it. Even the owl sensed it, circling tighter, crying sharper, as if the coming dark had already begun to close its grip.

Osric slowed the horse to a halt.

The wind clawed at them, relentless, but he gave it no heed. Beneath the bearskin, Elara trembled against him, her breath uneven, each draw catching with a faint rattle that set his teeth on edge. Every inhale felt hard won, as if the cold meant to take it back. She would not survive the night without shelter. He knew it with the same certainty he had learned to trust when the world came to collect its due.

He closed his eyes.

There were actions he could take. Deeds he had sworn never to do again. Acts that would draw the Commander's attention, bend the land, scar the night itself. Acts that would buy warmth, shelter, life for her. But they came with a cost that would settle into his bones and might never leave.

Osric rested his forehead against the horse's mane. For one fleeting heartbeat, he allowed himself the belief that there might be another way.

He had no choice.

Straightening, he made the decision. It did not feel like courage. It never did. Only acceptance. He adjusted the bearskin around Elara one last time, careful, reverent, as though committing her to something sacred. Then he turned his gaze toward the darkening horizon and reached inward; past fear, past pain, past the hope he no longer permitted himself to keep.

Let the cold come for him. Let the curse deepen. Let the night remember his name.

He dismounted.

The moment his boots struck the snow, the cold surged up his legs like a living thing, biting deep. He ignored it. Removing the two blankets from behind the saddle, he spread them on the ground. He yanked on the reins, bringing the mare down to her knees on top. He eased Elara from the saddle and lowered her against the mare's side, tucking her into the hollow formed by its folded legs, pressing her close to the warmth of its body, keeping the bearskin wrapped tight around her. Her eyes fluttered, unfocused. She did not wake.

"Forgive me," he murmured. He focused not on her, but his impending action.

Osric stepped away.

The wind screamed across the plain, tearing at him, clawing through wool and leather alike. Osric closed his eyes and opened himself instead; not outward, but inward, to the curse that had never once failed to answer him.

Take it, he thought. *All of it.*

The cold hit him like a wall.

Not the biting chill of wind and snow, but something heavier, something crushing and absolute. The air around Elara stilled, the wind faltering as if it had struck an unseen barrier. Snow fell more softly there, settling instead of scouring. Her shuddering eased. Her breath improved, still shallow but no longer erratic.

Osric staggered.

The cold poured into him, deeper than bone, deeper than marrow. His hands went numb instantly. Pain bloomed, sharp and merciless, as the curse dragged the night itself through his veins. Frost rimmed his lashes, his beard. His skin blanched where blood fled in retreat. His heart hammered once, twice, then slowed, laboring under the strain.

The land noticed.

The wind did not stop everywhere. Only around them. A hollow of unnatural calm spread wide enough to shelter one fragile life. Beyond it, the storm raged louder, angrier, as if offended by what had been stolen from it.

Osric dropped to one knee.

His vision tunneled, darkness pressing in at the edges. He could feel the cost tallying itself, precise and unforgiving. This was what the curse demanded: not power, but payment. Time shaved away. Strength leeched out. A night borrowed from death, repaid with interest.

Behind him, Elara stirred.

That was enough.

Osric's body shook uncontrollably now, the cold gnawing at him from the inside out. He positioned himself between her and the wind, becoming what shelter the land would not give. Snow crusted over his shoulders, his back, his hair, already marking him.

From a distance, the anomaly was unmistakable. A lone figure knelt in the open plain, rimmed in frost, unmoving amid a storm that bent strangely around him.

Osric remained motionless, a being more made of ice than blood.

Finally, the sky lightened from black to a thin, colorless gray. The wind eased, leaving behind a silence that felt heavier than the storm itself. Snow lay undisturbed around them, save for the shallow depression where Osric had knelt through the night.

He did not rise when the light touched him. He couldn't.

Frost had claimed him in earnest. His cloak was stiff as bark, his hair and beard crusted white, his lashes frozen together. One hand lay half-buried in snow, the fingers curled and unmoving, the skin beneath pale, waxy, robbed of color and life. When he tried to shift, nothing answered at first. The command to move reached his body and died there.

Pain came later.

It arrived slowly, blooming deep in his limbs as sensation crept back in jagged shards. Pins and needles turned into fireless agony, sharp and relentless. His legs buckled when he forced himself upright, and he had to brace against the horse's flank to keep from collapsing outright. One foot dragged when he stepped, numb and heavy, refusing his will.

He did not look at it.

Behind him, Elara stirred.

Her breathing was steadier now, no longer fighting every breath. Color had returned to her lips, faint but undeniable. She opened her eyes, unfocused, then drifted back into a restful sleep.

Osric exhaled, the sound tearing from his chest like something broken loose.

Only then did he allow himself to acknowledge the damage.

His hands shook violently now, the tremors beyond his control. He could not close his left fist at all. When he tried, the fingers remained stiff, half-curled, unresponsive. Blood seeped from cracked skin along his knuckles, dark against the white, already freezing where it fell.

He pulled the bearskin tighter around Elara with his good hand.

The curse had not spared him.

It never did.

Each dawn took something—strength, sensation, time—and this one had taken more than most. He could feel it in the way his heart labored, in the way the world tilted when he stood, in the dull certainty that some damage would not mend quickly, if at all.

With his one functioning hand, he worked the bundle of medicine free and tipped a few careful drops into Elara's mouth. He followed with several drips of the broth Ophira had packed, coaxing it past her lips with quiet persistence. When it came to him, he took nothing. The cold had claimed his face so completely that even the idea of swallowing felt impossible. The thought of taking a few sips of Elara's broth never crossed his mind.

Using his shoulder and upper arm, he somehow managed to get Elara back into the saddle. Raising the mare into a standing position, Osric mounted, swallowing the pain that threatened to pull him apart. He settled Elara before him. Unable to tie the blanket around Elara and himself, he laid it across Elara's legs. Using his teeth and one working hand, he positioned the bear skin around them both and tucked the eggs inside. He urged the horse forward.

The snow swallowed their tracks again as they moved on.

He did not look back. He didn't need to. He knew the snow was filling in the hollow where he had knelt, a ring of frost circling its rim, stained crimson with his blood.

His mark of payment. And proof that dawn, for him, was never free.

They rode through the day in silence.

The light brought no warmth. It only revealed. Every jolt of the horse sent a fresh lance of pain through Osric's stiffened limbs. His left hand remained useless, bound awkwardly against his chest, the fingers swollen and darkening beneath torn skin. Numbness crept where pain receded, a more frightening absence. He did not test it again. Some truths were better left unconfirmed.

Elara slept fitfully, her weight light against him, her breath steady. Each time she stirred, Osric adjusted the bearskin with clumsy care, shielding her from the wind, from the worst of the cold, from the sight of what he had become by morning's light.

By afternoon, his vision blurred at the edges. The world tilted when they halted to let the horse drink. He tasted blood where his lip had split, though he did not remember the moment it happened. His body no longer marked its injuries with clarity. It simply accumulated them.

As the sun began its slow descent once more, dread returned, heavier than the night before.

Like the previous night, no shelter rose on the horizon. Nothing but the same open land, stretched endlessly and indifferent. The horse faltered, head lowering, its breath steaming with exhaustion. It could not be pushed much farther. And Osric knew, with a clarity that cut deeper than fear, that he could not endure another night like the last.

Yes, he was immortal. His body could not die.

But immortality was not invulnerability.

There were limits even to flesh that could not pass into death. Thresholds beyond which damage did not heal, where sensation vanished forever, where the body continued in broken obedience, a prison that could no longer serve the will trapped inside it.

Osric flexed his numb hand; a sharp sting answered the motion, the first sign that sensation was creeping back.

Night was coming. The cold would follow. And the curse would demand its due a second time.

He lifted his gaze toward the darkening horizon, calculating distances that no longer mattered, weighing costs that now bordered on the irreversible. This time, his price would not be measured in pain alone. This time, he would not walk away from what he chose.

And still, he tightened his hold on Elara. There was no question which of them would survive the night.

After a brief ten-minute rest, he urged the mare forward once more. She obeyed, but the strain was evident. Before long, she would require several hours of true rest to go on.

Osric gasped as the air changed. Warmth brushed his face. It was impossible, yet unmistakable. A breath of heat rolled over him, carrying with it a low, resonant tremor that rippled across the horizon.

For a moment, he forgot to breathe.

"That wasn't there before," he breathed, blinking hard as if sight itself had betrayed him.

Where moments ago the land had stretched empty and bare, an oak now stood, vast and ancient, rearing from the earth like a titan returned, as though it had always claimed dominion over the plain. Its vast branches spread like a crowned canopy against the sky, a living monument of age and authority. The tree did not merely stand; it *asserted* itself, radiating presence, power, and the promise of protection.

A sanctuary.

The owl shrieked triumphantly and flew toward it.

Osric urged the horse onward. He wanted the beast to break into a gallop, to reach the safety and warmth of the tree, but he knew the mare's energy was spent. He allowed her to meander at her own pace.

The ground rolled again, harder this time. Cracks opened and branched out across the earth. Whatever was beneath them strained to break through. Osric held Elara tighter, wanting to assure both her and himself that they were safe.

The giant oak loomed ahead.

Twenty lengths.

I know you're exhausted, but can't you walk a little faster?

Fifteen

Ten.

Five.

The moment the horse crossed into the shade of its vast branches, the trembling ceased.

Silence fell.

Unable to force another step, the mare faltered and dropped to her knees at a tangled rise of roots. Osric swung down, gathering Elara and the two eggs in one careful motion. He carried her to the great trunk and eased her against its base. Heat seeped from the bark into Elara, into his frozen arms, and into the mare's chilled body.

"Thank you," he whispered, dropping to one knee. To whom he spoke to, he wasn't sure. The owl? The tree? The Elders themselves?

He crossed to the mare and rested his forehead against hers. "You as well," he whispered. "You bore more than you should have today. I'm sorry." He set to work, unstrapping their gear, though he left the saddle in place, a precaution he could not quite abandon. Still, something in the air had softened; for the first time since leaving Ophira's cabin, the need to flee did not press against him.

He poured water into a shallow pan and held it steady while she drank, then fed her four carrots from their dwindling supply. At first light, he would let her graze, a full hour at least, long enough to put some strength back into her legs.

He fed Elara some mushy stew, dripped medicine into her mouth, and redressed her leg wound before wrapping her tightly in the skin once again. With the warmth radiating from the tree, the feeling in his frozen face at last returned. He ate several slices of dried meat and tubers, washing the food down with several mouthfuls of water. He then pulled one of the blankets over him and curled up beside Elara. With gun in hand, he closed his eyes, drifting off into an exhausted sleep. He did not hear the dragon wings pass above them or hear its frustrated cry.

Osric tore awake with a sharp, ragged inhale that caught in his throat. Sunlight struck his eyes, too bright, too sudden, forcing them into a hard squint as they snapped open. For a split second, he did not understand what he was seeing, only that he had been ripped from sleep and something felt wrong.

His gaze flicked wildly across the sunlit space, from tree line to open ground, searching for a threat that refused to show itself. He shoved the cover aside and surged to his feet, breath coming fast, shoulders rigid. The gun was already in his hand, finger tight on the trigger, as his chest rose and fell in sharp bursts.

Even in the warmth of morning, his pulse hammered, his body refusing to believe the light meant safety.

No danger presented itself. The sun was already above the horizon, the sky a warm blue with no storm clouds. The mare was several yards away, straining to nibble on the fresh grass growing just out of her reach. He saw she had already eaten everything in her immediate vicinity. Bending down, he checked Elara and the eggs; all were well.

Only then did the tension begin to drain from him, slow and reluctant. He drew a long breath through his nose, held it, then let it slip out between parted lips. His grip loosened on the gun, though he did not lower it entirely. His eyes moved again, more measured now, tracing the edges of the clearing, the line of the horizon, the stillness of the trees.

Nothing stirred. No tremor beneath the ground, no shadow passing overhead. Just the quiet hum of morning and the soft pull of the mare at her tether.

Osric dragged a hand across his face, rough with fatigue, and blinked hard against the lingering haze of sleep. Whatever had torn him from rest had left no mark behind, yet the unease clung to him, faint but persistent, like a warning he could not quite hear.

He winced as a sharp pressure made itself known; his bladder's blunt reminder that he had slept far too long. He hurried behind the tree to see to it, silently grateful that the worst of the pain had loosened its grip on his frozen body.

Osric led the horse to a large patch of grass and tied her reins to a gnarled root. He returned to Elara and checked her vitals again. Her breathing had settled into a steady, even rhythm, quiet but sure. Each inhale came slow and measured, drawing deep into her lungs without strain, her chest rising gently beneath the bear skin. The harsh rattle that had once haunted every breath was gone, replaced by a soft, almost soundless cadence.

Now and then, her lips parted slightly as she exhaled, a faint whisper of air escaping, warm against the cool morning. There was still a fragility to it, a sense that her body was rebuilding itself breath by breath, but the fight for each inhale was over. What remained was recovery.

He administered her medicine and dripped the last of Ophira's broth into her mouth. While estimating how much time was left in their trip, he ate the last of the dried meat and mash-cakes. He longed for a good cup of coffee, but a fire was still out of the question. For the moment, they were safe; but a fire would definitely give away their position.

He broke camp and mounted with Elara. He turned sharply in the saddle, scanning the meadow's edge. Nothing moved. Yet still he could not shake the feeling of a presence, something unseen, something watching them.

The mare galloped off, reenergized, spurred by his tone. Before them rose the dark slopes of Dragon Mountain, its summit veiled in snow. He estimated another three to four hours.

They had gone less than four miles when the tremors returned. This time, they were stronger, closer. They pressed on despite it, the mare's ears flicking back with each distant shudder. The ground never fully stilled, only softened between pulses, like something vast far below. Time stretched thin under the strain of it. The rhythm of travel took hold, hoofbeats, breath, the quiet creak of leather, until the tremors began to feel less like interruption and more like a presence moving with them.

Then came a sound, so faint at first it could've been the wind. A slow, dragging whisper, like stone scraping stone. It followed their rhythm. Every time the mare's hooves struck earth, it answered.

"It's following us," he said under his breath. "I didn't imagine it before."

Elara's hand clutched his arm. "It chases the mark."

He looked down at her, caught off guard. Her gaze remained fixed ahead, unblinking, unfocused, her face drained to the color of ash. His attention shifted, almost without thought, to the mark above his wrist, the one burned into him when he bonded with his dragon. It pulsed with heat, alive with the fury of the Elder's fire.

Wrapping one arm around Elara, he drew her closer. A rush of heat struck him at once, radiating from her body into his chest, growing stronger, hotter. He shifted his hand to her neck, fingers searching for the telltale burn of fever, but her skin was cool, her pulse steady beneath his touch.

This was something else entirely, not sickness, not weakness. Something was rising within her that he did not understand.

The ground shuddered again, harder this time, disrupting his thoughts. Somewhere behind them, the earth split with a muffled crack. Crows burst from the giant oak, scattering in a storm of screeching wings. The owl uttered a high, piercing note and dived ahead of them toward the slopes.

Osric spurred the mare into a full gallop. The soil beneath her hooves pulsed, alive and furious. Behind them, something ancient rose.

Osric didn't look back.

From the abyss came the sound of life awakening. A scream born from a nightmare filled the air. Soil and shattered stone erupted skyward. From the wound, something vast rose. It was a shape hewn from shadow and stone. Molten veins glimmered faintly beneath scales of hardened rock. Two smoldering orifices opened where eyes should have been. Jaws stretch impossibly wide, exposing rows of jagged teeth slick with heat.

The creature's breath came in gusts that stank of ash and deep time. Each exhale bent the grass flat and carried the scent of lives long dead. When it moved, the land obeyed; roots tore free, stones rolled aside.

Osric's hand went to his sword. Whatever it was, it had come from a place beyond nightmare, older than dragons, older than flame. He didn't know its name, only that the world seemed scarier in its presence.

Two miles ahead, Osric saw where the meadow ended, and the mountain began. Grass thinned into rock, and scattered scrubs appeared as the ground began to slope upwards.

"Come on, girl, we're almost there. You can make it."

A cry blew past them, worse than the one his dragon had made when their Keeper's bond was stripped from him centuries ago. It was immense and unworldly, a raw, reptilian scream dragged through something dark, something ancient, something that should not exist.

Osric turned in his saddle. His throat closed. "By the Elders…"

It was not a dragon. It was what young dragons feared. Something even the Elders did not speak of.

Osric urged the mare faster. Her hooves struck sparks on stone. Her eyes wide in terror, she began to climb, straining against the slope, every muscle trembling.

The owl swooped past them, calling sharp and urgent hoots, urging them forward before vanishing into the higher mists.

The mare lunged up the climb, the path tightening into a narrow ribbon of jagged stone that threatened to give way beneath her. Her hooves slipped and skidded, each misstep a breath from disaster. Foam streamed from her mouth, flecking the rocks below, her lungs dragging in air in harsh, desperate pulls.

Osric fought to remain mounted, wrapping an arm around Elara, fighting to keep the eggs from rolling out of the blanket. He loosened his grip on the reins, allowing the mare to climb at her own speed and direction.

Behind them, the earth-beast dragged itself free of the meadow, each motion a thunderclap. It clawed upward, tearing gouges into the mountain's flank. The tremors shook loose gravel and shale, clattering down around them.

The owl returned, circling above his head before diving toward a cleft in the rock. "There!" Osric shouted, pointing to a narrow opening half-hidden behind a curtain of dead vines. Osric spurred the mare onward, but instead of advancing, she stopped. She would go no further. She stood trembling, nostrils flaring, whites of her eyes wide. Osric jumped down, leaning Elara against her main. Grabbing the mouth bit, he pulled, straining against her weight.

"Come on, we're almost there. Move, or get eaten by whatever that thing is."

The mare leapt forward. Osric ran beside her, leading her to their sanctuary. Both stumbled into the crevice as another quake split the ledge behind them. Rock gave way, tumbling down the slope in a roaring avalanche. Dust and falling debris rained across the entrance.

Osric pulled the mare further into the cavern, determined to put more space between the creature and them. Their lungs breathed in cool and wet air, filling their nostrils with the smell of iron and moss.

The creature's roar rolled up the mountain, voicing his anger over his quarry slipping away.

A blinding white flash split the heavens in silence. The world vanished in that instant, swallowed by brilliance. The mare reared and screamed, hooves flailing against the Keeper's grip. He caught Elara as she was thrown from the mare.

The air burned.

Then the mountain spoke.

"Stop!"

The voice was ancient, resonant, carrying the weight of mountains and the deep calm of the earth before time. Every tree bowed, every creature stilled. Even the mare froze. The storm held its breath.

And then, silence, broken only by the mountain's slow, steady breathing.

Osric blinked against the afterlight. The air shimmered with gold dust, fragments of brilliance descending like ash. He looked down at the dust dotting their bodies and clothing. His eyes opened wide with wonder and disbelief.

"By the Elders," he said softly. "The Elder Wyrm, Terrus. The Earth's own heart."

The ground beneath them thrummed, slow and alive. The mare bowed her head as though in reverence.

Above, the clouds split into a single luminous seam. Through it, Osric glimpsed the faint outline of colossal wings, carved of light and stone, spanning the sky. Terrus's gaze, vast and unseen, but unmistakable, fell upon them.

Then, as abruptly as it appeared, the light folded back into the mountain. The only sound was their own breathing.

Somewhere outside, the creature moved again, slow and patient. It slithered down the mountainside and burrowed back into the ground from which it came, silent, returning to its deep sleep, ready to awaken and protect Terrus again when needed.

Holding Elara in his arms and holding the mare's reins, he continued down the narrow pathway, the only sound the clicking of the mare's hooves on stone. The owl landed on the saddle, feathers puffed, head swiveling restlessly.

The fissure opened into a grotto made of gray stone. Ahead, a light beckoned them forward. As they continued, the air grew heavy, mixed with the taste of something old, like dust from the bones of the world. The tunnel sloped downward, winding through layers of rock. Every few steps, the walls expanded and contracted imperceptibly, as though the mountain breathed. Osric's hand brushed the stone; warmth throbbed beneath his fingertips.

"It's alive," Osric whispered.

He pressed deeper, the horse following, their footsteps echoing through the expanse. The hum in the earth grew louder. The light ahead grew larger as they neared. Then the passage widened abruptly into a cavern. The ceiling arched high above, vanishing into shadow. The floor and walls were covered with large crystal illuminous scales.

"It's like we are inside Terrus."

He found a small rise near the heart of the cavern, a natural platform surrounded by the soft glow of reflected firelight. It would do. Lying Elara on the floor, he spread the bear hide across it, then layered one of the blankets on top, creating a resting place that felt like a nest carved from shadow and warmth. Leading the mare closer, he unfastened the blanket and lifted out the two eggs with deliberate care. His gaze lingered on the orphaned egg. Its crack had widened further, a glowing seam threading across the shell.

Soon, Little One, He brushed a finger along its edge. *A few more hours.*

Gathering Elara in his arms, He carried her to the bedding. He laid her gently upon the makeshift bed, tucking both eggs safely at her side.

Once she was settled, he allowed himself to sink down beside her. He didn't even take the time to unpack the horse. The day's fears, the chase, the storm of uncertainty all faded into the hush of the cavern. Within moments,

Osric's eyes closed, and sleep claimed him before he could even draw another breath.

The sensation of wetness on the tip of his nose woke him. Half asleep, he raised his hand and wiped away the moisture. The wetness returned. He opened his eyes into narrow bands, the blur of sleep receding. At first, he thought it was a dream. But then reality reached him and he found himself staring into a pair of eyes that glowed like dawn through amber glass. A dragonet sat on top of him, damp from birth, her tiny chest rising with the fragile rhythm of new life. Her scales shimmered amber and bronze, the colors still finding themselves, the earth still deciding what tone this creature should be.

Osric drew in a slow, trembling breath. Five hundred years. It had been five hundred years since he had seen a hatchling open its eyes to the world. Although he had seen older dragons, he was not privy to newborns since Solarus cursed him. He had forgotten how silent that first moment was.

The dragonet tilted her head, studying him with uncanny focus. Her nostrils flared, testing the air, tasting him, the scent of fire-forged metal and time-worn dust. A flick of her tongue, a blink of gold-ringed eyes, and a faint spark shivered across its scales, like lightning learning to crawl.

Osric swallowed hard. So small. So impossibly alive. And yet, in that gaze, he saw the echo of every wyrm he'd ever known, Kaerath, the great Elder Wyrms, all the ancients folded into one fragile being.

He reached out. "By the stars…" he whispered. "You're real." A memory stirred: small hands he hadn't held in centuries, a tiny face he had chosen to let another family raise. He pushed the thought away. That life was gone. Better forgotten.

The dragonet answered with a soft hum, a sound older than language, and for the first time in centuries, Osric felt the impossible stir again in his chest: wonder.

"Welcome to the world. Little One."

The baby wyrm chirped.

Memory stirred inside him. The ancient ritual rose from the depths of his mind, etched there by a life he no longer had the right to claim. The Breath of Recognition.

He had not performed the ritual for centuries. The thought sent a hollow ache through his chest. He had sworn never again to reach for what had been stripped from him.

And yet, looking at her, he knew he had to try.

The dragonet tilted her head, nostrils flaring, watching his hand draw close to her. She leaned closer and exhaled. A warm mist swept across his hand, shimmering with flecks of gold and emberlight. The air thrummed, the ground humming softly beneath them.

Osric gasped as fire licked through his veins. Not pain, but life. The ancient scar in his palm, his Keeper's bond to Kaerath, flared bright, golden veins radiating outward. For an instant, he thought the curse would snuff it out. He felt Solarus's seal resisting, the light twisting beneath his skin, trying to die.

But it didn't.

The glow steadied, softer but sure, and a new light bled through, the hue of raw flame, untamed and newborn. Three faint sparks bloomed at the base of his thumb, forming a delicate spiral that pulsed in rhythm with the dragonet's heartbeat.

Her tiny claws gripped his wrist. The connection held.

"It worked," he whispered, voice cracking. "By the stars, it worked."

He bowed his head, overcome. He couldn't name her. Not yet. The curse forbade the rest of the Rite. But the first bond, the Breath, had answered him. Against Solarus's decree, against centuries of silence, the flame had chosen to live.

The dragonet trilled softly, pressing her snout to his hand, right over the twin marks; one old and broken, one new and flickering. Her warmth spread through him like dawn across frozen stone.

"I can't name you," he murmured, trembling, "but you know me already, don't you?"

She chirped.

Slipping the dragonet safely into his pocket, Osric rose and unpacked the horse. He carried the packet of medical supplies to the bed and redressed Elara's wound. He noted that the scaling on her leg had neither progressed nor declined. If that was a good omen, he did not know. He tried remembering centuries back when he dealt with Keepers who had such calamities, but the memories were faint and blurred.

Returning to the mare, Osric unstrapped the saddle and slid it off her back. He laid it against the wall, its service no longer needed. He returned to the mare and stroked her face.

"I know this isn't right, Girl, not after your bravery to get us here. But I have no choice. There is nothing for you to eat here. And we have no food left. You are our only chance of survival." The mare looked into his eyes. "But I guess I can wait one more day. Plenty of tunnels to explore. Ophira said there were some plants growing somewhere in this place. I'll search for some tubers to sustain me through until tomorrow."

Chapter 11

Osric moved quietly through the caverns, exploring their surroundings, considering the fissure's strengths and shortcomings. The soft glow from the walls guided his steps. The scales embedded in the stone shimmered faintly, stirred by his presence, ancient remnants of Terrus's slumbering power. Their light filled the passageways with a dreamlike glow, shifting from pale silver to deep amber as he walked, breathing life into the shadows.

He followed the first tunnel to its end, the air cool and sweet. A thin veil of mist drifted before him. An opening appeared in the rock, jagged yet graceful, letting in a spill of daylight that danced upon the surface of a clear basin. Water from melted snow fell from the heights above in a silver thread, constant and calm, gathering in a pool before trailing deeper into the earth. Osric knelt, cupped his hands, and drank. The taste was clean and sharp, like biting into new snow. It slid down his throat and settled in his chest.

He circled back to where Elara slept, his mind adrift in shadowed thought. His footsteps whispered against the stone… then the passage bent where none had been before, unveiling a chamber that breathed a low, living hum, as though it had been waiting for him.

A pool rested inside, its surface quivered like molten glass. Steam rose in slow, curling tendrils, carrying heat. Warmth kissed his face and hands, and he realized the air was alive here; Terrus's breath. The pool's ripples carried faint glimmers of light, each one pulsing in rhythm with something vast and hidden beneath the stone. He placed his hand into the pool, the water warm but not so hot that it burned. Wondering if the pool might contain Terrus's healing powers, he splashed several handfuls onto his newly suffered wounds. Within seconds, they closed and disappeared.

A healing pool, as Ophira said. Elara can bathe here and repair her leg much faster.

As he neared their sanctum, a third chamber to his right pulsed with a deeper hum. The air shimmered, the scent of minerals sharp in his throat. A vent cut through the rock near the far wall, glowing faintly red. When he stepped closer, the heat licked his face. Terrus's fire heart breathed through the mountain. Withdrawing a small piece of wood from his pocket, he dropped it near the vent; it caught flame instantly. A small smile tugged at his lips. *The perfect place for cooking our meals.*

Osric looked over the area, then dropped to one knee. The mountain was no mere refuge. It was a sanctuary. The breath of the Elder Wyrm warmed the stones; his light brought them sight; his body sheltered them in its folds. Osric looked back toward the passages he'd come from, where the luminous walls curved like ribs of some sleeping giant.

Thank you, Terrus. Even asleep, you guard your own.

Osric returned to the chamber where Elara slept. She lay where he'd left her, her breathing slow and even, one arm draped protectively around her egg. He reached inside his pocket and withdrew the small dragonet, placing her beside the egg. She wrapped her tail around the shell. A soft, trilling chirp rose from her throat: sweet, rhythmic, almost melodic.

A thrill answered from within the egg. It was faint, trembling, but alive. The wyrmling inside was singing back.

A quiet smile touched Osric's lips. "You're trying to coax her out, aren't you?" he murmured, crouching beside them. "I was afraid that without her twin, she'd never emerge. But you've connected with her."

The dragonet chirped in reply.

Osric reached out and lifted the egg carefully. Beneath his fingers, the shell was warm. The faintest red line appeared across its top. "It's begun," he whispered. "The smallest crack has appeared." Gently, he set it back beside Elara, letting the glow of the scales cradle them both in light.

The newly born wyrmling cried, looking into Osric's eyes. At the same time, the Keeper's stomach growled loudly. "I know. I'm hungry as well. I saved a piece of meat in case you hatched before I had a way to feed you." He extended his hand. "Come, Little One. Come with me." The tiny creature hesitated, eyes shifting between the egg and Osric, her tail twitching.

"She'll be safe," Osric assured her. "We need to let her rest, too, so she'll have the strength to break her shell. Come now."

At last, the dragonet gave a small chirp of agreement. She bounded into his hand, the warmth of her scales seeping into his skin. She clambered up his arm in quick, awkward bursts and settled on his shoulder, its tiny claws tugging gently at the fabric to steady itself.

Osric chuckled under his breath. "You're braver than you look, Little One." He, brushed her tiny chest with a fingertip. A soft sound emanated from her throat, almost purring. She enjoyed having her chest rubbed.

He walked over to where his saddlebag hung from a jetting piece of rock on the wall. Reaching into his saddlebag, he withdrew a small, wrapped bundle. The newborn chirped loudly as she watched Osric's fingers intently.

"Shh, you'll wake Elara," Osric said as he loosened the bindings. Inside lay two thin strips of meat. Biting off a piece, he held it out toward the hatchling.

"Go on," he coaxed softly. "Eat it."

The baby dragon sniffed, tilted her head, her unblinking eyes fixed not on the meat but on Osric himself.

"You don't trust it?" Osric asked with a faint smile. "Alright, watch me." He placed the piece of meat in his mouth, chewed, and swallowed, exaggerating the motion so the dragon could see. The taste of food made his stomach grumble again.

The hatchling watched, neck bobbing, eyes bright with curiosity. She chirped again, a questioning sound.

"Now it's your turn."

Osric offered another piece, but the dragon only sniffed it, hesitating, wings twitching.

"I know you're hungry," Osric murmured, studying the little creature. "So why won't you eat?"

He frowned, thinking back to when he was but an apprentice Keeper. He remembered the senior Keepers speaking of the problems with newly hatched wyrmlings. What had they done?

"Oh," he breathed. "Of course."

He threw the offered bit of meat into his mouth, chewed it briefly, letting his scent mingle with it, then offered it again.

This time, the baby sniffed and snatched it from his fingers, gulping it down with surprising enthusiasm.

A laugh escaped Osric's chest. "All you needed was your mother's scent on it, didn't you?"

The hatchling trilled, eyes gleaming, tail curling in delight, clearly asking for more. She ate the few remaining pieces before yawning. Osric placed her inside his pocket, where she snuggled deep inside his shirt and curled into a ball.

Osric looked around the room. "I need to find something that Elara and I can eat. She's growing stronger, but she'll deteriorate if I don't get some nourishment in her. You rest while I do some more exploring."

The moment he stepped out into the inner passage, a cool breeze blew over him, rustling his hair. He took a deep breath. "Earth! The air carries the scent of fresh dirt."

Hurrying along the passage in a near run, Osric headed toward the direction the wind seemed to originate from. After some minutes, the inner way opened into another large cavern, larger than the one he chose for their living area. He stopped, dumbfounded. At the far end, about a mile away, was an opening to the outside world, the cause of the cool breeze. He could see snow piled two-thirds up the opening. But it was what was between him and the opening that both mystified and confounded him; an area of rich dirt, filled with a variety of plants, including stalks of corn, vines of snap peas and beans, potatoes, and carrots. Drops of moisture dripped from the ceiling, watering the vegetation.

He ran to where the snap peas grew and dropped to his knees. His hands shaking, he carefully picked a pod, placed it in his mouth, and bit down. The pea split between his teeth with a sharp, wet crack. Cold sweetness flooded his mouth; green, raw, almost shocking after days of dried meat and mash-cakes. Juice seeped along his gums, clean and faintly sugared. His jaw worked without thought, saliva surging as his body recognized life where it had expected nothing. For a breath, the ache in his gut eased, the world narrowing to the simple fact of something fresh breaking open inside his mouth.

Crawling on his knees to where the tops of the carrots broke through the earth, he frantically dug into the soil and pulled up a carrot. Brushing off the dirt, he crunched it. Its taste was also divine.

When he could eat no more, he leaned back onto his heels. "Thank you, Terrus. Your bounty was delicious. Ophira said there would be food and a place to plant the seeds, but I never expected anything like this."

He stuffed his pockets with carrots, snap peas, an onion, broccoli, and sprigs of sage and thyme. He gathered a heavy head of cabbage into his arms and added four ears of corn, fodder for the horse.

A brief, unwelcome sadness tightened his chest at the thought of butchering the mare. He pushed it aside and turned back at once, hurrying to Elara.

Seeing that Elara still slept easily, her skin cool and free of fever, he turned to the small work of making dinner. Grateful for Ophira's insistence that he take her old cooking pot, he filled it halfway with water.

The small dragonet stirred and peeked out from Osric's pocket. She climbed to his shoulder, keenly watching his actions.

"Even though I cannot officially name you, I can give you a nickname. What name shall it be? *Little One* is a tender start, but names carry power. You need something forged of flame and sky, something worthy of what you are." The dragonet tilted her head, eyes bright and unblinking. "We can work on a name while I chop. What do you think?" The dragonet trilled softly in reply, curling her tail around his neck.

Osric chopped the vegetables with quiet efficiency, dropping them into the pot along with sprigs of thyme and sage. From a small pouch in the saddlebag, he measured out a careful pinch of salt.

Unwilling to leave Elara alone again, he set the pot directly over a nearby heat vent and stayed close. Before long, the water began to roll and steam, the air filling with the soft, green sweetness of vegetable broth.

"This should put a bounce back in her step," he murmured to the dragonet. He breathed in the aroma of the bubbling stew. "Lots of fresh vegetables and good herbs." He held out a small piece of root to the wyrmling. She sniffed the strange food, then moved to the other shoulder.

"Not a fan of vegetables?" Osric laughed. "I'm not usually a big fan either. But it sure beats another day of dried meat and mash-cakes."

While the soup cooked, Osric peeled the ears of corn and fed them to the horse. He then searched through a pile of stones in the corner, finding two that would suffice as bowls. Again, Ophira came to the rescue with the two spoons she had slipped inside the food bag.

The heat worked quickly, softening the vegetables to tenderness. Osric drew the pot from the vent and ladled the steaming mixture into a bowl, setting it aside to cool for Elara. With the back of the spoon, he pressed the vegetables into a soft mash, fit for feeding.

While the broth cooled, he checked her wound and administered another measured dose of the medicine.

Sliding an arm behind her shoulders, he drew her gently upright, feeling the weight of her sag against his chest. Her eyelids fluttered, unfocused, but her mouth parted when the spoon touched her lips. He waited, breath held, until her jaw worked and she swallowed.

She was not fully awake, but her body still remembered how to take what it needed. He felt no resistance, only the fragile, careful rhythm of feeding, one slow swallow at a time.

"So, have you decided on a name yet?" Osric asked as the dragonet sat beside him.

The dragonet twilled softly, a fluttering sound that trembled in the air: part purr, part birdsong. It rose and fell like breath through hollow reeds, delicate yet threaded with warmth.

A name brushed against his thoughts rather than his ears, a whisper that seemed to rise from within him instead of without. Osric stilled. "Tirra?" he murmured, the word tasting familiar on his tongue, as though he'd spoken it once before, lifetimes ago.

The dragonet twilled again, a silvery note that resonated through the air; a pulse that matched the rhythm of his own heartbeat. Osric smiled. "Tirra it is.".

Her head tilted, wings quivering in acknowledgment.

He smiled faintly. "Do you know what that name means, Little One?" The dragonet blinked. "It means *the spark that remembers*; the first warmth before the flame awakens."

"I don't know why you've come or what purpose you carry, only that you've waited for centuries for this moment. For me. And now you're here, born from the ashes of time."

The dragonet pressed her snout to his finger, eyes softening, and for a heartbeat, Osric felt something pass between them; an old promise rekindled, written not in words but in flame and memory.

So, life settled into a fragile rhythm over the next two weeks. Elara grew stronger with each passing day, her breath deepening, her color returning. The scaling along her leg advanced no further. Beside her, the crack in her egg widened, the shell easing apart as the wyrmling readied itself for birth.

Osric ranged deeper into the tunnels, scratching a rough map onto a new piece of horse hide. Between his forays, he pressed Ophira's seeds into the warm stone soil and tended them with quiet care. Always, he returned to Elara, watching and waiting for the moment her eyes would open and meet his.

On the eleventh day since their arrival, Osric was granted his wish. Elara awakened.

At first, the world was only sensation; the steady cradle of warmth beneath her, the muted thrum of stone, the faint, clean scent of herbs and cooked roots. Her body felt heavy, unfamiliar, as though it had been set back into itself after a long absence.

Then she opened her eyes.

A man sat beside her. Close enough that she could see the lines at the corners of his eyes, the roughness of his hands, the stillness with which he held himself, as if any sudden movement might break her. He was watching her, not with surprise, but with quiet, aching attention, as though he had been waiting for this moment longer than he dared to admit.

Panic flickered, brief and sharp, but did not take hold. Something in him steadied it. His presence pressed against her senses like shelter: solid, patient, unmoving. She did not know his name. Nor had she any memory of how she came to be in a cave with him. Yet her body understood him before her mind could.

Safe, it whispered.

Her throat worked, dry and weak. He noticed at once, reaching for the bowl of water, his movements slow, careful, as if giving her time to decide whether to trust him. When he spoke, his voice was low and even, shaped to calm rather than command.

"Don't try to speak. Here, drink some water." He held a cup of water to her lips. She took several small sips, the liquid partially spilling from her mouth. "Your throat has not spoken a word for some weeks." He took a cloth and wiped the water from her chin. "For now, know you are safe. And before you worry, your egg is lying beside you. A crack has developed across the top of the shell. I estimate your egg will hatch in the next day or two."

Elara watched him, her eyes searching his face, imprinting it. Whoever he was—stranger, guardian, savior—he had been here when she could not be. And that, somehow, was enough.

A soft trill drew her eyes to the side. Sitting beside her egg was another small bronze wyrmling, a newborn.

"This is Tirra. She hatched a few days ago while you were sleeping. She's been eagerly waiting to meet you and your dragon."

Elara tried to lift her arm, but it was too heavy. Her muscles refused to work properly. Using what strength she could summon, she pushed her hand across the bear skin toward the dragonet. Tirra cooed and pressed her nose into Elara's hand.

Her gaze returned to the stranger as she gathered the strength to do something more than watch. Her lips parted. Nothing came.

She swallowed, the motion small and painful, and tried again. Her throat felt raw, scraped hollow by disuse. A sound slipped free this time, but it was thin, uncertain, barely more than breath.

Osric did not move. He stayed exactly where he was, water in hand, eyes steady, as if even encouragement might fracture the moment.

She drew another breath, shallow but determined. Her mouth shaped a word.

"W…where?"

The syllables cost her. Her voice cracked, the sound fraying as it left her, but it was unmistakably a word.

"We're inside Dragon Mountain. To be more precise, I believe we're inside the sleeping Elder, Terrus. Do you remember anything?"

Elara managed to lift her hand a few inches off the bear skin. She rocked her hand back and forth.

"A little bit. What do you remember?"

She waved her hand through the air, then wiggled her fingers as she dropped her hand.

"You remember being on your dragon and then falling. Is that correct?"

Elara slowly nodded.

"Do you remember the battle?"

She froze. Then fear detonated. Her eyes flew wide, and she sucked in a ragged breath, twisting as if to escape a blow only she could see. Her hands scrabbled for purchase, nails biting into cloth and stone as she tried to pull herself away, legs jerking uselessly beneath her.

Pain stopped her where strength could not. She gasped, breath breaking, trapped between memory and the fragile limits of her body.

Osric moved at once. He caught her shoulders and drew her back.

"Easy," he said. "You'll hurt yourself. He can't reach you here. The Commander cannot enter this place. This is a sanctuary."

The words were simple, repeated with quiet certainty as he held her until the frantic strength bled out of her limbs. Gradually, her struggle slowed. Her breathing found a rhythm again.

She did not pull away. She clutched instead, her fingers curling into his sleeve, his strength giving her something solid to hold. She lifted her head and drew in a deep breath, then gave Osric an inquisitive look.

"Meat stew. I made it while you slept. Would you like some?"

Elara managed a partial smile as she nodded yes.

"Who?" Elara rasped. Osric lifted a small spoonful into Elara's mouth.

"Who am I?" She nodded. "My name is Osric."

Elara hooked her two fingers together.

"Your brother? I don't know. I never saw what became of him after he fell. I only know the Commander has his egg."

Tears filled Elara's eyes.

"But know this. Once the snow melts and you are strong enough, I WILL get the wyrmling back."

Elara turned her head and burrowed into the bearskin, her eyes closing as grief pressed down, heavy and inescapable.

Osric looked inside the bowl. Only half was eaten. He opened his mouth to protest and remind her she needed to eat, but thought better of it. He laid the blanket closer around her shoulders, granting her the one thing he could not take from her. Her grief.

Chapter 12

While Elara slept, Osric wandered the caverns. He drifted from tunnel to tunnel, following whichever path bent first, studying mineral seams and forgotten alcoves. He tried to keep his mind blank, but the wailing of the fallen wyrms echoed in his mind, the sound of wings turning to ash filled his thoughts, the sound of crushed bones filled his ears. Even after five centuries, he could not erase the sights or sounds he had witnessed from his mind.

He moved deeper into the mountain. He walked without a destination, driven by the need to escape himself. The tunnels twisted and opened without warning, as though the mountain shaped his path for him, and before he realized it, the stone opened up.

He stepped into a cavern unlike any he had ever known.

It was vast. So vast, it stole his breath. The walls glowed with a brilliance that no torch or vent could explain. Liquid sunlight poured from the stone, reflecting in countless shards across the ceiling. The air was alive with power, the low hum rising into a steady pulse.

Osric stopped. For an instant, in the light's heart, he thought he saw movement, a shifting form within the wall. The outline of scales? A vast head? A single eye opening, ancient, and knowing?

He stumbled backward; his breath froze mid-rise. "Terrus?"

The word left him barely above a whisper, yet it awakened the cavern. The hum deepened, rolling through the floor, vibrating in his bones. The golden light intensified, and from within it came a voice. Not sound exactly, but resonance. It filled the space and his mind all at once, vast and calm.

"You still walk in shadow, Osric of the Keepers."

He fell to one knee, the weight of the voice pressing down on him, not in wrath but in truth. "I…if you are Terrus, then you know I've failed you. I failed you all."

The light shimmered, shifting like breath. "All fail. Even dragons. Even gods. But failure is not the end. It is the beginning of what you choose to become after."

Osric's hands trembled against the stone. "There is no redemption for what I did."

"There is," the voice murmured, softer now, like embers whispering in the dark. "Through her."

"Elara?"

"Through both. The wyrmling and the child of flame. The dragonet ready to be born carries our spark, the last echo of our hearts. The blood of Solarus pumps through her veins. And the girl, she may yet become what I once was: the Wyrms' savior. If she does not falter."

Osric's head lifted, awe and disbelief warring inside him. "Elara? A savior?"

"One cannot know the shape of destiny until it breathes," Terrus replied. "But she bears the mark of blood and flame. But beware. Inside her burns the fire of a dragon.

The golden light swelled, flooding the chamber, and for a moment, Osric saw it clearly: a colossal dragon coiled within the stone, wings folded, eyes like suns. The image burned through him, too vast to comprehend.

"From the line of mercy shall come one born of fire and sea. She will wake the sleeping Wyrms when darkness forgets its name. Her courage will border on ruin, yet her heart will bind what time has broken. In her burns the wild warmth of beginnings; the fire that wakes what has been buried too long. When fire and restraint are born of the same blood, one must bend, or both will break."

"Are you saying that she is the person foretold in prophecy long ago that could hold a dragonfire? The Twin Flame?"

"Yes."

"But no human can hold dragon fire!"

"She was born to be the only one."

Osric looked back down the corridor, towards where Elara rested, trying to understand what Terrus was saying.

"But without her twin Vaelor to cool her flame, she could destroy the world. You must keep her flame cooled, keep her fire subdued until it is needed."

"But how do I keep her flame at bay?"

"When fire and restraint are born of the same blood, one must bend, or both will break."

"Terrus, I don't understand."

"Protect her and the new borns, Keeper," the voice said. "For in saving them, you may yet save yourself."

Then the light faded, leaving only the soft luminescence of the scales. The hum quieted to a heartbeat's echo.

Osric remained there on one knee, pondering the Elder Drake's words. He rose and turned away, walking slowly to Elara.

Elara still slept. Terrus' words reeling in his mind, he lay beside her on the bear skin. Tirra wiggled beneath the blanket and curled by his side, her warmth comforting.

How am I, a mere man, supposed to contain her flame? Not just flame, but dragonfire. Immortal or not, my flesh can still burn... can still melt.

A cold chill traced Osric's spine as an image entered his mind. His body was aflame. Flesh sloughed from his bones, falling in molten strips onto the ground. He immediately drove the thought away, not wishing to dwell on the possibilities.

Osric woke on a sharp breath, pain flaring as Tirra shifted. Her tiny claws bit into his skin as she scrambled up his chest, instinct and urgency driving her. An excited chirp escaped her as she wriggled free of the covers.

A low, ancient trill gathered in her throat, something older than language, older than memory. She leapt to Elara and scurried beneath her blanket, wrapping her arms around the eggshell.

Tirra's song sank into the shell, vibrating through its layers, carrying the cadence of wyrm-song, a call of recognition, of waiting, of the fire that remembers itself.

A faint answer pulsed back, the sound of an unhatched wyrmling preparing to enter the world. He remembered it well.

Osric pulled back the cover. Fine fractures spidered across the egg's surface, glowing faintly from within. Each tremor of Tirra's song drew another answering shudder from the shell.

The shell flexed, then cracked wider, pieces flaking loose as something inside pressed outward: small, urgent, alive.

Tirra's song deepened, no longer a lullaby but a summons, and the shell responded, breaking not from force alone, but from recognition.

Osric reached over and gently rocked Elara's shoulder. "Wake up, Elara. It's time. Your wyrmling is hatching."

Elara stirred at his words, her lashes fluttering open. Osric helped her sit up to watch the miracle of birth.

"Tirra's calling to her. And my egg is answering."

"Yes. As in the past, one hatchling calls to another. That's how an entire clutch hatches within minutes of each other."

Tirra's tiny claws hooked into the grooves of the egg. She pulled her body to the top and hooked her talons beneath the crack and pulled. A small portion of the shell broke and fell onto the blanket. She lowered her nose inside the opening, uttering several twills and clicks.

The fissure glowed brighter, widening, spreading until another thin piece of shell fell away. A tiny muzzle glistening and trembling pushed through until it gently touched Tirra's snout. The unborn wyrmling gave a weak cry, its voice small but piercing, answered immediately by Tiarra's joyous trill.

Elara's hand covered her mouth, tears glinting in her eyes.

The shell opened, light spilling across the bed as the hatchling emerged fully: slick, fragile, and radiant. Tiarra pressed close, crooning softly.

"You must perform the Breath of Recognition with her so you two are bonded," Osric said. "Hold out your right hand in front of her mouth, palm side up. Allow her to smell your scent. If she accepts you, she will blow a soft, warm breath across your palm and engrave the Keeper's sigil."

"And if she doesn't accept me?"

"She'll give you a nasty bite."

With some trepidation, Elara held out her hand. Her heart pounding, she watched as the newborn wyrmling cautiously approached, taking a large lungful of the woman's scent. Elara held her breath as she awaited the outcome.

The newborn paused, studying Elara's hand with uncanny focus. Then she breathed; a warm, golden exhale that shimmered like dawn. Stardust unfurled from her lips and swept over Elara's skin. The particles burned softly as they sank into her flesh, spiraling into place until the ancient Keeper's insignia blazed upon her palm.

From deep beneath them, Terrus's heart beat twice, rejoicing that there were now two newborn dragonets in the world.

*****

Tirra chirped softly from Osric's pocket, stirred by the scent of fresh blood as he sliced two steaks from the slab of horse meat. A flicker of movement caught his eye; something pale and round darted from beneath Elara's blanket.

The *other* hatchling.

It scurried straight for him, claws clicking on the rock floor, and before he could react, the tiny dragon launched its body up his pant leg, using him like a tree. Osric hissed through his teeth and tried not to laugh. "All right, all right, I see you."

The newborn reached his shoulder in a flurry of wings and squeaks as Tirra leapt from his pocket. Both dragonets chirruped hungrily.

"Okay, you two," he said, shaking his head with a half-smile. "You need to wait."

He set them both on a tall, flat stone, where they sat side by side, tails flicking in perfect unison. Their nostrils flared, delicate at first, then wide and greedy. Tirra lifted her head, tongue flicking in quick, uncertain darts as she tasted the air. Another trill sounded.

Osric shaved off several small strips of meat, fresh blood dripping across his blade and through his fingers. He held out two pieces. Both hatchlings lunged eagerly, their tiny jaws working with determined ferocity. They devoured their meal, eyes half-lidded in contentment, wings quivering with pleasure.

Elara watched from where she sat, her heart caught somewhere between awe and tenderness. The sight of him—the stoic Keeper, patient and gentle, two dragonets clinging to his fingers as if he were their world— drew a soft ache from deep within her.

Osric glanced up, meeting her gaze across the stone floor. For a breath too long, neither looked away. He gave her a quick smile.

"I'll take these down to the larger heating vent. They seem to cook better there. Be right back."

Osric grabbed the two steaks and hurried to the cavern he referred to as "the kitchen." Since both wanted their meat rare, he returned in five minutes.

The two ate in silence, the two dragonets asleep in Osric's shirt pocket, their bellies full. Osric removed a packet of powder from his saddlebag, holding it up for Elara to see.

"Time for your medicine," he said.

"Do I have to? It tastes like shit."

Osric mixed some of the powder into a cup of water and carried it over to Elara. "Most medicines do. Drink it."

"But my leg is so much better."

"Ophira said you had to take it until the powder was all gone or the infection might return. This should be your last cup."

"Then can't I skip it?"

Osric pushed the cup closer. "Drink it."

Elara tipped the cup back and forced the mixture down. Her nose scrunched, her eyes squeezed shut, and her mouth puckered tight as she shuddered. "Ugh," she muttered, wiping her lips with the back of her hand.

"Roll onto your side," Osric said quietly. "I need to inspect the wound."

Elara obeyed, shifting carefully onto one hip. The firelight traced a warm glow along her skin as he knelt beside her, his shadow falling across her leg. He lifted her cut pant leg in silence and unwound the bandage, the fabric peeling away in slow, deliberate turns.

When the last strip came free, Osric froze. The scaling had changed. The iridescent plates had softened in color. The skin beyond them was smooth and almost human once more. Relief flickered across his face.

"You're scaling is so much better. The hatchlings' birth has slowed whatever was happening."

He reached out, brushing the edge of the healed skin with the tips of his fingers.

Elara flinched; not from pain, but from *him*. The warmth of his touch rippled through her like a current, startling and unfamiliar. Her breath caught, pulse quickening before she could stop it. The sensation left her trembling, unmoored.

Osric drew back slightly, mistaking her reaction for discomfort. "Did that hurt?"

She shook her head quickly, voice barely above a whisper. "No. It… startled me."

He studied her for a moment longer, uncertainty flickering behind his eyes. Then he nodded. "I think a soak in the hot springs is called for. Terrus' healing waters will do your leg a lot of good."

"When? Now?"

"No time like the present. The sooner your leg heals, the sooner you can get around on your own. Plus, your body odor is getting a bit musky."

"Well, that's not very nice."

"Neither is your stink."

"I… I don't think I can walk that far."

Osric laughed. "Why does that matter? I'll carry you like I've been doing since I found you in the river. I can help you get in the spring. Then when you're ready, I'll help you out and carry you back."

Elara looked down at the bed, not wanting to see his reaction. "You know, I'll have to be naked to get into the spring," Elara teased, a twinkle in her eye.

"Seeing you naked will cause me no embarrassment. If it does for you, that's your problem." Elara thought she saw a brief look of mischievousness on Osric's face.

"You know, you could stay and join me."

"No, thank you. I soaked earlier today while you slept." This time, she was certain she saw a hidden smile.

"Come, Tirra, Kaura." The two wyrmlings ran onto Elara's shoulder.

"So, you decided on the name Kaura?"

"Yes. It means ember."

"It suits her. We'll need to conduct the Rite of First Flame within the next few hours to name her properly."

Osric scooped Elara and the two dragonets into his arms. "You're getting heavy."

"That's because you've been feeding me too well."

Osric laughed, one of the few times Elara ever heard him do it. "Off to soak."

"If I must."

"Can you undress yourself?" he asked when they reached the hot spring cavern. He placed her feet on the stone floor beside the pool. Elara wobbled, but was able to keep her balance, a good sign that she was getting stronger.

"I'll need your arm to hold on to in order to get my pants off. But I can take my shirt off by myself."

Osric held out his arm. She grabbed hold and tried desperately to slide her pants off. But the task was proving too difficult.

"Let me do it. You hold on."

She turned and placed both hands on his arm. She could feel the muscles beneath his shirt trembling slightly. Elara looked up into his face, but he avoided her eyes. He reached beneath her shirt, grabbed her waistband, and with one yank, pulled her pants down. One foot at a time, she stepped out of them. Using her good foot, she flung them to the side.

"You might as well do the top too. Getting undressed is harder than I thought it would be."

Osric took a deep breath. Although he had seen Elara's body during his tending to her, he had never seen her completely naked. He tried his best to keep his hands from shaking, but he couldn't completely stop them. Keeping his eyes directed to the floor, he grabbed the hem of her shirt and lifted. But when he tried to slip her arm through her sleeve, she lost her balance.

"How about you hold onto my waist, and I'll slip my arms through the sleeves. Then I can hold onto you again with both hands, and you can slip the shirt over my head?"

Osric said not a word, only nodded. He placed his hands around her waist, his fingers almost touching.

"Okay, my arms are through," Elara said, placing both hands on Osric's arms again. "You can take my shirt off."

As he lifted, his left hand brushed against her left breast. Both Elara's and Osric's cheeks turned bright red.

Elara wondered if his touch was intentional. She remained standing, waiting for him to place her in the water. But he remained motionless, his gaze locked upon her. "Osric, I'm ready to go into the water."

"What? Ah, yes…yes. Sorry." He scooped her into his arms, knelt, and lowered her into the spring.

"You have a beautiful body," Osric softly said, trying to dissolve the awkwardness of the situation.

"Thank you. A few scars, but for the most part it's decent."

He reached into his pant pocket and pulled out a small rag and a square bar of soap, another gift from Ophira.

"Wash up. Be sure to wash your hair; it stinks. I'll be back to get you out." He looked down at the two dragonets seated along the pool's rim, staring at their reflections. "You two remain here with Elara. But be careful not to fall in."

"See you in a bit. Scream if you need me." He laid his weapon down beside her. "In case you feel the need to shoot something. But be careful not to shoot me by mistake."

"Before you go, Osric, can I ask you something?"

"Sure."

"You said my brother sent for you to help us train the newborn dragons. How did Vaelor know you?"

"I've known your family for many years. In fact, I fought beside your father long before your birth."

"How is that possible? My father's been gone for ten seasons."

Osric's eyes widened, the truth filling them with remembrance. "I've lived more seasons than you can count. You may know me better as Osric Skaldvar."

That name was familiar to Elara, a ghost from men's stories. The Keeper who vanished after the Burning of Dravonar. A traitor, some said. A myth, others.

"I met your father," Osric softly said, "on the night the northern pass fell. He was young, ambitious, braver than most men twice his years. I remember him saying he fought because his wife was carrying twins. He carried a broken spear and a stubborn fire in his eyes that refused to die." Osric's gaze flickered to her, softer now. "Much like yours."

"We were outnumbered. The whole valley was burning. Your father should have fled, should have saved himself." A ghost of a grim smile tugged at Osric's mouth. "But he wouldn't abandon the villages. Not while even one soul still needed saving."

His eyes darkened with memory. "Your father and I held the bridge long enough for the last of the families to escape. Steel, fire, and shadow... it was a night carved in blood." He swallowed hard, a flicker tightening in his chest, not from a wound, but from what he remembered. "He bought them time. Bought *you* time. And when the moment came, he turned toward the enemy so your mother and the rest of them could run."

Elara pressed both hands to her mouth, tears gathering. "He... he died saving everyone?"

Osric nodded once, solemn. "He died a hero, Elara. And I have carried that night with me for many seasons. Your father was a good man. And the world is lesser without him."

"Why was the village attacked? We never had anything of importance or wealth. What did they want?"

Osric's expression shifted, his eyes reflecting something ancient and terrible. "Their leader of the opposing army was hunting a sign."

"A sign? What kind of sign?"

Ophira inhaled sharply. "The comet!"

Elara blinked, confused. "A comet? What comet?"

Osric turned his eyes to Elara. "Your father saw it first," he said. "The Comet of Ash and Dawn, an omen older than kingdoms, older than the dragon covenants themselves. It appears only when the balance of the world is about to change... and when new Keepers are about to be born."

Elara's breath caught. "Born... as in...?"

"As in *you*," Osric confirmed. "The comet foretold the rise of the Twins of Fire and Stone. And when that comet blazed across the sky, two dragon eggs were birthed in the sanctuaries at the exact same moment. Your father witnessed the omen, and Malachar wanted him silenced."

Elara whispered, "Two twins... and two Drake eggs... bound by the same prophecy?"

Osric nodded, jaw tight, eyes haunted. "The Commander knew the comet meant the dragons would return through twin Keepers. His entire empire trembled at that thought. He wanted the prophecy buried, burned before anyone could understand what was coming. And he wanted the eggs for his own evil usage."

He leaned forward slightly. "Your father understood. He saw the comet's tail split in two; an unmistakable sign that not one, but **two** dragon heirs had been conceived. And that meant two eggs. Two Keepers. Two forces destiny had paired to break Malachar's dominion."

Elara's pulse thundered. "So, he killed my father... because he saw a comet?"

"He killed your father," Osric said, voice thickening, "because your father told the truth. He warned the nearby clans that the prophecy had begun. He told them the world would soon see twin children with the power to awaken dragons."

Osric's gaze steadied on her, heavy and sorrowful. "And the Commander, fearing that prophecy more than any army, sent his vanguard to erase everything your father saw and everyone he could have told."

Elara trembled. "Because of us."

"Because of what you *will become*," Osric corrected. "Your father died protecting a future he believed in. The future the comet promised."

He leaned back, breathing slowly. "And now the Commander hunts you for the same reason. Fear. Fear that the prophecy will come to pass."

"Wait! You referred to this man as both the Commander and Malachar. Which is he? These two men lived a century apart."

"The Commander is Malachar. For some reason, he, too, cannot die."

"Was he cursed also?"

"Not to my knowledge. I am the only one the Elders have ever cursed. Something else gives him life, something dark and unnatural."

"I still don't understand," Elara said. "What difference does it make if Vaelor and I are these Twins of Fire and Stone?"

"Prophecy says the twins will restore balance," Osric said. "The Elder Wyrms will awaken, Keepers will return, and dragons will flourish. Evil will be driven from the land."

Elara's heart pounded. "So, the Commander hunts us because the prophecy says we can restore peace?"

"No. He hunts you because the prophecy says that if you awaken, if your dragons hatch under your bond, *he* will fall. His armies. His dominion. Everything."

"But... Vaelor is dead." Elara said. "If the prophecy needs both of us, Fire AND Stone, then what happens now?" Her voice trembled, barely more than a whisper.

Osric's expression changed instantly; anger fading into something deeper, older, and infinitely sorrowful. "I don't know."

"But with Vaelor gone, isn't the prophecy broken?"

"No," Osric said, his voice firm. "When Vaelor died, his half of the bond became dormant, freeing the unborn wyrmling to choose another to bond with. The Commander took his egg in the hope that he could be the new choice. He wants to twist that dormant bond, corrupt it, turn the wyrmling into something that serves *him*."

"Can he use another Drake to bond with the egg?"

"I know of no other unborn wyrmlings, so it's unlikely he can awaken the dragonet inside."

"What about his adult Drake?"

"Again, it is usually a wyrmling that can draw a newborn forth. And the only time I've heard of an adult dragon capable of such an event is when a mother dragon calls to her first born. To my knowledge, Malachar cannot use his adult male Drake to hatch the egg."

"But it could be possible?'

A darkness slid across Osric's face. "I don't know. Nor do I know how to defeat the Commander. Without at least one adult dragon, we stand little chance of rescuing the egg."

A soft rumble traveled through the air accompanied by a light vibration. Ringlets spread across the healing pool, lapping against the sides. Elara's gaze swept the chamber. "This place..." she whispered. "Sometimes it feels alive."

Osric nodded. "It is. It's Terrus. The mountain *is* him. His body became stone, but his fire-heart still burns beneath. The water, the warmth, the light, it's all him. We're inside his keeping."

"I've heard the old stories, how the ancients folded their wings and became mountains. But the tales never explained why. Or how."

"When the last cinder from the War of Ash and Ember dimmed, and my curse began its long echo, the world grew unbearably quiet," Osric said. "The Song of Making, once bright as sunrise, thinned to a single, shivering note. The Ancient Wyrms listened, each hearing the weight of what they had done. And one by one, they folded their wings." Tears filled Osric's eyes.

"Thus, the seven slept. Fire, shadow, ice, tide, stone, and wind all folded into the same long dream. The world cooled. The Song of Making grew quiet; its last note held in the breath between night and morning. And from that stillness, life renewed itself. Small, mortal, and free."

When you spoke of Solarus' fall, you said it was because he cursed YOU."

"He did."

"You knew him?"

An almost silent "Yes" escaped his lips.

"You're Osric the Cursed, aren't you? One of the original Keepers. That's why my brother sent for you. He knew you were the only one left experienced in taking care of wyrmlings, of training them."

"Yes."

Elara's eyes searched his face. "You were cursed to what?"

Osric exhaled slowly. "To witness and remember the demise of the Ancient Seven." His voice dropped, hoarse with the weight of what he had seen, what he had experienced. "And to remember every death I've caused, every wyrm I failed to protect. They don't fade like normal memories. They live in me. Their voices, their screams. Sometimes they whisper in my sleep."

Elara's expression softened, sorrow mingling with something deeper. "Then you carry their fire still," she said gently. "That's not a curse, Osric. That's penance. And proof you still have a soul."

"There's no penance for me." Osric turned, his head hanging low, and stepped away and left the area.

"Osric?" Elara shouted.

Osric paused, but he did not turn around. "Yes?"

"Thank you for saving me."

He walked slowly from the cavern. Elara's words offered no comfort. Only the raw memory of what had been torn from him the day Solarus condemned him. His body moved without him, step after step, until movement itself lost meaning.

Tirra's faint stirring dragged him back. He struck the rock wall with his shoulder and slid down it, the stone cold against his spine. His hands came up to cover his face. For the first time in a century, Osric wept, letting the grief he had entombed tear its way back into the world.

When he was able to bury his grief again, he stood and wiped his eyes with the tail of his shirt. Osric shuffled his feet as he headed back to the hot spring cavern. As he neared it, the smell of lavender and jasmine floated through the air. He breathed deeply, relishing the feminine smell.

"I brought you a change of clothes that Ophira sent with you. I'll wash your other clothes with mine later and hang them out to dry. Ready to get out?"

"Yes."

Osric tried to give her a warm smile, but it cracked under the weight of his sorrow. "Grab my arm and stand, and I'll lift you out."

Elara stood, droplets of water dripping from her body. The smell of the soap once again filled Osric's nostrils with its sweet smell. *Don't think. Don't think. Just pick her up and carry her over to the rock.* He placed his arm beneath her buttock and lifted her against his chest.

"You've got some bad scars," Elara murmured. Her fingers brushed across the mark of a fresh cut. "Is this where I stabbed you? It looks newer than the others."

Osric faltered, almost going down on one knee. He fumbled to keep from dropping Elara onto the floor. A sound between a scream and a moan escaped his throat.

"Did that hurt?" Elara asked, panic in her voice.

"No. I…I." He straightened up and hurried over to the rock, sitting Elara down. "It's been many years since a woman touched my skin."

"I'm sorry."

"Nothing to be sorry for." He wrapped a blanket around her. "Sit here and dry off. Once your skin isn't wet, we'll get you dressed."

"Might I ask how long it's been?"

"How long since what?"

"How long since you've been with a woman."

"Ninety. Maybe a hundred years."

"Why so long? You are still capable of being with a woman despite your age. Don't you like women?"

"Well, that's a stupid question," he grumbled, sharper than he meant to. *Why am I upset? Does the truth sting more than I care to admit?* "Of course I like being with women," he muttered, rubbing the back of his neck. "I've learned from experience that it's easier not to complicate my life. So, I stopped… getting close."

"DON'T CALL ME STUPID!"

"I didn't. I said your question was stupid."

"No, it wasn't. It was a legitimate question, especially after I saw the way you were looking at me."

"I wasn't looking at you."

"Now you're calling me a liar, too?" Her cheeks turned red, anger coursing through her body.

"What the hell is wrong with you?" Osric yelled, his temper now flaring. "You're acting crazy."

"So, you're adding crazy to the mix?" Elara kicked her foot, catching Osric in the stomach.

He staggered back three steps, the shock rolling through him before anger took its place. He advanced toward her, his pulse pounding.

"Elara, stop."

Then he saw it. A faint shimmering beneath her skin, deep, unnatural red. The air between them wavered, thick with heat. Even from several paces away, he could feel the warmth radiating off her, searing and alive. Terrus' words echoed in his ears: *Beware. Inside her burns the fire of the earth. Without Vaelor to cool her flame, she could destroy the world. You must keep her flame cooled, keep her fire subdued.*

It happened so fast, Osric almost didn't believe it. One moment, Elara's eyes blazed with fury; the next, fire flared beneath her skin.

Osric froze. Flames burst across Elara's arms; thin at first. Then racing upward, across her shoulders, and spilling through her hair. The glow painted her face in molten gold, her pupils narrowing into slits of burning amber. Heat rolled off her in waves that shimmered, bending light and shadow alike.

He took a step back without thinking, his instincts screaming danger even as his heart clenched in disbelief.

She's burning from the inside.

"Elara!" The word tore from him as the flames brightened, licking up toward the cavern ceiling. "Stop before it consumes you!"

But she didn't stop. Her jaw was set, her voice raw with anger and pain. "You think I can?" she cried, and the fire answered, roaring higher.

The heat struck him like a living thing. Osric shielded his face, eyes watering, the scent of scorched air and ash filling his lungs.

Without another thought, without even understanding why, he lunged forward, seizing her around the waist. Her skin seared against his hands; pain flashed through his palms, but he didn't let go. With a hoarse shout, he lifted her from the ground and darted toward the spring.

He hurled both of them into the water.

A hiss exploded through the chamber as the flames met the spring. The water flashed white, then surged into rolling clouds of vapor. For a moment, Osric thought he'd killed them both: the heat, the light, the choking steam. Then came silence, broken only by the gentle bubbling of Terrus' breath through the stone.

Elara surfaced first, coughing, her hair plastered to her face, the glow gone from her skin. Osric rose beside her, gasping, his hands stinging where he'd touched her.

Their eyes met; hers still fierce, but human again.

Osric's heart thundered in his chest. *I've fought dragons, but I've never feared one like this.*

And yet beneath the fear, a strange reverence kindled, a sense that what he had seen was not wrath, but power barely contained. Something ancient. Sacred. The thing Terrus warned him about.

Chapter 13

Elara held Osric's burnt hands, her fingers tenderly rubbing ointment on them. She cried inconsolably. "I'm so sorry, Osric. I don't know what happened."

"It's okay. I'll soak them in the healing pool several times a day. That, combined with my body's unnatural healing ability, after two or three days you won't even know they were ever burned."

"I'll know." Tears slipped free as her body shook, each breath breaking into a ragged gasp.

Osric wanted to pull her into his arms, make her world less sorrowful. Instead, he said, "Looks like we both have secrets. Any others I should know about?"

"No. Ah, yes…. One more…. I… sometimes …burst into flames …if I …become… extremely upset."

"When I said it was a stupid question, I wasn't criticizing you, Elara. I was simply making a statement."

"I know." She sucked in a mouthful of air. "I don't … know why…I got…so upset."

"Why wouldn't you be upset?" he said quietly. "We've been trapped in this cave for weeks. You can barely stand, let alone walk. Vaelor is likely dead, and his egg is in the hands of a madman. And on top of it all, you're stranded here with a cantankerous old Keeper like me."

"You are cantankerous," Elara said. A faint hint of a smile touched her lips. Osric pretended not to notice.

"We should get you into some dry clothes. And get me out of these wet ones. But this time, I'm going to need your help. There's no way I can get these wet boots, shirt, and pants off with these burnt hands."

Elara's tears returned, her cries echoing through the caverns.

"Please stop crying, Elara. I'm afraid to say anything because it makes you cry more."

She cried harder.

Osric hesitated, uncertainty tightening in his chest; then, with no better answer to reach for, he drew his arms carefully around her, being careful not to touch anything against his hands. "Grab my weapon," he said, kneeling so she could grip it. He thought of teasing her not to accidentally shoot him but feared it would further upset her.

He looked around for the two dragonets. Tirra poked her head out from behind a rock.

"You two want a ride or are you going to walk back?"

The two advanced cautiously. But when they saw Elara in Osric's arms, they stopped and cowered.

"Okay, I'll go slow so you can keep up."

Pulling Elara close, he began the slow trip back to the cavern. The sound of his soaked boots sloshing as water flowed out echoed through the halls. *It's going to take days to dry the damn things out.* Osric checked back every few steps to make sure the wyrmlings were still following. Elara clung to his neck.

When they reached the cavern, she was still crying, but her sobs had lessened. Seeing their bed, Tirra and Kaura ran to the fur and crawled beneath, hiding from the scary world they had witnessed.

"Don't start crying again, but can you help me with these clothes?"

Elara bit her lips, forcing herself not to cry. She nodded. Osric sat her down on her usual rock and leaned over. She grabbed the hem of his shirt and pulled it over his head, yanking at the sleeves as they stuck to his wet skin. Osric leaned back and lifted his feet up one at a time for her to pull off his boots. She yanked the first boot off and tipped it upside down. Water *slurped* and *splashed* onto the stone, pouring out in a cold gush. She started to cry again.

"We're almost done, Elara. I'm not mad at you."

"But ... you're…afraid of me."

"Not anymore. Get my other boot. It's okay if there's water inside. They needed a good rinsing."

She had to pull harder on the second boot; the leather had shrunk and tightened around his leg. As with the other one, water poured from it.

"Okay, now the pants. Unhook the belt and drop them down. I can step out of them."

Elara squinted to see the buckle through her blurred vision. After several tries, she unhooked the belt buckle. She unzipped his pants and gently pulled them down to his ankles, completely revealing his body. But she was too upset to even appreciate the fact that he stood before her naked, or that she did the same. He scooped her back into his arms and carried her over to their bed and laid her down. He lay beside her, pulling her into his arms.

"Can you cover us with the hide?"

She grabbed the bear skin and pulled it over their bodies, then rested her hand on his chest. He felt the two wyrmlings curl up beneath his armpit, too afraid to sleep beside Elara. Soon, her tears stopped, and her breathing evened out.

Osric could barely breathe as the nerves in his body felt her naked skin against his. Her skin was soft and still smelled of the lavender and jasmine soap. Instinctively, he drew in her smell. It was so tantalizing. He wanted to kiss her, to rub his burnt hands over her body, to make love to her. But he forced the thought deep into the back of his mind. As he had told her, getting involved carried consequences. And he already had a lot to manage without adding that to the mix. But he couldn't stop his mind from dreaming about it.

He woke sometime later to the sound of her sobbing again. She was still cradled in his arms, her face buried against his chest. Each tremor that wracked her body passed into his, her grief shuddering through him like a heartbeat he couldn't silence. "Oh, Elara. Please stop crying. What happened, happened. It's over."

"But what if it happens again. Without Vaelor, I can't stop it."

"We'll talk about it later. And I promise you, I will find a solution. Now dry your eyes and sleep."

"Are the babies beside you?"

"Yes, they're snuggled beneath my arm."

"Do you think they'll be scared to come near me?"

"Hold out some meat when they're hungry, and they'll forget all about what happened."

*****

The sound of Tirra and Kaura chirping from on top of Osric's chest woke the two from their sleep.

"I hear you," Osric yawned, opening his eyes. "You're hungry again."

"I'll feed them. You won't be able to cut the strips."

"And you can't reach the ledge where I put the meat. I'll get the meat down, and you can slice off two pieces for each."

"Okay." She threw back the bear skin and gasped, followed by an embarrassed giggle. The two were still naked. Osric stood, seeing no reason to get dressed now. Elara stood, gently placing her hand on his shoulder for support, and followed him to the ledge.

Unable to use his hands, he placed his arms against the bundle and lowered the meat. Elara grabbed it as it slipped from his arms. Placing it on a rock, she sliced off four thin strips. She rewrapped the meat and slipped it inside the satchel that had held Kaura's egg, securely locking its mechanism.

"The meat should be safe inside here. This way, I can get the meat without your help." She reached out and grabbed Osric's arm again. The two slowly made their way back to the bed.

"Here ya go," Elara said, offering both dragonets meat. Both chirped but would not accept the meat. "They're still afraid of me."

"Lay half of a strip over each of my legs." The moment Elara retracked her hand, the two quickly grabbed the meat and swallowed it. They remained at the edge of the bed watching, waiting for more.

"Try holding out a piece now."

Clutching the meat in both hands, Elara offered the strips. Tirra and Kaura bobbed up and down but would not accept the food.

"Guess it's too soon," Osric said. "They need more time and assurance. Place the remainder of the meat on the floor and rest your hands six inches back. That way they will encounter your scent while eating and see you are not a threat.

Elara did as asked. Both dragonets approached slowly, taking in deep breaths. Small cries emerged from their throats as they looked from the meat to Osric, then back to the meat. Their tongues flicked hungrily.

"Don't look at me. If you want it, you have to take it yourselves."

Tirra's stomach growled. She darted in and snatched a piece. Kaura followed within seconds.

"Way to go, Tirra," Osric said. "You're always the bravest one."

Elara's gaze lingered on the wyrmlings a moment, then shifted to Osric. "How are your hands?"

Osric lifted his arms and rotated his hands. "See, they're already healing just as I said. The blistering has lessened and I can already see new skin growing."

Both sat there in a moment of awkward quiet, neither moving, neither speaking. Elara shifted, drew a breath as if testing the weight of it, then spoke.

"Osric, you told me that an ancient prophesy spoke of the Twins of Fire and Stone, and you believed Vaelor and I are those twins. Am I correct?"

"Yes."

"Can you tell me more about the prophesy?"

"For hundreds of years, the Keepers carried the story in song. As the dragons dwindled and the bond between our kind thinned to almost nothing, it was all we had left, the promise that the Song of Making had not gone silent, that one day the bond would be restored and dragons would rise beside us again."

"Can you sing it to me?"

Osric laughed. "By the Elders, no. I have a horrible voice. But I can recite it:

> *In the age when dragons still dreamed beneath the bones of mountains, the world grew cold.*
>
> *The bond between man and dragon, once a song of flame and sky, had fallen silent.*
>
> *From the ashes of that silence came a comet of fire, cleaving the heavens in two.*
>
> *Where its light touched the earth, twins were born beneath a blood-red moon:*
>
> *One a girl, the heart of flame, the other her brother, the flame contained.*

"And you believe that's why I can bring forth flames, that I am the female component of the Twin Flames?"

"Yes, I do. In my five hundred and forty-two years, I've only heard of one instance of a person who could wield the dragonfire, and that's in that song. You, Elara, can wield dragonfire."

"But I can't control it."

"You said not without Vaelor. The ballad said *one would burn with passion fierce enough to wake the sleeping wyrms. The other would wield calm strong enough to master her fire.* You are the one who burns with passion. But Vaelor might not be the only one who wields calm strong enough to keep it under check. Ophira believed there was another strong enough to temper it."

"Did she say who?" Elara jumped to her feet. A redness glowed beneath her skin. Taking a deep breath, she forced herself to remain calm.

"She didn't mention a name." *But she did think I could harness your flame.*

"It's you, isn't it? You can help me harness my flame?"

"I possess many talents, but containing dragon fire is not one of them."

"Why not? You know everything there is to know about dragons. And you've already woken one dragon. Terrus."

"I don't think it was me who awakened him."

"Why do you say that?"

Osric smiled warmly. "I believe he stirred to protect you. The day you fought Malachar and fell into the river, I was still miles away. But I felt Terrus stir. I think he reached out to protect you and Kaura. That's why Malachar called off the attack. You're half of the prophesy; half of the Twin Flames. And the Elder Wyrms need you if they are to reawaken."

"If that's true, how do I wake the others?"

"I don't know."

Elara lowered her head, shifting her gaze to the cold stone floor. "I'm scared, Osric."

"I know. But the moment you start to feel angry or upset, concentrate on my voice. Can you do that?"

"I think so."

Osric stood. "I don't know about you, but I'm starving." He looked at his hands. "Since I can't cook, how about I teach you how to make us breakfast? That should keep your emotions down."

"But I still can't stand long. And now with your burned hands, you can't make the crutch you wanted to make me." Tears filled her eyes again.

"Tell you what. If you promise no tears today, I promise to show you how to make crushed grain flavored with honey. You'll love it. And you can make it while sitting down."

*****

As Osric predicted, his hands were healed by the third day, although still a little tender. He had spent hours trying to think of a method to keep Elara's body cooled, but to no avail. In desperation, he returned to the cave where he had seen Terrus.

"Terrus, are you here? I must speak to you about the Ballad of Twin Flames."

A face, reddish brown and filled with teeth, shimmered across the golden-lit walls. A hum in the floor traveled upwards, growing in intensity.

"I am here."

Osric again dropped to his knee, paying homage to the great Drake. "Oh, mighty Wyrm of Old, please tell me. Is Elara the Twin of Fire from the *Ballad of Twin Flames*?"

Terrus's golden eyes narrowed, the ridges along his massive jaw tightening. "Why do you ask, child of ash?"

Osric hesitated; his voice caught between awe and disbelief. "Because I witnessed her body burn with dragonfire."

A rumble moved through the cavern like the shifting of mountains. Terrus lowered his head. A warm breeze rippled Osric's hair. "You *witnessed* the flame and lived? Then perhaps the prophecy still breathes."

"What prophecy?"

"That when the fire is reborn within flesh not scaled, the line of the Elder will awaken from stone." Terrus's form blurred, his voice deepening, echoing through the stone like water flowing beneath mountains. "The *Ballad of Twin Flames* was not born from song. It was born from mourning."

149

"Mourning?"

"Yes, mourning. In the beginning, two wyrms, Solarus and Noctis, were forged of opposing fires. One carried dawn within his breath, the other night. They were balance. But even balance can fracture when pride learns its name. Solarus burned too fiercely, longing for perfection in all he made, while Noctis sought stillness to let the world breathe between the beats of creation. When Solarus demanded endless light, Noctis veiled the earth in shadow to cool it. Thus, dawn and night first quarreled. But, despite their differences, they remained dedicated to the other. It was the whisper from the Void, jealous of their accord, that broke their union. It sowed envy between them, teaching Solarus to fear the dark and Noctis to doubt the light. Their discord birthed storms, and when their breaths collided, the heavens bled. So began the War of Ash and Ember, the first wound in the Song of Making, when flame forgot it was born of love. Their war split the heavens. Their ashes hid the stars."

"The Ballad was our lament," Terrus continued, voice fading to a ghostly hush. "A remembrance that fire divided cannot endure. Yet in time, it was said the world would call forth their echo, two born not of dragonkind, but carrying the same spark, to heal what their ancestors destroyed."

The reflection leaned closer. "If Elara's flesh holds the fire, then Solarus's spirit sleeps within her. But remember this: reflections cannot lie, nor can they save. She will need her other half before the old sorrow burns anew."

"But her brother is gone, killed by Malachar. I'm all she has. What can I do to stop her from igniting?"

Terrus's reflection rippled. "His passing is unfortunate. Her twin was immune to her flame. He possessed the gift of ice and could still her fire by will alone. You, however, carry no such gift. Tell me, how did you quench it before?"

Osric hesitated, memory flashing behind his eyes. "We were at the hot spring. She lost control. I…" his throat tightened, "…I threw her into the water. The flames drowned. But we won't always be near water. When we cross the plains to rescue Vaelor's egg from the Commander, there will be nothing but dust and dry earth. If she burns then, I won't have a way to stop her. Is there *nothing* I can do to keep her from destroying herself … and the world?"

Terrus grew quiet, the veins of gold dimming as he searched the vast archives of his ancient memory. "There is no charm in your blood to shield you, no gift I can grant that will silence the dragonfire within her flesh. Only one thing may save her, and you."

Osric straightened. "What thing?"

"A distraction."

He blinked, uncomprehending. "Talking to her only makes it worse. The more I speak, the hotter she burns." His gaze fell to his hands, remembering the pain of charred skin and the scent of his own flesh burning. "Words won't stop her."

"Not words. Your *heart*. I have seen how your fondness for her has deepened into something you dare not name. You must call upon that passion, Osric. Let it meet her fire. Let it become the flame that consumes the fury and leaves only love."

Osric shook his head sharply. "No. I swore long ago never to mix love with duty. It weakens judgment. It complicates everything."

"Then complication is your salvation," Terrus answered, his voice rolling like thunder swallowed by the earth. "Only your love for her can quell the dragonfire. Nothing else will endure it. Nothing else will reach her."

Osric's chest rose and fell, breath trembling between denial and truth. "Nothing else?"

Terrus's image faded, his final word echoing through the cavern.

"No."

*****

Osric moved toward the living cavern as though each step carried weight, his body obeying while his spirit resisted. Terrus' words echoed behind him, but they offered no comfort. Only remembrance. The truth he feared most was not Elara's dragonfire, but what it would cost him to let his love for her surface, unguarded and real.

He had loved once. Only once. And that single act had shattered a life: his wife lost to death, his son to abandonment. Love, for him, had never been gentle. It was a blade that cut clean and deep, leaving nothing untouched.

As he neared the entrance, dread coiled tight in his chest. To care was to risk everything. To love was to invite ruin.

Do I have the strength to risk everything again? Will my love save her? Or condemn us both?

When Osric entered the chamber, he saw Elara pacing around a large rock formation, holding onto it for support. Her eyes were red and swollen.

Tear tracks marked her cheeks. Nearby the two wyrmlings sat, watching with intrigue, hoping it was feeding time.

"I don't want to hurt you again," she blurted out upon seeing him. "I don't want to lose control."

Osric said nothing.

"Teach me. Teach me to control the fire."

Osric froze.

He gave not a twitch. Nor a blink. He was utterly still, like a man hearing the first crack of an avalanche above his head.

"Elara, you don't understand what you're asking."

"I do." Her voice grew firmer, her spine straightening with a courage carved from desperation. "I choose this. I choose to fight what's inside me."

Osric's jaw tightened. He exhaled long and slow. He felt like a man trapped by a storm he could no longer outrun.

"This path will hurt," he said.

"So does burning everything I love," she answered.

Silence.

"So, what do you say. Will you teach me to control the flame?"

He held her gaze for a breath too long, long enough for something unreadable to flicker behind his eyes.

Elara watched him hesitate, his healed hands hovering at his side. For a heartbeat, she thought he might approach her; touch her shoulder, her face, something to anchor her to the moment.

He didn't.

He turned sharply, wrapped a blanket around his body, and walked toward the tunnel mouth. The shadows swallowed him quickly; his silhouette dissolved into the glow of Terrus's veins.

He kept walking.

Not fast. Not slow. But with the heavy, measured steps of a man trying hard not to feel anything. He didn't stop until he reached one of the abandoned side chambers. A small, cold, hollow pocket of stone where the mountain swallowed sound.

Only then did his breath break.

Osric braced both arms against the wall and bowed his head; the rock digging imprints into his flesh. The cavern's chill seeped into his skin. He pulled the blanket around him tighter.

"Elara…" he whispered. He squeezed his eyes shut. "How can I teach you?"

The words echoed in the empty space.

Training her meant standing close. Close enough to feel her breath, her fear, her fire. Close enough that her terror could erupt and burn him. Close enough for a connection that he'd sworn never to feel again to tighten its hold. He had spent centuries building walls: stone-thick, iron-bound, unyielding.

But they were cracking. Faster than he could repair them.

Terrus's voice echoed in his memory, deep and terrible: *"Only your love for her can quell the flame."*

Osric's jaw clenched hard.

"No." He shoved the thought away. "I can't… I can't go through that again."

But Elara's face, tear-streaked and filled with desperate resolve, rose unbidden behind his closed eyelids.

Osric cursed under his breath. *Why did I let myself care?* The question burned hotter than shame. And if he failed her, if he could not help her master the dragonfire, then the cost would be unending. She could burn him past the point of healing, reduce him to a ruined husk, condemned to endure eternity as little more than living flesh and unending pain.

He pushed off the wall, chest tight.

"But if I don't try," he whispered, "she'll burn."

He took two steps sidewise and pounded his fist into the stone wall. "And if I let myself feel, I will too."

Pain erupted in his burned hand, but he welcomed the pain. He needed the reminder of what his decision could mean. With a deep sigh, he headed back to where Elara waited. Waited for him. Waited for his answer.

*****

Elara sat on the bear skin, her knees drawn up, her chin resting atop them. When Osric stepped back into the chamber, she looked up quickly. Hope bloomed in her eyes before she could hide it.

Osric ignored the hope. He kept his expression locked beneath iron.

"We start at dawn," he said.

Her breath caught. "You… you mean it?"

"Yes." A muscle ticked in his jaw. "But understand this. I'm not doing it because you asked."

She blinked. "Then why?"

"Because if I don't," he said quietly, "you will burn yourself alive. Or me. Possibly even the wyrmlings. Their scales haven't hardened enough yet to withstand dragonfire."

He stepped closer. "But listen carefully. Training isn't safety. It isn't comfort. It's pain. Control comes through fire. Through endurance. Through facing the part of yourself that terrifies you most."

She swallowed. "I'm ready."

"Are you?" His voice dropped to a low, dark rumble. "Because this will hurt. Every day. Every moment. And you will hate me before it's over."

She held his gaze, trembling. But something fierce and new shone beneath her façade.

"I'd rather hate you," she whispered, "than fear myself."

"Then we begin," he said.

Chapter 14

Osric chose to conduct the training at the healing pool. If Elara lost control of the dragonfire, he could toss her into the pool and let the water choke the blaze. He desperately hoped it would work. He had begun to see her not as a burden, or a duty, but as a force that pulled him closer with every breath. And the thought of that fire consuming her, taking her away, terrified him.

Osric stood before her, face grim, the horse hide draped across his folded arms. "Stand," he ordered.

Elara rose, tottering on her new crutch.

"I want you to take in a long breath," he said.

She inhaled.

"Now release it slowly."

She did.

"Again."

She repeated the process.

"We're going to take this nice and slow. Remain calm. Remember I'm here with you. If I see you're losing control, I can use the horse hide to grab you and toss you in the pool."

She nodded.

He circled her slowly, predatory, each footstep echoing like a countdown.

"Your fire ignites when you lose control. So today, we test control."

"How?"

He stopped behind her. "By pushing you to the edge without letting you fall. Can you awaken the dragonfire?"

"No. It only comes when I'm threatened, stressed, or angered."

Osric stepped closer. "Okay. I will say words to provoke your anger. It should awaken your fire. Ready?"

"Yes."

"You know, you are a dumb girl," Osric said, circling her. "You're a spoiled aristocrat who's had everything handed to her. Did your servants spoon-feed you? Did they wipe the shit from your ass?"

Elara broke into laughter. Osric gave her a disapproving look.

"You're supposed to be getting mad, not laughing."

"Sorry. I can't help myself. I know you're not serious."

His brows fell. His eyes narrowed to slits. The muscles in his jaw tightened. "You think I'm not serious?" His voice did not rise; it dropped, hard and controlled, each word striking with deliberate weight. "It was your spoiled, sheltered life that got your dragon killed. You had no business being in that battle. None. And then you dragged your damned egg with you, risked your unborn wyrmling because you were too selfish to leave it behind."

Elara's smile evaporated.

Osric pushed on, voice deepening, sharpening. "Tell me, Elara, what idiot ever thought you were Keeper material? You'll never be steady enough, disciplined enough, or mature enough to care for something sacred. A wyrm isn't a toy. It isn't an accessory. It isn't…

A flush of red swept over her skin. "That's enough, Osric. You're going too far."

He stepped in close, voice a low, vicious snarl. "No. What's *enough* is this fantasy you've been living in. If you hadn't played hero, if you hadn't been so desperate to prove yourself, Vaelor would still be alive. He died protecting you. *You.* A reckless, naïve child who had no business being there. YOU killed your brother. You might as well have driven the lance through him yourself. His death belongs to you."

"ENOUGH!" Elara screamed.

The fire ignited in one huge ball. It surged across her skin. The air trembled. Pebbles skittered away from her feet.

"Tell me what you feel," Osric said, stepping back.

Her gaze locked onto him. Hard. Molten. Furious. Hatred flared in her eyes.

"Elara, tell me what you feel?" he shouted, bringing her back to reality.

She swallowed hard. "Heat."

"Where?"

"Everywhere."

"Good." His voice was calm, steady. "Now hold it."

The fire surged, curling up her spine.

She gasped. "Osric, it's rising…"

"That's the point." His breath ghosted her ear. "Control isn't stopping the flame. It's deciding how far you let it go."

The fire swelled.

"Breathe," he murmured.

She tried.

The flame grew.

"Again."

She dragged in another breath. Her shoulders shook.

"Elara," he said sharply, "listen to me. Ignore the fear. Ignore your memories. Concentrate on only ME."

Her jaw clenched. "I'm trying."

"Try harder."

The fire pulsed dangerously.

"Osric…"

"Fight it," he commanded. "Don't let it own you."

Her pulse spiked. The cavern blurred.

A flicker: the Commander's shadow, Vaelor falling, the river swallowing her screams…

Her breath shattered.

"Elara!" Osric barked, seeing the shift in her eyes.

She didn't hear him.

The memory seized control. The fire erupted. Flames spiraled from her hands, radiating in bright, blinding arcs.

"Elara, STOP!"

She screamed, the sound raw and animal, and her fire surged higher.

Osric lunged straight at her. He rushed forward throwing the hide over her and yanked her bodily off the ground. The flames scorched his sleeves as he spun her and threw her into the water.

Their bodies hit the water with a violent splash, the warmth seizing them both at once. The waters drowned Elara's fire in an instant and snuffed the flames devouring Osric's arms.

The sudden plunge tore a gasp from Elara's lungs as she sank beneath the surface. Darkness folded around her, the last of her flame dying with a sharp, hissing whisper. Then strong hands found her arm, hauling her upward. They burst through the surface together. Elara coughed, water streaming down her face. Osric pulled her toward the stone ledge, holding her there, both gasping for breath.

"Elara," he breathed, voice shaking from exertion, "look at me."

Her eyes focused, slowly, on his burned, blistered arms.

She gasped. "Osric, your skin. I've burned you again."

"It will heal," he said through clenched teeth.

"I lost control," she whispered, horror dawning. "I almost… I didn't even…"

"Yes," he said, voice harsh. "But it's only our first try. You can't expect miracles right away."

He grabbed her chin, forcing her to meet his eyes. Not cruelly. Not angrily. But with the fierce, unyielding intensity of a man refusing to let her drown in guilt.

"You hear me?" he said. "This is why we train."

"What if I lose control next time as well?"

"Then we go into the pool again."

Elara trembled, gripping the edge of the stone. "You can't keep grabbing me and throwing me in the water. You won't have any skin left to mend."

"Look, my arms are barely burned. The horse hide shielded my hands. My arms were injured because I left my shirt on. It caught fire and burned my skin."

"NO! We must find another way for you to get me into the water without endangering yourself."

"And how do we do that?"

"I don't know. You're the Dragon Keeper."

******

Elara's eyes swept over the small link iron chain lying at Osric's and her feet. "A chain? Couldn't you have thought of something else?"

"We're kind of limited to what's available," Osric said. "Be thankful I found this down one of the tunnels. It's the only element your fire won't burn through, unless you have some dragon sinew lying around somewhere I don't know about?"

"Sorry, fresh out."

"Then we use the iron. I'll need you to clamp it around your waist. I'll wrap the other end around my shoulders and hands and stand on the other side of the pool. If you lose control, I'll tug on the chain and pull you in. Okay?"

"Guess so." Elara leaned down and lifted the chain, clasping it around her waist.

"Ready?" He saw her eyes fill with tears. "No tears. Remember? You can't light your fire if you're crying."

"No, but my anger that I might injure you again might work."

"Good idea. Keep that thought. Now walk over to the other side."

Elara walked around the pool edge. She noticed the two wyrmlings cowering behind a distant rock.

"I think Tirra and Kaura believe I'll fail again. They're over there hiding."

"They don't think you're going to fail. They're being … ah, …careful. Now remember, this is only your second attempt."

"I'm ready. But do me a favor. Don't say what you said yesterday. I know what you were trying to do, but it was still hurtful. Let me try to bring forth the dragonfire on my own."

"Okay. Focus on the fact that my arms are burned again. Look at the burns and allow your anger to swell inside you."

She closed her eyes and reached for the flame. It came faster this time. No hesitation. No fear. Heat rolled up her arms in a powerful wave.

"I can feel it," she whispered.

"Good. Hold it there."

But the fire was stronger than she expected, its pulse quickening against her control.

"Elara, slow down."

"I'm trying," she said through clenched teeth, as heat surged past her grip.

The fire surged.

She clenched her teeth, forcing it down. A flicker of victory, small, fragile, danced in her chest.

I'm doing it. I'm doing it. I…

A shadow flashed through her mind.

Everything shattered.

Her body arched as the fire burst through her hands in jagged streaks of red light. The chain snapped taut.

"Elara!" Osric shouted.

She couldn't see. Heat blurred everything into searing brightness.

He pulled hard on the chain.

The world snapped.

Then **SPLASH**.

Steam exploded off the water as her fire died on contact.

Osric jumped into the pool, fearful the weight of the chain would impede her rise to the surface. He raised her up and brought her to the edge. "Elara," he panted, "you held it… longer."

She blinked water from her eyes, stunned. "I… did?"

"Yes. You fought it. You pulled it back. Not enough, but more than yesterday."

Her lips parted. "I thought I failed."

"You will fail," he said, brushing wet hair from her cheek with his hand. "Over and over."

She swallowed.

"But today..." His voice lowered, almost gentle. "You failed better. And that is progress."

*****

The air hung heavy and unmoving, the cavern's walls sweating with a thin sheen of moisture. Even the dragonets sensed something different; they huddled at the far end of the chamber, wings tight against their bodies, eyes wide and unblinking.

Elara stood at the center of the stone floor; the chain once again cinched around her waist. Her breath came uneven, shallow pulls that betrayed her before the fire ever could. She had not slept. Neither had Osric.

For two relentless weeks, they had trained; every other day, sometimes every day, until the chamber bore the scars of it: scorched stone, blackened seams, the lingering bite of smoke. Most days, Elara could hold the dragonfire, shape it, cage it within herself.

But not all days.

There were still moments when control slipped, when heat surged faster than will, and Osric had no choice but to drag her to the pool, plunging her beneath the water as the fire tore loose inside her.

"Osric, I have a bad feeling about today. I'm exhausted. The Commander has haunted my dreams for the past three nights. I barely contained the fire last time. Let's cancel today and try tomorrow. We could explore some of the tunnels we talked about."

Osric stepped behind the pool, bare feet planted, shoulders squared. He held the horse hide in his hands in case extra protection was needed.

"Today is the last time we push this hard," Osric said, circling her. "We'll take the next few days off so you can relax. I have a good feeling about today's lesson. The dragonfire is going to break."

She swallowed hard. "Or I'll break ... or you will. I don't want to hurt you."

His eyes flicked toward her. "That, too." He smiled. "You're not going to hurt me. Trust me."

She tried to smile. She did trust him, but each training carried a threat to his life.

161

"Remember, start slow. Think of something pleasant," he said.

She inhaled, her body already shaking.

"Begin."

The fire came instantly, racing through her veins like molten lightning. Her body jerked with the force of it.

"You're starting too fast. Slow your breath."

"I'm trying." Her chest tightened painfully. "It's rising on its own."

"That means you're thinking of something. What is it?" His voice sharpened. "Elara. What did you see?"

Her eyes clouded. "The river."

Osric froze.

"No," he said sharply. "Not today. Don't go there."

The memory slammed into her before she could stop it.

Water. Dark armor. The current forcing her under. The dragons' screams echoing inside her skull.

Her fire erupted.

"Elara!" Osric screamed. "Stay with me!"

She couldn't hear him.

She couldn't *see* him.

All she saw was black metal. All she felt was the cold crush of the river swallowing her whole. All she heard were those horrific screams of agony and terror.

She screamed.

Flames exploded outward from her body.

Osric threw up his arms, the horse hide shielding his body. But the fire traveled across the pool, slamming into him with the fury of a dragon's breath. Heat devoured the air around him.

"Elara, stop!" he choked, blinded by fire.

But she was gone, lost to the memory, drowning in it.

Her fire intensified, funneling into a spiraling column that twisted violently toward him. The ground beneath her cracked.

The dragonets shrieked and hid beneath a boulder.

"ELARA!" Osric roared as the horse hide erupted into flames. Heat slammed into him. Skin on his chest bubbled and split, blistering in a heartbeat. He threw his arms up, instinct over thought, shielding his face as fire crawled along his forearms and hands, flesh swelling and burning beneath the onslaught. "Look at me. LOOK AT ME!"

She didn't. She COULDN'T.

She saw the Commander. His armor. His hands.

Her shriek came without permission. Too loud, too much. Fire surged through her limbs, turning her body into something she could no longer command.

Osric.

He was still there. Burning. Not moving.

Panic flooded in, as the thought hit her with brutal clarity. *She was killing him.* And there was nothing she could do to stop it.

Osric stumbled backward, dropping to his knees as flames clawed across his torso. Every instinct told him to run.

He didn't.

"Elara!" His voice cracked. "Help me!"

She gasped.

The world flickered. The flames paused. For one suspended heartbeat, she saw him clearly. Osric, not the Commander. Osric, burning. Osric, dying.

Then the river memory surged again.

Osric saw it happen. Saw her eyes slip out of the present and into the nightmare. The fire rose again.

"Elara, NO!"

It was too late.

Osric was thrown across the cavern, body slamming into stone. The impact knocked the breath from him. His vision blurred. Unbelievable pain filled his body.

As the fire roared through Elara, it drowned all thought, swallowed everything. Then, somehow, beneath it, a sound broke through. One tiny, terrified squeak.

Elara's vision snapped into focus.

Tirra burst from her hiding place, stumbling over her own feet in haste, wings half-spread, body shaking. She ran straight toward Osric, as if her small, fragile form could stand between him and destruction.

She turned. A creature no larger than a hound, trembling so violently her claws scraped against the stone, held her ground, defiant and unwilling to yield. Her head lowered, a faint, broken hiss escaping her as she tried to be something she was not.

Something inside Elara cracked.

Not slowly. Not gently.

But shattering.

The fire faltered, its fury stuttering as if confused by the sudden fracture in its host. Heat still poured from her, but it wavered, lost its edge, its certainty.

Tirra's body quaked, her courage hanging by a thread, yet she did not move.

Elara stared at her, at the fragile defiance, at the raw, desperate love behind it.

And for the first time since the fire had taken hold, Elara felt something stronger than it.

She felt the need to stop.

Elara collapsed.

Osric lay motionless for several long, agonizing seconds before he rolled onto his back, coughing violently, smoke rising from his skin. Elara crawled toward him on shaking limbs, sobbing. "Osric... Osric, I'm so sorry..."

He didn't answer.

Unable to find an unburnt section of skin to listen for a heartbeat, she gently placed two fingers on his scorched chest, hoping for the rise and fall of his breathing. "Please. Please breathe. Please..."

His eyes fluttered open, unfocused. "Elara..." he rasped, voice barely audible. "You... almost... had me."

A broken sob escaped her.

He lifted a trembling hand to her cheek. "Next time..." His lips twitched, not a complete smile. "Aim lower."

Then his hand fell, and he passed out.

Elara stared at his limp form. At the burn marks, the blistered skin, the man she had tried to kill. Not knowing what to do and in shock, she curled around his unconscious body and sobbed.

Once more, Tirra's voice brought Elara back to reality. She wiped away her tears and stared at the small wyrmling at Osric's hand, softly blowing her breath across his burnt skin, trying to restore him.

Kaura ran from her hiding place and joined her playmate. Following Tirra's example, she blew healing breaths across the stilled Keeper.

"Yes, yes, we must help him." Grabbing the only part of his body not burnt, his legs, she carefully dragged his limp body closer to the healing spring, leaving a trail of dark blood behind. She scooped up handfuls of healing water and poured it over Osric's burnt body. His blisters hissed as the water washed over them, but his skin remained red and raw.

"Osric, please, open your eyes," she whispered, pouring handful after handful of water over his wounds.

He didn't stir.

"I'm so sorry," she choked out. "I didn't mean… I didn't want… I tried to stop."

Osric's lashes fluttered.

"Osric?"

He didn't wake.

She lifted his arm to clean it, and it fell limply from her fingers. She bent over him; forehead resting close to his ear. "Please don't die. Not because of me. Not like this."

She traced trembling fingers through the hair at his temple, brushing soot from his skin.

"If you die, I can't come back from this."

*****

Osric drifted in and out of consciousness, breathing raggedly. The dragonets remained curled beside him, lending him their small warmth and what healing powers they possessed. Elara sat close, knees drawn to her chest. Her hands wouldn't stop shaking.

She stared at them. How were they capable of burning a man alive, of killing innocent creatures, of destroying everything she loved? She clenched them into fists, willing the shaking to stop.

A ragged breath tore through Osric's throat.

Elara jerked upright, eyes wide. "Osric?"

His eyelids fluttered. He grimaced, barely, before exhaling a low, pained groan.

"Elara…" His voice was a ghost of itself.

"I'm here."

He looked around, disoriented, vision blurred. "What… happened?"

Her breath caught. "I nearly killed you."

He tried to push himself up and immediately collapsed back onto the stone with a brutal gasp.

"Don't move!" she cried. "Your injuries…"

"My pride," he rasped, "took the worst of it."

But he couldn't lift his arm. His fingers barely twitched. His body refused to obey him. Pain radiated through him in waves; even breathing hurt.

He tried again, pure stubborn reflex, and a strangled sound escaped him as agony flared across his ribs.

"Osric, stop!" she begged. "Please."

He stilled, panting through clenched teeth.

"You can't move. You can't fight this. You must let yourself heal."

His eyes closed for a moment. "You… stopped the fire?"

Her throat tightened. "Only because Tirra stepped between us. You would have burned alive if she hadn't. I almost lost you."

"I'm not that easy to kill."

"You are when you're with me," she whispered.

She removed a handful of herbs from the medicine bag and crushed them into a small cloth. "This will help with your pain." She reached into the spring and poured healing water over the cloth, then held it above Osric's mouth, allowing moisture droplets to drip down.

He swallowed, allowing the mixture to work its wonders. A dry, hacky rasp emerged. "Thank you."

*****

"No more," Elara whispered to the cavern walls. Her voice was hoarse, raw from sobbing, but firm. "I won't be a monster." Her gaze moved to Osric. "I won't hurt him again."

Her fingers tightened until her nails bit into her palms.

"I will control this fire," she vowed. "If it kills me, then so be it."

The cavern hummed faintly as Terrus listened.

She curled up beside Osric, covering herself with the blanket she had brought from their sleeping chamber. Before long, sleep overtook her.

She stood on an endless plain of black stone. Wind howled across it. The sky churned with fire and shadow.

"Hello?" Elara called.

Her voice echoed through the expanse.

The ground trembled. A shape emerged from the swirling dark, enormous and ancient, a silhouette of a titan carved from stone.

"Terrus... I didn't mean to hurt him. I didn't mean..."

The Wyrm's voice boomed. *"Intent... is not control."*

She flinched. "I'm trying. But the fire..."

"The fire is not the enemy."

The plane around her cracked, glowing red with molten seams. Terrus lowered his massive head until his breath washed over her like a furnace.

"You are its keeper."

Elara trembled. "I don't want to lose myself to it."

The Wyrm's eyes narrowed.

"Then stop fighting what you are."

She shook her head. "I don't understand."

The Wyrm's voice darkened. *"If you fear your fire, it will own you. If you accept it, you will own the world."*

Elara's heartbeat thundered.

"The Commander wants that fire, too. That is why he wants the wyrmlings. He seeks what he cannot hold. The flame is not his to claim."

Elara swallowed, stepping closer despite the tremor in her legs.

"What do I do?" she asked. "Tell me how to stop hurting the people I care about."

Terrus leaned so near she felt the heat of his breath on her skin. *"Control is not won by denial. It is won by understanding the part of you that burns most."*

Elara's eyes stung with tears. "And what part is that?"

The Wyrm whispered through the dream *"…Your heart."*

The world shattered in flames. She woke with a gasp, drenched in sweat, the echo of Terrus's voice still coursing through her mind.

*****

Osric moved like a man balancing on the edge of collapse. He tried to hide it: the stiffness, the pain, the burns that hadn't fully healed. But Elara saw through it instantly.

"Osric, you need to rest and heal. We can resume training in three or four days when you're better. A week is not enough time to allow your injuries to heal."

He sat on the stone floor, on the far side of the spring. A wet blanket rested beneath him as a precautionary measure against her dragonfire. Another wet blanket sat beside him, ready to cover him should her flame cross the pool again. His posture was straight, but his breath shallow.

"No. By my calculations, we should be able to leave this sanctuary in a month. You cannot leave here if you can't control your fire."

"But…."

"No buts. Trust me."

"You said that last time. And look what happened? Your body will bear those burnt scars forever because I lost control."

"I miscalculated. I shouldn't have pushed you as I did. I should have listened when you said you were too tired. But you've had days to rest. I know you're ready this time."

She looked at him with doubtful eyes. "Please don't ask me to try this again."

"It's your call. If you truly don't want to continue, or are too afraid to, we will agree to allow Malachar to keep Vaelor's egg. You and I will remain inside this sanctuary until you grow old and die."

"You know we can't allow Malachar to corrupt the dragonet."

"No, we can't. That's why we must continue despite what has happened. Besides, today, we're trying something new."

She tensed. "New how?"

"Close your eyes," he instructed. "Lift your hands above your head and clench your fists, but don't let your hands touch."

She did.

"Call the fire," he whispered. "But do not let it rise."

Her pulse spiked. "Osric…"

"You can do this."

She inhaled. She made herself remember Osric's burnt body, the raw flesh, how close he came to dying.

"It's not working. I'm too afraid to allow it to come."

"Relax. Go slow. Your dragonfire will come."

Elara tried again, but she couldn't concentrate. She lowered her arms. "It's no use. The fire won't appear."

"Okay, let's try this," Osric murmured. "Look at the burns on my chest. Remember what caused them…your fire, uncontrolled."

Heat surged through her at once, coiling behind her ribs. Her fingers tingled as the flame pressed outward.

Not too fast… steady…

"Tell me what you feel."

"Warmth," she whispered. "Everywhere."

"Good. Hold it there."

Her muscles tightened. The fire strained against her will, hungry to escape.

"I can't hold it long," she whispered.

"You won't need to."

Before she could ask what he meant, Osric spoke a single, low word:

"Release."

Her eyes flew open. "Osric, I can't!"

"You're not releasing the flame. You're releasing fear."

Confusion flickered through her.

"Let it out. Give the fear shape. Let me see it."

The fire pulsed inside her chest.

Her vision blurred.

The Commander's shadow flashed through her mind, followed by the river closing over her. Her breath broke into ragged gasps as old terror rose sharp and fast.

"Elara," Osric said softly, "let it break."

A sob tore loose, then another, shaking her to the core. The fire surged; then gentled, sinking back into her chest like a heated stone.

She drew a trembling breath. "Osric… it's quiet."

His eyes widened. "You suppressed it."

She stared down at her hands, shocked. "I didn't mean to."

"You did," he said, voice softening. "Fear is what fuels the flame. Today you faced that fear."

Elara froze, as if afraid the moment might vanish. Then she laughed, a short, disbelieving sound, and took a step, then another, feet moving before thought could catch them. She turned in a small, imperfect circle, hands lifting, shoulders loosening, her body celebrating what her mind scarcely dared to accept.

Osric watched, a look of joy on his face. No fire licked her skin. No heat surged.

She laughed again and did it once more, a clumsy, joyful turn on the stone, because for the first time the fire stayed where it belonged, and she was still herself.

A fragile smile tugged at her lips.

"I…I actually did it."

Osric smiled back. "Yes, you did."

For the first time, Elara felt something new beneath her skin. Control. And for one brief, precious moment, she believed they both might survive this.

Kaura tilted her head, her eyes bright and blinking with curiosity. She nudged Elara's foot with her snout. A faint pulse, warm and approving, fluttered as she climbed up Elara. Resting on Elara's shoulder, she sniffed her hair, exhaling a small puff of heated air that ruffled her damp curls. A staccato series of chirps burst from her throat, echoing like tiny bells. Osric glanced over from across the pool, startled.

"Kaura's celebrating," he murmured. "She can feel the change. Your flame pushed, but you pushed back."

Tirra joined in. Her trills mingled with Kaura's as she sat beside Osric.

"They're… happy," Elara whispered.

A low tremor rolled through the floor. Not violent, but warm, rhythmic, like the mountain taking a slow, pleased breath. The crystal veins brightened, their inner light pulsing in gentle waves.

The air grew heavier, richer, infused with the faint scent of minerals and old magic. The walls vibrated softly. Dust drifted from high crevices in lazy spirals.

Terrus did not smile. Elder Wyrms NEVER smiled.

But the mountain shifted. The ancient bones of the earth subtly adjusted in a way that felt unmistakably like approval.

Chapter 15

Winter crept over the mountain in slow, merciless waves. Early spring blizzards buried the opening beneath towering drifts, blotting out the sky. Each new fall sealed them in deeper, stretching their confinement far beyond anything Osric had prepared for.

He monitored the swelling drifts at the entrance like a sentry, but it was Elara he watched most closely, watching for any sign her dragonfire would return. So far, it hadn't.

Unaware of the month or whether it was day or night, the two devoted their time to exploring more caverns. When the weight of silence pressed too heavily, they worked the small garden near the warm vents where thin shafts of light filtered from cracks above. The seeds Ophira had given them, dry and wrinkled when planted, now climbed the stone in pale green vines, bearing roots and vegetables that sustained them. It was humbling work, but grounding. Life coaxed from the bones of the mountain.

Osric's clothing was beyond saving, reduced to scorched fragments by Elara's dragonfire. He needed new garments, and quickly. Under ordinary circumstances, he would have cured the mare's hide into proper leather, shaping it to fit. But the fire had taken most of that as well. What little remained was wrapped around the meat he had lowered into the deep freeze to preserve it.

Handfuls of scraps and meat wrappers were stitched together in rough sections to fashion trousers. For a shirt, there was no other choice: a blanket was sacrificed, cut apart, and refashioned to cover what the fire had left bare.

Elara took his measurements with twine and careful hands, circling him with a focus that made the air feel warmer. Each time her fingers brushed his skin, Osric stilled for a heartbeat, though he tried to hide it behind a gruff cough.

Osric cut the leather and cloth with slow, deliberate strokes, aware that she watched his progress. She leaned closer to compare a piece to her pattern, her shoulder brushing his arm. Neither of them mentioned it.

Using needles whittled from horse bone, they worked by firelight, stitching leather and cloth. Stories passed between them, traded softly, then followed by laughter, as each took a turn remembering another time, another place. The wyrmlings skittered through it all, scrambling over their laps, tangling themselves at their feet, demanding attention or food.

More and more often, their hands brushed as they worked, and neither withdrew. Beyond the cavern walls, snow pressed in, closing the world away. Inside, a different warmth took root, not of flame, but of nearness, shared breath, and the unspoken comfort of not being alone.

When completed, Osric slipped on his new outfit, the cloth still holding a trace of Elara's smell. Elara's eyes followed every motion, quiet and assessing, while he pretended not to notice.

"So, how do they fit?" Elara asked.

Osric ran his hand across his pant leg. "Soft. Almost like…" He stepped closer, voice lowering. "Like your skin."

Her eyes widened. "You think my skin is soft?"

He didn't answer; he simply closed the distance. He lowered his lips to hers. He kissed her softly, then deeper as her lips answered his.

His hands slipped beneath her shirt, tracing warm skin and the faint lines of old scars. She drew in a breath and tugged his shirt over his head, pulling him back into another kiss. Everything they had denied themselves: the careful distance, the restraint, the lie that this was nothing, gave way all at once, dissolving beneath the simple truth of his mouth on hers.

Her hands slid over his chest scars with a gentle caress. The faintly rough skin, still bare of hair where the dragonfire had touched him, skimmed across her fingers. "Does this still hurt?"

"No," he whispered.

He claimed her mouth again, deeper this time, capturing her breath, drawing her closer until there was no space left to pretend between them. His hand traced down her spine, slow enough to make her shiver, then slipped beneath the waistband of her pants. When she arched into his touch rather than away from it, a faint sound escaped him. Raw. Involuntary.

Keeping the kiss unbroken, he pushed her pants down her hips. She lifted her feet, walking them down the leg material, until they collapsed to the floor. She stepped free, her body brushing his in a way that almost undid him completely.

He lifted her effortlessly, her body molding to his as she wrapped her legs around him. Their hearts hammered as he carried her toward the bearskin. Osric guided her down. He stood over her for a heartbeat—bare, breathless, completely undone—before lowering himself toward her.

Elara reached for him first, fingers trembling as they traced the line of his jaw, the shape she had memorized in silence. Osric bent to her touch as though he had been starved for it, and perhaps he had.

Their hands roamed, learning each other's bodies with a kind of desperation, memorizing a language they had always known but never spoken aloud.

Every sound she made, every gasp, every broken whisper, cut straight through him. Osric felt something inside him crack open. She wasn't reaching for him; she was reaching *into* him, into the places he had locked away, the places he'd swore no one would ever touch again. And he let her. May the Elders help him; he let her.

Osric gave himself to her again and again until his control frayed and broke, and what spilled out of him wasn't longing. It was truth. Raw, unguarded truth. When he surrendered, it wasn't to the fire building in him, but to the certainty that his soul had always been moving toward hers, even when he was too afraid to see it.

In the quiet that followed, wrapped in warmth and shadow, they were not two broken lives clinging to a moment. They were one soul.

Newly formed.

Painfully honest.

Irrevocably bound.

At last, whole in a world that had never intended to let them be.

After three days of barely leaving the bear skin, the two lovers decided they needed to return to their normal daily routines, with an occasional break in the garden, in the healing pool, or the living area to reconfirm their love.

One afternoon, a narrow passage brought them to a vaulted chamber veined with gold and quartz. Along the walls were symbols: ancient spirals, jagged glyphs, and images of dragons coiled around human figures, wings merging with arms, scales with skin.

Osric reached out, tracing one of the carvings with trembling fingers.

"Those marks, they're like the one on your hand," Elara said.

Osric looked at his hand. The sigil on his palm burned a little brighter, its lines aligning with the carvings on the wall. The air pulsed in response, the light from the glyphs flaring.

The hum deepened to a low, resonant tone.

"It's remembering."

The carvings stirred. Dragons moved, coiling in the stone, their wings rippling in living flame. Scenes played out across the walls: wars of fire and shadow, the forging of the Dragon Laws, and the sealing of the half-blooded wyrms. Then, at the center of it all, a man appeared standing before a colossal dragon of burning stone.

Osric froze. He knew that stance. He had been that man.

A pulse resonated, filling the chamber with gold light until every surface shimmered. A voice sounded. Not Terrus's calm resonance, but a deeper rumble, molten and alive.

"Keeper."

Osric's chest locked, his body forgetting how to breathe. The name broke from him, raw and disbelieving. "Kaerath?" He could not move. Then, quieter, as if afraid to lose it, "Kaerath… is that you?"

"The bond endures," the voice thundered through the mountain. "My body sleeps, but my flame remains. You did not fail me, Osric of Karellin. You preserved what the gods sought to destroy."

Osric staggered back, his mind refusing what his ears had heard. "You're alive?"

"Entombed," the voice replied. "I remained where you saw me fall, buried deep in the earth at Solarus' mountain. Solarus sought to silence me, but mercy is not a sin that dies. The day you defied him, I was bound; not to stone, but to you."

Elara's eyes darted between them, her voice trembling. "Bound to him? Then he can still…"

"I can still answer the Keeper's call," Kaerath said. "And I will. The wyrmlings you guard must not fall into the Commander's hands. And the other twin must be rescued before his heart becomes dark like the dark dragon. The world has forgotten mercy. It is time to remind it."

"The stolen egg is safe for the moment," Osric said. "Malachar has no dragon that can call it into life, no breath to awaken its heartfire."

"You are wrong. The Commander used his dark art and the fire of his dark wyrm to force the wyrmling awake. They twisted the breath of sleep and tore it from its shell before its time. It is born with no guidance except evil."

Osric pressed his burning hand to the wall. "Then tell me what to do."

For a moment, there was only silence. Then Kaerath's voice came again, softer now, almost human.

"Find me. The bond will lead you. When you stand upon the soil that hides my heart, call out Solarus' name. He will listen to your words and break the earth."

"Why will he listen now?"

"Because even the sun can doubt its own light. For five centuries, Solarus has burned alone, his fire untended. He thought his judgment righteous, that by cursing you, he preserved the order of our kind. But time has a way of grinding truth from stone. The world has darkened, Osric. Shadows walk where light once ruled. Even Solarus feels it: the dimming of his flame, the weight of his own decree."

"Solarus listens now because he must. Not to forgive you, but to *understand* what went wrong. You were the only Keeper who ever defied him and lived. And the only one who still guards the wyrm's faith. He sees that now. Your curse did not break you. It made you something rarer than any dragon's scale; a man who still believes."

His voice grew stronger, louder. "Solarus does not bend easily, Osric. But even he cannot ignore what stirs in the blood of the girl. Nor the truth that your hand, the hand he condemned, may be the only one strong enough to lift the world from its ashes. Your heart may be the only thing to tame the dragonfire that lives within her, keep her from destroying the world."

"That is why he will listen. Because the age of wrath is ending... and the age of reckoning has begun."

The light dimmed, fading into the cracks of the stone until only the echo of silence remained:

The sigil beneath Osric's skin dimmed.

*****

Elara ran into their cavern. She began packing the saddlebags, stuffing them with their supplies, pushing the forgotten medicines into empty pockets.

"Run and get several chunks of meat. We'll wrap it well and take it with us. We don't have time to smoke it. We have to get what tubes and roots are ready for eating."

"What are you doing?" Osric asked.

"What do you think? Packing. You heard what the voice said. The Commander has forced Kaura's twin's egg to hatch."

"Elara, it's not spring yet. It's too early to leave the mountain."

"We can do this!" She scooped up their few dishes and pushed them into the bags.

"No, we can't. Snow still covers the entrance. Drifts taller than us block the hillside. We must wait a few more weeks until the snow retreats and the grass begins to emerge."

"We can't wait."

"We must. And even if the passage down the mountain was passable, how are we going to hide from the Commander? Both eggs are hatched. We can't hide their signature. He'll detect their vibrations the moment we set foot off the mountain. Ophira's spells that once protected us are gone."

"We still have The Veil of Noctis."

"It's not strong enough alone." He grabbed Elara's arm and spun her around. "I need Kaerath. We can't defeat Malachar without a dragon."

"We'll think of something."

"There is nothing to think of. You and I can't defeat him."

"We'll find others to help us."

"How? We can't show our faces."

"I don't care what you say, I'm leaving."

Elara's skin glowed, turning red as molten rock, the dragonfire waking beneath her flesh. Without thinking, Osric lunged forward, seizing her shoulders, pushing her against the wall.

"Stop, Elara."

Her eyes blazed. Her hands plummeted his arms. Osric grabbed her hands, pinning them against the wall. "I said, STOP."

"LET…ME…GO!"

He brought his lips forward, ready to feel them burn from her dragonfire. Terrus said his love could save her. Osric hoped he was right.

"No, Osric," she shouted, pushing him away and sliding out from under his grasp. "I'll burn you again. Your skin has finally healed. I won't hurt you like last time."

"Then stop the flame. I know you can do it. I've seen you conquer your fear. Use your love for me to return your dragonfire to the place inside you where it lives."

"I can't."

"Then I will burn." He moved towards her, ready to place his lips on hers, wrap his arms around her body, allow the fire to consume him.

Tirra and Kaura ran from their hiding place. Both emitted high-pitched calls.

"NO!" Elara shrieked, the sound reverberating across the room, shaking the walls. The fire dimmed. Flickered. Then retreated.

Osric ran forward, grabbing Elara into his arms. "I knew you could do it. You quieted the flame with your will."

"Your training worked."

"No, Sweet Lady. It wasn't the training, although it probably helped. It was our love for each other." He glanced at the two wyrmlings. "And the cries of our wards."

Osric stood there, Elara locked in his arms. Believing she was calm enough to approach the subject, he said, "So you agree. You'll wait three weeks until the snow has regressed enough to allow our passage?"

"I don't like it," Elara answered, her head resting on his chest. "But you showed me that there's no other way. The sun has not risen enough to melt the snows to allow for easy passage. And we have no horse to carry us through the heavier drifts." Elara bent down, lifting each dragonet into her arms. "Thank you for being my conscious and reminding me fire isn't the answer."

Tirra and Kaura purred, rubbing their snouts against Elara's cheeks.

"And you're sure we have to go to Solarus' mountain before storming the Commander's castle?"

"As I've said, I can't do it without Kaerath's strength. He has the power to defeat the dark Drake. Once he's gone, we can defeat the Commander."

"How long will the journey to Mount Pyraeth take?"

"Five to six weeks, if we can make it at all."

"That's a long time for the newly hatch wyrmling to wait for a rescue."

"I know, but I see no other way."

Do you have any idea how we can hide our presence? There's not a lot of concealment between here and Mount Pyraeth."

"No, I haven't a clue. But Terrus will. After all, he hid himself from humans for centuries."

*****

Terrus's reflection stirred in the gold-veined wall. His vast outline shimmered through the rock like molten memory, and when he spoke, the air bowed to his voice. Osric bent his knee.

"I am glad to see you are still alive, Keeper. I felt the dragonfire erupt once more in her veins and feared the worst. What reawakened the dragonfire after so many weeks?"

Osric diverted his eyes to the stone floor. "We had a…a fight."

A sound like laughter resonated through the stone. "Ah, females of your species do have a temper. Why did the flames diminish?

"I reminded her that she loved me, and if she continued, I would burn." He paused, then added. "And, the two wyrmlings sounded their cries."

"Ah… the presence of innocence. Even without them, she would have stopped before you burned again. Her fire is gentled now, bound by the love between you. It will hold… until the hour comes when she must wake it again."

"Wake? Why would she need to awaken the dragonfire?"

"The Commander has many talents. He is almost invincible. To defeat him, you will need all your arsenal."

"But Elara's fire? You said she could destroy the world."

"You will know when her fire is needed. But I believe you came here for another reason besides talking about your passions. You have decided to confront Solarus and need a way to cross the great field to his home."

"The Commander burned the forest we hid beneath on the way here. And the sorceress's spells dissipated long ago. The Veil of Noctis no longer holds enough power to shield the four of us. And we have no way to recharge it. I need a new way to hide us from Malachar's and his Drake's eyes. Can you offer us a way?"

"You cannot cross the plains unguarded, Keeper," Terrus said. "The Commander's gaze stretches farther than horizon or storm. His Drake smells fear and fire alike. He will know the newborns exist the moment you step away from my protection."

Osric bowed his head. "I feared as such. Tell me what to do, Ancient One. We have no spells, no cloak of the Elders left to us."

"There are still older cloaks. One wrought of shadow, one of stone. Both remember their purpose if you are strong enough to awaken them."

Light flickered along the walls, tracing two sigils in living gold: one swirling like breath drawn inward, the other angular, sharp as mountain peaks.

"The first," Terrus continued, "is the Veil of Noctis. In the War of Ash and Ember, The Elder Wyrm Noctis hid the wounded beneath her wings; not by erasing them, but by teaching them to *breathe with the world*. You must learn that rhythm. When you walk the plains, your hearts, and your dragons' hearts, must beat in time with the land. Breathe as the wind breathes, still yourselves until the world forgets you are foreign to it."

"You mean to vanish?"

"No, to *belong*. The unseen are not those who fade, but those who fit."

Osric's gaze drifted to his palm, the Keeper's mark faintly pulsing with inner fire. "And the second cloak?"

The light shifted, deepening to red-gold. The mountain seemed to exhale.

"Kaerath's Shadow," said Terrus. "When the sun-wyrm bound him in stone, the echo of your bond sank into the earth. He sleeps still, but he knows your name. Press your marked hand to the ground and speak the vow of your keeping: *'Flame for life, stone for silence.'* The land will answer, and the shadow of Kaerath will fall over you. Under it, scent, sound, and presence will be swallowed by the mountain's will."

Osric's eyes widened. "You mean the earth will hide us?"

"The earth hides what it loves," Terrus murmured. "And though Kaerath sleeps, his heart remembers you."

"And if we fail to hold the rhythm? If our hearts falter?"

Terrus's reflection dimmed to ember light. "Then the world will see you for what you are, fire against shadow, and the Commander will not hesitate. The Veil is not a trick, Keeper. It is a covenant renewed."

"I understand."

"Leave when the moon turns red and rises high, Keeper of Mercy. That is when it will be possible to cross the plains to Mount Pyraeth. But beware of the watchers beneath the earth that protect Solarus."

"Like the one that we encountered when we came here?"

"They are called *the Deepborn*, but the word is far too small for what waits in the dark before Solarus' mountain. No one knows what they looked like when they were first forged in the dawn age. Only that Solarus mixed living flame with molten stone, and from that union birthed guardians with no need for wings, air, or mercy."

"They have no eyes. They *feel* instead: every vibration, every footfall, every breath that touches the rock. The earth is their skin, their senses, their domain. A whispered word, a heartbeat, even the scrape of cloth against a cavern wall echoes through their bodies like thunder."

"They rise from the floor in towering spires that twist into monstrous forms: limbs too long, joints bending in impossible angles, faces shaped only by the suggestion of a skull. Their mouths reveal a furnace heat that can melt metal in seconds. Their voices are nothing more than grinding stone and the hiss of escaping steam."

"And worst of all is their *intelligence*."

"They do not charge blindly. They stalk. They listen. They flank. They retreat to lure prey into places where the land narrows, where sound cannot escape, where fear grows thick enough to choke on. They are patient. They have waited for half a millennium."

"Once awake, they do not rest. Once alerted, they do not stop. If Elara, you, or the dragonets are discovered, the watchers will not simply attack; they will *consume*, folding stone around you, crushing light, hope, and bone alike. Only Solarus himself can call them off. And even he might struggle against the fury of the creatures he birthed to guard his sacred peak."

"Is there no way around them?" Osric asked.

"No. But you will be safe until you are two days from the mountain. Once you cross the Barrier of Stone, know they are listening."

"What is the Barrier of Stone?"

"The Barrier of Stone is no mere wall, Keeper. It is the skin of the world itself, raised at Solarus' command in the Dawn Age. Cross the Barrier with a corrupted heart, and the Deepborn will devour you before you take a second breath. But enter with truth in your soul, and they will part like shadows before dawn, for the pure of heart have nothing to fear beneath the earth."

"But know this, Keeper; though you and the girl are pure of heart, no mortal walks without a shadow in the soul. The Deepborn can scent such darkness as easily as breath. To cross the Barrier unseen, you must mask what lies within you." He lowered his stone-hewn muzzle. "In the cavern of waters, behind the small waterfall, is a great vein of golden amber. It is from my body. Take two small fragments for the wyrmlings to swallow when you reach the Barrier. You and Elara must do the same. Divide a larger piece of amber into two. Carry the twin shards close against your hearts. The amber within your guts will blind the Deepborn to your breath and heartbeat; the shards will disperse the soul's scent. It is not a perfect shield… but it should be enough for the protectors to grant you passage."

"Return with your companion and the two wyrmlings. I will teach you the Veil of Noctis." Terrus withdrew.

For the next three weeks, the small band visited Terrus' cavern for four hours each day. Elara and Osric stood barefoot on the stone, Tirra and Kaura standing beside them, each feeling and learning the slow pulse of the earth.

"To wear the Veil of Noctis," the Elder rumbled, "you must first learn to forget the sound of your own breath."

Elara frowned. "Forget it?"

"Yes. If you breathe *against* the world, the world will hear you. To vanish, you must breathe *with* it."

"But how do we teach the wyrmlings to change their breathing?" Osric asked.

"I will teach you and they, in turn, will learn by watching you. When you were a Keeper over younglings, how did you teach them?"

"By repetition and example."

"It is the same principle here. Now, close your eyes. Do not think of air as something taken or given. Think of it as something shared. The earth exhales through you. Let it find your rhythm."

Osric obeyed, lowering to one knee. The stone beneath his palms pulsed faintly. He matched his breathing to it, the way he had once matched his sword-hand to Kaerath's wingbeat.

Inhale…

Pause…

Exhale.

The hum beneath him steadied.

Elara tried to follow, but her breaths came too quickly, rising and falling like the flicker of a flame. The younger dragonet beside her mirrored her restlessness, tail twitching, small puffs of smoke leaking from its nostrils.

Terrus's eyes glowed faintly from the wall. "Not fire, child," he murmured. "Stone. Do not command your breath. Listen to it. Feel how the world moves beneath it."

Elara stilled. She pressed her hands to the ground, palms flat, and waited. The tremor came, soft and low, like a sleeping heartbeat. She followed it, letting her breath fall into its rhythm.

The dragonets tried repeatedly. Their efforts were clumsy, their chests rising and falling out of sync. One let out a frustrated huff, scattering pebbles across the floor. The other tucked its head beneath a wing and whimpered.

Terrus's deep laugh vibrated through the stone. "Do not scold them," he said, as Osric's hand reached toward the nearest hatchling. "Even mountains stumble before they stand. The small ones will learn when the world is patient enough to wait for them."

Terrus's voice softened. "Now, listen to the silence between heartbeats. That is where the Veil lives. When you walk the plains, carry that silence with you. Do not fight to hide. Simply *belong*. The wind will forget your scent. The light will pass you by. The earth will close over your steps like water."

Osric opened his eyes. The chamber had changed. The air felt thicker, softer. Alive. Elara's outline shimmered faintly, her shape blurring at the edges as though she were being drawn into the mountain's rhythm. Even the dragonets, though still visible, had grown quieter, their restless movements subdued by the pulse of the world.

Terrus looked upon them, the light of his gaze spreading through the gold-veined rock.

"Remember, you are not walking upon the earth as a separate creature. You are a part of it."

Osric bowed his head. "We'll remember, Elder Wyrm."

"You will not need to," Terrus murmured, his voice sinking back into the stone. "When the world breathes through you, only stillness remains."

Chapter 16

Each evening, Osric walked to the mouth of the cavern and stood at its edge, neither fully within nor willing to step beyond. The darkness beyond the stone felt patient. Waiting. Above it, the moon continued its slow, inevitable swelling—night by night growing fuller, heavier, more insistent.

He felt the change long before it was visible. Immortality had taught him that much. Time did not pass through him as it did through others. It *pressed*. It accumulated. With every swelling phase of the moon, memories rose with it, unbidden: other plains, other skies, other nights when he had stood watching, knowing he would still be there long after the light faded.

When the full moon finally rose, it was red; the deep, ancient hue of dragon's blood spilled and never forgotten. Its light washed across the plains and crept toward the cavern, staining stone and shadow alike. Osric's chest tightened. He had lived beneath that moon before. He would live beneath it again.

That was the curse of eternity. Not endless life, but endless return. Cycles repeating while he endured unchanged, bound to witness, bound to remember, bound to survive what others were mercifully spared.

He did not turn away. Immortals rarely do.

He returned to the living cavern where Elara waited, passing her time by playing with the wyrmlings.

"It's time. We leave at first light."

*****

Osric wrapped his sword in a piece of cloth and slid it into his saddle bag. "Remember, nothing shiny. It will reflect off the sun or moon and give away our position. Also, no raised voices or flames of any kind. We can't make a fire. That's the reason for all the dried meat. No running, or allowing our blood to touch the earth. Blood is the loudest sound the earth knows. We sleep at the same time. And the dragons may only ride on our shoulders or beneath our clothing. They must not stretch their wings or cry out. Any questions?"

"No, I think I remember everything." Elara slipped Kaura beneath her shirt. "Tirra, you can ride inside here for a while." The dragonet scampered inside, curling next to Kaura.

Both travelers slipped a saddlebag around their necks and over their shoulders. Across his other shoulder, Osric placed their bag of dried meat and roots. The bear skin with critical supplies, he strapped to his back. Elara slipped the skin of fresh water over hers, along with the medical supplies.

The small group walked to the entrance. Osric paused and turned his vision back towards the caves. "Thank you Elder Terrus. May you return to your slumber until it is time for you to awaken and return to this world."

The two emerged from the throat of Dragon Mountain. The air outside was thin and crisp, carrying the scent of burned forests and old sorrows, along with the fragrance of new grass. Clear streams of newly melted snow raced in tiny rivers down the mountainside. The plains stretched before them in all directions. In the distance, the first light of morning kissed the slopes of Mount Pyraeth.

There, Solarus slept. And deep beneath his mountain, bound in stone and silence, Kaerath waited.

Elara studied the mountain's edge, her gaze drawn to the distant peaks. "That's where we're going?" she asked quietly.

Osric nodded, tightening the strap on his pack. "Terrus said Kaerath lies in the roots of Solarus' range. If we can reach it, he'll help us recover the stolen egg."

"You're certain?"

"No, but I believe Terrus." Osric shielded his eyes with his left hand, checking the sky for danger. "Terrus said the Commander still circles the plains on his Drake. We must call forth the Veil, or we won't make it even a mile across."

He knelt, pressing his palm to the earth. The sigil in his hand flared gold, its glow sinking into the soil. The mountain's hum rose in answer, a sound too deep to hear, yet felt in his bones.

"Elara," he said softly, "breathe with me. Slow. Match the rhythm."

She knelt beside him, closing her eyes. Together they breathed, hearts falling into unison. The dragons buried their heads, their wings folded tight. A pulse rippled outward, the echo of Terrus's lesson, and the air stilled.

The world shifted. Their outlines wavered, dissolving into the shimmer of heat and shadow. The grass bent beneath unseen feet, then righted again, untrampled.

Elara opened her eyes in awe. "Osric, I can only see a faint outline of you."

He looked down at his own hand and saw only the faint shimmer of displaced air. "The Veil holds," he whispered. He rose, turning his gaze to the horizon. "Now we cross. And pray the world keeps forgetting us long enough to reach the other side."

By the third day across the plains, the silence had become its own kind of sound. Every breath was measured. Every step deliberate. The world breathed with them: stone cooling beneath their steps, dust curling away without a trace.

But silence was a fragile companion.

They were nearing the low ravine that marked the edge of the next valley when Osric froze. Across the distant rise, he saw them. Black figures cresting the ridge, glinting faintly with steel. Soldiers. A scouting band from the Commander's ranks, no more than twenty men, combing the plain.

Elara caught the change in his breath before she saw them. "Osric?"

"Down," he hissed. They sank into the tall, dry grass. The dragonets burrowed deeper into the clothing, pressing flat against human flesh, tails twitching.

The patrol descended slowly, scanning the field. The rhythm of their boots thudded through the soil, a discordant pulse, heavy and alien.

Osric's hand went to the hilt of his sword.

Elara's whisper was sharp. "No. You'll break the rhythm."

But the instinct was already there, old as war. His fingers curled around the grip, knuckles white. In that instant, his heart lurched out of time. The world's hum faltered.

The Veil shivered.

Heat rushed into the air, stirring the grass. A shimmer rippled outward: brief, bright, like a mirage catching light. One of the soldiers stopped and turned, squinting toward them.

Elara felt the break. Panic threatened to rise, but she crushed it, forcing her breath steady. She reached across the grass, finding Osric's hand.

"Look at me," she whispered fiercely. "Not them."

His eyes flicked to hers. Sweat traced a line down his temple; his breath came too fast.

"Breathe," she said again. "Match me. In… out. In… out."

The dragonets whimpered softly, their small chests fluttering. Elara shifted, laying her other hand on Tirra and Kaura. "You, too," she murmured. "All of us."

Osric tried. His pulse hammered, his throat tightened. The air resisted him. But Elara's voice, low, even, unyielding, pulled him back.

"In," she said, her breath falling into the mountain's old rhythm. "Out. Feel it? The hum beneath your hands? That's the Veil. That's the world."

Osric closed his eyes. Beneath his palms, the ground trembled faintly. His heart followed it. The tension in his shoulders eased. His fingers relaxed. His grip around the hilt released, allowing the sword to sink quietly into the saddlebag.

The Veil steadied. The shimmer faded.

The soldier on the ridge frowned, scanning the horizon one last time, then turned away. The patrol moved on, their footfalls fading in the distance.

For a long while, neither Osric nor Elara spoke. The wind returned, brushing the grass in soft waves.

At last, she exhaled. "You almost broke it."

Osric nodded, shame flickering in his eyes. "I know. Old habits die slower than men."

She squeezed his hand once before letting go. "Then I'll breathe for you when you can't."

He looked at her, gratitude unspoken but fierce. "And when you can't?"

Her lips curved faintly. "Then you remind me of who I am."

They rose together, the dragons crawling out from their cloth shelter. Tiny claws snagged the weave as they clambered up, settling soundlessly onto Osric's and Elara's shoulders. The two humans set off again across the open plain, each step steady and measured.

As they walked, the world dimmed, color draining into silver and shadow. The Veil continued with them, delicate and alive.

Beneath the full moon, Osric unrolled their bedding onto the cool grass. Elara portioned a small meal of dried meat and grain. They ate in silence, the faint rustle of fabric and the sigh of wind the only sounds. Both fed the dragonets tiny pieces of raw meat in between bites. The newborns waited patiently, their tails intentionally stilled.

While Elara gathered the scraps, Osric dug a small hole with his hands and buried them, packing the earth down tight.

Settling for the evening, Elara lay down on her side, the curve of her back outlined by moonlight. The dragonets curled beside her, their small bodies soon twitching in dreams. Osric sat a little apart, watching the horizon where the black line of Solarus' range cut through the starlit sky.

His eyes drifted to the sight of her body rising and falling as she breathed. He longed to embrace her naked body, to ignite her passion and hear her joy. Every fiber of his being screamed to reach for her, to kiss her lips, to feel warmth that wasn't borrowed from memory. But the Veil breathed around them, fragile as spun glass, and every motion carried consequences.

When he spoke, his voice was barely sound. "Elara?"

She turned slightly, her eyes glinting in the dim light. "You can't sleep either?"

He shook his head. "No."

Silence pressed between them again, thick and alive. He wanted to tell her everything that filled his heart: how her courage humbled him, that her fire scared him and saved him in equal measure, how much he loved hearing her moans when he pleased her. But even words could fracture the stillness they'd fought to keep.

"I wish I could kiss you," he whispered.

Her lips curved faintly. "Me too. But don't think about that. You'll get excited and change your breathing. Keep your breath slow and rhythmic."

Once assured they were safe and he could maintain his breathing, he lay beside her; close enough to feel the faint warmth radiating from her body, but not close enough to touch. Their breaths found each other in the dark, two quiet rhythms merging into one. The hum beneath them softened.

Minutes, or hours, passed. He couldn't tell. Time meant nothing here, only the space between one heartbeat and the next.

He felt her hand shift slightly, fingers brushing against his. He didn't dare take it, but he didn't pull away either. Their hands rested side by side, close enough to bridge the distance.

The next morning, they rose. After feeding the dragonets again and eating a small breakfast, they continued their journey across the plains, drawing closer to Mount Pyraeth, wrapped in silence and dust. Twice more, they crossed paths with the Commander's foot troops and passed unseen.

But on the twenty-fourth day, as the sun hung low and heat shimmered across the horizon, the world changed.

They rested beneath a slender aspen that had somehow survived the burn. Its pale bark flaked like silver skin, whispering softly in the wind. The two dragonets nestled in the shade, their bellies full of dried meat and dew.

Then both lifted their heads. A soft whimper escaped them, a sound too small for alarm, yet filled with primal fear. Before Osric could react, they scrambled up his sleeve and disappeared into the opening of his shirt, trembling.

Elara looked up sharply. "What's wrong?"

Osric's expression darkened. "Shh." He raised a hand, eyes narrowing toward the southern sky. "Listen."

At first, there was only the wind. Then it came. A piercing shriek split the air in two.

A great Drake's cry.

The sound tore across the plains, followed by the deep, rhythmic thunder of wings. The air rippled beneath their power, each downstroke rolling through the grass in waves. The sound grew louder, deafening.

The blood fled Elara's face. Her jaw tightened, breath turning shallow as recognition struck. "The Commander."

Osric's tone dropped to a low, controlled whisper. "Calm your fears. Close your eyes and breathe with the earth. He cannot see us unless we break the rhythm."

He reached for her hand. She grasped it tightly, her pulse trembling against his fingers. She stared into his eyes, forcing herself to only see Osric, only his presence.

"Breathe with me."

Together they slowed their breathing, aligning it with the deep vibration beneath their palms, the heartbeat of the land. Their hand pressed into the soil while their other hand clutched each other. Osric whispered the ancient vow, barely moving his lips. *"Flame for life... stone for silence."*

The ground answered with a faint hum.

A vast shadow swept over them, swallowing the sun. Even with his eyes closed, Osric felt it pass, immense and suffocating. The wind struck next, a violent surge that ripped across the ground, flinging grit and sand that lashed at their faces.

They remained still, breathing in unison.

The air seared, choking with scorched metal and sulfur. Then the world slammed into them

The air seared, choking with scorched metal and sulfur. Then the world slammed into them.

Vorthryn claws tore into the earth, carving deep furrows in the hardpan. The hiss of its breath filled the silence that followed, long and low. His tongue flicked, tasting for life.

"Breathe," Osric murmured, the words barely sound at all.

The Commander sat upon the beast's back; a tiny dragonet tucked against his leg. The wyrmling cried out, calling across the plain for its twin. Kaura heard the whine and responded.

"No. Quiet, Kaura," Osric said, forcing his voice to remain calm as the Veil shimmered for a second. Staying in rhythm with the earth, he pulled Elara's shirt tight, burying the young dragonet's voice.

Malachar looked toward the tree, studying its form, searching for something that was hidden from him. As he searched, the world grew darker as a huge cloud in the shape of a dragon crossed the sun.

"I thought I heard a cry."

The Commander lifted his leg to dismount.

A desert sparrow burst from the upper branches, wings thrashing as it fled, its cry thin and frantic. The sound rang out across the hardpan.

The Commander paused, listening. He dismissed it at once. The bird was nothing. A creature ruled by instinct, screaming at shadows it could not understand.

Malachar settled back in his saddle, pulling on the Drake's reins. The ground shook as the dark wyrm leapt skyward, the thunder of its wings retreating slowly into the distance.

For a long time, Osric and Elara stayed as they were, hands buried in the dirt, hearts pounding in rhythm with the world's slow, steady hum. Only when the plains fell silent once more did Osric open his eyes.

Elara exhaled shakily. "Do you think he saw us?"

"No. But Kaura nearly gave him something to find." He looked toward the empty horizon. "We should move before he circles back. The earth has hidden us once. It may not do so twice."

The air still carried the scent of scorched metal, the aftertaste of fear clinging to every breath. Osric led, his gaze fixed ahead. The Veil held, but barely. It felt thinner, stretched.

Behind him, Elara stumbled, hard enough that the sound made Osric whip around. Her hand braced against a rock streaked with soot, her breaths quick and uneven.

"Elara?" His voice stayed calm, but his stance shifted, ready to catch her if she fell.

She shook her head, struggling for air. "I'm okay."

No, you're not.

"Elara," he said quietly, "your flame is erupting; it's breaching the Veil."

Osric reached for her hand. Her skin seared his palm. A pulse of light flickered beneath her skin, erratic and dangerous.

"Steady," he said, voice low and controlled. "Breathe with me."

"I…can't…" She pressed her hand to her ribs. "The air's too heavy. It feels like I'm drowning."

The grasses around them bowed in sharp, uneven gusts. The ground vibrated beneath their boots. Far overhead, something stirred the darkness. Not a sound, but a pressure.

Elara's pulse jumped. "He's coming. Osric, I can feel him."

"No, he's not," he said sharply." But if you lose control, if your dragonfire ignites, he *will* find us."

Her heartbeat jolted outward in a pulse of heat. The Veil flickered.

"Elara, look at me," Osric demanded. "Right here. Stay with me."

She tried.

But the world was tilting. Darkness flowed in from all sides. The Commander had seen them, taken Kaura and Tirra. She and Osric lay dead, their blood seeping into the earth.

Her breath seized. Her fire surged.

A thin thread of flame rolled across her shoulder.

Osric's gut turned to ice.

"Elara, stop."

"I'm trying."

"Elara!"

Flame leapt from her arms, spiraling upward. The Veil split open, streaks of light slashing through the air.

A single moment. A single mistake. In seconds, the Commander's Drake would see them.

Osric spun to the dragonets.

"Tirra. Kaura. Sing. **NOW.**"

Tirra released a trembling note, soft but piercing. Kaura joined her, their voices weaving together in a harmony older than life. A song taught to calm terrified wyrmlings in their shells.

A song dragons never forgot.

The melody shimmered through the air.

Elara gasped. The fire in her chest faltered. She turned toward the two little dragons, both pressed against Osric's neck, singing like their lives depended on it. And it did.

Her vision steadied. Her breath found the rhythm of their song.

Osric didn't move. He let the dragonets anchor her, their tiny voices wrapping around her panic. The glow beneath her skin dimmed. Her breath slowed. The heat receded. Her knees buckled. Osric caught her gently, lowering her into the grass. Above them, a vast shadow swept across the clearing. A scream tore through the night.

Hunting

Hungry.

The Drake.

Osric held her still, pulling the dragonets close with one arm. All four of them tucked together as the beast circled overhead. Another scream. Another pass. And then, the Drake turned. Its shadow thinned. It vanished into the clouds.

Elara sagged against Osric, trembling violently. Tirra and Kaura pressed against her ribs, exhausted, still humming faintly.

"Why didn't he see us?" she whispered. "I felt the Veil break. I know it did."

Osric brushed her hair back from her damp forehead. "You didn't break it."

She stared up at him, confused and shaken.

"You strengthened it," he said softly. "Fear fractures the Veil. But connection, belonging, pulls it back together." He nodded toward the dragonets. "Their song tied you to the world again. The Veil heard them and responded."

Elara looked down at the two little wyrmlings. "They saved me," she whispered.

"No," Osric said, tightening his grip around her shoulders as the last tremor left her body. "They reminded you who you are."

Chapter 17

The four travelers woke as the sun slipped over Solarus' range, its new light spilling across the plains. Shadows stretched long and warm, folding the world into life. Osric and Elara packed their meager belongings, ate a few dried roots, fed the dragonets, and refilled their flasks from the dew pooled in stone hollows.

It had been five days since they had seen any sign of the Commander's soldiers or his Drake. That, along with Elara's inner fire quiet once more, the world was bright. They walked without speaking. The air had that rare, sacred calm that comes only after danger has passed but before fate remembers your name.

Two days later, a knoll materialized in the distance. Upon climbing it, they saw a small ridge of rocks cutting its path across their way. Osric stopped, placing his arm to stop Elara from advancing further.

"Terrus told me about this: the Wall of Stone. Beyond that barrier lie the protectors, ready to devour anyone who dares step foot toward the mountain." He reached inside his saddlebag and removed the larger chunk of amber. Sitting it on a nearby rock, he hit it with a large stone, breaking off several small pieces. He handed two to Elara. "You and Kaura both need to swallow a piece. Tirra and I will do the same. Terrus said it will blind the protectors to our bodies."

Once all four had swallowed the amber, Osric used his knife to chip a small piece from the top of the rock. Inserting his knife, he used another rock to pound on the hilt. The rock split in two.

"Here," he said, handing Elara one of the pieces. "You must keep this in your pocket until we set foot on Solarus' mountain."

"Do you think we can make it?" Elara asked, watching the ground ahead for any sign of movement.

"Terrus said it was possible."

As they stepped closer to the barrier, the air grew heavy with the scent of sulfur and stone. Across the last few miles of their journey, the heat rose from the ground in wavering threads, distorting the horizon until the world seemed uncertain where earth ended, and sky began.

"Walk softly and unhurried," Osric whispered. "Keep your steps short."

With trepidation, Osric stepped across the barrier, Elara followed. Immediately, the wind died. Osric held up his index finger to his mouth, signaling for silence. Holding her hand, they moved across the barren expanse, each step placed with excruciating care. The ground between them and Solarus' peak stretched wide and exposed, a sheet of pale earth, rock, and ash.

No matter how carefully he placed his feet, each step struck the ground like a hammer in Osric's ears, too loud, too certain to be ignored. The silence beneath him felt alive, listening. Would the Deepborn sense the tremor of their passing, or were they already turning toward it? He swallowed, forcing another step, praying the watchers would not notice their presence.

A mile in, a rumble filled the air. Osric turned to his left. Sixty yards away, a patch of earth rose and fell as something moved below. Two minutes later, two more movements appeared further out.

Osric turned to face Elara. He saw that she was frightened but saw no sign of her dragonfire. *Good, she's keeping her fear in check.* He lifted her hand to his lips, kissing it softly and giving her a big smile. Using his free hand, he pushed down on the air, signaling for her to remain still. She nodded.

The two humans stood perfectly still. From within their shirts, the wyrmlings peered out, small heads barely visible, their eyes wide and unblinking as they watched, silent, as if they understood the danger beneath them. When seven minutes passed without sound or any ground upwelling, Osric nodded and started forward once more,

Halfway across, two more ripples rose, this time directly beneath them. The earth heaved upward, lifting them without warning, forcing both to shift their weight to keep their footing. Then it sank, slow and deliberate, lowering them back down.

Elara pulled back on his hand. "Osric…"

He shook his head sharply. *"No,"* he mouthed. *"Don't speak."*

Another vibration surged beside them, traveling west, stronger this time, rolling through the stone like a heartbeat awakening.

The watchers know we're here.

Before either of them could move, cracks of red light spiderwebbed in the distant soil. The mountain groaned, a low grinding moan of stone shifting against stone. A deep hiss followed. Steam forced its way through fractures as heat stirred below.

"Elara, run." Osric's voice was barely a breath, but urgency drove it like a blade.

They bolted.

Behind them, the ground erupted in violent jolts. The once-flat stone heaved upward in jagged pillars, twisting into the beginnings of monstrous forms: limbs carving themselves out of the earth, skull-shaped ridges forming in the rock. No eyes, yet each one *turned* toward the sound of their fleeing boots.

Spire after spire tore free, molten seams glowing down their bodies like veins filled with fire. Long limbs bent at impossible angles reached toward them, fingertips dripping with molten ore.

Elara stumbled as the earth buckled beneath her, but Osric caught her arm and yanked her forward. "Don't stop. Don't ever stop. Keep your feet moving!"

The mountain grew closer, but still too far.

Behind them, one of the watchers plunged a limb into the ground, and a shockwave split the earth open, racing toward them like a living fissure. Elara leapt over it, the heat searing her legs. Osric barely cleared it, landing hard but running harder.

They were being herded. Flanked. Driven toward a narrowing stretch of land, the way the watchers have done to prey for half a millennium.

Elara's voice cracked, breathless and terrified. "They're trying to trap us."

"I know," Osric rasped. "But we reach the mountain, or we die."

Another Deepborn burst from the ground ahead. Osric grabbed Elara's wrist and veered sharply right, barely avoiding the creature's spire-like limb as it slammed into the earth.

Their sides burned from running, a deep, tearing heat that spread with every stride. Each breath scraped raw through their lungs, too shallow, never enough, as if the air itself had turned against them. Their hearts hammered wildly, out of rhythm, threatening to burst free of their chests. Still, they ran, legs trembling, vision narrowing, driven by something far stronger than exhaustion.

Osric glanced ahead. The edge of Solarus' mountain was less than a mile away.

The watchers closed in. Grinding. Hissing. The earth shrank around them.

"Osric!" Elara's voice tore free, sharp and desperate.

The Veil of Noctis buckled. The air around them began to fracture. Threads of darkness snapped apart, dissolving into nothing. Sound rushed in all at once, a violent return, their pounding steps, their ragged breaths, the distant, hunting shrieks of the Deepborn crashing over them. The Veil shattered.

"We're not going to make it! It's still too far away."

"Yes, we are!" he shouted, more defiant than certain.

The ground trembled violently behind them, then roared.

Together, the Deepborns lunged.

Osric shoved Elara behind him, dropping to one knee and slamming both palms against the ground." Flame for life, stone for silence."

A whisper of ancient draconic left his mouth.

"Noctis vael'kaara... Kaerath, lend me your shadow."

The world dimmed.

A black ripple unfurled from beneath Osric's body, thin as smoke, cold as forgotten night. It spread outward in a widening veil that swallowed the light around them, wrapping their bodies in a shroud of living dusk.

Elara gasped softly. "Kaerath's shadow..."

Osric grabbed her hand again, his voice a whisper. "Don't break the shadow. Don't stumble. Move with me exactly. Try to slow your breathing."

A jagged spire erupted from the stone not more than ten yards behind them, twisting into the beginnings of a watcher. Its furnace-mouth opened, releasing a hiss that scraped the soul raw. But when it turned its eyeless face toward them, it hesitated. Confused.

The shadow cloaked them completely, bending their presence, muffling their heartbeats, smothering their warmth. Kaerath's essence wrapped around their bodies like coiled wings.

"Go," Osric urged.

They moved in perfect sync, steps soft, breath controlled, slipping through the expanse like ghosts. The Deepborns rose behind them. One spire, then another, then an entire ring of obsidian horrors forming a hunting circle. The ground trembled with their fury.

A watcher whipped a limb through the stone, sending a shockwave racing toward them. Osric tightened his grip on Elara's hand, pulling her into a sharp leap to avoid the molten fissure splitting the ground at their heels.

Still cloaked. Still unseen.

But the hunters were intelligent. Their limbs pressed into the stone, seeking, testing, sensing the faintest irregularity in the earth's vibrations.

Osric saw the shadow thinning. "Kaerath's too far away to hold the shadow much longer. He's losing it. We need to run as we've never run before.

They sprinted, their figures more suggestion than substance beneath the protective shroud. The Deepborns reacted instantly as they hunted for the disturbance they could sense but not see.

A limb slammed down inches behind Elara, heat blistering the air. Another tore a trench across Osric's path, forcing him to vault over it midstride.

The mountain was so close. The watchers, even nearer.

Osric gathered what strength remained and dragged the last scrap of Kaerath's shadow forward, one final surge of darkness enveloping them as they lunged toward Solarus' boundary.

A watcher's molten hand swept down…and struck only shadow.

Osric and Elara burst past the invisible threshold, collapsing onto the stone inside the mountain's domain as Kaerath's shadow dissolved behind them. The watchers slammed against the unseen barrier, their furnace mouths shrieking in frustration, heat spilling in sheets across the ground.

But they could not cross. Solarus would not permit it.

Elara lay on the jagged ground, clutching Osric as tremors ran through her. He wrapped both arms around her, pulling her close, his chest rising and falling in harsh, uneven breaths, the fragile truth settling in that they were still alive.

They were safe.

For now.

In the silence that followed, the mountain exhaled a deep, smoldering rumble. They didn't know if Solarus would greet them as visitors… or trespassers.

"It feels alive," Elara whispered.

Osric nodded. "It is, like Terrus."

Osric opened his shirt and looked inside. Two terrified eyes looked up at him. "You okay?" Tirra gave a small trill. He turned to Elara. "How's Kaura?"

"Alive, but terrified."

"Aren't we all. Look!" He pointed to the top of the mountain stretching above them. "On the other side of that crest is where Solarus cursed me and broke my connection to Kaerath. It's also the place where Kaerath sleeps."

"Do you think you can wake him?"

"No, I don't have the power to do that. But Solarus does. We'll rest here until we've caught our breaths. Then we make the climb."

For a handful of strained breaths, neither moved. Then, pushing past the weight in their limbs, Osric hauled himself up and pulled Elara with him, and together, on unsteady legs, they began the climb toward the crest.

With each step, the land grew sharper, the sparse grass giving way to glassy rock and rivers of black sand that hissed underfoot. By the time they reached the crest, the air shimmered. Heat rose in curtains, bending light into mirages. The dragonets remained hidden in their shirts, unwilling to make a sound.

Osric crested the peak. And stopped.

The sight below hollowed him. The valley yawned wide and broken, a wound of molten glass and ash ringed by ridges of obsidian. The air shimmered with trapped heat; each breath scraped dry against his throat, tasting of soot and old sorrow.

He hadn't meant to stop breathing, but he did. His lungs refused the air. For five hundred years, he had dreamed of this place only in fragments, but memory was kinder than truth. *This is worse than I remember.*

He stared at the dull-gold veins flickering below, unable to look away, because he could feel the beat in his chest matching it. The fire had known him once. It still did.

His knees weakened, not from exhaustion but from the weight of recognition pressing down, grinding centuries of penance into something sharp and immediate. He stepped forward, the ash crunching beneath his boots. The last time he had walked here, the world had been red. Kaerath's body had been a pillar of flame. And Solarus…Solarus had looked at him not as a Keeper, but as a traitor.

"Elara," he said softly, "this is where he fell."

She turned her gaze to the dark plain. "It's still warm."

"It never cools."

He stepped forward, step by step, until he stood at the center of the hollow. Heat licked at his boots. A hot wind evaporated the tears escaping from his eyes. His palm glowed where the Keeper's mark lay, responding to something deep below.

Osric fell to one knee and pressed his hand to the scorched earth. "Solarus!" he called, his voice echoing across the basin. "I have returned."

Silence.

"I know you can still hear me."

The mountain listened.

"I've come for Kaerath!" he shouted, his voice growing raw. "The dragon you bound for my defiance! The one who carried your light and my sin alike. He still breathes beneath this rock, still bound by a punishment meant for me."

The faint glow in the obsidian ridges brightened, threads of molten light bleeding through cracks that had lain dormant for centuries. The veins of gold beneath the ash quickened their pulse.

Osric knew that rhythm. It was the heartbeat of Solarus.

The sigil of the Keepers flared against his palm. He staggered backward, squeezing his fingers shut. The pain was intimate, familiar. It was a greeting and a warning, both.

The mountain exhaled again, harder this time. Dust spiraled upward. Sparks leapt from the fissures around him.

Osric raised his voice again, louder this time. "You cursed me to wander and remember! You made me watch the world die one age at a time. But I will not let another fall because of your pride!"

Flames ghosted across the cracked ground, rising without smoke, burning without consuming. Then came the sound, deep and resonant, impossible to mistake.

"Osric of Karellin."

It wasn't only Solarus' voice he heard. It was the memory of the curse, the judgment that had bound him to wander the earth, denied rest, denied light.

Osric dropped to one knee, bowing his head. His voice was unafraid. "The one you condemned stands before you."

"Did you think I would forget?" The light surged, blinding in its fury. "I am the will that condemned you. You chose mercy over flame, defied the order of fire itself, and so I unmade your place among us and set you to wander without end."

Osric rose, withdrawing his reverence of a bended knee. He looked up into the burning sky. "And I have wandered. I have seen the cost of your fire, the ruin your justice left behind. I come not for forgiveness, Solarus. I come for him. I come for Kaerath."

"You would unbind what I sealed?" the Elder thundered.

"I would *restore* what you destroyed," Osric said. "Kaerath's flame was never your enemy. It was your balance. He deserves freedom."

For a long moment, the air stood still. Then Solarus's voice softened. "Then prove it, Keeper. Prove your mercy is stronger than fire."

The ground beneath Osric's feet cracked open, revealing a narrow fissure that burned with molten light.

Elara gasped and reached for him, but Osric raised his hand. His mark flared brilliantly, answering the call.

"I will," he said. "Even if it burns me again." And as he stepped into the light, the earth roared, alive and remembering.

The fissure widened at his feet, a wound of molten light cutting through the bones of the mountain. Heat rolled upward in slow, searing waves. Whispers, screams, prayers, all burned into the earth long ago.

Osric hesitated only once, glancing back at Elara. She stood on the rim, hair whipping in the updraft, her face pale but steady. The dragonets crouched beside her, their eyes reflecting the golden fire.

"I'll find him," he said.

Elara's voice barely carried through the roar. "Don't forget who you are."

He gave a small, grim smile. "That's the problem. I never can."

He stepped forward and dropped into the light. The air swallowed him whole.

Heat struck first. Not the surface burn of fire, but the deep, devouring heat that lived inside stone. It pressed against his chest, forcing the air from his lungs, and for an instant, he thought his body would turn to ash. But the mark on his palm flared, spreading cool gold through his veins. The gift of Solarus, the curse that would not let him die, kept him intact.

He fell through light and smoke, through voices that were not voices at all but *memories,* alive and echoing.

He saw himself kneeling on the same ground five centuries earlier, Kaerath at his side, wings torn and bloody. Solarus stood above them, a god of unrelenting flame, his eyes bright with fury. He heard the decree again, spoken like a sentence carved into time.

"For mercy against fire, I cast you into endless wandering. Your dragon shall sleep beneath your sin."

The surrounding light pulsed in rhythm with those words, each syllable a blow of heat.

Osric cried out, pressing his hand to his head. The world spun. Fire and memory were one here, living entities that bled together. He staggered forward through the molten haze, boots striking what felt like solid glass.

Shapes formed out of the glow, dragons of fire and smoke, flickering through the air like echoes of the First Age. They circled him silently, their bodies made of flame, their eyes molten gold.

One lowered its head, exhaling a stream of white fire that curled around his body but did not burn.

"You still carry his mark," the apparition said.

"I carry his curse," Osric rasped.

The dragon's flame flickered, then dissolved into smoke. Others rose in its place, figures he once knew: soldiers who had followed him, the half-blood wyrms he had refused to slay. Their faces burned in the glow, eyes hollow, mouths whispering the same word repeatedly.

Mercy. Mercy. Mercy.

"You think I don't remember?" he shouted. "You think I've forgotten what my mercy cost?"

The fire around him blazed higher, wrapping him in a ring of light. But then a voice rose through the inferno. Solarus.

"Memory does not punish. It teaches. Will you let it consume you again, or will you learn?"

Osric knelt, pressing his hand against the glowing ground. He felt his palm sizzle, but beneath the pain was a pulse. It was *alive*.

"Kaerath." Osric closed his eyes. "I'm coming, old friend."

He rose, breathing through the heat, and stepped forward. The fire bent around him now, less like an enemy and more like a test, searing away fear, leaving only resolve. Each step carried him deeper into the molten corridor, the Heartway where fire glowed. The deeper he went, the more the heat softened into light, and the voices of judgment faded into the distant hum of something vast and sleeping.

The air cooled. Gold turned to crimson, then to a dull, embered glow. And there at the end of the corridor, stood a wall of glass, pulsing in rhythm with that familiar, thunderous beat.

Kaerath.

Osric pressed his hand against the surface. The mark on his palm blazed stronger.

"Flame for life," he whispered through clenched teeth, "stone for silence."

The wall shuddered. Cracks raced outward, spidering across the surface. A roar rose from deep within. The Heartway trembled.

Kaerath was waking.

The fissures widened with each heartbeat, and from within came the long, drawn-out sound of stone breaking around something that refused to die. A massive shape moved behind the molten veil.

"Come on," Osric whispered, pressing his hand against the glowing surface. "Wake up, old friend. You've slept long enough."

A roar erupted.

Flame burst outward in a spiral, throwing Osric to the ground. The world vanished behind brilliance. A shadow emerged, vast and trembling, scales of molten bronze cooling to deep crimson as it drew its first breath in an age.

"Kaerath."

The dragon's wings unfurled slowly, shuddering under the weight of centuries. Firelight ran along his body. His eyes burned with both rage and grief. He fixed his gaze on the fallen figure before him.

"Keeper, you came back."

Osric forced himself to stand, his hand still glowing. "I told you I would."

"You should not have," the dragon rumbled. "He will see you. He always sees what burns."

"He already has," Osric said. "I've lived long enough in his shadow."

Kaerath's massive head lowered. "You bear the same fire, Osric. It keeps you alive. And it chains you still. Why return to the flame that damned you?"

Osric stepped closer, his boots sinking into molten ash. "Because the world is dying again. Because a Commander hunts the last of your kin. And because mercy doesn't end with a curse. It begins with one."

A low rumble built in Kaerath's chest, half growl, half sigh. "Mercy," he said at last, the word heavy with memory. "It is the reason we both burn."

"I can free you," Osric said. "Solarus bound your body to mine. If my curse holds his light, it can also break it."

The dragon's great eye flared brighter. "And what will you become when the light leaves you?"

"Whatever I was meant to be before he named me sinner."

For a moment, silence. Then the dragon bowed his head, the gesture slow and deliberate.

"Then do it, Keeper. End this slumber. Let the fire walk again."

Osric raised his hand. The two marks upon his palm, one bound to Kaerath and the other bonded to Tirra, blazed gold-white, spilling lines of light that traced through the air and into the dragon's scars. The glow spread, seeping into Kaerath's body, turning his veins to rivers of dawnfire.

Osric cried out as the heat consumed him, his own body burning with mirrored pain. The curse that had bound them both for ages strained, cracked, and…

Broke.

The Heartway exploded with light.

Osric lay there on the scorched stone, chest rising and falling with uneven breaths. Smoke curled from his clothing. The mark binding him to Kaerath was dark, burnt out.

Kaerath's shadow fell over him, vast and trembling. The dragon's breath gusted across him, hot but gentle.

"Keeper," Kaerath rumbled softly. "You live."

Osric's voice was hoarse. "Do I?"

He pushed himself up slowly, every movement stiff, heavy, *finite*. His muscles ached. His heartbeat was too loud, too fragile. There was no steady hum of divine fire beneath his skin anymore. Only the small, rhythmic pulse of something beautifully mortal. He looked down at his hand. The faint scar existed no more.

"I can feel it," he whispered. "The weight of time. I haven't felt it in…I don't even know how long."

Kaerath lowered his head until one golden eye, still glowing with inner fire, met his gaze. "He released you?"

Osric shook his head. "No. *I* released *us*. The curse was a tether, divine light bound to mercy's defiance. When I broke it, the fire returned to its source… and left me behind."

"Then you are free."

The words struck deeper than the dragon knew. Freedom. Osric had dreamed of it for so long. Yet the truth of it frightened him more than death had.

Osric exhaled. "I can die now."

"All life born of earth must," Kaerath said gently. "It is not loss, Keeper. It is balance."

Osric smiled faintly, resting his hand on the dragon's warm scales. "You sound like Terrus."

"Perhaps even gods learn."

Osric tilted his face toward the sky. "So, this is what it means to be human again."

Kaerath's eye softened. "Then live well, Keeper of Mercy. The world will need your heart more than your flame."

Kaerath burst from the fissure in a column of fire. Osric climbed out from the fissure after him. He looked up at Kaerath, free at last and blazing with life, and whispered hoarsely, "You're home."

Elara pushed her way through the settling ash and ruins. Up ahead, she spotted Osric sitting hunched on a blackened stone, his head bowed, his body steaming from the heat. "Osric!" She ran to him, dropping to her knees. "Can you hear me?"

He looked up slowly. His eyes were tired; their shine dimmed to a weathered gray. He tried to smile, but it faltered.

"I hear you," he said. "For the first time in a long while, I hear everything."

She reached for his hand. His skin was hot to the touch but no longer burned with light.

"Osric, your mark."

He followed her gaze and turned his hand over, studying it as though seeing it for the first time. "Yeah, it's gone," he murmured. "All that's left of eternity is a dull scar."

Elara shook her head, confusion and awe mingling in her expression. "But how? The curse, the fire that kept you alive…"

"All gone," he said softly. "I broke his hold when I freed Kaerath. The light that bound us both returned to its source."

"You mean…"

"I'm mortal again."

The words hung in the heated air. Elara stared at him, her throat tight. "You can die?"

He nodded, the faintest trace of a smile in his eyes. "Yes. I can die. I can bleed and grow old. At last, I can stop wandering."

Tears welled in her eyes. "You gave up eternity."

Osric's gaze lingered on her face, on the trembling light reflected in her eyes. "No," he said. "I gave up punishment."

Kaerath landed beside them. He lowered his massive head. "The Keeper lives as the world lives. Not bound by light, but by choice."

Elara turned toward the dragon, then turned back to Osric. Without thinking, she cupped his face in her hands. "Then don't die on me," she whispered, kissing him lovingly.

"Not today."

The sky split open with a scream of light. Clouds tore apart, and thunder rolled across the mountains. From the wound in the heavens, a storm of fire and radiance poured down, and within it came wings vast as the horizon.

Solarus descended.

He was light made flesh. Flames coiled around him like living serpents, his wings veined with molten gold. The air burned in his wake; shadows fled before him.

The First Elder did not descend as a god in peace, but as judgment.

"Keeper."

Osric rose to his feet. He stepped forward as one who would not bow again. "You have seen it with your own eyes. Kaerath lives. The fire you bound us with was never yours to silence."

Solarus's brilliance pulsed once. "You defied me again, and still you stand. Do you understand what you have done?"

"I've undone your cruelty," Osric said. His jaw tightened. "The world cannot endure beneath one will. Not even yours. It needs balance, or it burns."

Solarus did not answer.

His wings shifted, scattering sparks across the sky. The heat lessened. His glare softened. When he spoke again, his tone was quieter. Immense still but touched by something almost human.

"I did not summon you here to destroy you, Keeper. I summoned you because your defiance has ripened into wisdom."

Osric frowned, wary. "You summoned me?"

The light bent, folding in on itself as if gathering weight. It thickened, taking shape, until radiance hardened into scale and sinew. Solarus emerged, no longer formless, but vast and draconic, flesh and blood forged through with living light, his body gleaming like molten metal. He was terrible in his enormity, beautiful in his design, a being of substance and brilliance, as if the sun itself had chosen to wear a body. He lowered his neck, his molten eyes meeting Osric's.

"You are not the only one who kept the truth of what it means to perish."

Behind Osric and Elara, a second fissure split the ash field. A burst of blue light filled the air, followed by a cry: thin, searching, unbearably human. Ash spiraled upward in a twisting column as the light thickened, gathering itself into something like breath. Osric staggered back, shielding Elara with his body.

From the heart of the light, a shape rose.

At first, it was only a wavering silhouette, edges dissolving in and out of reality. Then a shoulder formed. A hand. A bowed head. Mist clung to the figure like unspun thread, refusing to decide whether to become flesh or memory.

Elara gasped. "Vaelor…?"

The figure flickered violently; vanishing, returning, vanishing again. The light folded around him, struggling to knit back together something that had not entirely survived the journey home.

Solarus blew a breath of light over the half-formed figure.

Vaelor's body lifted from the ground, suspended between the living and the dead. A deep vibration rippled through the air. Across the clearing, two other shapes flickered into being.

A broken whine escaped as Thymorion, Vaelor's Drake, materialized in a burst of shadowed flame. His wings were half-formed, membranes blinking in and out of existence. His scales rippled like heat-haze, no longer certain which world claimed him.

Solyndra, Elara's Drake, followed in a sputter of fading firelight, collapsing beside him. Her scales were dimmed to ember hues, cracked with glowing fractures. She tried to stand but buckled, breath rattling in her throat.

No dragon roared. They had not returned strong enough to do so.

Solarus' voice reverberated through the stone. "Come forth," he shouted to the remnant of a soul clinging stubbornly to the world.

Vaelor blinked into form…

But not wholly.

Not cleanly.

His edges bled into vapor. His outline trembled as if the world refused to hold him. His eyes drifted, unable to settle, sliding past Elara again and again, seeing movement but no meaning.

He opened his mouth to speak.

No sound emerged. Only a shuddered breath that vanished like smoke.

Solarus's jaw tightened. "He has not fully returned."

Elara stepped forward despite her shaking knees. "Vaelor," she whispered.

He flinched, not in recognition, but in confusion.

His gaze skittered across her, failing to land. For a suspended moment, he looked through her as though she was a memory he had not yet earned back.

Then, slowly, the world began to resolve.

"El…" The sound died.

He tried again. This time, it reached her.

"Sister?"

Elara fell to her knees. She reached for him, her hand passing *through* his arm before his body remembered how to be solid again.

Behind him, Thymorion lurched forward, collapsing. His wings drooped, trembling. Solyndra pressed against his sides, sharing what little strength she had with him.

"This is the price," the Elder Wyrm said. "No life returns whole. Nothing taken by death comes back unchanged."

The fissure sealed itself. And in the silence that followed, the three stood not as victors returned from death, but as souls dragged back at a terrible cost.

Osric stepped forward, his eyes ablaze with anger.

"Explain yourself, Solarus. By what right do you return the dead? Why bring them back now, broke and half-formed, when the world had already claimed them? What gives *you* the authority to decide which deaths stand?"

"Because your task has changed, Keeper. The Commander hunts more than the newborn. He hunts the Song itself. You will need their help. You cannot defeat the Commander without them."

He turned toward Vaelor and Elara. "You are the Twin Flames, fire and mercy born to balance what my pride broke. But Malachar ended the bond, and therefore the prophecy. It is time for the fire to walk again."

Vaelor took a step forward. "I know what must be done. Thymorion and I are ready."

Osric stepped between the two and the Elder Wyrm, fury sharpening every word, his fury growing.

"You took everything from me once," Osric shouted. "My life, my choices, my Keeper's bond. And now you give me *this*? A boy who can barely stand? Dragons who can barely breathe? You call this a gift?"

Osric took a step forward, close enough now to feel the Elder's heat on his body. "You speak of cost as if you bore it. But look at them, Solarus. Look at what you returned. They are alive, yes, but they are *wounded*, and this wound belongs to you."

The mountain trembled.

"Even gods learn, Keeper. Fire without mercy is ruin. Mercy without fire is death. The world needs both."

Osric's fists clenched. "Do not speak to me of what the world needs. Speak to me of what *you* took."

Solarus's eyes dimmed, ancient regret threading through the molten glow. "I did not return them to ease your pain," he said. "I returned them because the world turns toward darkness, and only the bonded flames can hold back what hunts them."

The Elder Wyrm looked again to Vaelor and Elara. "You needed each other once to survive. Now the world needs you both to endure."

Osric's breath shuddered. He did not thank the Elder. He could not, would not.

And Solarus did not expect him to.

But Osric did bow. Not in submission, but in agreement.

Solarus bowed his head as his light faded. "Go, Keeper. Go, Twin Flames. The dawn of the last fire is coming, and only those who remember mercy will survive it."

Chapter 18

Osric took Elara's hand and turned away, the heat of the Heartway falling from his shoulders. They had words to say, plans to make. Too many lives balanced on the edge of a single choice. For a breath, he simply held her hand, the world narrowing to the press of fingers and the steady, mortal thud of his own heart.

Solarus' voice cut across the hush. "Wait, Keeper. There is one thing left that I must speak to you about. But it is for your ears alone."

Osric turned. Solarus's tone was not a command but a summons. He inclined his head toward Elara. "Take Vaelor. Ride with the dragons down to the base of the hill. Keep the wyrmlings safe until I hear his words." He smiled. "And this time we'll fly over the protectors."

Elara's face registered confusion and stubborn loyalty, but she did as asked. Vaelor bowed, and together they mounted Solyndra and Thymorion, their silhouettes folding into the molten light as they dropped toward the lower slopes.

Osric watched them go, their flight uneven as they regained their strength. When only stirring dust marked their passage, he turned and planted himself before Solarus. The Elder hung in the air like a brilliant statue, silent. For a long moment, the only sound was the slow settling of ash.

"I am here, Lord of Light," Osric said. "Tell me what you will."

Solarus's light shifted, drawing the air taut. "You proved your mercy was stronger than fire," Solarus said at last. "You unbound what I bound.

You kept your oath when cruelty would have been easier. For that, you have earned my attention. Now I ask one more favor: show me that your mercy is stronger than hate."

Osric frowned. "I don't understand."

The sun-wyrm's wings folded a fraction. "On the plain to the west, on Mount Vulkaran, the Commander wields his evil like a sword. He twists the young wyrmling's heart, bending it toward shadow. You know him as the Commander, the dark rider who drives the armies of ash. But he answers to another name."

"Yes, Malachar."

"His real name is Lucan of Karellin."

"Lucan? How can he …"

"He is your son; born of the wife you lost before his first birthday. He is the one you could not raise and, therefore, gave to another couple to do what you could not. Love him."

Osric staggered, his hand reaching to balance himself against the stone. But the shock of Solarus' words was too great. He fell forward onto both hands.

"That is not possible," he gasped. "He…he …he would have died centuries ago. He CANNOT be Lucan. You are wrong."

"I assure you, I am not. The man who awaits on Mount Vulkaran for you was only a boy when the War of Ash and Ember ended. When his village was reduced to cinders, it left him with nothing but smoke and silence. His foster mother lay among the fallen, and something inside him refused to accept she was the last of his family."

"Lucan clawed through the ruins for days, bare hands torn and blackened, turning over charred beams and broken stone, certain he would find his father beneath it all. He called for him until his throat split raw, until each word came out as a rasp, then a whisper, then nothing at all. Still, he searched. Because as long as he kept looking, he did not have to face the truth that the man he needed would never answer."

"Grief carved a hollow in him, a place where hope should have lived. The Void found that emptiness and offered him the one thing he could never earn — certainty. He turned to revenge, killing everyone he could find. It did not matter if they were innocent or guilty. Their existence was crime enough. And the more he slaughtered, the more he became alive."

A warm tear slid down Solarus' cheek.

"When Lucan broke covenant, when he chose dominion over balance, the world did not strip his power. It stripped his name. The Void did not transform him into Malachar. It forced him to choose. He had to abandon the name that still answered to mercy. And so, Lucan was sealed away: alive, aware, and unreachable."

Osric swallowed hard, the words scraping raw against his chest. "I should have been there for him. But when his mother died, it tore the heart out of me. I couldn't breathe, couldn't think. I told myself that loving anyone again would only end the same way. So, I turned away. I called it strength, but it was cowardice. The truth is... I abandoned him because I was drowning, and I let my grief decide his fate."

Solarus inclined his head. "Grief is a teacher, Osric. You bore its weight and kept walking. Malachar... he laid his grief down at the feet of the Void and asked it to take the pain away. And the Void did...by taking everything else with it."

"But Malachar's darkness and hate are not of his own doing," Osric said. "The Void shaped him into the monster he is today. How can I punish him for something that is not of his doing?"

"Even monsters have a choice."

"So, to save the wyrmlings and the world, I must kill my own son?"

Solarus watched him. "Or you can show him mercy." The Elder's tone carried no softening. "Hate will burn him, and in burning him, you will feed the very Void that made him whole. Mercy, true mercy, might shatter the chain that holds him. It might not. But only mercy can destroy the hunger that bred him."

Osric closed his eyes and felt the faint scar on his palm, cool and ordinary as stone. The mark had once kept him alive; now it was remembered only as a lesson. Mercy had cost him everything. Would mercy now demand the impossible: save the hand that tried to destroy the world?

He spoke, his voice low yet sure. "If he can be spared, I will spare him," he said. "If he cannot, then I will end him. And I will bear that weight."

Solarus's light flared once. "Go now, Keeper. Begin the journey that will determine your fate. Your destiny waits, and so does your choice between your heart and justice. Remember. Mercy is not weakness. It is decision. Make it well."

Osric let the words fall into him. He rose, shaking, the hollow of the world now full of consequence. He looked to the west, toward Vulkaran and the dark that had a name he had never thought he would hear again.

Osric climbed onto Kaerath's back, the dragon's scales warm beneath his hands. Once more he felt the pulse of Kaerath's heart through his legs: steady, thunderous, ancient. It was like straddling the heartbeat of the world. He remembered. And he rejoiced.

Kaerath rumbled low, wings unfurling with a sound like torn storm clouds. Heat and wind exploded around them as he leapt skyward, his massive body cutting through the air with terrifying grace. For a breathless moment, Osric could do nothing but hold on, the rush of air tearing at his cloak, the horizon spinning below. His fingers clutched the dragon's spines. Even in his best riding days, he had trouble riding without a saddle.

Dragon and man crested the hill. With a single, earth-shaking beat of his wings, Kaerath descended and landed beside the other dragons. Osric swung down, his boots hitting the ground with the quiet finality of a man returning to destiny.

"What did Solarus want?" Vaelor asked.

"To remind me of my mortality."

Elara caught the lack of color in his skin, the sorrow behind his eyes. "Are you okay?"

He exhaled, steadying himself. "I will be. My body is not accustomed to being mortal. But enough of me. We need to move. It will be night soon. We will use its cover to begin our journey to rescue the wyrmling."

"Toward Mount Vulkaran?" Vaelor asked.

Osric nodded. "Yes. If we ride now, we can fly half-way there before the sun returns tomorrow. Lucan of Karellin will not see us coming."

Elara frowned. "Lucan of Karellin?"

Osric met her gaze. "The Commander's true name," he said softly. "My son."

The words fell like stones into the silence that followed.

Elara stared at him; disbelief etched across her features. "Your son? Malachar is your son? How is that possible? You said your family was gone, buried centuries ago."

Osric's eyes darkened. "So, I believed. But Solarus told me the truth." His body sagged to the ground. "In my early days of wandering, I allowed myself to love a woman. We had a son together. She was killed when he was still a baby. I was so devastated and confused, plus I knew I could not watch someone else I loved die. So, I gave him to a family who I knew would love and raise him. When he was a young adult, his adoptive parents were killed. Lucan escaped death, but the loss devastated him. He bartered with the Void and bought forgetfulness at the price of his soul. And became Malachar, the bringer of death."

Elara's hand drifted toward him, then stopped, uncertain. "And now you have to face him?"

"Yes."

"What are you going to do?"

"I don't know."

"Are you going to tell him you're his father?"

"I…I have no idea. Would it change things if he knew? Would he even care? I have no answers except for one: I either end him… or save what's left of him."

Elara swallowed hard. "Then may the Elders favor mercy, Osric. Because no one else will."

Without another word, Osric rose and climbed back onto Kaerath's back, settling as best he could between the spines. Holding on with both hands, he braced himself as Kaerath rose into the fading light with a single, mighty thrust. Vaelor and Elara followed, climbing onto their Drakes, the tiny wyrmlings nestled in Elara's shirt.

Below, the earth beside Solarus' mountain rumbled. Waves of movement rippled across the dry grass. The Deepborns. They sensed the passing of the three humans on their Drakes, furious that they were out of their reach. Once the humans passed the Wall of Stone, the guardians quieted again, sinking back into the bowels of the earth.

The plains below stretched vast and empty, their surface dulled by centuries of ash. No bird sang. No wind stirred. Only the heavy rhythm of wings broke the stillness.

Elara rode close beside Osric, Solyndra's glide smooth and quiet. Ahead, the horizon was no longer flat but fractured: an uneven rise, black against black.

"Is that it?" she asked softly.

Osric nodded, observing their destination on the horizon. "Mount Vulkaran, the Broken Forge." He turned to the east, the first rays of daylight slipping over the valley below. "I don't want to arrive during daylight. We'll have to hold up until night returns."

Kaerath sailed through the thinning clouds. The wind carried the scent of rain and ash, and something in it made Osric's chest tighten, as if the air carried both salvation and ruin.

As the sun climbed higher, Osric scanned the terrain below. Before him stretched a lush valley cut by a winding stream, its grasses silver with dew. "There," he said, motioning Kaerath downward. "That clearing near the water."

Vaelor and Elara followed, landing softly in the glistening meadow. Trees arched around the clearing, their leaves dripping with morning moisture. Kaerath folded his wings with a weary groan, lowering himself beside the stream. Elara's dragon settled nearby, while Vaelor's gave a low rumble before lying down in the grass.

"The dragons need rest and food," Osric said.

"We could use something to eat ourselves," Vaelor said, rubbing his stomach. "I don't know about you two, but it's been months since I tasted food."

"Thankfully, it hasn't been that long for us," Elara laughed, brushing her wind-tangled hair from her face. "But I am starving. And sore." She rubbed her buttocks.

"We could all use food, water, and rest," Osric said, surveying the small glade. The sound of running water mingled with birdsong. "We'll rest here till dusk."

"What do we do about hiding?" Elara asked. "We can't use the Veil of Noctis. And Kaerath's Shadow is no longer an option. How do we prevent Malachar from seeing us?"

"We don't," Osric said. "He will know we are coming, and he will wait for us upon his mountain."

"What about his army?"

"Malachar doesn't have enough time to deploy them to attack," Osric said. "More than likely, he will station them in front of his fortress as his first line of defense."

"With three massive dragons, we'll cut them down."

"Probably."

The faint bleating of sheep drifted in the air through the trees. A small flock grazed in the morning mist, unaware of the danger settling nearby. Their white coats shone like drifting clouds against the emerald grass. Kaerath lifted his head, nostrils flaring as their scent reached him. Vaelor's dragon rumbled low, his tail flicked with impatience. Even Elara's mount, usually calm, shifted restlessly, her pupils narrowing to slits.

Osric glanced toward the sound and gave a faint nod. "Go on," he murmured. "You've earned it."

The dragons needed no further encouragement. In a flurry of motion, they moved through the sky, silent shadows of scale and muscle. The flock scattered, cries echoing briefly across the valley before fading into the sounds of rushing water and rustling leaves. They fed quickly, each taking several sheep. When the dragons returned, the air carried the heavy scent of blood and steam. Each settled again beside the stream, content and drowsy. Kaerath laid a sheep carcass on the ground beside Osric.

"It appears our dinner has arrived." Osric knelt near a carcass, drawing his blade. He cut several slices of meat and carried them to where the two wyrmlings waited near Elara. They chirped softly as he approached, their tails flicking with excitement.

"Easy now," Osric held out the raw strips. The wyrmlings snapped them up eagerly, their tiny teeth clicking as they tore the meat apart.

Elara smiled faintly. "They trust you completely."

Osric looked down at the young dragons, feeling the warmth of their breath against his hand. "Their trust isn't given," he said quietly. "It's earned."

Vaelor joined them, wiping sweat from his brow. "Then let's make sure we're worth their trust."

Elara opened a package of tubers and dried meat. "We've only got two bundles left. Then there's nothing to eat."

"By then we'll either be dead, or Malachar will be defeated. If the later, we can restock our supplies from his pantry. If the first, it won't matter." Osric returned to the sheep carcass and sliced off three large chunks of meat. "So, in case this is our last meal, we eat like kings. Vaelor and Elara, gather firewood. We don't need to hide our presence any longer."

"I was hoping you'd say that." Vaelor ran off, gathering a large pile of wood.

The twins wove through the trees, quick and sure-footed, returning with armfuls of deadwood. They built a tight pyramid of branches; dry leaves tucked deep within to catch the first breath of flame.

"Kaerath, a little help, if you please," Osric said.

The dragon gave a slow, indulgent roll onto his side, as if the request amused him. He exhaled once, a controlled ribbon of fire that kissed the pile. The leaves caught first, then the wood, flames climbing in a sudden rush.

When the fire settled into a steady burn and the coals glowed hot beneath, Vaelor set the chunks of meat on sharpened sticks and angled them over the heat. Fat hissed and dripped, the scent of roasting flesh thickening the air until it drew saliva to their mouths. Elara wrapped tubers in broad leaves and nestled them deep into the coals, where they would soften and sweeten in the heat.

"Mind if I ask you something?" Vaelor asked, turning the chops over.

"Wondering if it's true, that I'm over five hundred years old."

"How did you know I was going to ask that?"

Osric smiled. *Damn, it fills good to smile again.* "Because that's the first thing people want to know. And yes, it's true. I'm five hundred and forty-two years of age."

"What's it like to live that long?"

"The first year was the hardest, although I didn't realize it until I had lived many more. I walked because I had no reason to stop. The curse did not compel my feet to move. I retained full agency over my body. But without Kaerath's presence, without purpose, without even the ability to end my own existence through simple surrender, walking seemed as reasonable as anything else."

"About a hundred and ten years ago, I figured out my purpose: to be a protector. I used my training as a fighter and Keeper to help those who needed protection from others. Remember, that's how I came to be in your service, although I arrived too late to be much use."

"How can you say that? You saved her. Had you not been there, Malachar would have both twin wyrmlings. Besides, you gave Elara something no other human being has ever given her."

"What's that?"

"Happiness. I've never seen her so happy."

Elara reached over and gently kissed his cheek. "He does make me happy. And I even tried to kill him several times."

"Stuck me once in the gut," Osric chuckled, lifting his shirt and showing the stab scar. "She's deadly with a knife, so do me a favor. Now that I'm mortal again, keep your knife hidden well. I wouldn't want her to stab me again."

Vaelor's eyes opened wide, his mouth partly opening. He swallowed, staring at his sister. "You stabbed him?"

"I'm afraid so," Elara sheepishly said.

"Even set me on fire a few times," Osric added. "Good thing I was immortal at the time." Osric brushed a lock of hair from her eyes. "But that's a story for another time. Let's eat and get some sleep."

*****

The air changed.

It started as a shiver, a tremor that crawled through the bones of the mountain and up Malachar's spine. The torches lining the cavern flared, then dimmed to dying embers, their flames bending toward the northern tunnels as though drawn by an unseen tide.

Malachar froze. His pupils contracted to pinpoints of molten red. A taste of ash and lightning filled his mouth.

It was *Him*.

A blinding pressure, vast and golden, radiating from somewhere far beyond the mortal veil. *Solarus*. The Elder's fire had stirred again. He felt the world bow beneath his awakening.

Malachar's heartbeat thundered in his ears. He felt the rules of the world shift, the careful balance of dark and light tilting, the game he had mastered for centuries no longer his to command.

Then came the second pulse, fainter, but sharp, defiant. Osric. And beneath that, deeper still, the slow, steady rhythm of a sleeping inferno. *Kaerath.*

Malachar staggered back, his breath breaking as if the air had turned against him. His nails clawed into the stone, dragging lines as he tried to steady himself.

"No…" The word tore free, brittle with panic. He shook his head, once, then again, as if he could force the realization away. "No. Solarus sealed you in glass. Your fire died."

The cavern seemed to exhale, wind whispering through unseen cracks. The wyrmling in its nest whimpered, its coal-black scales reflecting the red of his eyes.

Malachar turned toward the small creature, voice low, almost reverent. "They're coming," he said. "The fallen Keeper and his dragon. They're coming for you."

The torches died completely, plunging the chamber into shadow.

Behind Malachar, the black dragon stirred, lifting its head from the coals. Its great wings unfurled with a thunderous crack, scattering ash across the floor. It bellowed. His sound shook the wall.

A grim smile cut across the Commander's face, cold and certain. His voice rolled through the darkness, certain and unflinching "Let him come. I'll end this once and for all."

*****

As the sun began its journey behind Mount Vulkaran, the three humans woke. Osric's gaze traveled westward, toward the dark silhouette of Mount Vulkaran fading into the horizon.

As they waited for darkness, they ate another meal of roasted lamb and some fresh strawberries and walnuts Elara found. The three Drakes helped themselves to the remainder of the sheep herd, licking their lips in satisfaction.

The moment the shadows stretched into eerie beings, the three riders and Drakes rose into the air. Within an hour, they reached the edge of Malachar's domain. Vaelor guided Thymorion higher, scanning the wastes. "There's no movement below. No wind. Nothing alive."

"It's not absence," Osric replied. "It's corruption. The mountain's heartbeat drowns everything within miles."

The air continued to grow heavier. Faint murmurs rode the currents; half-heard whispers that seemed to twist around their names.

"Do you hear that?" Elara asked.

"Name-seeking echoes. Memories that latch onto the living, whispering whatever fragments of language they once possessed. Names are common because names are the last memories to die."

From further below, another sound rose, one that didn't belong. A faint hiss. Then another.

Thwip.

Thwip-thwip.

Osric's eyes narrowed. The sound grew, thin and sharp, until it became a storm of whispering steel rising through the clouds.

Arrows. Hundreds of them.

"Piercers!" Osric shouted, his voice carried above the whispers. "Bank left. Keep your body low against your Drake."

The air exploded around them. The hiss became a roar as the first volley sliced upward, shafts of black wood tipped with crimson flame. They tore through the mist like a swarm of hornets, cutting bright lines through the gray.

Kaerath's wings didn't falter. The arrows glanced off his scales with the sound of metal striking stone, bouncing harmlessly into the abyss below. But where the dragons were invulnerable, their riders were not.

Osric ducked low against Kaerath's neck, feeling the air split inches from his head. A burning shaft passed close enough that its heat seared the top of his glove.

"Elara! Stay close!" he shouted, twisting to see her. Her dragon veered through the storm, arrows hissing past her shoulders like angry sparks. Vaelor shielded his face with his arm, shouting something lost to the wind.

Then the clouds tore open.

Beneath them stretched an army black as pitch; hundreds of soldiers in perfect formation, their bows firing, their armor gleaming with dark fire. Each release came like the beating of a monstrous heart: a hundred strings drawn; a hundred deaths loosed into the sky.

"Higher!" Osric ordered, and Kaerath answered, folding his wings slightly before surging upward with a burst of force that made the air scream.

The others followed, their dragons vanishing briefly into the churning gray. The arrows pursued, singing through the mist in endless, keening waves.

Osric's heart hammered in his ears, matching the rhythm of the arrows' deadly song. He whispered in Kaerath's ear. The mighty Drake growled in response, and immediately the scales around his lower neck raised enough for Osric to crawl beneath.

Elara's dragon climbed beside them, her hair whipping across her face. "They can't reach us forever!" she shouted.

"Long enough to bleed us dry if we're careless," Osric answered. "Tell Solyndra to raise her neck scales and crawl under them. The pierces can't penetrate her scales."

Elara did as Osric instructed, amazed. "I didn't know she could do that."

"All dragons can. The knowledge comes from being a Keeper for so many years. But not all dragons are trusting enough to show their vulnerability. While it does protect their rider, it does leave the Drake open to injury, even death."

They continued, past the army, rising above the clouds. The arrows fell short; their sound diminished until only the sound of their wings remained.

Osric fixed his eyes on the horizon. "Remain above the clouds. We should clear the ridge at any moment."

As they flew over the summit, their hearts saw what awaited them. Mount Vulkaran rose from the earth like a black monolith, its jagged peaks pulsing faintly red from within. Rivers of cooled lava carved its flanks, glowing in slow, dying veins. Around the summit, a storm of ash circled endlessly, turning the sky into a whirl of gray. And from deep within the mountain came a sound.

Not wind.

Not thunder.

The slow, heavy heartbeat of something alive.

Osric's eyes narrowed, pointing to the second mountain from the right. "He's inside that one."

"Malachar?" Elara whispered.

"Yes. And the wyrmling is with him."

"How do you know?"

"Kaerath senses both. He told me."

A tremor rolled through the air, a wave of heat so intense it rippled their vision. The mountain's shadow shifted, longer, reaching outward.

"Down!" Osric barked. "To the lower ridge!"

The dragons folded their wings and dived, cutting through the heavy air. Ash swirled around them, coating the leathery scales in gray. The ground rose swiftly to meet them. Their feet landed on a ledge of broken stone.

And far above, at the summit of Vulkaran, two red eyes stared through the dark.

Chapter 19

Inside the heart of Mount Vulkaran, the wyrmling lay coiled upon a bed of scorched rock. Once, his scales had been pale gold, innocent. Now they were dulled to pewter, rimmed with black. With each breath he took, his body trembled. Malachar stood before him.

He spoke softly, his voice low enough to pass for kindness. "You feel it, don't you, Little One? The ache inside your fire."

The wyrmling raised its head. Its pupils, once clear and bright, were rimmed with red.

"Your flame hurts," Malachar continued, stepping closer. "It burns because it was born to serve. But they…" His voice dripped with quiet contempt. "They will tell you to hide it, to smother it in mercy. Mercy weakens the flame. Mercy lies."

He stretched out a gloved hand. Shadows crawled from his fingers like tendrils of smoke, brushing the wyrmling's snout. It flinched, whining softly, but did not pull away.

"That's it," Malachar murmured. "Feel how cool the dark is. No pain. No fear. No obedience."

The shadows spread. The light in the cavern dimmed further. For a heartbeat, the wyrmling fought. Its tail lashed, claws scraping the stone, a few sparks breaking loose from its throat. But the struggle faded. The black veins along its body pulsed brighter, sinking deeper into its scales.

Malachar's mouth curved in satisfaction. "Good. Now you witness the truth: fire does not heal; it consumes. The sooner you learn that the stronger you will become."

A faint glow appeared far down the mountain: Kaerath's fire. The wyrmling lifted its head, sensing the presence of another flame. Before he could stop it a whimper broke free from its throat. For an instant, the shadow faltered, and the gold beneath its scales glimmered faintly.

Malachar's voice turned sharp. "No. Look at *me.*"

The wyrmling obeyed. Its eyes darkened once more.

Malachar smiled, lowering his hand. "That's it, My Little Ember. Concentrate on me. They have nothing that you want or need. Together we can show them what mercy costs."

The cavern shuddered, dust falling from the ceiling. The wyrmling's wings unfolded slowly. It hissed once, testing the new strength in its body.

Outside, the mountain's heart pulsed black.

And far below, on the lower ridge, Osric felt the echo of that heartbeat vibrate through the stone beneath his feet. "He's twisting it," he whispered.

Kaerath's great head turned toward him. "We must reach the wyrmling before his light goes out completely," Osric said. "Before Malachar turns it into a weapon."

"This place reeks of death," Vaelor muttered, dismounting. He pressed his palm to the ground, grimacing. "The heat isn't from the magma. It's from corruption."

Elara leaned against Solyndra's neck, resting a hand on her dragon's shoulder. Solyndra's scales had dulled since they'd entered the Ashlands, their sheen masked by soot. "She can feel it," Elara said quietly. "The darkness is trying to corrupt her, too."

Osric scanned the slope ahead. Black fissures crisscrossed the hillside, glowing faintly from within, like veins of blood under dying skin. "We'll go on foot from here. The tunnels will be too tight for wings."

He looked at Kaerath. "Stay alert. If the mountain breathes flame, get the others clear." Kaerath's great head lowered, eyes burning faintly gold. "The mountain breathes more than flame. Be wary."

Osric leading the way, the three pressed on, slipping inside. The path wound upward through stone that steamed beneath their boots. Each step carried them deeper into shadow, until even the moonlight vanished behind the ridges. The only light came from the molten veins threading the walls, flickering, unnatural.

Elara paused, brushing her hand against the rock. "It's alive," she whispered. "The mountain's skin is alive like Terrus' mountain was."

Osric's eyes narrowed. "No, no Elder lives here. It is something else." He placed his unmarked palm on the wall. "It's not alive, Elara. It's infected with the darkness of the Void and Malachar's lust for dominion."

A low rumble rolled through the tunnels. The air shifted. Vaelor drew his blade, its edge catching the faint light. "He knows we're here."

"Yes," Osric said, voice low.

Rounding a bend, the tunnel opened into a cavern. The floor sloped sharply upward, leading into a hollow where molten cracks traced strange patterns, like runes drawn by a shaking hand. At the center lay a smear of scorched metal, glowing faintly. Within it, a carving twisted and pulsed, as though it were breathing.

Elara stepped forward, her brow furrowed. "It's the same mark that was on Kaura's egg," she said softly. "But it's wrong. It's reversed."

Osric's jaw clenched. "Malachar's corruption runs deep. He's trying to twist the language of creation."

Before he could speak further, the ground *moved*.

The molten cracks shifted, coiling like serpents. The air filled with a faint hiss, and from the fissures rose black vapor. It was thin at first, then thickening into columns that coiled and joined.

Figures took shape.

Scaled.

Winged.

Hollow.

They were not dragons, but imitations, shadows molded from memory and ash. Their eyes glowed dim red, their mouths open in silence.

Elara drew back, horror flashing in her eyes. "What are they?"

"Echoes," Osric said. His sword rasped free of its sheath, the sound harsh in the suffocating dark. "Remnants of the first fire."

The first of the creatures lunged, its shape rippling like smoke. Osric met it head-on, his blade cutting through its chest. It exploded in a shower of sparks. No blood, no cry, only the smell of burned iron.

Vaelor slashed at another, his blade flashing red in the molten light. "We'll never reach Malachar this way."

Elara turned toward Osric, desperation rising. "We need Solyndra's flame. She's small enough to squeeze down here."

"Summon her," Osric shouted.

Elara lifted two fingers to her lips and whistled, sharp and commanding. Solyndra answered at once, rearing onto her hind legs as the stone floor shuddered beneath her weight. The dragon surged forward, claws scraping sparks from the rock as she charged the tunnel mouth. At the last possible moment, Solyndra snapped her wings inward, folding them tight against her powerful frame until scale brushed scale. The walls rushed past in a blur as she dropped into the narrow passage, her body twisting with instinctive precision, scales scraping stone. Talons tucked, neck low, she slid through the constricting dark, her breath echoing in harsh bursts.

"Burn bright, Solyndra."

The dragon's throat glowed faintly. She roared and unleashed a jet of pure fire. The blast struck the advancing shadows and tore them apart, the light illuminating every crevice of the mountain for a single blinding moment.

When the flame died, the cavern was empty.

Only their breathing filled the silence.

Osric lowered his sword, scanning the scorched walls. "He's testing us. He wants to see how much we'll burn before we break."

Elara stared into the dark ahead, her hand still trembling from the echoes. "Then he'll learn that mercy burns hotter than hate."

Osric looked ahead. The tunnel tightened. "No dragon can fit through that, not even Solyndra's slim body. Send her to wait with the others."

"Thank you, Solyndra," Elara said, pressing her face to the dragon's snout. "Back to Kaerath and Thymorion."

They climbed without pause, always upward as the tunnel narrowed and steepened. Frost spread across the stone beneath their hands and boots, clashing with the unnatural heat pulsing in the air. Each breath burned, fire and ice tightening the chest. The walls shimmered with rime, bending the faint light into sharp, distorted reflections.

The sense of being watched grew heavier, an invisible pressure that pressed between the shoulders and whispered of inevitability. Somewhere above them, beyond the last bend and the final rise, Malachar waited. The mountain knew it. The cold knew it. And deep within Elara's chest, her dragonfire knew it. It stirred, answering the silent promise of what awaited at the summit. She fought to keep it contained, hidden from Malachar's knowledge.

Osric walked ahead in silence. Solarus's words echoed through his mind, circling and returning, each repetition cutting deeper than the one before. The weight of his words grew heavier, pressing down on him, demanding reckoning.

"He is your son."

Forgive me, Son. I should not have abandoned you in my time of loss and despair.

He clenched his jaw, trying to anchor himself in motion. But guilt crept in. He had thought himself cursed alone, a wanderer born from mercy's sin. But now the truth carried another face, another name. If blood tied him to Malachar, then what did that make him? The son of light, or the father of darkness?

Over the years, Osric had heard whispers carried from distant lands; some of Malachar, others of the Dark Commander. The tales were spoken as though they were two separate men, two separate evils. He had never known Malachar's full name, nor had he ever suspected the truth that bound those rumors together. To him, they were fragments of different stories: one a name murmured with unease, the other a title spoken in dread.

Yet the deeds were unmistakable. Burning villages reduced to cinders. Wyrms twisted by another's will, their fire fouled, their spirits broken. Black banners rising from ash-choked ground, heralding conquest through terror.

Solarus' revelation had torn the veil away. The quiet, undeniable truth that he had helped shape the man who now stood against him coursed through his veins. The sin was shared. That knowledge did not stay his hand; it bound it tighter to the task. This was no longer justice, but necessity.

I put his foot upon this path. It is my duty to remove it once and for all time.

Osric stopped, resting a hand against the rock wall. It was hot enough to sting, but he didn't move it. He needed the pain. It kept his thoughts from unraveling completely.

But he is my son. If I destroy him, do I destroy part of myself?

He closed his eyes. He could almost hear Solarus' voice, a distant thunder rolling through memory. *"Show me your mercy is stronger than hate."*

How could I grant mercy to a man I've never known, a son I gave away, a boy twisted by shadow in time of need?

Elara's voice broke the silence behind him. "Osric," she said softly, "you've gone quiet."

He didn't turn. "I'm thinking."

"About him?"

He nodded. "About what it means."

Her footsteps drew closer. "You did what you thought was right."

"And that might be worse. How many lives have I taken in the name of justice, never knowing my own blood was behind it all? How many sins are shared between us, simply because I chose the easy way out?"

"His choices are not your sin, Osric."

"Isn't that what every failed father says as an excuse?"

Osric looked down at his hand, the faint scar on his palm catching the red glow from the veins of molten rock. "I spent half a lifetime believing that choice was enough. Now I'm not so sure."

He turned his gaze toward the tunnel ahead. "I'll save the wyrmling. But if I must kill him to do it, I will. Whatever blood runs between us, it ends here."

Elara searched his face. "And if there's still something human in him?"

Osric's eyes hardened. "Then may the Elders help him because mercy may be all I have left to give."

He drew a steadying breath, feeling the weight of both guilt and duty. He started forward again, deeper into the heart of Vulkaran, where his destiny awaited.

"Keep close," Osric warned.

The ground beneath them bucked. A wall of molten rock burst open ahead, spilling liquid fire down the corridor.

"Move!" Osric shouted.

They scattered, diving into a side tunnel as the lava rushed past, hissing and steaming, flooding the path they'd just taken. The roar of it filled the world, drowning out thought. When it passed, they emerged into another cavern.

One where the walls moved.

At first, it appeared like solid stone shifting. Cracks opened and closed, exhaling gusts of sulfur and heat. Dark shapes formed in the walls, carved by the Void.

"Keep vigilant. More shadow shifters are coming to try and stop us," Osric shouted.

The nearest wall split open, and something clawed its way out. A creature of molten slag and ash, roughly shaped like a man, its body dripping fire from its limbs. Its eyes burned white-hot, its mouth opening in a shriek that sounded like stone grinding against bone.

More followed, tearing themselves free of the rock, forming an advancing line of burning silhouettes.

Osric drew his sword. "They're not real," he said. "They're pieces of the mountain's will. If we fall here, Vulkaran keeps us."

"Then we don't fall," Vaelor shouted. He raised his blade.

"There's too many of them. We can't fight them and win," Osric shouted. "Run for your lives."

The three ran. The ground trembled underfoot, the ceiling groaned, collapsing behind them. Blackness engulfed them, plunging them into the night. Osric flicked his flint and lit two torches. "This way."

A black mist rolled in without warning. It coiled around Osric's boots and crept higher, swallowing the faint glow of his torch until the light stuttered and died.

"Elara? Vaelor?" His voice vanished into the fog.

Somewhere ahead, the wyrmling screamed, a high, piercing cry that cut through the suffocating dark and lodged itself in Osric's chest. He moved toward it before reason could stop him, hand brushing the damp wall to steady his steps. The scar on his palm flared faintly, reacting to something unseen.

Behind him, Elara's voice rose in alarm, distant and muffled. "Osric! Where are you?"

The mist thickened, a living wall separating them. Elara stepped forward, but the tunnel ahead of her was gone, replaced by blackness that breathed.

Chapter 20

"Hold on," Osric muttered, quickening his pace. "I'm coming, Little One."

He was alone now. Whatever waited ahead, whatever horrors lay coiled in the mountain's depths, he would face them unaided. He had no choice. He alone was capable of reaching the wyrmling… and saving it.

The wyrmling cried again, closer this time, thin and desperate. The sound was both beacon and curse, pulling him ever deeper into the mountain's heart. Stone groaned around him as the mountain shuddered in protest, the reverberation so vast it swallowed his thoughts whole. Osric bent forward, clamping his hands over his ears, teeth gritted, fighting to remain upright as the roar threatened to tear him apart from the inside. Still, he pressed on, driven by the knowledge that there would be no one else.

Then…

Silence.

Even the beating of his own heart had gone still.

The mist peeled back in slow ribbons, revealing a vast chamber carved not by tools, but by force. The walls rose high and uneven, fused in places to a glassy sheen where heat had once burned hot enough to melt the mountain itself.

The floor sloped inward toward a central hollow, a blackened basin ringed with jagged spikes of warped metal and fractured rock. Chains stretched from their tips toward the center, their links etched with symbols that flickered faintly, as if struggling to hold their shape.

At the heart of it all lay the wyrmling.

It was bound within the basin, chains fastened to each wing and foot. A dim, pulsing glow seeped from beneath the structure, casting long, trembling shadows across the chamber. Every flicker of light made the runes along the walls shift and crawl, as though the entire sanctum watched, waited, and fed on the small life it imprisoned.

Osric took a cautious step forward.

"That's close enough," came a voice from the shadows, low and calm.

From the darkness stepped a figure cloaked in black, eyes burning. "Welcome, Keeper," Malachar said, spreading his arms as if greeting an old friend. "I was wondering how long it would take you to follow the sound of his suffering."

The wyrmling whimpered, and Osric's scar pulsed in answer. It still beat as a Keeper. And it remembered a Keeper's responsibility to always protect the innocent dragonets.

But the trap was sprung.

Chains of fire lashed out from the runes, seizing Osric's wrists before he could draw his blade. He hit the stone hard; the breath ripped from his lungs.

Above him, Malachar stepped closer, his armor glinting like obsidian bathed in blood. In the reflected light, Osric could see his face clearly: the angles of his features, the familiar line of the jaw, the set of the brow, the eyes that mirrored his own too closely to be chance. The image that greeted him was a reflection of himself as he had been when cursed…and as Lucan had been as a boy. Any doubt he had vanished. Malachar was Lucan, flesh of his flesh.

"Still fighting for them?" Malachar asked, his voice laced with a tinge of disgust.

Osric strained against the bindings, teeth bared. "Always."

Malachar grinned. With a flick of his hand, the chains yanked tighter, dragging Osric toward the edge of the chamber where the wyrmling writhed in its prison of rune-fire.

"I'll show you mercy," Malachar whispered, summoning a pulse of black flame that surged outward, shattering the stone roof above them. "You can die under open sky."

The world exploded into blinding light and roaring heat. The mountain cracked, spewing dust and cinders as Malachar pulled Osric into the storm. They rose up through the chasm and emerged on a jagged cliffside. The

Moon's light bled through smoke and cloud. Below, rivers of magma tore through the valley floor.

The wyrmling lay crumpled near the cliff's edge, its cries weak but defiant. Osric lunged toward it, breaking one chain free. A searing wave of Malachar's power struck him in the ribs. The blow threw him to the ground. Pain bloomed in his side. He could feel blood pooling beneath his body.

Malachar advanced, sword drawn, ignited with shadowfire. "Where's your strength Old Man? I thought you were invisible, but your blood runs out in rivers onto my floor."

"My immortality never stopped me from bleeding; only dying."

"Today you do both." Malachar raised his sword into the air and brought it down with all his strength.

Osric rolled aside and, with a desperate roar, drove his own blade upward. The strike caught Malachar across the chest, splitting his armor. Black smoke hissed from the wound.

Malachar staggered, eyes blazing. "You shouldn't have done that."

Before he could retaliate, a deafening screech tore through the clouds. The ground quaked as Kaerath descended, his wings vast as thunderheads, scales gleaming. The dragon's claws slammed into the rock between father and son, a wall of living fury.

"Kaerath!" Osric gasped.

The wyrmling cried again. Kaerath blew a tiny breath of molten light at the dragonet's bonds. They shattered. The small dragonet leapt from the table, across the floor toward Osric. The Keeper quickly grabbed the young dragonet and shoved him beneath his shirt, determined he would never suffer from Malachar's cruelty again.

"Vorthryn," Malachar shrieked, summoning his own beast from the storm. From across the torn sky, Vorthryn answered Malachar's cry with a scream that curdled the air. It wasn't sound; it was a corrosion, a Void-born cry. The Drake descended, slamming into the rock beside the Commander.

"Let the dawn judge us both," Malachar said.

Osric climbed onto Kaerath's back, pain flaring through every nerve. Malachar did the same. Both dragons took to the sky: one blazing with light, the other cloaked in night. The wind howled as they rose above the broken mountain.

Sunlight broke against the horizon.

And as day met darkness, father met son, blades drawn, fire and shadow entwined, in a battle that would decide the fate of every dragon left alive.

Osric gripped Kaerath's neck ridge, teeth clenched against the gale-force winds. His side burned where Malachar's strike had torn through flesh, blazing agony with every breath. But Kaerath's pulse throbbed beneath his palms, strong and unyielding, anchoring him in the storm.

"Steady, old friend," Osric rasped. "We end this now."

Malachar rode the updraft of destruction like a general commanding the end itself. Each wingbeat of his Drake rippled through the shredded clouds. Each breath exhaled shadow thick enough to drown sunlight. For a heartbeat, Osric saw his son clearly through the smoke: not as he was, but as the small infant he loved.

"We don't have to do this. You don't have to die," Osric shouted.

"But you do."

The two dragons collided.

Vorthryn slammed into Kaerath's flank with the force of a falling continent. The impact sent both titans spiraling across the sky, carving a burning helix of gold and darkness. Osric's grip slipped, his body whipped to the left, ribs screaming, blood flung into the air and snatched by the wind.

Kaerath retaliated with ancient fury.

His jaws clamped down on Vorthryn's shoulder. Dragonfire ignited, devouring Void-scorched flesh in a blaze of brilliance. Vorthryn shrieked. His shadow exploded outward in jagged spines that raked across Kaerath's flank, carving deep gouges that pumped blood into the wind.

They spun.

Over and over, two celestial beasts locked in a death spiral, wings shredding the clouds, roars shaking the ribs of the world. Osric's vision blurred from the spinning, pain, and blistering wind. He pressed himself flush to Kaerath's neck, muscles screaming as he held on.

Vorthryn lunged again.

His jaws snapped inches from Kaerath's throat: fangs scraping scales. Kaerath twisted, using momentum and gravity, and hurled the shadow Drake downward. Vorthryn crashed into a ridge, cracking the obsidian mountainside.

But the shadow reformed as a cathedral of darkness. Vorthryn surged upward with impossible speed, half his face burned to gleaming bone, wings serrated, eyes burning with starvation for light.

Kaerath braced himself.

Osric felt it: the coiling of ancient muscles, the gathering of flame deeper than breath. Kaerath folded his wings and dove.

Fire and shadow collided midair, braiding into a single, blinding detonation. The blast sent Osric flying backward, but Kaerath snapped a wing beneath him, catching him before he could fall.

"Did Solarus not tell you?" Malachar called. "Light always dies first."

Kaerath spun, light bursting from his scales in radiant arcs that blinded Vorthryn for an instant. Osric seized the moment, driving his blade downward as Kaerath dove. The weapon blazed white, striking Malachar's shoulder.

The two dragons locked talons mid-air once again, tumbling end over end. Kaerath twisted free, wheeling through the updraft. But Malachar was not finished. From his dragon's jaws erupted a spiral of darkness, liquid night that swallowed the flame whole and slammed into Kaerath's chest. The great dragon shuddered, faltered, dropped a hundred feet before regaining his balance.

Osric clung tight, coughing blood. He could barely see through the smoke and glare, but he felt it: Kaerath's exhaustion, his heartbeat slowing. The Drake's cry echoed faintly from the mountain below, raw and frightened.

He raised his sword, voice hoarse. "For them. For every life you turned to ash."

Kaerath surged upward once more, wings blazing gold. Malachar charged headlong to meet him, both dragons screaming, their riders silhouetted against the sun.

When they struck, dawn shattered.

For a breathless instant, the world vanished in white.

Then came the fall.

Kaerath's wings crumpled, smoke trailing from torn membranes. Osric clung to the ridge spines, his fingers slick with blood. The world spun. Sky, mountain, and fire tumbled until he couldn't tell which way was up. Wind screamed in his ears, a thousand voices of dying flame filled the sky.

"Kaerath, pull up!" Osric gasped, but the great dragon did not answer. The light in his scales dimmed, his strength spent. Below, the valley yawned open, jagged and drawing near.

Across the churning sky, Malachar and his Drake spiraled too, both bleeding shadows. Father and son locked eyes through the chaos, a single heartbeat of shared recognition. Not forgiveness. Not hatred. Something older. Something broken.

Osric forced himself upright, bracing against the plunge. His sword was still in his hand, its edge glowing faintly with what little power remained. He could end Malachar now. One throw. One strike. One moment before they hit the ground.

Kaerath groaned beneath him, a sound that shuddered with pain. Osric felt it through the bond, felt the dragon's heart falter, then rally weakly. If he swung, if he gave everything to destroy Malachar, Kaerath would die with him.

"Don't," whispered a voice within him. Elara's voice, distant, remembered.

Save him. He's your son.

Osric hesitated, eyes burning with tears and wind.

Malachar's wyrm roared, banking toward him for the final strike. The beast was half-dead but driven by its master's fury. Osric steadied himself and made his choice.

He dropped the blade. It fell away, swallowed by light.

"Kaerath," he said softly, pressing his hand to the dragon's neck. "Fly."

With a sound like the sun breaking free of night, Kaerath flared his wings. The dragon veered upward, barely clearing the valley's rim. Behind them, Malachar's Drake plunged into the ravine, smashing into stone and flame. The impact thundered through the mountain, shaking the world to its core.

For a moment, all was silent.

Kaerath's flight wavered, his breath ragged. Osric leaned forward, forehead against the dragon's scales. "You did well, old friend. Rest now."

Below, the chasm burned, a wound in the earth where darkness and light had met.

High above, the first true rays of dawn broke through the smoke.

And as they flew forward, Osric did not look back. He didn't need to. He knew Malachar was still alive. Somewhere in the ruin, the shadow stirred.

*****

Smoke drifted through the dawn like ghosts, curling over shattered stone and the blackened skeleton of Mount Vulkaran.

Elara stumbled across the scorched slope, one arm shielding her face from the heat. Her lungs burned from the ash, but she kept calling his name. "Osric!" Her voice broke, carried off by the wind. Behind her, Vaelor combed the ridge, his torch weak against the rising sun.

A faint tremor stirred the earth. She turned. There, on the far ledge, a massive bronze shape moved beneath a veil of soot.

"Here!" she cried, racing toward it.

Kaerath lay half-buried in rubble, wings shredded, breath coming in low, wheezing bursts. His scales flickered dimly, the once-blinding radiance reduced to embers. Elara's heart clenched. If Kaerath had fallen, then…

She climbed over the debris, scraping her knees raw, until she saw him. Osric lay slumped against the dragon's neck, his body covered in blood, his skin pale as moonlight. His hand still rested over Kaerath's heart, fingers twitching with the faint pulse of their bond.

"Osric!" She knelt beside him, brushing the ash from his face. He stirred weakly, eyes half-open, gaze unfocused.

"Elara?" His voice was a rasp.

"Thank the Elders you're alive. Did the wyrmling survive?"

Before he could answer, a tiny cry came from inside Osric's shirt. As she watched, the wyrmling crawled out from beneath the fabric, its wings dragging, eyes luminous with grief and recognition. It pressed its small head against Osric's face, keening softly.

Osric exhaled, a sound caught between pain and relief. "You are safe at last, Little One."

Elara did her best to smile. He looked nothing like his twin sister, Kaura. He was small, undernourished, abused. She reached out her fingers toward the wyrmling. It immediately hid behind Osric's neck, shivers running through his tiny body.

"How could anyone abuse such a beautiful creature?" she whispered.

Elara looked to the west, to where Malachar and his Drake had fallen. Something felt wrong. The air shimmered, not with warmth, but with a cold ripple that slid through her bones.

Kaerath's one uninjured eye snapped open, pupils narrowing to slits. The wyrmling hissed.

Then Elara heard it; the faintest whisper riding the wind. A voice, low and broken, carried from deep within the chasm.

"Did you think the shadow dies with the dawn?"

Her blood ran cold. Somewhere far below, a black mist stirred anew, curling upward like smoke from a reborn fire.

She clutched Osric's hand, fear clawing its way up her spine. "He's still alive."

Osric's eyes opened fully, their pale gray turning hard as tempered steel. "Then it isn't over."

The earth trembled beneath them. Pebbles rolled toward the edge of the chasm as the black mist thickened, spreading like spilled ink across the scorched ground.

Kaerath struggled to rise, his claws tearing deep grooves in the stone. His great chest heaved, his breath labored but defiant.

A column of fire and shadow erupted skyward. It coalesced into a towering figure, arms spread wide and dripping darkness.

Malachar.

Half his armor was molten; the other half fused to his flesh. His eyes burned white-hot now, no longer human, no longer *alive*. Shadowfire poured from the cracks in his skin, and his voice boomed like the breaking of the world.

"You cannot kill what was forged in night!"

Kaerath roared, his light flickering defiantly. But he was too weak to stand against what rose before them.

Elara moved instinctively, stepping in front of Osric. "Stay down," she said, her tone leaving no room for argument.

Osric tried to push himself up, blood streaking his lips. "Elara, don't. I will finish this."

Malachar lifted his hand. The ground exploded, sending Kaerath sprawling and Elara tumbling back. The wyrmling shrieked and darted in front of Osric, curling around his hand to shield him.

Malachar advanced, the ground freezing beneath each step, his voice dripping venom. "Osric, the great Keeper, the Wanderer. Solarus blessed you with immortality. You could have ruled beside me. Together, we could have reshaped this world. But you chose the light."

Osric gritted his teeth, forcing himself into a half-upright position despite the agony burning through his side. "I will always choose *life*." He reached into his waistband and withdrew his gun. In vain, he tried to raise it and end the life of his son. But his hand shook involuntarily. The gun fell to the earth, his strength gone.

Malachar smiled and raised his arm. Darkness gathered in his palm, a spear of living shadow pulsing with flame shot forward. "You end now."

Osric's eyes met his. The blue eyes he had witnessed in his son contained nothing but darkness and hunger. Cold, endless hunger.

Would it make a difference if you knew I was your father?

Solarus' warning echoed through him: *Show mercy when none is deserved. Mercy is the only blade that can cut the cycle clean.*

But this, this was more than mercy. This was placing his throat into the jaws of the Void and hoping it remembered how to love.

Osric wanted to say it, to shout it to the heavens, shout so loud even the sleeping Elders would hear. He ached to give Malachar what he himself had never had. A father's truth. A father's love. Even if it was too late. Even if it changed nothing.

If he didn't speak the truth now, Malachar would die not knowing…, and Osric would have failed him *twice*: once as a father, and once as a man who forced his dying son to carry guilt he could not undo.

No. Not like this.

With the last thread of his strength, Osric lifted his head. Not to plead, not to explain, but to meet the darkness with the only weapon he had left.

Mercy.

His voice broke, barely more than breath. "I forgive you."

Malachar staggered back a single step, more from instinct than weakness. His spine locked. His jaw clenched.

"I have **nothing** to be forgiven for!"

The words tore from his lips. The Void surged in answer, black fire rippling along his veins, screaming for blood, for certainty, for annihilation. Forgiveness had no place here. It had no teeth. No dominion. No power.

The moment lingered.

Something inside Malachar hesitated. Not fear. Not doubt. Something far more dangerous.

Memory.

Osric did not lower his gaze. "I know," he said softly. "That is what makes it unforgivable."

The Void shrieked, coiling tighter around Malachar's heart. It did not feed on absolution. It could not use it. Forgiveness slid through its grasp like light through smoke.

Malachar's hands shook with something he had not felt since before the dark took him.

"You speak like you **know** me," he growled. "Like you were there."

Osric took a step forward. His legs trembled. If he faltered now, there would be no second reckoning, no endless tomorrow in which to try again.

"Because I was," he said.

The Void recoiled as Osric's voice fractured, not in weakness, but in truth.

"Lucan," he whispered. "That was your name."

The name struck deep, slipping past the Void's grip. Malachar froze. His breath caught. Blue flickered in his eyes, thin and fragile as a dying star.

"What... did you say?"

Osric swallowed. The confession burned, heavy with lifetimes of silence and a future he would never see.

"You are my son."

Silence fell; absolute and terrible. Malachar's face softened. The darkness in his eyes receded, and beneath it, blue returned, faint at first, then clear.

For one unbearable instant, Malachar *saw it*; his features mirrored in Osric's face.

The ache that had trailed him since childhood eased, then shifted, settling into a quiet, undeniable clarity. Fragments of memory, once jagged and misplaced, began to find their place, aligning with a truth he could no longer turn away from.

"No," Malachar whispered. "No… you're lying."

"You are my son, Lucan," Osric said, his voice breaking. "I could not care for you, so I gave you to a loving family. I thought my absence would spare you. I thought silence would protect you." His breath shuddered. "It only gave evil a place to grow."

The Void screamed in panic, thrashing through Malachar's veins, desperate to crush the truth before it could take root.

Malachar dropped to one knee, torn between revelation and annihilation.

"I do not ask for forgiveness," Osric said. "I only wanted you to know, before it ends, that you were never unwanted. Your mother and I loved you."

The Void rippled violently, sensing the fracture, hissing through Malachar's blood like static. It pressed against his spine, urging him forward, urging him to kill the thing that dared see him.

Malachar's hands curled into fists.

"Stop looking at me like that."

"Like what?" Osric asked gently. "Like you **matter**. Like you were not forged only for destruction. For becoming what you were **forced** to be."

Malachar reeled inward from the thought and roared to bury it beneath fury. The spear of light in his hand dimmed.

The Void screamed.

Osric saw his son's eyes change back to a being possessed by the Void. "I don't believe your lies." A torrent of rage erupted from Malachar's throat. "Goodbye, old man."

Fire flared, but it was Malachar's that faltered and died. He turned toward Kaerath, expecting the surge to be his, yet the new flame did not come from the dragon. Nor did it come from the sky.

It came from *her.*

Elara stepped between them, the ground cracking beneath her feet. Her eyes blazed amber, and from her body and hands burst the unmistakable fury of dragonfire, white-hot at its core, edged in crimson and gold. The air warped around her, heat waves rippling outward.

Malachar stopped, the spear of darkness dead in his hand. "I didn't imagine it the day you fell. You can wield dragonfire. But how? Law decrees no human may hold the flame of dragons."

Her gaze did not waver. "Solarus spoke true when he said the fire can pass to one who bears a dragon's heart. But not to a man like you. You've blackened yours, hollowed it with cruelty and hunger until there is nothing left for the flame to claim. You killed Ophira, along with thousands who stood in your path. You tried to murder Osric, your own father. You tortured an innocent wyrmling to bend it to your will. Your desire for the flame will always be denied."

She stepped closer, each pace leaving scorched prints in the soil. The fire within her built, a roaring inferno that danced along her arms, weaving up her throat.

Malachar's sneer twisted. "Then burn."

He unleashed a torrent of black fire, the ground splitting beneath its path. Elara met it head-on, her own dragonfire exploding outward, devouring his shadowflame. The two forces collided, sending shockwaves through the valley, lighting the sky in a blinding inferno.

Osric shielded his eyes, the heat searing even from where he stood. "Elara!"

But she didn't hear him. The fury had taken her. And it was unstoppable. The fire within her howled with the voices of every dragon lost to Malachar's corruption. It wasn't light she wielded. It was vengeance.

Her flames surged higher, engulfing Malachar. His scream split the heavens. The darkness melted from his flesh, his form crumbling as the fire tore through him, consuming everything it touched.

"You can't destroy me!" he shrieked, his body breaking apart. "I am the…"

Elara raised both hands, her voice a thunderous roar. "Then let the dragons reclaim you!"

The final blast erupted, a storm of pure dragonfire that blotted out the sky. It struck like the judgment of the heavens, a pillar of searing gold that swallowed the darkness whole. The ground split. Air turned to flame. Malachar's form shattered, fragments of his being scattering like shards of obsidian into the inferno. His final scream dissolved into a thousand whispers, each one fading until only silence remained.

The black mist evaporated, curling away into nothing. Drifting embers fell softly through the air.

Elara stood in the center of the devastation, her chest heaving, hair haloed in flame, eyes two molten suns. The dragonfire had not dimmed; it raged still, coiling around her like a living aura, bending the air. She turned slowly toward Osric.

"Elara," he shouted, reaching for her. "It's over. He's gone. You can stop now."

But she didn't hear him.

Osric saw that the look in her eyes was not her own. It belonged to the dragons. Ancient. Unyielding. Consuming.

Then a voice came from behind. Calm. Grounded.

"Elara."

Vaelor stepped forward through the haze, his armor cracked, his face streaked with soot and blood. His dragon stood behind him, low and watchful. As he moved closer, the flames around Elara surged in warning, flaring higher, testing him.

"Stay back!" Osric cried, but Vaelor didn't stop.

"She'll destroy herself," Vaelor said quietly, eyes locked on her. "The fire's taken control. It doesn't know where to end, and she doesn't know how to stop it this time. It is too powerful, the heart of all the Elders into one flame."

He took another step. The heat rippled against him, scorching the ground at his boots, but he kept moving, his hand outstretched, steady.

"Elara," he said again, softer now. "It's me."

Her head turned toward him, the flames twisting violently. "Vaelor…?" Her voice cracked, distorted by the roar inside her. "It hurts…"

"I know." His voice was steady, calm, the tone of command she trusted, threaded with love and fear. "Let me in."

The fire roared, a dragon's bellow bursting from her chest. The air rippled, pushing him back a step, but he didn't falter. His hands glowed faintly, a cool blue light spilling from his palms. The mark of Solarus' gift, the power to balance flame with stillness.

He reached her, pressing both hands to either side of her face. The heat was everywhere, but he held on. "Come back to me," he whispered.

The fire resisted. It screamed through her, lashing outward in violent bursts that lit the horizon. Vaelor stood firm, his own power weaving through hers; light and fire, two halves of the same essence. Slowly, her flames wavered, their color softening from white-hot to gold, then to amber.

Elara gasped, clutching his wrists. "I can't, Vaelor. I can't stop it."

"Yes, you can." He pressed his forehead to hers. "Because it's yours. You're not the fire. You're the heart that holds it."

The dragonfire let out one final surge before collapsing inward, retreating beneath her skin. The glow faded from her eyes, leaving behind the soft blue he knew so well. Her knees gave out, and he caught her, holding her as smoke curled gently around them.

Her breath shuddered. "I almost lost myself."

Vaelor brushed her hair from her face. "You didn't," he said softly. "You simply forgot you weren't alone."

Elara leaned into Vaelor's chest, the faint shimmer of flame still flickering beneath her skin, subdued but alive. "It's still here," she murmured. "Sleeping."

Vaelor nodded, his hand wrapped around hers. "Then we'll guard it together until the day it's needed again."

The dawn broke fully then. For the first time in five centuries, the valley knew peace.

Chapter 21

The world was quiet. As Elara awoke, a warm breeze brushed across her face, carrying the scent of damp earth and crushed grass. The last embers of dawn had cooled to the soft gold of afternoon. For the first time in what felt like ages, there was no sound of battle, no screaming wind, no thunder of dragons, no person or beast trying to end their lives. Only the whisper of the stream and the steady rhythm of her own breathing reached her ears.

She blinked slowly. Her vision cleared, and she found herself lying on the familiar bear skin near a quiet stream's edge. Kaerath slept a few yards away, his body half-submerged in the shallows, smoke still curling from the gashes in his scales. The new wyrmling nestled against his side, his tiny chest rising and falling in rhythm with the great dragon's breath. Tirra and Kaura curled beside him. Behind them slept Solyndra and Thymorion.

Her gaze shifted and found Vaelor sitting beside her.

He was pale, his face drawn with exhaustion. The edges of his clothing were seared and covered with soot. His eyes, when he lifted them to meet hers, were alive and filled with something deeper than relief.

"You're awake," he said softly.

She swallowed, her throat dry. "How long?"

"Since dawn yesterday. You've been out a full day."

Elara tried to sit up, but her surroundings blurred and a wave of nausea engulfed her. Vaelor reached out to steady her. Warmth from his palm flowed into her; not the heat of skin, but something *inside* him, pulsing faintly, like an echo. Yet, he could not look directly into her eyes.

"Vaelor, how did you stop my flame?" Her brother hesitated, his eyes flicking to the ground. "What did you do?"

Vaelor closed his eyes and took a deep breath. He held it, then slowly let it out. Keeping his eyes averted, he said, "When your fire consumed you, I used my gift, the balance the Elders gave me at birth. But it wasn't enough to draw it out. It needed something to hold onto."

Her pulse quickened. "You didn't."

He looked up, his eyes shining with quiet resolve. "I couldn't take it from you, Elara. No mortal can steal dragonfire. But I could give it another anchor. My own life so it wouldn't consume yours."

She stared at him, her lips parting in disbelief. "It's inside you?"

"Not actually inside," he said. "It's anchored to both of us. One flame, two hearts. When it stirs in you, I feel it. When I steady it, it quiets in you." He smiled faintly. "The fire is alive, Elara. And now, so long as I live, it will never consume you again."

She reached for his hand. The moment her skin touched his, warmth rippled through them both, a rush of power so intimate and ancient that it stole her breath. For an instant, she could see what he felt: the memory of fire coursing through both their veins, two souls fused by something older than magic.

Tears filled her eyes. "You risked your life, your soul, for me. You know dragonfire cannot live in a mortal indefinitely. What will happen to you?""

Vaelor brushed a strand of hair from her face, his thumb grazing her cheek. "I might live a few years less. What does it matter? Solarus already blessed me with new life, gave me years I shouldn't have had. Besides, the world still needs your dragonfire. I couldn't let you die."

A silence fell between them. Elara leaned forward until her forehead rested against Vaelor's.

"Vaelor?" Her voice cracked, barely a whisper. "Osric, did he...?"

For a long moment, Vaelor said nothing. The silence stretched, heavy as the wind blew between them. Tears welled in his eyes. "He lives. But he's badly injured. Burns cover his arms and part of his face. His left arm is broken in two places, as are his right two ribs. His right leg is pretty messed up also. Plus, he's lost a lot of blood. But with rest, time, and a good nurse to care for him, he has a chance of surviving. But he will carry the scars of the battle for a lifetime."

Vaelor paused, his mouth twitching.

"What aren't you telling me?"

"With so much damage on the outside, he had to sustain injury to his lungs and internal organs. We can't heal those. Only he can."

"Can't we take him to a nearby village, somewhere where we can get him some better care than us?"

"The nearest village is several days' flight from here. He'd never make it. Besides, Kaerath is gravely injured as well. He isn't strong enough to make the journey."

Elara narrowed her eyes against the brightness, scanning the quiet field. "Where is he?"

"Asleep, beneath the hemlock," Vaelor said softly, pointing to the tree.

Her brow furrowed. "Why isn't he lying beside me on the hide?"

Vaelor's lips curved in a faint, knowing smile. "He feared his pain might disturb your rest. He asked to be placed beneath the tree."

She forced herself upright, the world tipping sharply around her again. Determined to remain vertical, her hand shot out and gripped her brother's arm for balance. "Oh, this will not do. I cannot ensure he lives if I am not near him. Help me to the tree. Bring the bearskin."

Vaelor slung the heavy pelt over his shoulder and steadied her as they crossed the grass. His arm curved protectively around her as though afraid she might fall apart if he didn't hold her together.

When they reached the hemlock, Elara stopped. She gasped in horror.

Beneath the sweeping boughs lay Osric's still body. Much of it was wrapped in strips of cloth stained dark with blood. What flesh did show was raw and blistered, glistening with the weeping burn of healing. The air around him smelled faintly of smoke and iron…and crisped flesh.

"He's so badly burned," she whispered, her voice trembling, tears filling her eyes. "I'm not sure his mercy was worth this."

"To him it was," Vaelor murmured, lowering the fur and spreading it beside Osric's still form. "I gave him something for the pain. He'll sleep until evening, perhaps longer. We'll need to keep asleep for several days. It's been centuries since he's felt the true agony of mortal flesh."

Elara knelt beside the scarred man, her gaze tracing the rough line of his jaw, the fragile rise and fall of his chest. "True. He's not used to being mortal again. Although he is familiar with pain, he is accustomed to his body healing within two or three days. With mortality comes the realization that the healing will take weeks, maybe even months. That is, if he even survives."

*****

Osric slowly opened his eyes. They burned like the gates of hell. He tried focusing his vision, but everything was a blur. Except for two large golden eyes staring into his, belonging to something sitting on his chest.

"Well, hello there Little One. I am glad to see you made it and are well."

"He wanted to thank you for saving him from the Dark Commander," came Kaerath's voice inside his mind. "He said without your help he never would have been reunited with his twin sister and would have been forced to do the Void's bidding."

Kaura climbed up beside her brother, her claws pricking Osric's tender skin. He winced in pain.

"No sitting on Osric's chest until he gets better," Elara said, lifting the two dragonets down and placing them on the bear skin. "That goes for you too, Tirra." She grabbed the third wyrmling as she tried to scamper up. "You can lay beside him, but no walking on any part of his body. Do you understand?"

Tirra chirped as the others looked at her with blank stares. "I mean it." They snuggled beneath the blanket, curling up close, but careful not to touch his skin.

"Those little claws do hurt," Osric grumbled. He gazed into Elara's eyes. "I didn't think I'd see you again."

"I feared the same." She carefully lifted his bandaged hand in hers. "How are you doing? How's the pain?"

"Pretty bad. I forgot what real pain feels like. This shit doesn't stop!"

"Worse than when I stabbed you?"

"On a scale of one to ten, where your knife wound was a seven, I'd say it's about a twenty."

"Worse than when I burned you in the cave?"

"Lots worse." Osric tried to smile, but stopped as pain filled his body.

"Here, drink this," Vaelor said as he held Osric's pain medication to his lips "It will help some.".

"How long have I been out?"

"A little over three days," Vaelor said.

"No wonder I'm so hungry. Another sensation my body needs to get used to again: being hungry."

"I'll get you some stew. After you're done eating, I want you to take more medication and sleep. Sleep is your friend right now. It will help your body mend."

Vaelor walked over to where a pot sat beside a small fire. He scooped up a small bowl.

"How's Kaerath doing?" Osric asked Elara as he waited for Vaelor to return. "That Drake did some damage to his wings and chest. And he landed pretty hard on that ledge."

"He's recuperating like you," Elara said. "His injuries are serious, but nothing a dragon can't heal from."

"And Malachar?"

"He will never hurt anyone again."

"Then I didn't imagine it. You burned him with your flame."

Elara hung her head, avoiding Osric's eyes. She said not a word.

"Elara, tell me the truth. Did you destroy him with your dragonfire?"

"Yes," she screamed, jumping to her feet, startling the three dragonets. "He was going to kill you. I know he was your son, but I couldn't allow that. I'm sorry."

"But Solarus said to show him mercy. You reminded me of that when I confronted him, my sword drawn. Because of your words, I let my sword fall and spared his life."

"Solarus said for you to show him mercy, not me. I showed him what the Elders blessed me with. Their fire."

"How…how did you stop it?"

"Vaelor intervened," she said, reining in her anger. "It got too strong, too hot. I forgot all our training to allow the dragonfire to pass through me into Malachar. I couldn't control it. Vaelor couldn't either. So, he became a second anchor. He grounded it, allowing it to pass through both of us."

"I don't understand."

"He divided it and took one-half into himself. His cold white flame was able to control what raged inside him. Since our flames are connected, his anchoring also anchored my flame."

"But what happened to the dragonfire after it consumed Malachar? Did it remain inside you?"

"I don't know." She lowered her gaze to her hands. There was no glow, no trace of fire, only the plain, mortal color of skin. "I don't feel it raging beneath my skin as before. It's like it's there, but not completely. One moment it was consuming me, out of control. Then Vaelor anchored it and it…it…vanished."

Osric looked over at the sleeping Kaerath. "Then it must have gone back home, into a dragon where it can live without consequences."

"Does that mean that we don't have to worry about it returning?"

"I do not know. I guess time will show us."

Elara paused, biting her lip, her eyes tearing. She said nothing and locked her eyes on the ground.

"Are you okay?"

"Can you forgive me?"

"For what?"

"For ending Malachar's life."

"There is nothing to forgive. As you said, you ended Malachar's life. Not Lucan's. The boy who was my son died centuries ago."

"Here you go," Vaelor said, returning and handing Elara the bowl of stew. He saw the look on both of their faces. "You two look intense. Everything okay?"

"Everything is fine," Osric said, forcing a smile.

"Then perhaps Elara will be kind enough to feed you since your hands are bandaged."

"Thank you, Vaelor," Osric said.

"For what?"

"For saving Elara when I couldn't."

"I think it was you who saved her. And me. If you had not eliminated Malachar's Drake, she never could have defeated him." Vaelor fetched the saddlebag with the bandages and ointments. "While she feeds you, I'll change your bandages and apply new ointment."

"Open wide," Elara said as she filled the spoon's bowl with stew.

Osric opened. He chewed the small portions of meat and vegetables, allowing them to slide down his throat with the broth. Moving his mouth stung, the burnt skin pulling tightly. His eyes watched as Vaelor unwrapped the cloth around his right hand.

"Can you move your fingers at all?" Vaelor asked as the bandages fell.

Osric grimaced as he flexed his fingers. "They're pretty sore, but I can move them some."

"It's going to be a while before you can hold any type of weapon."

Osric gave a faint, bitter smile. "A fitting punishment," he murmured, eyes on his hand. "Once I held the flame of creation. Now I can't even hold a spoon."

Elara paused, spoon hovering near his lips. For a heartbeat, neither moved. Then she whispered, "You're still here. That's what matters."

Osric met her gaze, the faint reflection of firelight glimmering in his gray eyes. "For now," he said softly, and opened his mouth for the next spoonful.

Osric heard a soft, trilling chirp. He glanced down and found Tirra perched beside Vaelor, her luminous eyes fixed on his seared hand. Curious and intent, she crept closer, claws clicking softly against the stone.

The scent drew her; the sharp tang of burned flesh mixed with the bittersweet musk of healing salve. She sniffed once, then snorted, the acrid odor wrinkling her tiny snout. With a faint growl of displeasure, she leaned forward and parted her jaws.

A thin breath escaped her. Not flame, but warmth, ancient and pure. It drifted across his palm like sunlight breaking through clouds. The Keeper's mark beneath his skin flared, searing white-gold, illuminating the hollows of his hand.

Osric dragged in a breath. The pain vanished, replaced by a tingling heat that pulsed through his veins. Before their eyes, the raw red of his burns softened, fading to a tender pink. The torn edges knit themselves together, smooth and whole once more.

Tirra chirped again, pleased with her work, and nestled close to his knee, her eyes fluttering closed.

"She's trying to heal you," Elara said, watching in awe.

"Like Kaura did when you were hurt, and she was still inside her egg. I kept her wrapped in your blanket. She healed your injuries and protected your heart."

"Do all dragons have the capability to heal?" Vaelor asked.

"To some extent, although some, like Kaura, have a greater capacity. And from what Tirra showed us, so does she."

Elara looked over to Kaerath lying beside the stream. "What about Kaerath, Solyndra, and Thymorion? Could they combine their breaths and heal your injuries?"

"No." Osric leaned his head back, exhausted from the sparse activity of sitting up and eating. "Tirra was able to heal a small part of me because on a minor scale, we have bonded. I now wear a second Keeper's insignia, thanks to her. Solyndra and Thymorion have no bonding with me, so their healing would be minimal. But Kaerath? I don't know. Before Solarus broke our connection centuries ago, he could have cured me of almost anything. While Solarus' curse kept him entombed, he probably maintained some potential. But now that only a meager scar remains of my Keeper's connection to Kaerath, I doubt there is little he can do."

"But it could work?" Elara asked.

"Possibly."

"Then let's test it," came Kaerath's voice inside Osric's mind.

The giant Drake rolled over, stretched, and rose. He walked over to where Osric sat. Vaelor held out Osric's other burnt hand, the one with the fading scar of his bondage to the dragon. Softly, Kaerath blew a breath over the tender flesh. Like with Tirra's tiny breath, the red angry flesh diminished to a soft pink with splashes of beige skin.

"It worked," Elara whispered, too afraid to say it aloud in case it wasn't real. She looked up into the behemoth's eyes.

"But he's still weak," Osric said. "He needs to heal more before attempting to heal my body. Healing me could weaken him."

"I have healed sufficiently, Osric of Karellin," came Kaerath's voice. "Why live another hour in such pain?"

"Because pain is my penance," Osric said silently. "Malachar did not die in mercy, but vengeance."

"No, not vengeance. Protection. He had every intention of killing you … and Elara. He would have turned the wyrmling into something evil. She stepped in and allowed the fire of dragons to pronounce judgment on him. It was as it had to be."

"Kaerath is willing to try," Osric said. "But I have spent my strength and need more rest. Besides, the act of healing works best at sunrise when Solarus' light rejuvenates the world anew. Let's try it then."

Before anyone could answer, a soft snore rose from his parched throat, exhaustion once more claiming his body.

The next morning, Osric rose. Elara and Vaelor undressed him and unwound all his bandages. Tears slipped from Elara's eyes as she saw the condition of Osric's injuries and burnt flesh.

"Take me down to the stream," Osric said. "I need to dip my body into the water first to wash off some of the dead flesh. Then Kaerath can heal me."

With an arm looped around his waist, Elara and Vaelor guided Osric to the stream. The walk *should* have been short. But every step tore a sound from deep within him. His legs trembled beneath the weight of his own body, sweat beading across his brow despite the cool air.

"I can't," Osric moaned, collapsing onto his knees. "Too weak. Too much pain."

Vaelor motioned Thymorion beside the Keeper. "Outstretch your wing so we can place the Keeper upon it. Then, gently carry him to the stream's edge."

Thymorion opened his mighty wing. Holing it alongside Osric, Vaelor and Elara gently laid him down. Lifting it slightly so the Keeper would not slide off, the dragon walked to the flowing waters. Once there, he again lowered his wing and let him slide onto the soft grass at the stream's edge.

Biting his lip, he lowered one foot in. Pain surged upward, sharp as shattered glass. The cold bit through skin and sinew, wrapping around bone. His face twisted; his teeth clenched so hard his jaw ached. A muffled sound slipped from him, half growl, half moan.

Fire would have been kinder.

He forced the other foot in. The shock struck like lightning. His body convulsed, a cry tearing from his throat before he could stop it, a sound wild and raw, not of this world.

"Let's wait a few days to do this," Elara said, tears again cascading down her cheeks.

"No," Osric whispered. "We do it now."

Elara and Vaelor eased Osric into the water. The air filled with his scream as the cold invaded every wound, every nerve. It was unbearable, and yet he clung to it, forcing himself not to pull away.

If I can endure this, then I am still human.

"I'm sorry," Elara said, her words almost lost on the breeze.

Osric did not answer. He only nodded. His breath came in short, desperate bursts, but behind his pain, a flicker of resolve burned. This agony, this proof of flesh, was the price of mercy. And he would pay it.

Vaelor's tears broke free when they eased the Keeper onto his back, the stream closing around him until only his face remained above the water. The sound that tore from Osric's throat this time was the worst. It was raw, something nightmares carried.

His chest heaved; breath came in ragged gasps. Then, drawing one final lungful of air, he surrendered and sank beneath the surface.

For several heartbeats, the world went still. Beneath the water, the pain sharpened to a thousand burning needles. Then it dulled, then vanished. The icy current numbed everything, claiming his agony, silencing the fire that had devoured his flesh. In the cold's merciless embrace, he found something close to peace.

When he emerged, Elara and Vaelor grasped his arms and lifted him upright. The color had drained from his skin, leaving it pale as river stone. Thymorion dipped his wing into the stream and scooped Osric out, carrying him to a grassy area.

Vaelor guided his body down the dragon's wing onto an earthy mound. Osric's teeth chattered, his shoulders quivered. The faint warmth of the rising sun brushed his face, but it barely touched him; he was all shivers and fogged breath, a fragile silhouette of the Keeper he once was.

From the shadows beneath the hemlock, Kaerath moved. The earth trembled softly under the weight of the dragon's approach. Steam curled from his nostrils; his eyes, vast and ageless, glowed with quiet sorrow.

The great Drake lowered his head and drew in a deep, deliberate breath. When he exhaled, it was not fire he released, but warmth, a living wind that shimmered with golden light. It washed over Osric's body like sunlight.

Under that breath, flesh renewed. The angry burns softened, dark red blisters fading to tender pink skin. Oozing wounds sealed and smoothed, leaving only faint traces where agony had once ruled. Beneath the skin, the slow grind of bone mending could be heard, a sound both unsettling and divine.

Osric's eyes opened. He rose slowly, his movements sure and steady. The Keeper's faded scar within his palm pulsed with brilliant life again. For the first time since the battle, his voice was steady. "Kaerath," he whispered, "your fire remembers me still."

Tirra scampered forward, blowing her breath across Osric's little toe on his left foot. A small cut across the toe had been missed by Kaerath's great breath, and Tirra quickly corrected the omission. Osric bent down and picked up the tiny wyrmling. "Thank you, Little Lady."

"How do you feel?" Vaelor asked, wrapping a blanket around Osric's body.

"Still weak, but the pain is gone." He looked up at the Drake. "Let's get me dressed before I catch a cold. And then I'd like a big slab of mutton, that is, if the dragons haven't eaten all the sheep."

*****

The sky above Solarus' mountain was alive with drifting embers, remnants of ancient flame caught in the wind like fireflies. Osric climbed the final ridge alone, his body aching with every step. The air grew thinner as he neared the summit, colder, touched by that strange stillness that always accompanied the presence of an Elder.

At the mountain's peak, the world opened wide. The great stone spire that crowned Solarus' domain pulsed faintly with inner light. When Osric stepped into the glow, the resonant voice of the Elder filled the space around him.

"You return, Keeper."

Solarus' vast form coalesced from the mountain's light, his wings folded, eyes burning with ancient warmth and sorrow.

Osric bowed his head and bent his knee. "I needed to speak with you."

"Then speak."

Osric drew a slow breath, his voice quiet but firm. "I know what you took from me, the fire that kept me beyond time. I don't regret it. I never wanted immortality." He looked down at his hands; the lines were deeper now, his skin rougher, mortal once more. "But I can feel it… my body weakening. Each day, I lose a little more. I've found a life again, Solarus. With Elara. She's my light, my home. I'd like…" His voice faltered, then steadied. "I'd like enough time to live it. To raise children. To grow old with her. Forty or fifty years is all that I ask."

For a long while, Solarus said nothing. Finally, he spoke, his voice deep and kind. "You ask not for eternity, but for meaning within it. That is rare among those who have tasted timelessness."

Osric met his gaze. "Death isn't what I fear. Leaving her is."

Solarus' eyes softened. "You've grasped something few ever comprehend: love's flame burns hotter than ours, possessing greater peril."

He lowered his massive head until his breath warmed the ground where Osric stood. "As you wish. I cannot restore what was taken, nor return you to the eternity you once carried beside your dragon. But when a Keeper's bond is broken and reborn, the mortal heart follows an ancient measure. Forty years. That is the span granted to those who walk between flame and flesh."

"It is not a mercy I invented. It is the law set when the first Keeper survived the loss of his dragon. The world gives forty years to rebuild what was broken… or to lay it to rest. I can grant you that measure, Osric. Perhaps a few more. Enough to share the life you still dream of."

Osric exhaled, relief flooding him. "Thank you."

Solarus' voice deepened again. "You kneel before answers you do not yet have the courage to ask. Speak, I am listening."

Osric nodded. "Elara and Vaelor. The dragonfire now burns in them both. It's bound their lives together. Is there any way to remove it before it consumes them?"

Solarus' eyes dimmed with thought, and the mountain seemed to sigh. "No. The fire cannot be taken. It can only be balanced. Once it enters mortal flesh, it will burn their bodies from within. If torn away, it would kill them both. But…"

He leaned closer, light shimmering from his scales. "You know that no mortal can contain full dragonfire for long. When Vaelor joined with her and gave the fire another anchoring point, it allowed it to flow through them both and enter Kaerath. There it sleeps until needed again."

"Needed again?"

"Elara has not completely fulfilled her destiny yet. The day will come when she must take back the dragonfire. But as her heart will give it warmth, his will give it restraint. Alone, either would burn or fade. But together, they will endure. It is the nature of balance."

Osric lowered his head. "Then it's enough. I cannot deny Elara her destiny."

Solarus studied him for a long, silent moment. "You have changed, Keeper. Once, you sought redemption through duty. Now, you seek it through love. That is the greater courage."

"I'm not sure I'd call it courage," Osric said with a faint smile. "I think I've finally learned what matters."

The Elder's eyes brightened, a deep rumble of approval rolling through the mountain. "Then take your borrowed years, Keeper of the Dragons, and make them worthy. When your time comes, the light will remember."

A warmth spread through Osric's chest, a pulse of golden energy, steady and strong. The ache in his body eased; his breath deepened, freer, stronger. He felt… whole again. Not immortal, but alive.

He stood and bowed deeply. "I'll spend them well."

When he turned to leave, Solarus' voice echoed one last time through the mist.

"Guard the fire, Keeper. For though the shadow is gone, its echo lingers. And every fire, even love, must be watched lest it consume what it was meant to warm."

Osric paused, gazing out across the vast expanse below. "Then I'll keep watch," he said softly. "For all of us."

*****

The sun rose across the valley when Osric descended from Solarus' mountain. His light clung to him faintly. The climb had drained him, but the pulse in his chest reminded him that Solarus had kept his word.

Forty years. Perhaps a little more. Enough to build something real.

Osric sat on a nearby stone, his gaze lingering on Elara and Vaelor as they slept. Vaelor stirred first. He blinked, disoriented, then rose to a sitting position, brushing ash and dew from his clothing. The faint lines of fatigue were already returning to his face, though he tried to hide them.

"You found him," Vaelor said quietly, not as a question.

Osric nodded. "I did."

"And?"

Osric's eyes moved to Elara, still sleeping, her features soft in the early light. "Solarus granted me forty years. It is long enough to live, but not long enough to grow careless."

Elara stirred, her eyes fluttering open. When she saw him standing there, she smiled.

*****

Solarus was true to his word. Osric lived another forty-one years, bringing his total age to 583.

The valley, once blackened by war and flame, became a place of green rebirth. Wildflowers grew where ash once lay, and the rivers ran clear, singing softly through the meadows that stretched below Solarus' mountain. It was a land of peace, fragile but real.

In that haven, Osric and Elara built a life. The Brotherhood of Dragon Keepers was rekindled. And once more, dragons flew the skies. And the dragonfire that slept inside Kaerath waited until needed again.

The war is over.

The cost has only begun.

Malachar is dead. Osric lives, though barely. Elara's fire no longer burns in her veins, it rests within Kaerath, contained… for now. And against all odds, six dragons still walk the world.

But death was never the end for Malachar.

What burned on the surface was only flesh. His essence bled into the world itself, seeping through fissures in the earth, sinking into trenches older than memory, coiling through volcanic chambers and the unseen veins of shadow beneath every living thing. Silent. Waiting.

Now those scattered fragments are awakening… and drawing together.

He is not returning as he was. He is becoming something far worse.

As the ancient Pillars of Balance begin to fail, something even more dangerous is set in motion. The Elder Wyrms, bound to the Pillars and to one another, are waking out of sequence, torn from their slumber at the wrong time, in the wrong order. Their unity fractures before it can form, their combined power slipping through the world's grasp.

The one force capable of restoring balance… cannot assemble.

And the only one who might stand in their place is no longer whole.

To save the world, Elara must reclaim the dragonfire she surrendered, take it back from Kaerath, and wield it once more. But the flame was never meant to be divided… and taking it again may destroy her before she can use it.

A race ignites. Osric and Elara must reach the Pillars before Malachar's essence gathers enough strength to corrupt them, to invert their purpose, and claim Dominion not just over dragons… but over the world itself.

Because if the Pillars fall, nothing will remain untouched. Not sky. Not sea. Not soul.

And this time, there will be no second chance.

Not the cartoon versions. Not the hollow CGI beasts. ***Ember and Ash Magazine*** returns dragons to their rightful place; as ancient forces of power, mystery, and meaning. This is a publication for readers who know dragons are more than creatures of fantasy. They are symbols woven into the oldest stories humanity has ever told.

Each issue delves into dragon lore, mythic symbolism, and codex-style entries that feel pulled from forgotten libraries. Original illustrations and carefully curated quotes create an immersive reading experience. One meant to be savored, not skimmed. This is slow, intentional storytelling for readers who value depth and atmosphere.

Ember and Ash is designed for fantasy lovers, writers, artists, and collectors who crave something richer than surface-level fantasy content. It speaks to those who sense that dragons represent something vast and eternal, guardians of memory, fire, and fate.

This is not a disposable magazine. It is a keepsake. A volume to return to, to display, and to reread. If you're ready to rediscover dragons as they were meant to be known, step into the fire and remember the myth.

Get the first issue at the link below. The magazine is pay-what-you-want, even $0.00. It is my gift to you for loving dragons as much as I do.

Issue #1 https://mimmiverse.gumroad.com/l/ucxeuh

Issue #2 https://mimmiverse.gumroad.com/l/sdsta

ABOUT THE AUTHOR

PR Garcia, the youngest of three children, grew up in rural Michigan, where her love affair with science fiction began on a childhood movie outing. The moment she heard Patricia Neal utter *"Klaatu barada nikto"* to the robot Gort in *The Day the Earth Stood Still,* she was captivated. Those words sparked countless adventures in the fields behind her home, where she and her dog battled imaginary aliens and explored distant worlds. When *Star Trek* premiered during her high school years in the late 1960s, it deepened her fascination with the cosmos—so much so that she famously skipped Friday night football games to catch each week's episode, a choice her friends still tease her about.

Ms. Garcia's creative pursuits took an unexpected turn in her thirties when she became an award-winning basket weaver, a craft she practiced for three decades. After retiring from a thirty-year career, she relocated to San Diego, California, where she spent five years as a volunteer guide on whale-watching boats, sharing her knowledge of gray whales and Pacific marine life with visitors from around the globe.

At sixty-two, Ms. Garcia embarked on her most ambitious project yet: the Europa Saga, a ten-part science fiction series that reimagines the legend of Atlantis across 6,000 years and three generations. This epic tale of intrigue, suspense, and mystery launched her into bestselling author status. Her deep concern for environmental issues—global warming, deforestation, pollution, species extinction, and Earth's fragility—permeates her later works, including books seven through nine of the Europa Saga and *Extinction 2038*. The Guardians of Earth series followed, with three novels published between 2021 and 2024.

In 2024, Garcia combined her passion for fairies and healing crystals in *The Magical Fairy Guide to Healing Crystals*, a comprehensive guide for novices and enthusiasts alike. Most of her novels are available through Kindle Unlimited.

Beyond her science fiction work, Ms. Garcia writes children's books that blend imagination with real-life inspiration. *A Cat for William* tells the true story of how a stray cat helps a man navigate a disabling disease, while *The Christmas Crayons* recounts the touching tale of a neglected homeless girl who discovers joy in a simple box of crayons on Christmas Day. She has also launched the Granny Ducks series.

When she's not writing, Garcia designs adult coloring books, adding yet another dimension to her creative repertoire. All are available on Amazon under the author's name of Pamela Garcia, or you can find them on her website: http://www.prgarcia1.com.

In 2024, Ms. Garcia added her fairy designs to Redbubble and Zazzle for sale at the following stores:

www.redbubble.com/people/Labadie2024
www.zazzle.com/store/whisperingwillows

In 2025, in honor of her new upcoming book "The Dragon Keeper's Mark: A Song of Fire and Stone", she began a digital magazine publication about dragons. From birth to death, the reason our fascination for these creatures doesn't die, and so much more, can be learned from this FREE magazine:

THE EUROPA SAGA

She was never meant to be human.

When Europa wakes, her world is already gone. Her mother was assassinated. Her life, a carefully woven lie. And now, she's the next target.

The Europa Saga is a bold reimagining of the myth of Atlantis, told through the eyes of a twenty-year-old woman whose entire existence is a deception of lies and falsehoods. Spanning four generations and 2,000 years, this sweeping saga reveals the hidden truth: Europa's parents are not human but the exiled rulers of an aquatic alien race from Jupiter's ice moon, Europa.

Driven from their dying homeworld by civil war, the Atlanteans fled to Earth and built a secret city beneath the Pacific Ocean. But time and betrayal have nearly wiped them out. No Atlantean child has survived beyond the age of five in over two millennia. Their last hope: a child born human to survive the enemy's curse.

Now, with her mother dead and her enemies closing in, Europa must uncover the true history of her people, claim the throne she never asked for, and transform herself into what she was destined to become—an Atlantean.

But to save them, she must sacrifice the one thing she has left: her humanity. And if she fails, Atlantis will fall forever.

For more information, go to www. prgarcia1.com

MORE STORIES BY P. R. GARCIA

The Bounty Hunter: Before they were legends, they were BiiJun and Li-ara.

A savage bear attack nearly killed him. Saved by a stranger and her two wild canines, BiiJun—a Huntsman Bounty Hunter known only as Hunter—is thrown into an unfamiliar world of vulnerability, needs, and hope.

Helpless. Defenseless. Dependent on a woman he barely knows, he begins to question everything—a life without armor, without killing, without the creed that has ruled him for decades. Is there life without the helmet? Can a Huntsman walk away… and still be himself?

The Bounty Hunter is scarred, tender, and unfinished—like its characters. Like all of us. It's vulnerable. Fierce. Deeply personal. And maybe that's exactly why readers don't just read it—they carry it with them.

Hunter II: The truth didn't disappear. It was silenced.

For generations, Kolorian Huntsmen fought beside their genetically bonded canines, until the bond was abruptly severed and the dogs vanished without explanation. No records. No answers. Now, millennia later, that silence breaks with blood. When Suemay, daughter of legendary bounty hunter BiiJun, is attacked by her own trusted canine, the incident is dismissed as a tragic anomaly until similar attacks erupt across the galaxy. A mutating virus spreads, transforming the infected into something terrifying, and the truth behind the vanished canines begins to surface.

As Suemay struggles to survive both the bite and the changes it may have triggered, her family uncovers a conspiracy buried deep within Kolorian authority; one designed to protect power at any cost. With galactic stability crumbling, loyalties tested, and love pushed to its breaking point, uncovering the truth may be the only way to stop history from repeating itself… if it doesn't destroy them first.

Extinction 2038: When Antarctica's ice finally yields to global warming, a discovery thought to be the greatest scientific breakthrough of the century turns into humanity's deadliest nightmare.

Beneath the melting glaciers, a perfectly preserved dinosaur corpse emerges, carrying inside it the original, prehistoric strain of Ebola. Within hours, the virus claims its first victim. Within days, it spirals into a global extinction event.

As the death toll explodes, civilization collapses. The Internet dies. Electricity vanishes. Fuel and food become relics of a lost world.

Now, the few survivors must fight not only the deadly plague but also the brutal lawlessness rising from the ashes of a shattered society.

The clock is ticking. Humanity's final chapter has begun.

Guardians of Earth: An unstoppable alien force is racing toward Earth, determined to strip the planet of its water, minerals, and life itself. One guardian, sworn to protect Earth, stands in their way. But he can't do it alone. He needs help from an Earthling he has never met—a woman who holds the key to humanity's survival.

Her name is Sarina Spalling. She thinks she's launching a science fiction novel.

Sarina's new book about alien guardians defending Earth from annihilation is a work of pure imagination. Or so she believes. Until the impossible starts to bleed into reality.

A secret government agency, exposed in the pages of her novel, abducts her, accusing her of espionage. Her husband is implicated. Her life, as she knows it, collapses overnight.

Held against her will, Sarina is desperate to prove her innocence until a message from the Moon reaches the facility. She is ordered to call her childhood home, a house demolished years ago.

When the line connects, her dead mother answers.

With everything she believed shattered, Sarina is thrust into a hidden war for Earth's survival, where fiction is fact, guardians are real, and her destiny is greater and more dangerous than she ever imagined.

Guardians of New Earth II: The Watcher. Six months from New Earth, humanity's future shatters when a catastrophic breach cripples the great space station ferrying Earth's last survivors. Systems fail. Tensions ignite. Survival hangs by a thread.

When Head Commander Glogg is gravely injured, reluctant but battle-tested Renn Spalling is thrust into command, and into a nightmare he never saw coming. The breach wasn't an accident. It was sabotage.

What begins as a desperate repair mission spirals into a deadly hunt through a maze of lies, conspiracies, and secrets buried deep within the station's android core. Enemies walk among them, hidden, calculating, and deadly, even as the station's structure buckles around them.

Now Renn must uncover the traitors, protect the last living cargo of Earth's animals, and save the station before it collapses into the void. But survival demands sacrifices Renn may not be willing to make—sacrifices that could cost him everything.

In *Guardians of Earth II*, alliances will fracture, loyalties will be tested, and the fate of humanity's last hope will rest on the shoulders of one man, a man who never asked to be a hero.

Guardians of New Earth III: The Emissary: For the first time in thirty-eight years, Earth has sent a desperate signal to the Interstellar Space Coalition. Captain Tim Spalling, grandson of the legendary Renn Spalling, is ordered to lead the mission to find out why.

It's a journey he never wanted. A burden he fears he can't bear.

Haunted by the shadow of his family's legacy, Tim arrives to find Earth worse than he ever imagined. The northern hemisphere is a wasteland of ash. Of eight billion souls, only 200,000 individuals cling to life in the radiation-choked south.

Every decision he makes could save them or doom them all.

Now stranded on a dying planet, Tim faces an impossible task: stop the radiation that's killing the survivors and his own advanced android team. But something far darker lurks in the ruin, a hidden alien threat watching, waiting to strike.

As the pressure mounts, Tim's growing bond with an Earth woman threatens to blur the lines between duty and desire, clouding his judgment when he can least afford it.

With time running out and betrayal closing in, Tim must confront the question that will define his legacy. How far will he go to save a dying world?

Amazon Author's page:

https://www.amazon.com/stores/PamelaGarcia/author/B00GH4F8TG

Gallary

Osric

Elara

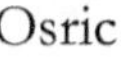

Vaelor

Ophira

Malachar

Solarus

Tirra

The Twin Dragons

Terrus

Noctis

The Battle

Malachar's Mountain

www.ingramcontent.com/pod-product-compliance
Lightning Source LLC
Chambersburg PA
CBHW051553030726
47592CB00001B/268